FROM
QUIET
HOMES

FROM
QUIET
HOMES

From quiet homes and first beginning,
Out to the undiscovered ends …

Hilaire Belloc: *Dedicatory Ode*

MICHAEL KELLY

Published by Michael Kelly

ISBN 978-0-64694-435-7

First printed 2015, reprinted 2020 as Print on Demand

Cover: Painting of Halifax bomber courtesy Paul Hobbs.
        The photograph is of a German nurse, taken during
        World War II. Attempts to identify her and to trace the
        provenance of the image have been unsuccessful. It is chosen
        both for its authenticity and for its dignity. It is used with respect.

Cover and Text Design by Paul Taylder – Xigrafix Media & Design

Also available as an eBook.

For Rita and Owen, my parents

Contents

Acknowledgements

During the Second World War I was a primary-school student in Sydney, far removed from German prisoner-of-war camps. In order to write about them I approached a number of people for advice. In no case was my request rejected, and I have to express my appreciation for the help so freely given.

This is especially true of those ex-prisoners of war who replied willingly to phone calls and emails from a stranger. They include: Owen Doherty; Cyril Gilbert, National Secretary of the ex-Prisoners of War Association; Vern Hallinan, Secretary of the 6th Division Association; Arthur Leggett, President of the West Australian ex-Prisoners of War Association; Bill Rudd (who set up the website *www.anzacpow.com*); W.S. Sinclair, Secretary of the 9th Division Association; Garth Turner; J.J. Wade, President of the 9th Division Association; Ron Zwar.

I also have to mention the generous help given by staff at the New South Wales branch of the Returned Services League of Australia; at the Australian War Memorial; and at the Australian Defence Force Academy, where Bill Huston, Garth O'Connell, Martin James and Greg Gilbert patiently answered questions or directed me to sources. Neil Chippendale, of the Hornsby Council Library, New South Wales, who was in

London at the end of World War II and whose father was in the British Occupation Forces Across the Rhine, also shared his memories with me; and Eberhardt Pfeiffer, of Boroko, Papua, very kindly replied to my request for information about the German presence in New Guinea. Rob Davis, author of *Nor the Years Condemn* and of the website *RAF Bomber Command 1939–1945*, advised me on the training of airmen.

At a more personal level, I wish to thank the friends who read the manuscript and those who worked on various tedious editing tasks, Margaret Knowlden, Bente Jensen and Irina Dunn; those who helped me with the German language, Jacqui Calandra and Barbara and Walter Fuchs; Cecile Yazbek for generous practical suggestions; Paul Taylder for his cover design and for preparing the book for publication; Paul Hobbs for permission to reproduce his painting of the Halifax bomber *Beer is Best*; and most particularly, Blanche d'Alpuget, whose support has been invaluable, Margaret Hetherton on whose encouragement and help I have constantly relied, and Jeremy Nelson, without whose patient advice and hard work this book might still be a collection of pages at the bottom of a drawer.

Part 1: Stalag

CHAPTER 1

The Stalag
(Germany, 1944–1945)

The Stalag housed more than three thousand Allied prisoners – soldiers, mostly. Tim was expecting a camp exclusively for aircrew. It made little difference. Abruptly he was back in the world where men fought and were captured and sometimes tried to escape: he was back in the war. Those around him thought as he had thought, or had tried to think, before being shot down.

There were four compounds. Three formed a large open rectangle, designed to hold army officers, senior non-commissioned officers, and other ranks in segregation from each other. But the threat of over-crowding had forced the German guards to place large numbers of soldiers with the airmen in the fourth compound, the Stalag Luft, in the middle of the rectangle. It was here that Tim was brought.

His fellows at first treated him with a reserve bordering on hostility. He had not been interrogated at a transit camp, or subjected to the period of solitary confinement almost routine with captured airmen, and these considerations reeked of the possibility that he was a "plant". But the suspicion was not long sustained – his Australian accent, and even more his Australian manners, counted against it, and he certainly did not ask too many sensitive questions. It remained possible that he was a sleeper, a real Australian who had somehow been "got at"; but gradually the prisoners reasoned that the Germans would hardly have inserted a spy in so obvious a way, and dropped their suspicions for simple lack of evidence. So they shrugged and tried to welcome him into their company and chaffed him with their slang and assumed that he shared their attitudes. His slight limp and scarred hand were after all badges of honour – not only captured, he'd been wounded.

Initially he did not respond. He felt that few of them would share his revulsion from saturation bombing. This was doubly true of Army men, many of whom had seen the devastation of the Blitz. They had watched in helpless anger as firemen, standing in rubble with hoses rendered puny by their task, were silhouetted against buildings set ablaze by incendiaries. But they had not seen the destruction from the sky; they had not seen a city ringed with fire. To an extent they were in a shell of ignorance that he half-envied and half-rejected. There was no point in trying to explain – still less in telling them that he had a personal reason for identifying with the Germans on the ground as *victims*.

At times old feelings did course through his blood, producing a sense of unreality about the interlude at Tannhofen. For more than five months he had allowed the detachment of that small, safe region in the mountains to close around him like a protective fog; all that now confronted him had retreated from his thoughts until it seemed a distant dream. But it was no dream. Since 1939 the logic of conflict had become the new common sense – the foundation of all practical decisions. Everybody took that much for granted. The world really was locked in this bitter struggle to the death and, returning to it from his enforced retreat, he found himself deeply torn. Old questions, shelved rather than solved, reasserted themselves. Bomber Command's strategy – had Alan's defence of it been right? Tim could not accept that; he could not be so clinical in his judgment. But neither could he deny the immense risk, the great leap of faith, in a mere flight sergeant rejecting a mind-set embraced, it seemed, by the whole British people.

And even more acutely, part of him now felt something like guilt because, for a while, he had not only managed to put the world's agony aside but had even thought little about the Halifax crew. Now anxiety resurfaced. Alan, Phil, Ron – what had happened? Almost certainly they had lost their lives. And Bruce, Don and Tony? According to Berndt, three men had been captured. Surely they were the ones. But if so, they had not been sent to this camp. No one knew of them. Could they have made it after all?

That concern for men who had become dear to him was a simple human response, independent of the war. But it had matured in the context of taking sides, of dividing humanity into "us" and "them". It was difficult now to disentangle grief from something approaching hatred of the enemy. Such feelings were reinforced because he could see, clearly and beyond doubt, that among the mix of prisoners around him most were at base ordinary, decent men. They had little taste for war, for all that they might have bombed cities or fought hand-to-hand in France or Crete or Libya. Indeed, what he admired most in his comrades was the way they combined extraordinary courage with unassuming ordinariness. And he could not escape the suspicion that their courage included something his lacked. The men around him had not, he felt, really evaded the questions that plagued him. But having decided that the fight was necessary, they had put those questions aside – not callously, but regarding them as answered; they must turn now from consideration to action. Why could he not share that sense of closure – and its relative peace?

That was one side of the tension that dogged him constantly. It was rooted deep in instinctive solidarity with comrades, family, nation, traditions, as well as in the hard logic that Alan had espoused.

But there was the other side. And it, too, could be seen in the same men around him. Few hated Germans. Their response to their enemies was closer to that of his father than that of his uncle Jim. There were some guards who were reviled as trigger-happy brutes only too ready with a rifle-butt or even a bullet, but not many – most were humane; and, though a certain distance was preserved, it was not unknown for prisoners and guards to address each other by Christian names. What did all that mean, if one really stopped to think?

Did it mean anything?

Practically speaking, the war rendered such touches of humanity peripheral. From its perspective, they were insignificant – unreal. Perhaps the Tannhofen experience, with its anodyne quality, had in fact led him away from reality, enabling him to submit externally to an imposed routine while in the citadel of his soul he could stay safe in his own detached world.

Away from reality? But – no. Anna at least was real. Her love was real. The values they had shared were real. A hundred times each day, and even more in the quiet of the night, she was more real than all this. War or not, there was something ultimate about that. That deep affirmation of life survived: at least in their one, small, personal relationship it survived even this cosmic madness and its pressures.

It was a balancing act. He was confronted by two absolutes, neither of which he could dismiss: the fight against tyranny, the love transcending that fight. He felt now like a traveller returning home, unable to communicate the changes his experiences had wrought in him, yet recognising in himself a deep commitment to the friends and the country he had left.

The contradiction produced intense stress, opposed attitudes contending in his consciousness until at moments he doubted his own sanity. So long as he was not again asked to drop bombs on cities, he did not have to resolve the dilemma to the point of a public declaration, like a martyr declaring his faith before the executioner; but wrestling with it was still enough to send him into a state of serious depression.

The prisoners in general knew nothing of his struggle. They had difficulties enough of their own – not least that of keeping their spirits up sufficiently to survive years of incarceration. To that end, they were determined to present a "good show" to their captors, and though in private there was plenty of gloom, in public they challenged the hardships and irritations of their confinement with cockiness when they could and with discipline when they couldn't.

Tim did make some early efforts to join in this, but his anguish at being separated from Anna remained with him like a great weight bearing down on his spirit, and his sense of moral confusion added to the burden. No chirpiness, no enthusiasm felt possible. For a while even eating gave him no pleasure beyond that of fulfilling a rationally recognised need. Here, in the camp, food mattered enormously, for the fare was several degrees worse than the hospital rations, meagre as they had been, and the prisoners were always hungry. With the black bread, rumoured to contain sawdust, some coped by slicing it into tiny portions and eating a little five times each day; others wolfed the lot at once, putting up with the stomach cramps that came at normal meal times; but in any case it was a rare prisoner who actually rejected anything in the way of food, and without fortnightly Red Cross parcels they would barely have survived. Nevertheless, Tim experienced a brief period during which he could not eat even the camp's thin soup and scrawny potatoes, and hunger was replaced by an absurd feeling that his stomach was already over-full. He hardly slept, and could not sit in one place for five minutes. His speech became oddly hesitant, as though forming familiar words required a conscious effort. He gained something of a reputation for moroseness, not – as had happened back in the squadron – with one or two perceptive observers, but more widely, until the Senior British Officer took him aside.

"Look, Rogers, none of us likes being here, but it's dangerous to let it get you down. Can't you make more of an effort to snap out of it?"

This, though kindly meant, was little help. There was a moment when he almost told of his experience at Tannhofen, but just then a particularly unpopular German guard walked past and the SBO muttered "buggers." Suddenly he was certain: no one here would sympathise – not with his falling in love with a German girl.

The depression lasted for about three weeks, and then, for no reason that he could discern, simply passed from him. It was as though through emotional exhaustion he had found a new calm; as though some catharsis had run through his being. His love for Anna had not gone away, but it had become more tranquil. He realised, now, that he must enter into the life of the camp.

And it was a life of surprising creativity. Less so in winter, when the hut stoves petered out after burning the little coal allowed and when men, simply to combat the cold, spent whole days in bed wearing every stitch of clothing they possessed. But in the warmer months every effort was made to combat the ever-present enemy of simple boredom. There was of course work – cleaning, cooking, washing – such tasks were done largely by the prisoners. There were sports, mainly football and volleyball and some boxing. There was a market every Thursday where trestle tables were littered with all sorts of odd items on sale for the only currencies that would be accepted or, indeed, allowed – *Lagergeld* or, preferably, cigarettes. A scarf sent from home might be offered at "50 cigs", a writing-pad for "15 cigs", a bar of Red Cross chocolate for "70 cigs". On other days there were courses run by prisoners who were expert in some field – electronics, perhaps, or law or languages or navigation or history, for the war had funnelled many with skills into these closed communities; and it was even possible to study for a degree from London University. Poetry became popular with men who had no experience of it, and esoteric courses in fine porcelain or Sanskrit had their enthusiasts. Instruments supplied by the Red Cross enabled an orchestra to form. There were drama groups which mounted plays (much appreciated by the guards) and there were dance classes (with no women) and classes in sketching. Chairs for these activities were fashioned from boxes in which Red Cross parcels had arrived. There was a lending library, stocked with Red Cross books ranging from Bulldog Drummond to Shakespeare. The volunteer librarians were driven to distraction by prisoners who had not returned books because they had not "had time".

And, of course, there were attempts to escape – more difficult for airmen since, being all officers or NCO's, they were confined to the camp; whereas ordinary soldiers could be taken outside on work parties, and this greatly increased the chances. Some army NCO's contrived to exchange identities with privates for this reason, while others volunteered to supervise – which, though it might be done simply so that the men were not left completely to the oversight of Germans, also made absconding easier. There were a few attempts to feign madness sufficiently to be repatriated with sick prisoners who were exchanged for counterparts interned in Britain; and since, in that confined world, a well-counterfeited mental disorder was not easy to distinguish from the real thing, and might even promote the illness it mimicked – or its first cousin – some of these masquerades were continued until no one was quite sure of the truth. There was one man in particular who may have been acting, or genuinely unbalanced, or intensely religious in a sincere way, or perhaps all three: he would meditate for hours sitting on the ground, apparently unaware of attempts to attract his attention, and he would interrupt conversations suddenly and unexpectedly to speak of his spiritual insights. His behaviour became increasingly eccentric, until the day when he appeared naked on *Appell* and, leaving the ranks during the count, went up to the German officer and asked, "Who gave you these numbers?" Some prisoners tittered, and a few cast anxious glances at a particular guard who was considered trigger-happy. The officer, taken aback, made a sign to his *Feldwebel* who approached the man and ordered him roughly to get dressed. Ignoring the order, the prisoner repeated, "eins, zwei, drei … Where did you get numbers?" Then, raising his voice gradually, he went on: "They are not yours. You did not make them. No man made them. They are a gift to us all from God. They are given to us in our minds to understand the structure of the world. That is a holy reality. And you are abusing it. You are using numbers to keep us in this prison!" The guards laughed as the man was taken away, and he was eventually repatriated. But, Tim thought, was that madness? From a practical point of view, perhaps; but the ideas – did they touch some reality?

The great day in the camp was the one when mail arrived, courtesy of the Red Cross. Men pored over letters and read them twenty times, and if the wounds of parting from loved ones were thereby re-opened, they accepted the pain gladly. There were those who had bad news: those whose families had suffered losses in the war, or simply experienced social upheaval; and those whose wives had "found a baby left on the doorstep", and plaintively asked whether they could keep it. There was one man whose fiancée told him that she could no longer be tied to a coward who had surrendered to the enemy. And there were those who simply received no letters, and had no idea why.

Officially they had no war-news except that provided by the Germans, but in spite of constant searches by the guards some prisoners managed to secrete tiny radios that could pick up the BBC on clear nights, and new arrivals could add to what they gleaned from that source. Occasionally letters from home contained material that had evaded the censors. In a piecemeal fashion, supplementing such information with their own interpretation of the German propaganda, sifting the fanciful rumours and subsequent denials that abounded, they were to an extent able to follow the progress of the war. A "newspaper", its articles cobbled from such of these sources as would not alert the guards to clandestine activities, was pinned weekly to a notice-board.

The Allied invasion of Sicily had been getting under way when Tim was shot down; now the prisoners followed the long struggle for dominance in Italy like men working on a jigsaw puzzle with more than half the pieces missing. As 1944 dragged on, they were heartened and let down and heartened again by the destruction of Berlin and the slaughter of the Americans at Anzio and the final Allied victory over what had long seemed an invincible German garrison at Cassino. The news of D-Day brought by newly captured men changed the mood radically. Prisoners from Australia and New Zealand heard that the Japanese were being expelled from New Guinea and driven back through the Marianas, Guam and the Philippines. Indians heard of the bitter see-sawing as the British, Indians and Chinese liberated Burma. Everyone was aware of the Russians entering Poland and Czechoslovakia, and slowly forcing their way towards the Baltic. Recent arrivals said that what was left of the Luftwaffe was almost unable to operate because of lack of fuel, that wholesale bombing of German cities had pretty well ceased, and that the Allied Air Forces were now concentrating on railways, bridges, oil wells and synthetic oil plants.

An expectant sense increased almost daily. They could smell victory, some of them after nearly five years of captivity. A sort of contagious light-headedness ran through the camp. It was mixed with restraint – for false hopes were worse than none – and it was severely dented when a large contingent from the soldiers' compound was given one day to prepare to leave: they were to be taken to Poland, where they would work as miners. It seemed a bad omen. But underneath the fears confidence grew steadily: the end was coming.

Of course Tim wanted that victory, and wanted it soon. He had never doubted that the Allies, in a broad, over-arching way, had the right of it, and in spite of the moral hesitance which he had first expressed in a letter from New York, and which had continued to torment him with increasing intensity during bombing raids, he would always have regarded a German victory as unthinkable. Now, in addition, the war had become a monster separating him from Anna. All this, somehow, would be over when peace came.

Yet he was aware that a final German surrender must bring new problems. He and Anna, by an instinctive, unspoken agreement, had avoided discussing the underlying questions of right and wrong. But it was obvious that she must have many ties to her nation – emotional, historical, cultural, linguistic – and he wondered what the crushing of her country might do to her, or perhaps in her. Conceivably, she would feel a purely personal liberation with the end of hostilities; but her friends, her parents, her memories, the customs she had always accepted, even the architecture – all these dear things would form her idea of Germany, and Germany would never be the same again.

He was above all relieved to hear that cities were no longer major targets. He remembered vividly the bombing of Hamburg, where reconnaissance photographs had shown half of the buildings destroyed; where there was talk of a terrible gale generated by the heat which sucked people into the fires, and where estimates of the dead had reached fifty thousand in ten days. At least Anna would now be safe from *that*. Previously he had hardly faced the possibility. But it had been real enough. For though her hospital was nowhere near any military target or industrial town, her immunity was not thereby guaranteed: periodically she visited her family home in Hildesheim, and Hildesheim, like any German city, might have been attacked.

So he disciplined himself to be a normal "kriegie", and made an attempt to rise out of his personal quagmire. Seeing his efforts, the men around him met him halfway and, since things happen quickly in a closed community, he was soon accepted and as at home as most. His self-absorption receded and he realised with full clarity that he was not alone in feeling extreme stress. Indeed, the symptoms were all too obvious for those who cared to notice them. It was, in a way, consoling when he overheard a recently captured Yorkshire man saying, "If you chaps are sane, you've got a shock waiting for you when you get back to Blighty. They're all as mad as hatters there. Don't even mutter to themselves all day."[1]

In some ways it helped that the camp allowed no opportunity whatever for privacy or solitude. But his emergence from depression was aided immeasurably when he received a bundle of letters stretching back almost to the time of his removal from the hospital, neatly tied in chronological order. He read them starting with the last, and spent a day in a kind of dazed relief, nostalgic for his parents and Walgabran and the sun of Australia, but also immeasurably comforted. On one letter there was a small ink-blot: his father's fountain-pen sometimes leaked, and usually Ben Rogers would re-write the page, seeing it as a kind of discourtesy to send a blotted letter. But on this occasion, no doubt, he had not had time; and the blot was something Tim valued – a homely token of humanity, an emphasis on the reality of the hand that had put the words on paper.

And there was a special bonus – a letter written by Willy from the internment camp at Tatura in Victoria. "We are both prisoners now". Suddenly the war was only an interlude rather than, as it had become for millions, a reality that no one could see beyond.

And then he received the first letter from Anna. She had taken a dreadful risk, aided by Doctor Berndt and a friend.

It was possible because the camp was not absolutely segregated from the civilian population. People from outside came in to work on the electricity and the plumbing and the leaking roofs, to collect the officers' laundry and the camp garbage, to give dental and medical treatment and even, rarely, to remove the body of a prisoner who had died. And some of the prisoners went out from the soldiers' compounds

---

1   See Appendix: McKibbin's *Barbed Wire: Memories of Stalag 383.*

on work parties – farming, timber-getting, taking part in any industries not immediately connected with Germany's war effort. This opened possibilities of contact and even what was euphemistically called "fraternisation" between prisoners and local women – not unknown in spite of the fact that draconian penalties could be imposed. Some Red Cross cigarettes, a bar of Red Cross chocolate, could sometimes be a bribe.

So there were channels, discreet and difficult but open to a trickle of contact. However, it was radical and dangerous to use such channels to get a message *into* the camp, and a *written* one was absolutely foolhardy. Yet that was what Anna had done. She had confided in Berndt, who had made delicate and painfully careful enquiries to discover where Tim had been taken, and had come back to her with good news. He knew a dentist who attended both guards and prisoners in the camp, and on whom he had a double claim: they had been undergraduate friends, and he had once successfully treated the dentist's daughter for a condition which others had described as hopeless.

The dentist, though a loyal German, had little love for the Nazi party ... and he was an old-fashioned romantic, apt to become sentimental over young love. And he was extraordinarily brave.

Nevertheless he was reluctant ...

But – if he were assured that there was nothing in a message that could harm the Reich ... well, very occasionally, once, possibly twice, he just *might*, if it was safe – if Tim himself could be trusted ... No, he would not tell another prisoner to bring Tim to see him – that would be to invite trouble; but if – fortuitously – Tim happened to present himself for dental work ... well, he might be able, if they happened to be alone together ... as he usually would be much of the time when working ...

Anna's letter was brief and written in a tiny hand on a piece of paper small enough to be secreted in a wallet. It told of her love, and her belief that they would meet; and it mentioned, in the inconsequential manner that can sometimes infuse humanity into a bare statement of facts, that she felt better after spending two weeks' holiday with her family in Hildesheim.

A few lines – but for Tim they let light, air and joy in through the barbed-wire surrounding the camp. His mood changed radically. He would not risk writing to her, for if the letter was discovered she could be called a traitor. But he exacted a promise from the dentist to tell Berndt to tell Anna that he loved her and that she must not take any more chances – that after the war he would join her, somehow. She ignored this warning, and the dentist, having once thumbed his nose at fate without mishap, became emboldened, and two more letters followed. Yes, she had received the message, and understood why he would not write, but he was too careful. It would be all right.

That night he fell asleep with the letter in his hand. It fluttered to the floor, and the man who picked it up read enough to guess what it meant. He was a man who did not understand caution or even privacy. He told the hut. There was no longer any hope of concealment, and the story got around. Tim blamed himself – the danger to Anna was greatly increased by his carelessness. But it became an open secret that he intended to marry some *Fräulein* as soon as the war was over.

Against his expectations, most of the prisoners seemed sympathetic. Not all. Some presented Tim with a dismissive, cold shoulder, accompanied by an occasional pointed comment about a "Hun girl-friend". One offered to fight him. A few approached him with winks and prurient questions. The SBO took him aside again: "You were in a queer situation, Rogers. No one to talk to – one kind girl. Affects a man, that. War-time romances are dangerous at the best of times. Lots of problems. Even back home. You and this nurse don't really know each other. Where would you live? Here? Australia? Would she be accepted there? What does she know about the country – different way of life, eh? Could she leave her family, everything she loves? Classic situation, Rogers – marriages started that way don't last."

He didn't care. He'd had advice of this sort before. In spite of his limp he did fight one man who sneeringly voiced his opinion of all "Hun women", and emerged with a bloody nose but a better heart. Every word of her letters was read and re-read, and he was restless with the unpredictability of the war, but if a man in a POW camp can be happy, he was happy. Among the soldiers in his compound was a major who taught classes in German. He would join. It wouldn't be fair, when they were married, to ask Anna to speak English all the time.

Late in February 1945 there was another letter.

"*Tim,*" she wrote, "*I love you very much, and that is why I have never said you this, but I have wept for the people in Berlin and Munich and Cologne. I know the Luftwaffe bombed English cities, and if the British and Americans have done it more it is because they have more power. But now it is something else. They have bombed Dresden. Why have they done this? Tim, I know that you always hated the bombs. That is why I am able to love you. But Tim, the fires! Tens, perhaps hundreds, of thousands died! Will we – will the world – ever be able to be human again? Can we ever forgive each other – all of us?*"

The news of the Dresden raid had not penetrated to the prisoners; still less could they know of the controversy that followed even in Britain, where a public debate threatened to erupt and where the word "terror-bombing", long current in Germany, now appeared in some newspapers. Some argued that the city was a legitimate military target, one of the last great nerve-centres of German industry and communications; others claimed that it was full of people fleeing the Russians, pulverised in a pointless attack on German morale in a war already nearly over.

Tim could know none of this; but a cold shiver seemed to pass through his heart, not only because he had never before known Anna to mention his part in the bombing of Germany, but because his confidence that all targets were now precise military ones was swept away.

For two months no letters came. Finally there was a note from Dr Berndt; it contained a new, sharp tone that Tim had never before associated with the doctor. Anna had gone in March to visit her parents. Hildesheim was bombed and her house was destroyed. It was hard to get reliable news. The *Bürgermeister* had contacted the hospital to say that she had survived, but her mother was killed, her father seriously injured, and for now she must stay with him and with her sister. Perhaps she would be able to return to the hospital in time, though of course she had already been replaced. Dr Berndt thought it possible that she would no longer wish to communicate with a British airman … in any event he was no longer willing to help, he did not relish sending even this message, but he thought that she would wish it. Ever since Tim had first been his patient, he added, he had tried to refrain from discussing politics and the war. But now he felt obliged to pose one question: why Hildesheim? Why such a town? Why now – when everyone knew Germany was beaten?

This question, echoing Anna's, closed the letter abruptly, followed only by the signature "B". There was no expression of regret or sympathy. Berndt was clearly performing a task which had become distasteful.

Tim could no longer receive or send messages, nor could he know what changes had occurred in Anna's life. He could only wait with mounting anxiety mingled with wild hope for the end of the war in Europe. Inevitably, at times, he found himself remembering all that had led up to this. In the restricted life of the camp, it was easy to let his mind form the habit of going back – back through Tannhofen and Netherholme, and Broken Lake and Brisbane, back to Walgabran; and back through the history of his friendships with Fay and Barbara and Reg and George and Alan and Bruce and the other boys – back, right back, to his first encounter with Willy. Back through that growing unease with war that had been with him in some measure since boyhood.

The Stalag (Germany, 1944–1945)

This journey, that now seemed so long to a man not yet thirty, kept recurring to his mind ... piecemeal, not in true sequence, but yet with an order to it ...

Part 2: Childhood

CHAPTER 2

Rough Cricket (Walgabran, 1928)

The trees seemed braced against the sun, their leaves moving and sighing in a light air. The rustle and drone and smell of the bush, restless with early summer, filtered into the playground where a rough-and-ready cricket game engrossed some nine-year-old boys.

John had the bat. A magpie wandered almost to his feet pecking some crumbs, and fluttered away when he shifted his stance.

The stumps were painted on a garbage tin, the bat leaked rubber at the handle, the ball was an ancient and forbidden six-stitcher. Only tennis balls were allowed in the school grounds, but as always on the third week-end in November the Brothers were away on retreat, and no one else was likely to bother.

Except for the batsman, everyone fielded. Bruce, inspired by Wall bowling to Hammond in Saturday's newsreel, swaggered to his mark, rubbing the ball on his shorts. Tim was at slips, his cousin Alan at silly point. Ken kept the wicket, Barry and Owen crouched ready for catches at mid-on and mid-off. The fielders were sparse, but the school walls would prevent a ball from travelling far.

The boys called out mock-abuse to each other and enjoyed the game immensely, feeling the thrill of competition in their hearts and the caress of the sun on their bare legs and feet.

Tim, idle in his position, allowed his attention to wander. Dreamily, half-watching Bruce walking back to bowl, he was aware of a faint hum. The sound grew into the snarl of an aero-engine, a flood of sound that spread across the landscape, and his thoughts flashed back to the balsa models that littered his bedroom. He looked for the plane but could not see it. Then it moved out of the glare of the sun – a biplane painted orange, and he scanned it for features that would allow him to recognize the type. The wings waggled a little – the grace of the thing! Was it a de Havilland? He was aware of the inherent balance of the machine, the way it agreed with the demands of the air – the way it answered a problem men had tried to solve for ages.

"Rogers! Wake up! What're you doing?"

The lofted ball had passed him and fallen less than two yards away. A childishly easy catch – if he had been alert.

There was nothing he could do except mutter "Sorry!" Shamefaced, smarting at his own stupidity, forcing himself not to look up, still entranced by the fading drone of that free thing in the sky, still aware of the paradox of its energy-filled frailty, he watched Bruce coming again, changing his run, swerving in from the leg side, sending a ball that would pass well outside the off-stump. A mistake, Tim thought; a wide. John thought the same. He took a chance, danced forward to meet it, was half out of his crease when the ball switched direction off the ground, heading straight for his knees. Swivelling a little, trying to convert his stroke into a desperate block, he only succeeded in a fierce mis-hit that sent the ball hard and fast – straight to the hands of Alan.

It was a magnificent bit of courageous fielding. The ball had been in the air perhaps a twentieth of a second. Alan had not flinched. A smile creased what was already his good-looking face, and yelling in triumph he tossed the ball into the air.

John grinned, and handed the bat to Tim. "Your turn," he said.

Tim took it and faced Bruce, tapping it twice on the ground, determined to efface the memory of his lapse. Bruce, savouring the opportunity, called out, "Bet yer miss again."

"Yair, bet yer," echoed John.

"Bet yer," replied Tim.

"Don't let 'em rag yer," interposed Ken. "Have a go."

Bruce bowled, and Tim missed. The ball went to the keeper.

"Told yer." That was Bruce.

"Y'r not swatting flies," said Ken. "Hit the ball."

"Miss again y'r out!" Owen put in.

The ribbing was innocuous, friendly – it would not have been offered to any player genuinely less able than themselves. But Tim felt piqued.

"Hit yer fer six," he called to Bruce.

"You and what army? Bet yer can't."

"Just watch."

Bruce bowled and Tim jumped forward with open shoulders to meet a full toss. He connected sweetly. The ball drove fast on a low, rising trajectory. There was a crash, and a jagged hole in a classroom window.

Alan exclaimed: "Ow! Now yer've done it! Billo's in there. He'll tell Hilary!"

Willy Schultz's future was about to be determined.

"A warm climate." The doctor had stood with a sigh and gone to the window, staring at the heavy Bavarian sky. "You need somewhere where the sun gets into your bones. No, it wasn't tuberculosis; but you're weakened; and with your arthritis …

"To be honest, I almost envy you – I wish I had a reason to leave this damned mess myself. Revolutionaries, *Freikorps*, half the country in mourning, half the rest turning to absinthe – or to nihilistic satire. There's nothing left to believe in. And now this newfangled 'hyperinflation'. He laughed mirthlessly. "Better sick lungs than a sick nation."

The advice had been welcome. Willy had his own reasons for being fed up with the culture that had nurtured him. So he had obeyed, selecting New Britain as his place of exile. An odd choice, the doctor had thought, and not a wise one. But Willy had distant relatives there – cousins of his mother, they had run a copra plantation on the coast for twenty years; and though most Germans had either left or been deported under the new Australian administration, these were among the few who had stayed. Their reasons were obscure. Their business was hardly flourishing. It had suffered in the war, and was plagued by recurrent arguments between the three tribal groups who periodically came seeking work before retreating to immerse themselves again in village life. But letters back to the wider family were infrequent and uncommunicative, and Willy had hardly heard of these problems. Nor would he have greatly cared. He simply wanted to be far from Germany.

So he had gone, and had tried to be at home on the fringe of a tropical island, working hard and learning something of accountancy and a little of Papuan life. When he came to understand the straits the business was in, he redoubled his efforts, giving all his energy in an attempt to restore its prosperity. At first he was troubled by the relationship between planters and natives: they lived in worlds almost wholly disconnected, intersecting only at the points of work and pay. He would have liked something less distant. But to bridge the cultural gaps proved next to impossible. Here Europeans and Papuans were alike persuaded that all, white or black, rich or poor, had their place in a great static scheme and could, if they were lucky, find a kind of settled happiness in it. It was foolish to disturb that equilibrium. Willy accepted this and shook off his unease as a dog shakes off water.

And for a while he did achieve a sort of repose. New work in a new environment brought a freshness that laid a calming film over the turmoil of his memories. He was good with his hands in a practical way – he had learnt this at the museum –

and it proved a useful skill on the plantation where mending and building were recurring necessities. It was also pleasant: everything from a little carpentry to a little agricultural planning became a welcome relief from his main work of book-keeping. To all such tasks he brought a German attention to detail and care for a job well done.

Nevertheless, after some months it became clear that the experiment was not working. This cousin from the Fatherland fitted awkwardly into a *milieu* that observed its surroundings with severely practical eyes. To his relatives, the forest was sometimes an obstacle and sometimes an opportunity, but it was never an ancient, living wonder. A river could be a commercial highway or a place of danger, where crocodiles lurked and snakes slithered and mosquitoes were at their worst, but it was never a metaphor for the moving story of life. Coffee and copra were potential money, but never part of the miraculous bounty of the earth. To these people, Willy was slightly suspect; to him, they were half-asleep and, in their indifference, largely responsible for the troubles on the plantation.

And he was ill-at-ease in other ways. There were no unmarried women. The coast was too humid. The mountains were too remote. Australians were in charge. No one could understand them. They never spoke without making jokes but somehow they did a good job. Their insensitivity could mask a rough, humane innocence, or it could go deep. Many of them, when circumstances demanded it, suddenly turned into natural gentlemen; others – a few – could be as hard as any *Unterfeldwebel* out to impress his superiors. And you could never tell, when dealing with a new individual, which category he fell into. Willy didn't know whether he liked them or not.

He persevered for more than a year; then, still wheezing at night, glad to have Germany on the other side of a psychological fence but deeply unsettled, he tried to take stock. No, he was not a planter, that was clear now. And the minor tasks of each day were diverting him endlessly from the greater challenge of finding a direction in life – a direction that made sense for him. But . . . who was he? If he did not fit in here, then he had failed twice. Even three times, if you counted the army. What did that leave?

And he thought at last, "If I must put up with Australians I might as well try Australia. At least it's not far away, there's work there – and it's dry, isn't it?"

In the event, Brisbane hadn't been dry. He had tried it anyway, hoping that surely in time he would land a good job – something like managing the Australian end of a Pacific trading company, with copra or palm oil coming in and machinery, food or liquor going out. The business skills he had acquired in New Britain would have stood him in good stead. But there were too many men back from the Great War with similar ideas; and even though German settlements had existed in Queensland for eighty years, in the aftermath of that enormous conflict his nationality was against him.

Willy was a stayer. All his failures were worked out the hard way, and it took two more heavy, humid summers and two more surprisingly cold winters handling mail sacks in the Queensland General Post Office before he headed west.

And there at last, in the town of Walgabran, he found a climate where the sun beating on hard earth leached the water from the topsoil, and where the summer's heat, though it could drain your energy, did not lay an extra garment of sweat on your back nor spread a soggy mist over the clarity of your mind. He got a job. It was a far cry from managing an export-import company. In a formal sense – though no contract or paper was ever signed – his employer was the Parish Priest. He would work as a general caretaker and repair man, sometimes in the church but mainly around St Aidan's school. The pay was moderate, but its mix of creative improvisation and manual activity was appealing, and he could believe in its underlying value. On the plantation he had missed this sense of humane purpose; not that he rejected commerce as such, but he could not be at home with the single-mindedness his relatives brought to it.

And now with each passing month his arthritis troubled him less, his cough diminished until it was merely an occasional tendency to clear his throat. Though his wispy hair thinned further, and he looked older than his thirty-four years, at least his physical ailments seemed contained – here – in this bush school in this bush town in this bush country. So in a dissatisfied, resentful sort of way he became more or less settled. With the small group of teaching brothers he remained affable but distant while with their young charges he was taciturn when he could not avoid them.

Still, there was a dimension lacking. He needed to explore ideas through and through, to share speculations, to express the visions locked inside him. For this there were no companions. The brothers were friendly and open-minded, interested in a way, but for the most part not well attuned to this part of his spirit. And they were overworked and always busy.

So Willy began to paint – again.

Soon dozens of small canvases littered the caretaker's timber cottage where he lived alone. They were his secret – almost his secret indulgence. It was easy to keep them private. No one in this country knew or cared that he could hold a brush. And anyway, he didn't want his efforts seen. He knew they weren't good – not good enough for a *real* painter. They were the product, not of ambition, but of compulsion. It didn't matter. He lived now at a slight remove from the world, and from reality, in a half-comfortable compromise which didn't repay too much thought. He was aware of this but, after all – wasn't that life for most people?

In that mood of subdued resignation he continued for some time. But a few days ago this *modus vivendi* had been disturbed. Brother Hilary had said: "We need to freshen up that hall and especially the stage, Bill. I've got a special reason for that. Very pale green, I think – nothing too bright. Something that'll be a quiet background when the boys get their prizes. You know the sort of thing – not gloomy but dignified – I'll leave the details to you. Get the paint from young Tim Rogers' dad – he always gives us a good deal."

Willy had started, but it wouldn't work. He couldn't – in the mood which had revived with his painting he really couldn't just slap green paint onto a wall. He kept tracing outlines: a peak here, a stream there; a random sweep of his brush would turn unbidden into the branch of a tree. He felt the garden beginning to come to life again, under his hand.

It started old memories ... those days ... Vienna ... the war ... the hospital, the valley ... memories that surfaced as he went about his duties, refrains that echoed in against a pillar outside the portico of the *Kunsthistorische*. He'd thought they were his friends, but he could remember every word:

"Willy's going to fail."

"He's an idiot. Lives in the past. Ignores Kokoscha. Dismisses that new Spanish fellow."

"Yes. He just hangs around here and the Albertina. Schiele, Cezanne, Braque might never have existed."

"Have you seen the room he calls his studio? It's full of romantic landscapes."

"Well – he is German."

"What – you think he's a throwback? Wagner? Friedric and Heine?"

"Well ... not Wagner. Maybe Waldmuller. Or those Hudson River people. Tranquillity – tranquillity and grandeur - that's what Willy's after. He should have been around a century ago."

"Even then he'd have been third rate."

The other student laughed. *"Maybe it won't matter anyway – the war won't leave any of us much time for painting."*

"You think it will come?"

"It'll come – this year, next year ... not that they'd take Willy with his eyesight and that stoop. He was rejected for his military service."

"Yes ... I'm a bit sorry for him sometimes – he doesn't seem to have any real friends – but – well, he is so gauche – and a bore – it's

embarrassing. He drifts into grandiose philosophical speculations at the most inappropriate times. I invited him to a party once. After a few people wandered away from him he just sat in a corner looking as though he didn't know how to speak. Never again."

It wouldn't have mattered quite so much if Willy hadn't respected those students – their work and their judgment. Yet surely, he'd felt, there was room for many styles – one didn't have to belong to the latest trend.

But damn it all, those criticisms – once they had been spoken aloud, they sounded so right.

Yes … yes … he *was* third-rate!

A romantic. Once that had meant a man who looked forward. Now it was a man who looked back. Without energy. He was not part of Cubism or Expressionism or any other vital new movement.

"But – that's how I paint. That's me."

And Willy had turned in on himself, almost a recluse. Submerged doubts came to the surface and flowed like cold lava in a destructive tide over his hopes. He knew then that he would never be a painter – not a *real* painter.

And there was nothing else he wanted to do.

He dropped out. He became an assistant to the caretaker in Munich's National Museum. It was a limbo of pleasant manual activity, dulling his artistic instincts. The first retreat into such work.

And the war *had* come. The student had been half-right: Willy had not been accepted by the army – then; but within two years they were glad to have him. They winkled him out of his job, gave him a number and a rifle that was too heavy and a helmet that was worse, and denied him any privacy or time to think.

At first, the other men tried in their way to be kind, but Willy could not respond in their language, laced as it was with rough camaraderie and rougher jokes, and he knew that he could never shoot anyone. He aimed at empty space, and froze in the trenches and the mud, and picked at the lice, and muttered to himself, and they had left him alone as much as possible – until his chronic cough began to show blood in the sputum and he was invalided out.

The hospital in the southern hills was not far from his home. Six months, on his back at first and then mostly in a bath-chair.

It was in some ways an unfortunate place for a failed landscape painter. On three sides the hospital grounds fell away into sudden valleys surrounded in the foreground by folds and ridges and in the far distance by high mountains, and anyone using the outdoor benches was a guest at a feast of natural beauty. Willy used to sit there through the early afternoons, a rug over his knees, a book dropped by his side, while alternately he fought the nightmares that invaded his memory from the trenches and, exhausted, retreated into a grateful numbness. But by slow degrees he looked up and allowed the mountains and the sky to seep into his soul, smuggling in a kernel of hope that there was some good thing still in human life, some lingering remnant of innocence.

He stared at these scenes and sometimes dreamed what a *real* painter might do here – what Waldmuller might have done. What he could never do – he would make a fool of himself if he tried.

It was the back valley that fascinated him most – where the visitors attended the garden parties around the lake on Sundays. Rich visitors, sleek and laughing, looking for all the world as though the war had not touched them. It was another world – unreal, private, detached from pain, like the fairylands of childhood. Unreal but beautiful – in every detail.

Sometimes, he let himself wonder … could he?

But no, he wasn't a painter.

He was reclining in a bath chair, looking at that same scene, when the real world intruded in a way that no one could possibly ignore. A nurse came running, shouting, and spontaneously planted a strictly forbidden kiss on his cheek. She was waving a newspaper. He read the headlines.

DAS ENDE!

The end?

THE END?

No. The word had lost meaning. It had joined the dictionary of fantasy.

But it was real.

The end of what had become the interminable, horrible yet normal condition of life. It had come.

He stared, stunned.

Then he thought: so many men – dead in France, Belgium, Russia, the Middle East. So many sailors at the bottom of the sea. So much courage and effort and heroism and promise cut off.

No more. At least, no more.

He knew that he should rejoice, but his heart was too tired to leap up and join in the relief that his mind urged upon it. He tried to overcome this hollowness and gathered some feeling of celebration by sheer force of will, and he joked with other patients and nurses and doctors. Not to have done so would have been a sort of blasphemy.

And then the news of Versailles supervened … Dimly he sensed it even then: no, the war was not over … not really. Not yet.

In time, however, he recovered enough – the lungs more or less clear, the cough gone, the depression more or less lifted – to take up life again.

But not in Germany. A warm climate, the doctor said.

And here he was. A *verdammter* caretaker-handyman in a bush school. How far from Vienna? *Spiritually*, how far?

Here he was, surrounded by the smells of boys and of the brown-paper bags that had held their lunches. At the bottom of the world. What was he doing here? What was it all about?

Did it matter?

How had the enthusiasm of a young student in a city full of creative energy turned to this?

His bad luck? His lack of talent – or lack of effort? The war? How did it all fit together?

He didn't know. He hadn't the resources left to retrace the journey.

He knew that he was here, an alien in this dry and dusty land, bearing traces of an utterly different past and even now a kind of bewilderment at the hard logic that had led here. Something deep within him protested: he belonged where streets were alive with laughter and sadness, where life played against a background of exuberant architecture in the Schubertring or the Stephansdom or the Hofgarten – or even in that other garden, the garden of beauty, where the nurse had kissed him … the garden he could never paint …

And then it came to him quietly, unbidden. It was suddenly strong. He *would* paint it – he was going to paint that garden – paint it in the school hall, even if Brother Hilary had him sacked for it. He would plant a little bit of Germany in this land that seemed not part of the same planet. He would start now and finish by February – he'd have about ten weeks.

And it was just after he had formed this irrevocable resolve that the cricket ball came through a closed window of the classroom, scattering glass on the floor and striking him on the head.

It is not good for anyone's nerves to be unexpectedly hit by a cricket ball, and Willy's nerves were already wound to a critical pitch. He was nonplussed for a second, and then, as the full meaning of the tinkling glass registered, he exploded. Storming to the door, he unleashed a series of expressions learnt in the service of his namesake, the Kaiser. Though his English had become quite exact, his memory now slipped, reverting to half-German forms. His voice rose to something like a scream and then subsided, but it remained full of barely contained anger as he addressed the boys in more controlled terms.

"Idiots! Demonkinder! You – you wit' der bat! Com' here! How are you called?"

Tim walked slowly forward, while the others hesitated, caught between running and staying to listen. "S-sorry", Tim said. "It was an accident."

The word was like petrol on a fire. "Accident! For you boys everything is accident. You never thinking are! Maybe you ein accident are! Go! I will see Brother Hilary the moment he comes! Go – go now!"

Subdued, they turned, starting to walk – except for Alan. Piqued, he stood his ground and retorted: "Who're you to give advice? You're just a kraut! We're not going to listen to you!"

Willy understood the Americanism. "Who am I? I will tell you who I am. I am a human being. You – you may become a human being some day – if you ever learn that rudeness is not strength. How many years have you – nine? By now you should have learnt some wisdom! But no, I see that you are still a very little child. It is grotesque at your age! Grotesque – do you know what that means, eh? You may become a true man with dignity some day, if you ever grow up. But I do not think so. You have a long way to go! Now – go!"

Alan looked at him and could think of no reply. He pouted, shrugged, and waved his hands in front of his face as though to banish a smell. It was a gesture that conveyed contempt for someone who could not be reasoned with. "C'm'on, kids," he said.

The boys left, under Alan's lead moving with a deliberate slowness to show that they were not cowed.

CHAPTER 3

Alan's Revenge (Walgabran, 1928)

Brother Hilary, though a quiet introvert, preserved a wry humour under the stern facade required of all headmasters in the nineteen-twenties. So when the boys had been made to apologise and received the customary "cuts", two on each hand delivered with a long cane whose swishing noise was almost worse than the pain it inflicted, accompanied by a warning about rules having reasons, the matter should have been forgotten.

Life, however, mocks what should have been. Two weeks later Alan McCleary still nursed a sense of injustice. The accident, he felt, might have happened to anyone; the punishment was absurd. That kraut – he didn't have to make this great fuss.

Alan had never known his father. It had been a pregnant wife that Noel McCleary left waving from the dock when his troop-ship sailed, and he had arrived in France only to die within days. Alan's uncle, Jim Nolan, had gone two years earlier, and had brought back the scars of a bayonet-wound and a detestation of all things German. He had also brought a souvenir – a black spiked helmet, filched in 1917 from No Man's Land and now decaying, half-forgotten in an old trunk under the house which he shared with Alan's mother, Louise, and where he tried to be a father-figure to his nephew.

For Alan, Willy's splenetic outburst merely reinforced what he had so often been told: that Germans were a mixture of madness and badness. And, casting in his mind for some way of responding in kind, he had thought of the helmet. Suppose it were placed high on the roof of the caretaker's house – in some position visible to anyone who passed, and difficult to reach. A German hat on a German roof. The idea satisfied some instinct in him.

The house, like all others in Walgabran, was a white timber cottage raised from the ground on thick piles called "stumps". In its tiny garden there was a majestic silver sentry: a lemon-scented gum. A little above its first fork a heavy limb divided, reaching outwards to form a pair of still substantial branches which remained roughly parallel. These meandered together over the slope of the roof. There the sturdier of them hovered close above the corrugated iron, while the other seemed to accompany it, four or five feet above. And hardly more than a boy's arm-reach away from the lower branch, there rose at the front of the house an ornamental finial.

Could it be done? Alan thought it could.

In this he was not wise. There are trees which might almost have been designed by God for agile children to climb – trees which have a tangle of branches difficult to see through, and which have a solid, unyielding strength, so that they present a sporting challenge without being seriously dangerous if a boy or girl has common sense. Gum trees are not like this. Mostly their branches are sparse and lonely wanderers, spreading widely in their search for space and light, and the lowest is always well clear of the ground. They sway easily in the wind, and not infrequently they break off.

Alan's thoughts did not run to such considerations. He was gripped by a resentment that crowded prudence out. And, he reasoned, the helmet belonged to no one now. He could take it without permission. Of course he wouldn't get it if he asked, but that was just adults being fussy. Really it would only be carrying on the fight against the Germans, who thoroughly deserved it. Pity the war had ever stopped, anyway.

Of course, he'd have to wait a couple of weeks until the start of the Christmas holidays when the school would be almost deserted.

So he brooded until the time came, and then he gathered the boys. They were all there – John, Bruce, Owen, Barry, Ken and Tim – in the little hollow by the river that was their unofficial den. Alan was holding a sack and smiling secretively.

"Look't I got," he grinned, tipping the helmet from the sack onto the grass.

"Gee, that's German!" exclaimed John.

"'Course it is! My uncle Jim got it."

"D'you mean he took it off the German?" asked Ken. "Did he have t' kill him?"

"Yair – he killed lots! Good thing, too."

Tim moved uncomfortably, thinking of his father. Ben Rogers, like most veterans, was taciturn about his war experiences; but once, at a Sunday dinner there had been a revealing incident. It came back now to Tim.

It was, he remembered, an unusually large gathering: Beth Tosh, recently married, and her husband Ned, up from the city where Ned was a jeweller; Joe Carey whose small farm produced a sharp cheese and who kept bees; Andy Dayball, who could break horses. And, as always, Jim Nolan was there with Louise McCleary.

In the course of the chatter Tim's mother had mentioned the German caretaker at the school. Wondering a little, she added "He seems all right – nothing at all like the Germans we used to read about."

"Of course not. That was made-up stuff." Beth spoke sharply.

To Jim she was an enigma, having opposed conscription but soon afterwards gone to France with the Nursing Service.

Reminiscences on the war followed. Ben Rogers and Jim Nolan stayed silent, listening quietly as things they had witnessed were recounted by people who knew them only from half-remembered newspaper articles. The conversation ebbed and flowed. Mingled pride, compassion and pathos were stirred. Someone mentioned Beersheeba, its heroism and the rumours of its shame. There was an embarrassed pause.

Joe broke the silence. "Bloody war!"

"Bloody's right," grunted Ned. "Blood and mud. I don't know how Beth did it."

The talk moved to the nurses, to their sudden introduction to the wounds caused by shrapnel and bullets and mines, and to what they had meant to the men.

"We'll never know half of it," said Beth. "Even over there we saw it the way you see a play – you only get the bit on the stage but you know there's all the stuff behind. Who made the big decisions? Who was right and wrong?"

"And who got rich?" added Louise.

"No," said Andy. "All that'll get written one day. It's the little things – why did a gun jam? Why did a company get stuck? Maybe it was just a sick horse. Those little things could be life or death. And we'll never know."

Beth came back: "Yes, ordinary people bore the brunt. Often for trivial reasons."

Ned, wary of his wife's ability to politicise any conversation, tried a diversion: "Maybe it was a bit better at sea, though. I mean, maybe the attitude was different. That German count with the sailing ship – what was his name? – At least he was old-fashioned and chivalrous."

Joe laughed: "von Luckner was his name – but he was a loner, a brilliant eccentric who ignored the rules."

"I dunno about the sea being much of a place," said Andy. "A lot of men went down. Often both sides lost ships in the same battles."

Jenny Rogers, still thinking of her recent meeting with the caretaker, mused, "Yes – I suppose it was just the same for them as for our boys – poor fellows, it must be awful to drown …"

Throughout this conversation Jim Nolan had fought with rising anger, knowing that he could not speak without displaying violent emotion. Mention of those days always touched a blinding nerve in him.

Louise, too, had said little, and only the slight whitening of her face betrayed her controlled tension. But now Jenny's comment stung, and she spoke tersely. "Well, didn't they start it? Maybe this German seems all right to you, Jen, but I can't ever forgive them – any of them."

"Oh Lou, I'm sorry. Of course it's different for you – I mean … It's just that – well, I met him shopping, and I had too many things, and he carried them home for me, and he was polite."

Beth, not alert to the undercurrents, said inconsequentially: "I don't know why men have to fight."

An awkward pause followed until Jenny Rogers spoke again. "I suppose," she sighed, "that Mr Wilson was right. There'll be another war. I worry about our boys."

Her sister seemed not to hear. "Noel was so young," she whispered, as though to herself.

"Noel?" Ned wondered aloud. The name was new to him.

The simmering anger in Jim boiled and burst through his restraint. "Yes, mate – Noel. Lou's husband. My brother-in-law."

He turned to Beth and then to Jenny. "I'll tell y' why we fight them", he said. "Because that's the way the Huns are – the lot of them. Yer don't get a choice."

"Oh, Jim, they can't all be bad – I mean, I don't think a whole nation can be bad."

"Don't tell me! They love war – always have! You'll see – yair, there'll be another one all right!"

"But men like Mr Schultz …"

She was cut off. Jim was almost shouting. "Bugger Mr Schultz! We saw what they're like! Don't fool yourself, Jen. They'll do anything! What about Charlie Armstrong still down at the Repat Hospital in Brisbane? I didn't get the gas. But he did. The Huns don't fight like men! Y' can't fight gas! If y're lucky y' get time to run – if the wind's right. And that's only going to happen if the wind changes. No one knew what it was, the first time – men just waited, and it came, and they died, slow and nasty. Charlie – he only got a small dose. Just the same, his lungs are shot to pieces. He'll never work again. Can't walk a hundred yards. The mongrels! You don't want another war, Jen? Well, don't take that attitude. Don't trust 'em. Wake up t' yerself."

Tim's father would not have spoken, but after this rebuke to his wife he said quietly, "We all had a bad time, Jim. There's blokes will never come back to this town, and there's girls will never marry. But there's always two sides. When I saw those German prisoners – kids, half of 'em – just like us – sitting there in the Cas' Clearing Station, I knew it was all a bloody great furphy. They didn't order the gas. Jenny's right. They had good men and bad men, just like us. Mostly good, same's our blokes. They were just caught up."

"Look, Ben, you were there. You bloody well know! Don't be stupid! You're sounding like Jen."

"Like Jen! I reckon you'd better apologise, Jim."

"Let it go, Ben," said his wife. "Jim didn't mean it that way."

But he swore, and stood up at the table with the just-served course of his meal untouched, claiming that "they" were all the same, and that Tim's father wouldn't be so bloody charitable to the bastards if he still felt pain in his chest when he worked hard. "Do you know what that bugger was doing when he stabbed me? Laughing! Laughing – that's what! Don't tell me!" And he stumbled out of the house and down the wooden steps in a fury.

"Bloody fool!" said Tim's father.

The meal continued in a constricted atmosphere, with everyone attempting to ignore what had happened. When, after a few minutes of pointless tension, Jenny Rogers got up to follow her brother, her husband said, "Not now", but she replied "I've got to try, Ben." She returned minutes later, white-faced and tight-lipped, on the verge of tears.

"He'll be all right," said Ben. "We've had blow-ups before. Next week it'll be fine."

He was wrong. Relations between the two men continued strained for months. And though, at last, their wives managed to repair the damage, the exchange remained half-submerged in Tim's memory.

Now, behind Alan's last, vicious, "Good thing, too", he could hear its echoes. He felt challenged to speak: this was something he felt his father would not have let go. But his words had to pass through a problem he had never resolved. Everyone knew that the Australians had been heroic – and there was the War Memorial in the park, with all those names … all those good men, fallen; surely the Germans who caused that couldn't have been good. *Both* sides couldn't have been good. Otherwise nothing made sense. Yet … he trusted his father …

All he could think of was to repeat Ben Rogers' words, and a nervous catch came into his voice, robbing it of its intended force. "My father says the Germans were good. Most of 'em, anyway."

Alan grunted: "Oh, yair? You heard Billo! How good d'yer think he is?"

"I dunno. Maybe he's one of the bad ones. There's got to be some like that, same's here."

"Well, he got us all the cuts! I reckon he's mad! And I'm goin' to put this on his roof!"

Tim was startled: "What?"

"It's goin' on his roof – on that little wooden thing that sticks up at the front!"

Barry asked excitedly, "How y' goin' t' get up?"

Ken chipped in: "S'easy. Look at how close the tree is."

John, always the group's sceptic, demurred: "Yair, but … that's a hard tree to climb."

"Yair, I reckon," added Owen.

Alan dismissed the cautionary advice before it could divert his mind. "Not once y'r up t' the first branch. And Billo always leaves a ladder on his verandah – I've seen it lots o' times."

John insisted: "I dunno. I reckon it's a mad idea."

Owen again supported John: "And y'd need two – yer can't reach down to that wooden thing just yerself. Someone'd have t' hang on t' yer."

"'Course. Me'n Tim. But yers've all gotta come."

Barry and Ken nodded. "Gee – up on the wooden thing. I'd like to see that," said Ken.

John, bowing to the pressure of the group, neatly switched sides. "O'course, if there's *two* – yair, that'd be all right. Like Owen said."

Bruce, silent until now, came in on Alan's side: "That's terrific." He turned to Tim. "'Course, I'll do it if y' don't wanta."

Of the group, Bruce was the one Tim especially admired, and it was hard to resist his lead. He knew that his parents would never approve of such an escapade, both because of the very real danger it entailed and because of the mocking character of the attack it represented on the German. He knew, too, that if he refused to take part now, he would at once be called a coward. The group was excited both by the riskiness of the project and by its illicit character, and its technical problems lent an added fascination. Only Tim was sensitive to its injustice. The others would feel some guilt if he or Alan was injured, but they suppressed this thought, and they were too young to understand that they were deceiving themselves.

Tim hesitated, and gave way. It was a moment he would always remember with remorse.

So the boys waited for the vacation and chose a moment when Willy was well away, repairing some dilapidated blackboards in the now deserted school, and they quietly commandeered his ladder. With its help Alan, followed by Tim, clambered to the fork and surveyed their task. They would have to edge up a thirty-degree incline, their bare feet on the lower of the parallel branches and their hands at head-height steadying themselves against the upper one.

At first several smaller limbs twisted in and out of their path, offering added support, but these soon swung away, leaving them exposed on their makeshift scaffolding. The boys progressed sidewise, one foot following the other. Alan, leading, had the helmet perched on his head. It kept threatening to slip off, and in the end he held it in his teeth by its strap, letting it slap against his chest. He was surprised at its weight and the drag at his mouth.

Tim could feel the bark, smooth and cool under his feet. Glancing down, he was appalled to see how far he could fall. In his ears an unaccustomed pressure began to throb, and his head seemed to swell. Fortunately the lower branch seemed perfectly stable; but the upper began to vibrate slightly with their combined weight. Tim wondered whether it could break. He admitted it now to himself – he wanted to turn back. And then he realised for the first time that the descent might be even more difficult. He feared he might freeze. Nothing but Alan's *sangfroid* and the knowledge that the others were watching below kept him going.

The slope became shallower and the shuffling steps easier, and the two branches drew closer together. Tim could now lean on the upper one and twine his arms around it. Alan, because of the helmet, could not do the same; he was forced to crouch a little, and he felt the increased pressure on his bent knees. Determinedly he remained in this chimpanzee posture until at length he was over the corrugated iron of the roof, and actually descending towards it. Tim, a step behind, came closer, reassured that the drop onto the silver metal was at least short. Whether, if he fell, he could then stay on its slope did not bear thinking about.

Alan continued his scrabbling progress, drawing towards the finial until he could get no closer. There was a slight cracking noise. He seemed not to notice. His vaguely imagined intention had been to lie on the lower branch, holding it with one hand and clinging with his thighs. Even if he could have achieved this, it would not have been a stable position, but in the event he found it impossible. Given the space between the branches, it required him to let go with both hands at least for a short time, and without the support of at least one he could never maintain his already precarious balance. And the strain on his body, bent almost double now, had become next to intolerable.

"Hang on t'me," he called through teeth still gritted about the helmet-strap. The words came in an almost unintelligible gurgle. Tim could not have obeyed unless his own right hand had encountered a small projection extending upwards, a tiny secondary branch just small enough to grip. His other hand reached for and held Alan's belt. Alan took the helmet from his mouth. He swayed a moment and recovered. He reached out experimentally towards the hip of the roof.

The gap was far too great. He stretched further.

It happened in slow motion. Tim knew that he could not keep his hold as Alan began to rotate sideways. There was a clear, horrible moment when the fall was not yet but was inevitable. The helmet, half-flung, landed on the roof, and rolled and clattered down the iron slope to lodge in the gutter. Alan was in the air. His head hit the corrugated iron and he seemed to bounce, twisting as he fell to the ground. There was a snapping noise followed by a hollow crack. The upper branch, freed of his weight, swayed horribly, nearly causing Tim to lose his own balance, and it did not quite return to its original position – something *had* happened to it. Tim, aghast, hung on for dear life and stared with a white face at his fallen friend.

The watching boys ran to Alan, who lay motionless. They bent over him, unsure what to do. Blood streamed freely from a wide cut extending from his temple to his ear-lobe, opening his cheek so that bone could be seen. One eye was hidden under the flow. His left leg was twisted under him.

"Y'r all right?" asked John, stupidly.

Bruce looked at Tim, clinging to his branch. "What happened?"

Tim didn't try to answer that – it wasn't a real question in any case. He just stuttered, "I can't move."

The boys hesitated, knowing that this time there would be serious trouble. They stared at Alan, alternately moaning and snuffling, writhing a little. Then they ran for their mothers – all except Bruce, who stayed watching, hoping in some confused way to be of help.

Willy sat with his head in his hands. He thought that he had left the war behind him. But those boys! That helmet – on his roof! A helmet such as he had seen men – good men – die in. A wave of homesickness, mixed with national sentiment, moved over him. He felt alien here. These people – they had no culture, they knew nothing …

He seldom got drunk, but he did that night.

CHAPTER 4

The Mural
(Walgabran, 1928)

Brother Hilary's office was utilitarian: a desk and three chairs, a cupboard and a bookshelf, a crucifix, a picture of Mary with Jesus as a toddler in her arms, and a print of the Matterhorn which made Willy feel a surge of nostalgia whenever he was there.

But it was a seething Ben Rogers who stood there now. He faced the Headmaster angrily.

"A monkey couldn't have done it! Couldn't someone have *seen* them?"

The monk grunted. In the holidays boys were given the run of the playgrounds. The supervision which on school days was standard would have been a sort of intrusion. "We can't be everywhere. No one even knew they were coming on Thursday. I'm extremely sorry that this happened."

"Sorry! My son risked his neck. Young McCleary has a broken leg and a scarred face. There could be brain-damage! Sorry's not enough!"

"Yes. Alan's mother was here an hour ago. Fortunately, I understand that the concussion is slight. I don't want to minimise these matters, but at his age I think he might heal fully. And, you know, that's boys – they're still finding their limits."

"Finding their limits! What about common sense?"

"Of course they've got to learn that too."

"Well, they don't seem to have any yet! And I don't think the school's helping."

"Mr Rogers, I am not a parent, but I can understand something of how you feel. I don't mean to oppose you. I'm trying to be objective – not very successfully, it seems."

Ben Rogers stared. This monk was being so damned calm about what might still prove a crippling accident. With an effort, he returned to the conversation: "Well, first off I'd like the school to apologise."

"I've told you I'm sorry. Really, I am. If there's any other way I can help ..."

"All right, we'll leave the apology there – I suppose that's the best you can do. But it wasn't just the stupidity. It was the nastiness. That helmet up there like a sort of beacon. The war – still with us."

"Yes. It was unpleasant – it might even have caused someone to attack Mr Schultz. Not that the boys would have appreciated that side of it."

"I don't know about that. Young Alan's had a funny upbringing. And I don't want Tim picking up these prejudices. I'm actually embarrassed. In fact I'd like him to do something to make it up to this Mr Schultz. I want to know if you have any ideas."

The monk looked around as though for inspiration. "Well, I'll give it some ..." He broke off. Schultz would be taking advantage of the vacation to do jobs he couldn't manage during term. Could the boy assist him for a day or two? As a sort of reparation?

But ... Germans could be exact about rules. Would Schultz be too strict?

Thinking of Willy, bringing his character into focus, he was convinced that it would be all right. He spoke before he realised clearly that he had decided.

"Look – Mr Schultz could use a bit of help. Christmas is still nearly three weeks away, but he has a lot to do first. Afterwards he has a break himself. Could Tim give him a hand? A few days' work, it would be."

Ben Rogers had wanted some meaningful gesture, but this took him unprepared. He found his mind shifting gear, his protective instincts suddenly dominating.

"Well ... how well do you know this man? I don't want to question your judgment, but ..."

"I'm sure there wouldn't be any problems."

"No, he's too young. At nine, working for 'a few days', as you put it, is pretty tough. I don't even let him help in my business – half an hour here or there, but that's it."

"Well, I was milking cows at that age. I can't think of anything else. And you asked my advice."

Ben Rogers hesitated.

"A nine-year-old boy working alone with this bloke: look – what sort of cove is he? Can I trust my son to him?"

In the nineteen-twenties such reservations were seldom voiced. Apprentices and child assistants a few years older than Tim were routinely entrusted to adult supervisors. No one gave it a second thought. The monk bridled. "I wouldn't have employed him if he wasn't, Mr Rogers. And I resent the suggestion. He's a German – but I believe him to be a gentleman."

"Well – it's an idea. Sort of. Suppose it backfires? Tim could wind up blaming Schultz even more – and you, and me into the bargain. I suppose you'd keep an eye on them?"

"No, I'll be away for a good month. But I'm sure Tim will be all right with Bill for a few days."

"Well ... "I'll talk to Jenny about it."

"Do. You know, it wouldn't be really hard – and boys *like* hammering nails and holding ladders."

❖ ❖ ❖

When Brother Hilary proposed the scheme to Willy, the German almost exploded again. Controlling himself, he said curtly, "I want nothing to do with those boys!"

The monk felt awkward. "I understand," he said. "But his father is concerned – ashamed, I think – and he thinks that it might help him to mature – to understand about prejudice."

Willy sighed. What did these Australians expect of him? To be a nursemaid to the brats who had insulted him?

"This Tim – he was not the one who called me a – cabbage?"

It was a tiny weakening. "No, he had the bat. Look, Mr Schultz, I know that boy. He's all right. I would appreciate it if you gave him this chance."

"A chance – how? I thought this was to punish him."

"A chance to make a gesture. Deep down, I think he needs for his own sake to do a bit of penance."

"You make it difficult, Brother. I do not want to do this."

"Well, I suppose I'm in the middle, Mr Schultz. It would help *me*, too."

Another sigh. "It is what you call the blackmail. All right. I will give him the chance. Only he must be polite, and do what he is told. You know and I know that I could get more work done alone. But we will try."

Unexpectedly, Tim's mother welcomed the suggestion. She made it seem less a punishment than a piece of fun. So Tim turned up at nine on the Monday. "I've got t' help yer," he said, shame and resentment contending in his heart.

Willy was gruff. "Ja. I have some t'ings for you to do."

Tim then discovered, for the first time in his life, what it meant to work for three hours without a break, carrying, fetching, sweeping, holding, and, when he had munched on the sandwiches his mother had packed, to return to the job for two more hours in the afternoon. At times he was pressed and the minutes flew; at others, working at a drearily repetitive task, he looked at a clock and was unable to believe that so little time had passed since his last glance. He found Willy reserved, for which he was grateful – he didn't want to talk to this strange man.

Willy, on his part, watched. His first surge of anger subsided, and the Brother's claim that he was somehow helping this boy struck a nerve in a man who felt that his own chances had been whisked away.

Still, it was the matter of the snake that changed the relationship. Willy was working under a classroom, surrounded by its supporting stumps, clearing away a clutter of old timber and blown leaves in the dark, moist space. He was inspecting the damage done by termites to the steps that led up to the door through a gap in the verandah, and was musing on all the sawing, filling, bolting, creosoting that the job would demand. It was Tim who saw the death adder, still and silent, almost under Willy's foot, and who pulled him back by the arm; and it was old Charlie Armstrong – a tough, experienced bushman, skilful and indomitable in spite of the gassing that Jim Nolan had bitterly referred to – who killed it with a piece of fencing wire while commenting on the process with a wry humour that showed Willy no rancour. Willy had acquired a healthy respect for snakes in New Britain, and he readily believed Charlie when he said that the bite of this one could be fatal. Tim, he realised, may have saved his life. The thought nudged him over an edge. After all, he conceded to himself, the ill-directed cricket ball was simply bad luck, and all it had set in train was – childish.

Through his gruffness, something of this thaw communicated itself. Between the man and the boy arose the first beginnings of fellow-feeling, fostered by working together. As the contact deepened, Willy guessed that Tim had not been the leader in the matter of the helmet – he was somehow not cast in that mould. But he would not ask. The boys were too young to have a code of silence surrounding their little conspiracy, and Willy would not trade on that youth by probing.

By the second afternoon Tim's tiredness was less. He could see things newly mended, and he began to feel that he had helped make the world somehow more finished. Willy, remorseful that he had been pressing the boy too hard, announced a break for what he had come to call "tea" – though it was in fact coffee that he brewed in an old enamelled mug to drink on his battered garden-seat. Tim sat on the ground and contemplated the tree which had played a part in bringing him here.

Willy noticed and nodded. "Ja, some trees are not good to climb, eh?"

Tim looked embarrassed. Willy, suddenly, laughed. "OK, I was angry. But I think maybe you are a good boy. You like lemonade?"

Work in the summer sun had built a thirst in Tim that he had been about to slake at the school bubblers. But lemonade, once mentioned, was infinitely desirable.

"Yes. Please ... Bro' ... Mister." Tim had unthinkingly used the boys' abbreviation when speaking to their teachers.

Slowly the ice was broken. As the days progressed Willy showed Tim how to use tools without harming himself and where to place them for safety. He would not let the boy climb his ladder – "You have climbed enough, eh?" – but a slight smile touched his lips as he said this. The scattered remarks that passed between them – on Tim's side monosyllables at first – grew into increasing chat, until Willy found himself fielding endless questions: "What d'y use this for, Mr Schultz? ... Why's it harder to saw the wood this way than that? ... What's wrong with this putty – why's it all gone hard?" Another man might have told him to be quiet, but Willy, lonely as he was, found himself welcoming the role of mentor, and soon, as he had predicted to Brother Hilary, whatever time he was saved by Tim's assistance was being more than lost in discussion which ranged over many topics.

"He's actually nice, Mum", said Tim at home. "We talk about everything."

"Well, don't ask him about the war," put in his father.

"Why not?" asked Tim.

"They lost, son. We don't know how bad it might have been for him. You've already insulted him once. Leave the war out of it."

"But Dad, he talks about New Guinea and Germany and everywhere."

Tim's parents looked at each other without speaking. "Well, don't talk about the war unless he does first, dear," said his mother.

By the fifth and last day of his penal servitude, Tim had become a sort of handyman-scout, wandering about finding things that might need Willy's attention. Eventually his search led him into the hall, where he found, roughly hidden behind some old movable partitions, and still in its early stages, Willy's mural. Running excitedly, he called out "Mr Schultz – I've found a picture on the wall. It's beautiful."

Willy felt three emotions at once: a burst of anger, that his secret world was breached; a stab of fear, lest Brother Hilary should hear of the work and forbid it; and a glow of gratification, because this nine-year-old who knew nothing of painting had called it beautiful.

A short fuse sputtered quickly in him and died as quickly. "Tim," he said, "that is my own painting. I am making a big surprise – for Brother Hilary and for all you boys. I do not want to tell anyone until is finished."

"Aw, gee, Mr Schultz – can you really paint pictures?"

" 'Really' is a big word, Tim. I paint a little."

"Aw, but that's terrific! It's beaut! You mean it ain't finished?"

"No, it is not finished. And even I who come from another country know you do not say 'ain't'."

"I mean it isn't. When're yer goin' t' tell Brother Hilary?"

"Maybe I can finish it before he comes back for the new term. Then I shall tell him – then, when he can see what it is. You have made the model aeroplanes, Ja? You do not show your parents when they are half-complete. Now – this is a secret.

Can you keep a secret?"

"'Course I can."

Willy directed his most serious look at Tim. "Even from your friends?"

"'Course."

"Even from your parents? – No, I cannot ask that. But Tim, you have made things difficult by finding my painting. I do not want people to know."

"Mr Schultz, this isn't a *bad* secret. It's a good one, like a secret Christmas present. 'Course I won't tell – not anybody!"

And Tim didn't. He completed his days of work and then returned to the life and games of a nine-year-old with his friends. They were intensely curious about Willy and they badgered him for information, and at moments he thought he would burst with his private knowledge. But if he was resolved not to speak about the mural, he was open about the German's friendly character. The assertion that a nice man lived behind the unwelcoming exterior mystified the other boys at first, but they accepted it as just another of the wonders of which the world was full. They were accustomed to things being not always what they seemed, and discovering this new example was simply part of the fun of growing up.

Except for Alan. They visited him in a body, to find his bravado undiminished. After everyone had admired the stitches sealing the livid cut on his face, and signed the cast on his leg, he threw out: "Aw, how'd y' put up with Billo? D'd he belt yer?" To this Tim answered "I reckon he's nuthin' like that. He's beaut. We shouldn't 'a done it."

The ensuing argument kept them apart for a couple of days, during which Tim, faced with a blatant example, began for the first time to understand what ignorant prejudice was. He noticed, too, that when Alan thought no one was looking he would sometimes run his fingers along the developing scar; and he wondered what thoughts accompanied the action.

Yet, in the manner of boys of their age, the dispute was

quickly forgotten. And for once Tim looked forward to school recommencing, for then the mural would be unveiled. He would share the drama of the moment; and more, he would have the special glory of being the first to have seen this blazing display of unfamiliar beauty.

CHAPTER 5

The Mural Unveiled (Walgabran, 1928)

Willy was nervous. Brother Hilary had returned, and tomorrow he and the parish priest would engage in an annual ritual: their inspection of the school's bricks and mortar. The German's private indulgence would become public knowledge. As the critical moment loomed the reckless confidence that had sustained him during the work seemed unreal.

And on top of this, the Headmaster had sought him out for a moment's chat, and as he was leaving had added "I've been noticing the good work you've done, Bill – you're a real craftsman. I'm especially pleased because of our guest."

This struck an ominous note. "Thank you, Brother – do you mind if I ask who is this guest?"

"It's the bishop, Bill. Bishop Maguire. Come to Walgabran to check up on us all. He'll join us for the inspection."

Willy had paled and found an urgent job in a remote part of the school, weeding an overgrown strip of untended land. Even among Australians, whose love of informality had diluted the impact of such customs, bishops were still addressed as "My Lord"; and Willy was a European, subject to the full force of centuries of that tradition whereby they had ranked as nobility.

A bishop! Somehow, he felt, it would make it much worse if he was sacked.

For a week now he had been on tenterhooks: would the Brothers accept the Garden or would they obliterate it under a veil of green paint? And if it came to a dismissal, where could he find another job? These were his immediate worries, shrill in their insistence. But in a sense they were superficial; beneath them was an apprehension of a different sort. Tomorrow would, in effect, be an unveiling – a showing of the work into which his frustrated artistic instincts had been poured with an intensity that only he could know; and, though clerics in provincial Queensland would hardly be experts or perhaps even sensitive to art, they were still educated men with a spiritual dignity that somehow mattered: Willy did not want them to – laugh.

Largely, Brother Hilary shared the awe which had flowed over Willy at the mere idea of a bishop, but it affected the parish priest not at all. He was a rough-and-tumble sort of priest, whose frequent insensitivity men – though not always women – readily forgave. Thirty-five years ago he and Tom Maguire had tackled each other in "footy" games at the seminary; later, they had worked together in two parishes, where their ministry relied on tough faith, bush humour and common-sense practicality. The two were out of the same stable; as Brother Hilary ruefully put it, they "just clicked"; whereas he, one of those men whose shyness has been deliberately thrust aside by an inner courage, felt insecure in their combined presence.

And he could not afford to show this – he had financial demands to make, and they must be put with confidence. He did not think Father Sullivan had ever given the school the priority it deserved, and he intended this inspection to make it clear that at least one new classroom was urgently needed. The bishop's presence, he feared, could work against him, reminding the priest that the parish finances were subject to wider, diocesan demands; it could tip the scales towards a kind of prudence in which Brother Hilary, for all his retiring personality, did not believe.

But to his surprise his anxiety diminished as the tour progressed. The long-standing rapport between his guests bubbled up in good-humoured banter, and in spite of himself he caught the mood. He realised that he was actually enjoying himself. He had come to this meeting full of plans about what he should say and why; and, more importantly, what he shouldn't say and why not; but he found himself chattering about peripheral issues – the boys' appalling taste in popular music, their favourite items at the tuckshop, the work Willy had accomplished in his absence. "We've been really fortunate to have this German chap as a caretaker-handyman," he commented, after they had done most of the rounds. "He's invaluable. Been painting the hall, too – I'd just like us to look in at that. I asked him to smarten it up."

He took a deep breath then and came to his real point. "I haven't mentioned this until now. But enrolments are increasing, and our policy is to turn away no one. In the immediate future we'll make do putting boys in here, up on the stage, but they deserve better than a makeshift classroom. Really we need another building. It's difficult – I know that the parish is strapped for cash. Of course, if we could get help from the *diocese*, our problems would be solved for a few years."

They entered the hall by a side door and glanced around, and the priest, noting the impression of freshness that Willy's caretaking had achieved, nodded approvingly. The bishop too was reminded of an old-fashioned naval ship, scrubbed and tidied, every rope's end spliced and in its place. The great hanging cords that enabled the upper windows to be opened were new and white. The window-frames that had once borne signs of white ants, the skirting-boards that had been scuffed by hastily stacked chairs, the scarred floorboards – everything timber – had been neatly restored. The faded paintwork was gone from the walls and replaced by a quiet green. Nothing seemed amiss.

Brother Hilary felt he had done well. He had shown his guests a well-kept school but one that clearly needed to expand.

He had primed the bishop and he had made his request as bluntly as he could. He'd have to follow it up later, but for now he could relax.

There was little more. One last thing – the stage at the end of the hall was invisible behind its drawn curtains. He hauled on the lanyard that opened them. The three men's eyes came simultaneously to rest on the wall at the rear.

Nothing, perhaps, could have prepared Brother Hilary for the shock. He had expected a neat, plain green wall. The scene he encountered could hardly have been more different or more arresting: a mural whose extraordinary harmony of composition touched a nerve of instant appreciation. Seeing it for the first time, the three clerics become suddenly still.

What they saw was something wholly unfamiliar: as in Tennyson's lotus-land there was an eternal afternoon bathed in gentle sunlight where, on grassy banks dotted with flower-beds, clusters of men and women in elegant and formal dress held lazily vivacious conversations under the protective arches of trees unknown in Australia. A small lake gave back the sky's pastel blue, and the lapping of its water could almost be heard. The scene was perceived through painted French windows, and in the middle distance it receded to a sort of false horizon where a low stone wall marked its fringe, evidently the last built object protecting this place from the contrasting wildness of some deep and sudden valley. Further off rose pine-clad hills, backed again by far-distant mountains which soared to meet a crystal sky and to declare the real horizon.

Reduced in size the painting might have decorated a chocolate box. On the wall it didn't feel like that. Willy had achieved a depth into which the viewer was slowly drawn. Romantic and Impressionistic influences were discernable, but the mark of Willy's own personality emerged in the contrapuntal blend of slowly flowing notes and lightly tripping ones. In the dappling of shade and light, in the interweaving folds of the hills, in the disposition of the human figures, there was a sort of dance. A poise in this woman, caught at that exact moment when turning to glance aside is supremely graceful, set off a tension in that man whose head was thrown back in an unrestrained laugh. A surge of colour bursting from the flowers was vivid against the repose of water, the gentle waving of grass was playful against the settled strength of trees, and in the contrast there was nothing discordant. People, nature, seemed in tune on every level. The mountains, subdued by distance though they were, lent their own dramatic note. In the early twentieth century the subject was traditional enough, but the execution had a remarkable force.

Brother Hilary gazed for perhaps two minutes before he tried to speak, and when he did his words turned into a swallowed cough. His first thought was that he was entranced. His second was that he had forgotten some arrangement he must have made. His third was, who had done this? His fourth was, how was he going to pay for it? Would the bishop think that he had been wasting the school's meagre resources on some fancy project? And his fifth was, where was Bill Schultz, who was supposed to paint a green wall and who must at the very least have connived at this mural – especially since the subject was so clearly European?

Gathering himself, he was about to explain that there had been a mistake. But, before he could do so, the bishop clapped him on the shoulder and exclaimed: "Wonderful! No wonder you kept this till last! The best wine, eh? Who on earth painted that?"

"Who, indeed?" wondered the monk to himself, though he had little doubt. "Just a minute," he said, unwilling either to contradict the bishop's reaction or to admit that he wasn't quite sure. "Excuse me a moment."

He found Willy working in the part of the school which approximated most to a hiding place – the toilets. "Well," he demanded, "a green wall it was to be, wasn't it, Bill? I think something happened to it."

Willy felt no confidence – only a sickening sense that he was about to fall into a pit that he had dug for himself. "I am sorry, Brother," he said. "I cannot explain. I had to do it. I had the paint sent from Brisbane. I hoped you would like it."

And that was the trouble. Brother Hilary *had* liked it. But he doubted that it would provide the right environment for the Seventh Class which he would be teaching this year. Moreover, it was a direct contravention of his instructions, and a headmaster's training did not predispose him to welcome that. Momentarily unsure what to say, he hesitated – just long enough. For the bishop and the priest, tired of waiting, emerged from the hall to see Brother Hilary and Willy standing foolishly silent in the sun outside the toilets, looking at each other.

"Good afternoon, Mr Schultz", said Father Sullivan, smiling. "I have been wondering who painted that new mural in the hall. Perhaps you know?"

"Ja, Father. I painted it."

The bishop intervened. "*You* did? Well that's absolutely wonderful!" He turned to Brother Hilary. "You said this man was useful – he's a treasure! What a great backdrop if the boys want to put on a play or a choral show for the parents!"

Brother Hilary back-tracked a little. This was happening too suddenly. Then his personal convictions surfaced. If there were objections, he had to voice them. "Well, I don't know. We do have to use the stage as a temporary classroom – there's no escape from that for the time being. And this picture – will it be suitable? We don't want the boys dreaming over it when they should be analysing subordinate clauses and conjugating Latin verbs. Besides, even when the hall is being used as it was intended, that mural will hardly be appropriate. We can't have mountains and gardens and lakes distracting the parents on Speech Night, surely."

Father Sullivan was perplexed: "But surely, Brother, you arranged this?"

"Well …"

The bishop jumped in again. "I think it would be splendid on Speech Night. And why *not* have it in a classroom? The boys won't notice it after the first week – they don't notice anything except things they can eat or tackle on a football field. Anyway, don't you have something to cover it with? Rush matting or something." He turned to Willy. "You know what I'd like, Mr Schultz? Would you be able to do *others* – in other schools?"

A few minutes ago Willy had more than half-expected the sack. Now he was apparently being offered an open-ended commission. And, curiously, he felt a sudden reluctance. The Garden had been something in his heart, waiting to get out. He *had* to paint it. But the sense of failure went deep in him, and he was afraid that the effort had drained him artistically – that other landscapes or other paintings of any sort would not have the same burning life. Yes, he knew he could paint almost any natural scene with a certain journeyman competence but – was that enough? He felt an unexpected tug from his job – now that it might terminate. He had become – comfortable. It was like the cosy, unadventurous niche he had found years ago in the museum.

How did one say "no" to a bishop?

Did he *want* to say "no"?

"Well ..." he said, and hesitated, leaving a silence.

The bishop understood – only in the vaguest outline, but enough.

"Of course," he said. "You must think about it. How did you learn to paint like that? And why aren't you using your talent – working as an artist? Surely you are burying yourself here."

"It is – a long story," said Willy. "It is hard to tell."

"I shouldn't push you. But, Brother, what about teaching? Your congregation has the boarding school over at Mitchell Plains. St Kevin's. Most schools have visiting music teachers – why not something similar for art? Perhaps Brother Columban would welcome it. Mr Schultz could travel there on the train a couple of days a week – we couldn't pay a lot, but I'm sure we could manage, say, thirty per cent of a normal teacher's salary."

With bishops, a theoretical question can sometimes be a polite way of expressing a direct command. Whatever Brother Hilary might have felt given more time, there was now no question of sacking Willy, who in a moment had become partly a handyman, partly a decorator, and partly an art teacher.

The mural remained in the school, touching the imaginations of those of the boys who were open to its message. For there was a message. It was subtle, unobtrusive – when the sweat from grimy fists smeared the ink on exercise-books, and the day's heat washed around bare knees, and equally when the morning chill made concentration impossible, it retired almost completely. But it was always there, hovering at the edge of school-room servitude, suggesting an alternative to learning long division. It hinted that somewhere, around some undiscovered corner of life, a world where elegant people endlessly dallied *ought* to exist. In the twenties the post-Edwardian clothes were already impossibly old-fashioned, but this only reinforced the impression of something *almost* real. The garden had a transcendent, Platonic quality, like a glimpse of some more perfect thing behind the common furniture of experience: it seemed a mythical place, a metaphor for something elusive but important.

And for a few students it had a more personal significance. For Bruce, John, Owen, Ken and Barry it was a lasting reminder of a maturing episode. For Alan it was an irritant, something invading his personal space. And for Tim it was a recurring stimulant to an already restless imagination.

But even he did not take it too seriously. Not in his most extravagant dreams could he then have suspected that the painted garden might have a real effect on his future.

CHAPTER 6

St Kevin's (Mitchell Plains, 1932)

Primary education in Queensland was relatively prolonged, and was followed by a mere two years of junior secondary school. Tim and his friends were twelve years old when they arrived as new boarders at St Kevin's. Willy, seeing them file into the school induction ceremony, realised with a start that he had now been a teacher for two years. Two years of catching the five-thirty on Sunday evenings to Mitchell Plains and of being rushed to the station for the return trip on Wednesday mornings, at first in the school's sulky and later in the Essex Six. Two years of learning to manage the many-headed monster that was a class.

The commuting was tedious but the work was congenial. Willy discovered that he was a natural teacher. Boys responded readily to him, and he survived the hump of his first beginning to win respect. Charged with the task of setting up something original, he made foraging trips to Brisbane, where he managed to collect enough books, prints and photographs to make a start with his History of Art course – though with these young charges, and in any case admonished by Brother Columban, he included no nudes. He encountered Australian painting for the first time, and at once saw that the boys would respond to artists who could open a new perspective on their familiar bush. McCubbin, Streeton and von Guerard were quickly included in his armoury. On Mondays he mixed some theory with what he called "Appreciation", while on Tuesdays the boys were set loose with brushes and paint in a large but dilapidated hut known in the school as "The old gardener's shed."

So, as the world slid into the Depression, Willy had a secure job and was infinitely better off materially than if he had stayed in Germany. His sense of failure receded and his own paintings became infused with a new energy.

His classes were small electives, timetabled as an alternative to choir practice, and the students looked forward to them: the work was never dull and digressions were allowed to range freely. Once, for instance, a preceding French lesson had as its theme *à l'atelier*. An accompanying cartoon had shown a figure dressed in a beret and smock, sporting a Dali moustache, and waving a brush at a canvas. Bruce asked Willy why anyone would embark on such a life.

Willy paused in his exposition of perspective on the blackboard. "What makes an artist," he said, "is that he must paint, the way a dog must run and feels bad if it does not."

Joe Duncan's hand went up. Joe was the one student who might become a painter; a little too easily satisfied with his own efforts, he was nevertheless undoubtedly talented. "But sir, just wanting to paint – that doesn't make you an artist, does it – not by itself?"

"I did not say 'want to paint'. I said 'must paint'. If you must paint it will not make you a famous artist. It will not even make you a good artist. But it will make you an artist."

A boy called Tom McGrath chipped in: "Sir, my Dad says he couldn't do any work except farming. He says the farm's in his blood. Is it like that?"

"Yes – in a way, I think it is."

Joe wanted more. "Sir," he asked, "all these things we are

learning – composition and vectors, light and shade, fading colours and mixing tones and brushwork – can't all those things sort of – get in the way? Can't it stop us painting the way we really want to?"

Willy paused a moment, then darted away to rummage amongst the prints jammed into the niches between crowded benches, untidy tables, and the deep concrete sink. He selected one, rejected others, found three more. He propped the first in front of the class.

"Do you like it?"

There was a murmur of approval from the boys. "That's really nice, sir," said Bruce.

"Ja. That is really nice. It is called *The Stonemason's Yard*. Do you think the artist could have painted it without knowledge of perspective and colour?"

They looked with wonder at the meticulously detailed work. It was again Joe who spoke: "No, sir. But …"

"Wait. Now look at this. It has a long name. It is called *A Childless Millionaire and a Poor Woman Blessed with Children*."

The boys were not sure how to react. One giggled, and Tom muttered "Anyone could paint like that."

Willy's hearing was exceptionally good. "No, Tom," he said. "Anyone could not."

Joe said: "It's beautiful, sir. It's like you can – sort of – feel the people. Like you know them."

"Ja. You are right. Now this. It is *The Blue Ship*."

"It's all out of proportion," said Tom, glad to use a word Willy had taught him. "It's not real at all."

"And yet the painter is well known. He was not educated but he is admired. Do you not feel that he loved that place? Does he not make you love it – a little? Now look at *The Sleeping Gypsy*."

Around the class there was an intake of breath. The unreality of the colours immeasurably enhanced the drama of the scene in which a lion was nosing a sleeping woman with her lute resting beside her.

"Gee, sir," said Tim. "Yair, wow!" said Tom.

"It is a work purely of the imagination. Every artist must find his own way. Whatever that way is, boys, *revere* your subject. If an artist feels the wonder – even, say, in a small apple – he will paint with care, with a kind of love for the world."

Joe's attention was gripped: "You mean he thinks the apple is beautiful, sir?"

Willy did not answer directly. "Beauty? Have you heard it said that beauty is in the eye of the beholder?"

Tom interposed: "My Mum says that."

"Well, it is partly true. But – I hope you mother will not mind if I say, only partly."

And Willy embarked on one of his folk-wisdom expositions, expounding something of his own theory of beauty. The boys listened, half-understanding, a little sceptical, but fascinated. The eye of the beholder, their teacher said, was important, for there could be hidden beauty, or beauty in ugly things, and it took the right eye – the right beholder – to see it.

"But then," he continued, "it is not *only* in his eye. The artist *discovers* the beauty. And he helps others to see it. So – was it not there before *anyone* perceived it? Were the sea and the forest not beautiful before there were people on the earth?"

"But," asked Tim, "can a thing *be* beautiful if there is no one to see it? Would beauty mean anything then?"

Willy nodded approvingly. "You are the young philosopher. This is a profound question. I give you my personal answer. I say beauty does not exist without some consciousness. And I say the sea and the forest were beautiful a million years ago. Whose consciousness was aware of that beauty? I say this leads us to be aware of God who always sees.

"Creation is good. That is almost the first thing the Bible tells us. I believe beauty reflects that goodness – opens it – not to our understanding but to our *sensibility*."

"D'you mean our common sense, sir?" chimed in Bruce.

"I said 'sensibility'. Look it up in your dictionaries for your homework."

Joe reached at once for his. At the same moment he asked, "You mean, sir, the beauty's sort of stuck on the top of things?"

"No, no no! The beauty is not a mask. It is real. It is in the things. Given with their existence."

"But sir," said Tom, "that means everything's beautiful."

"No, boys, I do not say that – not in any ordinary sense. But there are many kinds of beauty, and not all of them are seen with our eyes. There is a transparency in beauty: we see something *through* it. The beauty we see alerts us to the beauty we have to learn to see, and that in turn can alert us to the wonder in things, beautiful or not – they all have a depth we never know fully. The world is not a closed system that makes sense by itself. It is a gift whose final meaning is in the giver. It is a personal gift to each of you. And if you see the wonder even in an apple, then, when you paint it, you are making a tribute: to the apple, to the universe, to the giver – the Creator – who made the world for love."

This struck a chord in Tim. Brought up in a devout Christian family, beginning now to seek for deeper answers, he felt that life itself was an endlessly unfolding mystery, an immensity breaking every day upon his developing consciousness. To this mystery he was convinced God was the ultimate answer; and religious services in the school chapel intensified that conviction. But he was vaguely aware that a thousand practical and theoretical questions still hovered in some untrodden hinterland of thought; and whenever one of them was answered before he knew it was there to be asked, he experienced a sense of expanding clarity.

Willy, however, dropped from his metaphysical brooding back to his immediate job. "Now you boys must work with your own eyes and your own paint, eh? Each of you will see the same thing, but you will see it differently. And that is good. You see your own truth. Truth is one; but we each see our own – aspect."

He came and peered at Tim's work. "Ja, the *bowl* is very nice. But the peaches – would you like to eat them? Are they not to bright, too red? You must make them soft. Use your smallest brush – here, mix these colours – yes, then dab it, like this. Later you can smooth it over. That is, unless you want to say something about peaches that most of us do not realise."

Tim hesitated, and said: "Mr Schultz, I can't really paint. Not properly."

"Let us look. Here – you need a lighter hand, and that spot of light – you must make it more – how do you say? – more gentle, more subtle. It should not have these sharp edges like a button on your shirt."

"Sir, c'n I ask you something?"

"That is why I am here."

"Well, Joe Duncan's the best of us, we all know that, and you're always criticising him. You said my bowl was "nice". You never say that to him. I think you only say "nice" when something isn't really good."

Willy sighed. "Ach, sometimes you can be too clever. Well, yes, maybe I am hard on him. It is because he is very good. Maybe he will be a painter. That is not so many people. I am afraid for him."

"Afraid!"

"I am afraid because he is Joe. He cares too much. There is a type of painter who does not mind if he eats, he is devoted only to his work. He is a man driven, and mostly he will be poor, and often he will be a failure. Sometimes he will be great. Sometimes he will be a failure and be great also. That could be Joe."

"But sir, you're a great painter, and you're not like that!"

Willy laughed. "Am I a great painter, Tim?" For a moment he winced as his mind flashed back to an overheard conversation at the *Kunsthistorische* in Vienna. "A *real* painter, maybe?" He recovered. "It is good of you to say this. Go now, finish your peaches. They are OK"

Not that Tim minded not being destined for a career as a painter. Emerging from childhood, he was filled with a taste for the future. And the times promised exciting opportunities, ones his parents had barely glimpsed. It was not long since the Lusitania had bettered twenty-five knots across the Atlantic and Henry Ford had brought cars within the financial reach of many people. The gloom of the Great War had given way to a sense of adventure. The rhythm of the twenties had spread across the world, innumerable scratchy phonographs beating out the sounds of the Charleston and the blues; the rich and bohemian young had embraced a wild optimism that contained a sort of defiance, a mood in which counsels of restraint faded to oblivion like sparks spat into the night from a Catherine wheel.

Since then, the Depression had intervened, bringing desperation for many and despair for some. But the surge of the new ways was not halted. Movies acquired sound, almost every house had a radio, many were getting telephones. Popular music was dominated by the subtle energy of Gershwin and cleverness of Berlin and the wit of Porter. The world was being swept along with all its contradictions. It was going somewhere. Few could guess where. But in the western world, even in those towns whose skies were shrouded in industrial smoke, confidence had followed progress, riding it like a surfboat carried on the falling front of a wave.

For most of Tim's fellows at St Kevin's all this ferment meant little. Some would stay at school to matriculate, and later would study at Queensland University. For others the end both of school and of childhood would occur at the Junior Public Examination taken when they were fifteen. They would return then to the rural properties and businesses established by their parents or their grandparents, or move into whatever employment they could find. Often this meant decisions made almost without thought. Tim however, did know what he wanted to do.

For years he had been thrilled by aeroplanes, and felt a special pride in the early Australian aviators: in Charles Kingsford-

Smith and Charles Ulm and Bert Hinkler; in Harry Hawker, who had discovered how to get a plane out of a spin; in Lores Bonney, who that very year had flown around the country and who was Australian in Tim's eyes. At times he felt it was impossible ever to be part of this. It seemed ridiculous, a lad from a modest Queensland town getting above himself. At others he asked himself, *was* it impossible? Really impossible? Someone had to do it. And – he was someone. Why not?

He read stories of flight: of journeys over deserts and seas and glaciers, and of the still-recent memories of the air war, where his imagination placed him in the cockpit, savouring the sound of the wind screaming through struts and singing in bracing wires while his Sopwith Camel looped and rolled to return again and again to the battle.

Such tales, as written for boys, were simply adventure stories in which fair play and courage were primary, portrayed against the essentially joyous background of men playing like birds in the air. Fallen enemies were respected; and, though there were narrow escapes in plenty, few deaths occurred – on either side. In so far as they expressed any philosophy of war, it was that ordinary people perforce assumed that their own side represented what was good and right, and got on with it, embracing a difficult task with that enthusiasm which is sometimes called "spirit". In the meantime, like any widespread disaster, war did bring to the surface of life strengths and weaknesses, heroisms and betrayals – things that had been the stuff of legends for millennia.

Yet as he read such books an ambiguous sense of something like infidelity itched at the back of his mind; for they sat uncomfortably with the attitude to war he had learned from his parents.

In the meantime he was not unhappy as a boarder at school, though he felt the loss of home. He enjoyed the classes, the games, the company, and in his final year he joined the debating club. By then his relationship with Alan, a little distant at first, had been repaired: the episode of the German helmet had slipped well into the past, over-ridden both by their blood-relationship and by the length of their childhood friendship; and Tim increasingly admired his cousin who achieved a sort of prominence as someone brilliant at sport and more than competent at study. Tim's own academic results were middle-of-the-road, but in his last term he worked intensely, and to his own surprise was awarded a prize for Mathematics. He came out of that morning's assembly holding the framed certificate and glowing.

It was perhaps the worst day for the letter to come. The news was bad – and good. Ben Rogers' hardware business was teetering under the impact of unpaid debts and reduced supplies, but the local bank had an immediate position vacant for a junior clerk. The manager had actually contacted Ben to suggest Tim for the job. In these times, it was a rare opportunity; and it might tide the family over. Who knew? Perhaps in a couple of years something would happen to the world's economies, lifting the Depression. In the meantime, banking was a good career. It would actually be a good start for Tim if he was to leave school now …

Tim felt the news in his stomach, like a blow. A bank! It was the opposite of every dream he had. How could he join the select band that flew aeroplanes if he worked in a bank at Walgabran?

He had forty minutes free, before study and the evening meal. He wanted to talk, but not to any of his mates. Willy would still be in his classroom, putting things in order.

"What can I say, Tim? If your father says he needs you … You know, you can still get your Certificate. You can do the exam as a private student. I will help you. Brother Hilary will help you, I think. Mathematics and English and whatever you will need. And you should not despise honest work. In the bank you can have a good career."

Tim knew then that there was no alternative.

Part 3: Growing Up

CHAPTER 7

Margaret and Willy (Walgabran, 1935)

The citizens of Walgabran could leave its streets behind in a half-hour's walk. Earthy smells from nearby paddocks mingled with bush perfumes, and the resulting cocktail drifted through on every breeze. The houses were of white timber, and raised on their stumps they sat lightly on the ground. Their open verandahs had lacy railings of cast-iron, interspersed between narrow wooden columns that rose to support bull-nosed roofs of corrugated iron. At the joins fretted supports added a playful note. The whole effect was welcoming.

A larger and more elaborate version of the same architecture could be seen in the cluster of shops where the two central streets crossed, and in the three pubs. The sawmill, the one industrial building, was on the outskirts, half-hidden in sparse bush. The entire townscape blended comfortably with the surrounding natural environment.

Except for the bank. It alone was alien; a remote descendant of a Greek temple, built of sandstone and red brick, it had an atrium flanked by imposing granite pillars. It seemed to boast that the heavier culture of commerce had marched through and elbowed aside the simplicity of the unresisting land.

And this had its psychological effect. In a country where a

good farmer could improvise wonders with bits of old machinery and a length of fencing wire, and a good bushman would thrive where a new chum would die, and where manners might sometimes have rough edges but rested more on simple good-will than etiquette, the social structure nevertheless contained subtle distinctions, and the overhang of centuries of transplanted European tradition lent a mystique to certain occupations – to the doctor, the teacher, the banker. A man might be a master in his own domain but nevertheless show some nervousness in the precincts of these professions.

This was even truer if he had a private reason for feeling foolish. So Willy removed his hat and turned it self-consciously in his hand as he pushed open the heavy door of Jarrah and glass. He approached the single teller on duty and said quickly, "I have an appointment with Mr Rogers."

The teller looked at him and grinned unprofessionally. "Good morning, Mr Schultz. Tim's waiting for you. He's our new assistant in loans – between you and me, it's pretty good, at his age. What's in the suitcase? Money?"

There was indeed money in the cheap suitcase in his hand, and Willy knew that the fact might give rise to those half-kindly, half-mocking jokes he had come to associate with Australians. Shrugging, he went past the tellers' windows to an office where Tim sat behind the smaller of two desks. The other desk, a grand affair dominating the room, was unoccupied.

Tim rose and held out his hand. "Come in, sir. Take the load off your feet."

Willy sat and gazed around. Time, he thought, flies. Time tricks us. The shy boy who had once raised a lump on his head with a cricket ball, and on whom he had kept a distantly solicitous eye at St. Kevin's, had become mysteriously transformed into this young man who, at seventeen, shared an office in the bank, wore a three-piece suit to work in winter, stood when anyone entered the room, was never in the street without a hat, and still called his old teacher "sir".

The half of Willy that remained German appreciated the "sir". The half that had become Australian found it too formal. But certainly, Tim had matured.

"Ja, they promote you quickly. You should have your own office."

"Not likely, sir. I'm the dogsbody."

"Dogsbody? The body of the dog?"

Tim laughed. "It means someone who runs around doing everything that no one higher up wants to do."

"So. Like the sheep dog, eh? But you do well. You did not want to come to this bank. And now I think you like it?"

Tim had indeed become comfortable. A blurred regret stirred in him on the rare occasions when an aeroplane crossed the Walgabran sky, but these were small ripples on the surface of life, quickly disappearing. Yes, he thought – his dream had faded. He had become settled; perhaps a little too settled. "I guess I do," he responded. "It's not bad."

"Not bad? Australians – you never say anything is good. But you have this work, you concentrate, you learn, you progress. It is good. Your boss – how is he?"

"Mr Rainier? We all call him Cloudy. Fits his personality – a bit gloomy; overcast, you might say. But he's been a friend – got me the job in the first place."

"Well, in these times a friend in the bank is good. Tim, I have saved a little money. I leave it here – for now."

"Well, that's good, sir. Have you withdrawn it from some investment? I'd say you're wise. It's not like in 1930, and I guess the depression must break some time. But who knows when?"

"So – I give you advice, you give me advice. Well, here it is." And Willy hefted the suitcase onto the desk.

Tim's eyes widened. "What – in there? Look – it's got a broken lock …"

"Oh, it is all right. Here people are honest. But I should not keep it at home."

"Sir! You've had it at home? Where? Not – not under the bed, surely?"

"Well ..."

It was almost a shamefaced admission. Tim understood then why it was to him that Willy had come for what should have been an over-the-counter transaction. He shrugged and smiled. "Maybe it is true, sir, that artists really are impractical. Well, I can open an account for you. Better have two." And he talked at length about savings accounts and cheque accounts and pass books and the rules governing them, and secured Willy's signature in six places on official-looking documents.

"Now, sir, I'll take it to a teller. You go round to the front – over there."

The young man behind the counter took the suitcase and papers and, warned by Tim's momentary wink, strove to preserve a solemn demeanour as he counted the money, filled in the receipts, and entered the balance in the pass book. It took the better part of ten minutes. Then Willy, his business finished, walked quickly back to Tim's office to say goodbye.

"Come back in, sir. We've a moment. I've wanted to ask how things are at St. Kevin's – Brother Columban treating you well?"

"It is good, Tim. I like the teaching. You remember Joe Duncan? He is starting next year at the Brisbane Institute of Art."

"Sure I remember Joe. And I remember you said once you were worried about him."

"Yes – I worry still. He will do well – as an artist. I know that now. But as an ordinary man –who knows?"

At least, Tim thought, he would not keep his money in a tattered suitcase. "He always seemed sensible. I'd bet he'll be all right."

Willy sighed and seemed unwilling to say more. He changed the subject abruptly. "Well, I came here for business, and you are a busy young man – I must leave you. Oh, excuse me."

The last exclamation was occasioned by a near-collision. As Willy stood to go in the confined space, he was forced back by the opening door. The brief knock had given no real warning. Miss Flaherty, personal secretary to the manager, aide to the accountant, typist, maker of tea and the *real* dogsbody, put her head in and said, "Tim, I am sorry to interrupt, but could you see Mr Rainier as soon as you're free? – Oh, I am sorry." The last remark was directed to Willy who was recovering his balance.

"We're just finishing, Margaret. Thank you for coming, sir."

Miss Flaherty let her hand remain a moment on the doorknob and glanced at Willy as she withdrew.

Willy, startled by a stab of unexpected emotion, asked: "Who was that, Tim?" But without waiting for an answer he went on, "Well, I must not keep you. Goodbye."

Later Miss Flaherty reappeared. "Who was that, Tim?"

"It's a long story. He's one of my old teachers – an artist. He came here from Germany. He's a nice bloke, but – not like most people. Sometimes he talks about all sorts of things. He'll go on for a long time and – well, you might think he was boring, but I don't. I like to listen. I think he's a – what do you call it? A philosopher."

"A philosopher? Here, in Walgabran?"

"Sort of."

"He has an interesting face. Oh! Now – don't you tell him I said that."

"Who? Me?"

The trifling episode gave Tim the idea. Why should not Willy, wandering soul, and Margaret Flaherty, like many women in the aftermath of war unmarried at thirty-four in spite of a bright personality and a nice taste in frocks, be made into a match?

In a sense it was easy. He urged Willy to make appointments with the manager, strictly unnecessary but inevitably taking him by Miss Flaherty's desk and scrutiny. He asked her to run after

Willy with the cheque book he had forgotten to give him. To each he praised the other as subtly as he could, dropping pieces of information that he judged might be intriguing. And, after a month of this preparation, knowing that she would be with her brother at the local racetrack on the following Saturday, he declared that he would attend and persuaded Willy to accompany him – not difficult in a country town where a race meeting was an important social event and which, Tim suggested, might well provide subject-matter for a painter. He feigned great surprise to find Margaret there, but he introduced them formally for the first time, laughing against a background of prancing thoroughbreds and colourful jockeys – a background where conversation was easy and it was natural for people once connected to remain together in a relaxed camaraderie; a background, Tim hoped, that might promote a more intimate friendship.

His efforts, somewhat to his own astonishment, had borne fruit; and now, two months later, it was a newly engaged couple that he had asked his parents to invite to Sunday dinner. Waiting for them on the front porch, he felt a touch awkward. At work he and Margaret would joke and chat as equals, they would greet each other at the shops and after church, but she was fifteen years his senior and suddenly in this new context it mattered; while Willy, more than an acquaintance, was still less than a friend. So when he welcomed them, dressed in his best suit and beaming, he adopted a stilted formality.

"Welcome, Margaret; good afternoon, sir," he said.

Willy laughed: "I think now you must call me 'Bill'. It is the Australian way. Especially when I am a guest in your house."

Tim was saved from replying by his mother's arrival, surreptitiously whipping away her apron as she ushered her guests to the room known as the "lounge" and called to her husband, "We're ready, Ben – open the beer." Turning to Margaret, she went on: "We were *delighted* to hear the news – it's wonderful! Oh, and that colour does look *perfect* on you, Miss Flaherty ... Congratulations, Mr Schultz ... " – and so the sentiments went on, uncertainly breaking the ice, a little restrained until all were taken to the table and seated, when the talk shifted here and there and became more voluble as the initial stiffness succumbed to the beer. The baked dinner was served on the best dinner set, and Ben made a ceremony of carving the lamb and passing the vegetables. There was talk of Willy's work as a teacher, and of where he grew up, and of how different were Vienna and the Alps and the Rhine from the sparse gums and struggling rivers of Queensland west of the Great Dividing Range.

Then Ben Rogers unwittingly turned the conversation into heavier channels. It began with the most inconsequential of questions – "How d'you find this brew, Bill?" he asked.

"Ja, it is good. Very good. Maybe it is the second-best beer in the world."

Jenny laughed. "Only the second?"

"Well. Perhaps I am prejudiced. But I have to say this – it is not quite as good as the best in Munich."

"Do you think you will ever drink Munich beer again, Bill?" asked Jenny.

It was Margaret who replied. "We thought of going there for a honeymoon – but travelling is so expensive, and just getting there and back would take at least twelve weeks. We'd need four months at least. For me it wouldn't matter – I'll have to resign, of course; but Bill couldn't take the time off work. He wants to see his family, but in a way he's glad not to go – it's such a mess over there."

Tim asked: "A mess? You mean the politics – those new people running things?"

Willy nodded. "Ja, the *Nationalsozialisten*. Hindenburg was the only one who could do anything with them. And he is gone. I am afraid for Germany."

Ben Rogers tried to be reassuring. "Your people have always been great managers, Bill. They're even beginning to recover from the war."

"My people? Margaret's people are my people now."

Excited, Tim called out: "You mean you'll take out citizenship? I'll say that's great!"

Willy's smile carried a hint of sadness. "Ja, I will become Australian. But my other people – my people in Germany – they have always followed men who make big speeches and tell them to obey. That is why I am afraid. I do not know where this will end."

"Yes," replied Ben, "I know. I used to think this new German government might do some good – that it might hold Russia back. But they are becoming just another dictatorship."

"Becoming? Already they have given themselves the powers of dictators. They have banned other parties. There have been assassinations. They are building a new army."

Jenny sighed. "Where will it stop?"

"They will not stop. I do not think they wish only to control Germany. Certainly not Germany with the borders she was given in 1919."

"D'you mean other countries will be involved? Again?"

"Yes. And other countries will resist."

"So – what Jim Nolan always says is right? There'll be another war?"

"It could be. I must be Australian."

The full meaning of this struck Tim for the first time. "But sir – I mean, Bill – that's impossible! Wouldn't *we* be involved? Wouldn't you be sort of – caught in the middle?"

"Ja, Tim. If there is war, it will start in the East. Maybe France will object. Maybe Britain. And if Britain, Australia. Yes, I would be in the middle. Margaret and I have talked of this. Where my wife is, that is my home."

"Oh, goodness! This could be terrible for you!" exclaimed Jenny.

Willy glanced at Margaret, and smiled. "No," he said, "it is not terrible – not for me. Nothing can make me unhappy now. But ... I have read some writing of this man Hitler. He thinks the Allies have squeezed Germany to death, and he is right.

Even America withdrew its investments after the crash on Wall Street. So he wants Germany to have increased territory – he wants secure resources for industry and what he calls *Lebensraum* – room to live – living space.

"But I think he wants more. The word "Reich" can mean a kingdom, a state; but it can also mean an empire. He wants it to last for a thousand years. They are a little mad, these people. They talk of honour and pure blood and superior races. They get drunk on these ideas; and they can make the people drunk, because the people think they were betrayed by people inside Germany as well as crushed by people outside – and if people feel they are betrayed, they get resentful, and if they are resentful they like to get drunk. Maybe I would be the same. But I am here, and I can see my country from far away, and I am glad."

"You think it's that bad?" asked Jenny.

"Ja, it is that bad."

Ben spoke very quietly: "I don't know how old you are, Bill – too old, I suppose – but suppose you had to fight – on our side – what could you do?"

Into Tim's mind there flashed a memory. He had once noticed Willy sitting on a bench in the municipal park, unaware that he was observed. He was gazing up fixedly at a figure on a pedestal, a digger sculpted in sandstone, head bowed and arms reversed. Around him was a well-kept lawn, and nearby an ornamental arch. Apart from the eternally meditating digger, there was no hint of anything military. The place was lent privacy by the U-shaped hedge that surrounded it, and Willy seemed lost in thought. Tim for a moment had felt absurdly furtive, as though he was intruding. He had walked quietly away. Now however that moment had a vivid significance. He interposed: "Bill wouldn't fight – he hates war."

"Mightn't have any choice, if he becomes an Australian," said Ben.

"Then he won't! I'm not going to have Bill fighting the people he grew up with!" cried Margaret.

"No, Tim," said Willy. "I will never fight again. Ben, I was at Verdun. It affected my lungs, my back. No army would accept me now. But even if they would – no, I will never fight again!"

Ben paused. To himself he murmured, "Yes ... Verdun ... yes ... " and he drifted into silence – a silence that became contagious, like a moment of dramatic stillness in a play. Willy, now the centre of attention, remained very quiet in a way that no one wished to interrupt. Then, slowly, almost as though he had forgotten the company, he spoke in a monologue, a man thinking aloud.

"In the sights of your rifle there is a man – your enemy. It is not hard to kill someone – physically. With a rifle it is just pulling a trigger. But then, no action is really just physical. It also has motives, consequences, meaning. And to squeeze that trigger is very hard if you let yourself think *really* think ... really care ... he is not a target ... he is a man ... once he was a baby, helpless, and then a small boy, sometimes playing, sometimes confused. Still he is confused ... he is confused about why he should kill you and you should kill him. There flows through him the gift of life – something immense, yet something that can be torn out of this world by a small piece of lead. At home he has a mother, a wife ... a child waits for his return ... if you pull the trigger he will not return – ever ... a whole family will be destroyed ...

"There is a force – something evil – that takes over nations and sweeps them along to destruction. Twenty-three years ago the great nations of Europe treated their youth as chaff – as nothing, to be sacrificed. And the youth went – we went, we went in pride ...

"Until we learnt ...

"In an army, a cook on one side can talk to a cook on the other side, or a general to a general, as friends – if they can meet. They cannot meet. Each cook is linked to his own general, each general to his own cook, though they could not say much to each other over a drink. But that link is real. So – what is it?

What unites them? Nationality? No, not if that just means geography or political arrangements. Some nations are artificial – absurd. No, it is because they are a *people*.

"But the link between the two cooks, the two generals, is also real. There is something deeper than nationality – much deeper; deeper even than shared culture. It is our humanity. In war, you fight your brother."

Then he repeated, almost inaudibly, "Nothing can make me unhappy now. Not even these Nationalsozialisten … "

And they heard him whisper: "But … my country … my country …"

Jenny Rogers saw the tears in his eyes, and raced to get the stewed fruit and custard. Everyone made an effort, the meal recovered and finished brightly enough; yet under the surface there was something unsaid, something to be afraid of.

As the guests were leaving, Margaret drew Tim aside, and astonished him by giving him a big, smiling kiss.

"Thank you, Tim," she said.

CHAPTER 8

Three Conversations (Walgabran, 1935–1938)

In the years following Margaret and Willy's marriage, the Depression was receding into the past. People who had been impoverished and sometimes ruined took what jobs they could get and tried to re-build. In Walgabran individual lives began to flow more or less contentedly. A few people came, a few went. There were weddings and funerals. A man was arrested for trying to burn down the Drover's Rest. A child went missing, wandering in the bush. There was a flood, and the river ran between the stumps of the houses without reaching the floors. Ben Rogers' business began to recover. Tim's superiors at the bank continued to approve of his work, and his social life expanded, drawing on the Church of Mary Immaculate Social Society and the tennis and the bush-walking clubs. He took several girls out in a half-serious way and was generally well-liked in the town. Margaret and Willy had a son. Willy continued teaching, painting and meditating on life and the universe.

Those years contain only three events that bear on this story, and these are no more than short conversations.

❖ ❖ ❖

The first occurred early in nineteen thirty-seven when Tim encountered Willy in the middle of Walgabran's single pedestrian crossing. Fumbling in a futile attempt to juggle his over-full shopping bag with one hand while holding out the other, he spilt groceries onto the road. Contemptuous of the sparse traffic, he knelt to collect them, and Willy did the same. Their heads collided. Tim looked up and grinned.

"Still the Good Samaritan. You've got a bloody hard head. Great to see you, Bill. Since young John was born I don't often get the chance."

Willy rubbed his temple. "A hard head is better than a hard heart. Ja. They keep me occupied – Margaret and my job and especially Hans."

Whenever Tim heard the artist's pet name for his son, he felt as though he had just driven over some invisible bump in a car. There were still plenty of people in Australia who saw red at a hint of anything German. But he was unwilling to comment. Instead he asked: "Have you got time for a quick beer?"

"Always for you, Tim. But it cannot be long."

Gathering the groceries, hustling, avoiding an erratically driven 1932 Vauxhall Cadet, skirting the barber's pole and the horse-trough, they went around the corner to the pub, and when they both held chilled glasses, Tim asked at once, "Bill, what do you think of this business in Spain?"

"The war? It will be bad."

"Which side do you think is right?"

"There are not two sides. There are two coalitions. Each has four, five political groups. Moderates, extremes, crazies. Most try to use the others. What unites them? Anger and fear."

"Bill, that's fence-sitting."

"No, it is the truth. Newspapers make it simple, but war is never like that."

"Well, I don't know much about politics. Working in a bank I've seen how necessary the enterprise of individuals is – for us all. But I've also seen that the wealth doesn't get spread around unless people fight for it tooth and nail."

"Yes. Capitalism has led to many injustices. Communism has reacted from those. At its heart there is a sort of idealism, but it also has an arrogance; it wishes to force its vision, and it does not see that its vision is limited. It does not respect human nature. It too breeds injustices."

"Not Capitalism. Not Communism. So – what is the answer?"

Willy put down his glass. "Of course we need some system. The big parties in this country – the UAP, the ALP – they are OK. But something further is needed – something not economic and not political but cultural. You know what matters most? It is how people think about each other. How they value each other. As individuals."

He paused, musing, and continued: "Capitalism sees society like a tent – like a structure held in place by tension, by self-interests in opposition. And so long as human beings can be selfish, I suppose that has a place. But there is another structure – the dome, where the curved walls lean together and give mutual support. Centrifugal forces are replaced by centripetal ones. Taking is replaced by giving. That too is present in society. But we need it – we need less of the tent and more of the dome."

"Isn't that the Communist idea?"

"Thinking it is so is what attracts some people to Communism. But a dome rises from the ground. The Communists want to impose it – from above. They say it will emerge from historical progress, but still they will hasten that process – help it begin as a violent eruption. They do not see that giving is only creative and free and stable when it arises from a culture of gentleness. They do not understand – giving needs love, and love needs God."

"Bill, that's too simple."

"Of course. Great truths are simple. But their application is complex, difficult. And in dealing with the complexities we forget the foundation – we forget why we began."

"Well then, I'll tell you why I wanted to ask. Do you

remember Joe? Back when I was at St Kevin's? A thin kid with big ears? You said that you were worried about him."

"Joe Duncan? Young Joe? Of course I remember. He went to art school in Brisbane after he left school. Have you heard from him?

"No, *I* haven't heard from him. But it seems he went on to study in London. Bruce had a letter. He said Joe talked about how all the students were supporting the Republican side, and some of them were volunteering for something called the International Brigade, and he was going, too."

Willy said nothing. He put his head in his hands, and rocked forward over the bar like a man in pain, then seemed to recover. Almost to himself, he muttered: "Waste, stupid waste …"

Disturbed, Tim said: "Maybe he'll be OK – after all, he can still be an artist when it's over."

"Yes … if he survives, and then if his soul survives …"

"But Bill, do you think he was right?"

"No, I do not think he was right."

"But, I mean, about the side he took?"

Willy sighed. "For years Spain has been a tangle I cannot unravel. There are reports of Nationalists murdering teachers, of Republicans murdering priests and nuns. Each side hears what it wants to hear. Young students from Britain, France, America go and think they are defending humanity. Those countries do not send arms, but Russia and Germany send more than enough. Germany is supposed to be neutral, but she is given rights to Spain's minerals. Why does she need more minerals? To make motor-cars? I do not think so. Perhaps to make tanks? For the German government, this is the experiment."

"Experiment? You mean a sort of test?"

"I am afraid of it. Spain is terrible. But I think there will be a bigger war – soon."

"Bill, are you sure? Some people say that Hitler, and Mussolini too, have been good – made their countries efficient. Even helped poor people."

"Efficient, Tim? Efficiency can be monstrous. Even if only

half what the newspapers say is true, the *Nationalsozialisten* have made life impossible for Jews and for other people. I get letters from my family, and I know that many people want Germany to be great again, and many are angry, and many are afraid. Anger and fear – just as in Spain. And national pride. About Mussolini I do not know. But Italy invaded Ethiopia and the League of Nations condemned this. I can smell war. It is not a smell I like."

He paused for a time, and Tim sensed that he would drift into one of his impromptu reflections.

"Twenty years ago nations fought with all the effort of all their people – their bodies, their courage, their minds. Millions died. Even the land seemed dead. We became like men drilling down, through the earth, searching for water but finding only rock; so we were satisfied with rock.

"War – is it caused by the leaders of nations? They make the final decisions. But they too are victims of their cultures, of events. Perhaps it is also the little people; everyone who contributes to – what we call the *Zeitgeist*."

Then he exclaimed in a startled way, realising that twenty minutes had passed, and said: "Good-bye, Tim. I go quickly."

And Tim too went. But he went slowly and lost in thought.

The second conversation took place about a year later, in the bank where Tim worked. Even now, after more than four years on the staff and some rapid promotion, his knock on the door of William Rainier's office was slightly hesitant. Somewhere, in the byways of life, Cloudy had acquired an aura of genteel toughness. Tall, thin, with melancholic good-looks, his face heavily lined, his dress impeccable, he always knew what to do, what to say, how to be generous with some clients and, in the most agreeable way, firm with others. It made Tim feel homespun. It was a reminder of how far there was still to go, both in life and in the banking profession.

"Ah, come in, Tim. A fine September morning. A nip in the air, though. Heavy frost earlier. Would you sit down a moment?"

A little stiffly, Tim sat on a hard chair. Facing the manager across the polished hardwood desk, he felt the need to clear his throat. "Good morning, Mr Rainier."

"How is everything, Tim? Work going well?"

"Yes, I think so."

"I think so, too. Mr Piggott says you've been doing a fine job, and I agree. In fact, there's a possibility of something that might interest you."

Tim was gratified to hear of good report from the bank's second-in-command. But he said simply, "A possibility? That sounds fine, Mr Rainier."

"I hope more than a possibility. Tim, you must realise that you can't progress in the bank if you stay in this town. Head Office is asking country branches to send selected candidates to Brisbane for six months. At the end of that time, if they think you're up to it, they'll offer you a traineeship as an accountant. I'd like to nominate you, Tim."

Tim uttered a swallowed gasp, and replied in some confusion. "It's a great opportunity, Mr Rainier. But I don't know … there's Mum and Dad."

"I'm sure your parents would want it, Tim. After all, you were away at boarding school, and you could come home sometimes for week-ends – one week in three, in fact. They'll give you those Saturday mornings off. Brisbane's only five hours away by train. It's not much of a service, but if you're quick you can catch the 6.42 on Friday evening and get the 3.05 back on Sunday. Talk to your parents. I'd like your answer by Monday – that's all right, isn't it?"

The third conversation took place at Tim's home that same evening. Ben Rogers had once hoped that Tim would eventually take over his hardware business, but its near-failure a few years ago and Tim's success in the bank had altered his mind. Sadly, he admitted to himself that this offer was better, though he would not speak without consulting his wife. And when he did, Jenny did not hesitate. Disguising her real feelings she said brightly, "Of course you must – it's a wonderful opportunity. *I* would if it was me, Tim." And even as she said these words, within herself she wondered – yes, for a while he would come home regularly; but would that last? Was this the moment when she would lose her son?

"That's right," said Ben. "So would I, mate. And with Alan studying law down there, you'll have a friend to show you around."

CHAPTER 9

Alan, George, Reg, and Mrs Campbell (Brisbane, late 1938)

In spite of his father's expectations, when Tim went to Brisbane he did not re-establish the close friendship with Alan that had enlivened their childhood. There was some early contact, and he was invited to a dinner party where Alan, with an arm round his shoulder, introduced him to Brian and Victor, who intended to become solicitors, and to Charles, a budding barrister. But about the meal there hung an unspoken awkwardness. As the evening progressed Tim felt increasingly like someone excluded from a charmed circle. The pranks of friends wholly unknown to him were recounted with glee, and outrageous exchanges between a king's counsel and a judge were wittily satirised. With a touch of envy he realised that these students of the law had been drawn into a sub-culture with its own jargon and anecdotes and style of humour. He began to suspect Alan of regarding anyone not at a university as no longer in his world. And he was unwilling to cling to the fringe of that world as a sort of tolerated visitor.

He might nevertheless have remained in touch with his old friend had the argument not happened. It was inevitable that the talk should turn to the news from Europe. Hitler wanted Austria to become a protectorate of Germany and had demanded self-determination for German-speaking Czechs. About the wider significance of these events Alan's friends were divided. Brian thought that a Germanic bloc would remain economically powerful but be contained by its neighbours. Victor and Charles were less sure but hopeful. Alan himself took a simple, and opposed, view: "War's in their blood. It's all they understand."

Tim, feeling somewhat out of tune with the company, preferred to remain silent, but he did not bargain for the diatribe that was to emerge. Alan went on to claim that the Germans could never be trusted, and he actually mentioned the prurient posters and cartoons which, early in the Great War, had presented them as grinning bloodthirsty monsters.

"I know," he said, "that some of that stuff was made up. But was it *all* made up?"

Tim could almost see Jim Nolan in the background. Suddenly he heard himself arguing.

"Alan," he said, "that's bullshit. Yes, there *were* atrocities in Belgium in '14. But do you know any real Germans? My Dad met prisoners, and he says that they were just ordinary, like us. Many of them were glad to be captured. Some were just sixteen. They had been forced to fight – just like the English and the French, and the Americans too, at the end. I know you weren't fond of Bill Schultz at school, but he was a decent man – a good man. And he was an ordinary German."

Alan's eyes narrowed and – Tim was certain that the action was unconscious – absently ran a finger along the faded scar across his cheek. Brian, Victor and Charles, sensing undercurrents, sat back, a detached audience at a debate.

"No, Tim, I wasn't fond of him. But cut the red herrings. Schultz isn't the point. There's going to be another war. And this time we'll have to finish the job."

"Alan, *millions* died. War's no answer. Does it *ever* do more good than harm?"

"Mate, are you a pacifist? A conscientious objector?"

91

"Maybe I am."

"Come off it, Tim. What do you expect people to do if someone's trying to massacre them?"

"I know. A mob of thugs running amok through a village. Resistance is instinctive. That's one thing. But *big* wars? Look – when we were kids we read war stories. Not just set in the Great War, older ones too. In all of those stories the enemy doesn't really matter – not as people. When they're shot it's just a skittle knocked over. Why? Because they're *not* people – not really. They're the enemy. They're there to fill a sort of slot in the story. They have faces like men, but they're not human. In westerns they're 'outlaws' or 'Indians'. In King Arthur they're dragons and giants; in Robin Hood they're the sheriff's men. I had books where they were Spanish sailors or Caribbean pirates. But really, it's always the same enemy – with different names. They're all just part of a universal myth about a force we oppose. The 'baddies'.

"And all right, they're just stories. But the trouble is, *real* wars rely on the same myth. They divide humanity into us and them, and then they see "them" as sort of non-people; as a – what's the word? – an impersonal force. Almost an – an abstraction.

"Look at the air war. Men could shoot each other from the sky and then, if they survived, take them to the mess and toast them almost as comrades. That's the same myth. They were the enemy. They're people again now – once they're captured.

"But France was drenched in real blood. That myth is based on lies. Maybe the German nation *is* caught in it now. If we join in it as well, we play the same game back. And so it goes on – a bloody great ping-pong game of death. Alan, I reckon that's what keeps wars going."

Alan began his reply quietly, but Tim could see the passion rising in his boyhood friend. "Tim, you seem to believe we can just pretend that everyone's nice; instead of fighting we can all just shake hands and go home. Do you have any idea what really led to the Great War? It was national pride – pride and fear and jealousy and greed and the desire to dominate. And half the nations of Europe were guilty of it! Why? Because that's what people are really like. Face the bloody fact.

"You don't like the word 'enemy'. You believe a soldier can think of his opposite number as he thinks of the man beside him. But no. It's not like that. It's like a surgeon at sea who has to operate without anaesthetics. If he let himself feel too much he couldn't do his job – couldn't help the patient. Well, soldiers have a job to do – a job they risk their lives for and give their lives for. They're only human. They'd go mad doing that job if they thought as you want them to. They'd be beaten before they started – beaten by their own minds. They *have* to regard the enemy *as* an enemy – because that's what he is! Someone menacing them!

"Your ideas sound pretty, but they lead to something ugly. There *is* evil in the world; some people *do* attack others; and then – then it's part of human courage, even of human *dignity*, to resist them. We can't evade that – not honourably. Britain went into the war because she had a moral obligation to defend Belgium – and then an obligation to help France when she was invaded. Do you think obligations aren't important? It's all very well to worry about your brothers on the other side – what about your brothers on this side? Are we supposed to abandon them? Doesn't it *matter* to stand up to defend your own? That's what we expect of a *man*!

"In fact it's what the whole world expects. Always has. You ask if I know anything about real Germans. Well, *I* know something about real people. You know whose fault it'll *really* be if there's another war? It'll be sentimental dills who won't face things! Don't join the dills, Tim! Wake up to your bloody self!"

Alan was unaware that within two years most of the world would agree with him. So was Tim. But in the context of the moment, their disagreement was less important than the words and tones in which they had expressed it. Alan had been accused of something near hypocrisy, Tim of something near unmanliness. Brian intervened at this point, doing his best to pour oil on troubled waters, offering everyone a glass of port from Alan's sideboard and changing the subject to university rugby. Victor shrugged. Charles laughed and said, "Just as well you two aren't running the country. Pair of extremists!"

Brian's overtures worked for the moment; but when the time came for him to leave, Tim felt that there was little point in contacting Alan again. It was not the dispute – not really. It had merely been a catalyst. He did not belong with this crowd. In Walgabran no one would be called Charles – it would be Charlie. That somehow typified the difference.

The truth was, he felt inferior, and at the same time self-righteous. But it was another eighteen months before he would admit this to himself.

And he was fortunate that other friends came his way. In accommodation organised by Head Office, he was assigned to share a rented house with two others, and he found George King, from the North Coast, and Reg Billingsly, from the far West, congenial companions. Another thirty-odd plucked from Queensland's regional branches were similarly billeted in small groups around Brisbane's central suburbs.

Provincial as the city had seemed to Willy, it was to these young men a metropolis. They were unused to crowded streets, and to being surrounded by a wealth of restaurants, cinemas, theatres, sporting facilities and week-end resorts. In Walgabran the bank's assertive architecture had seemed brash and incongruous; here the large commercial buildings were at home. They stood as monuments to progress, and their sheer presence reminded Tim and his new friends that they were at the very bottom of an institution founded on generations of sweat and toil and brains and courage. That brute statement in stone worked a subtle change in the young men's attitude.

It gave them a lift, a sense of being part of something large and concentrated and going somewhere. Because of their jobs, they had long known that the ebb and flow of money affected lives, and on a small scale they had seen its effect in and around their home towns. But now, in the streets of a provincial capital with an international working harbour, jostling with a medley of strangers whose work meshed mysteriously with theirs, they were aware of the endlessly complex structure that was modern commercial life. Here that structure could be *felt*, not just *known*. And there was a satisfaction in being a useful part of it – in aspiring to a role that mattered in that half-conscious conspiracy called society.

Such thoughts influenced them secretly, like underground water. None of the young men could have articulated them. Nor wished to. Reg especially. He engaged in a joyous and humorous pursuit of life's comedy; his conversation was larded with irreverent bush sayings, constantly skirting the edge of irresponsibility and never quite crossing a line from which he could not retreat. By contrast George was sober-minded, and he sometimes affected a slightly formal mode of speech. Since both had friends in Brisbane, the foundations of a social life were ready-laid, and into this camaraderie Tim was gratefully inducted. In the first two months, the three had gone to dances and been invited to parties; George and Reg had joined a golf club and Tim, after one abortive attempt at eighteen holes, had opted for tennis. In most of these activities alcohol played almost no part. Tim had been and was resolved to remain a light drinker. George and Reg, though they had fewer inhibitions, instituted a regime that limited its use. Each Thursday evening they brought home a cargo of beer and played the rickety piano that came with the house, adding their own sometimes scurrilous words to well-known songs and laughing uproariously at the trivia of the day and the events of week.

These habits brought complaints from the neighbours about "those rowdy young men". Houses in Brisbane were little different from those in Walgabran – "Queenslanders" with nothing in the way of sound-insulation; and each Friday evening when they came home from work they would find their landlady, Mrs Campbell, waiting.

"I'm sorry," she would say. "It's too much. I've tried to put up with you boys, but if you keep making this row every Thursday you'll have to go."

They had divined, however, that she had the misfortune to combine a soft heart with an unexpressed liking for them, and they took these warnings with a grain of salt until one Thursday evening which happened to be George's birthday they outdid themselves. What Mrs Campbell received the next day were not complaints but angry demands. That evening it was Tim who opened the door to be greeted by a grim-faced woman, and he heard her saying, "It's too much. You've all got to go. I'm giving you a week's notice."

This was serious. The bank had got them the billet and would take a jaundiced view if they were kicked out. Reg leaped to contain the damage. "We're sorry, Mrs Campbell, but you see, it was George's birthday last night, and – well, we got a bit shickered. We didn't mean to disturb anyone."

"Now don't you give me that, young man. You can't get around me this time. Your playing up has happened before. Birthday indeed! I didn't come down in the last shower!"

"Honest, Mrs C," said Reg. "We wouldn't want tell you a fib!"

"No," said Tim. "We were carried away. We are sorry. We wouldn't want to upset you!"

Mrs Campbell was not impressed. "Humph!" she exclaimed. "Well, I'd hate to see what would happen if you *did* want to."

George interposed: "No, it really was my birthday, Mrs Campbell. We wouldn't have done it otherwise. Would we, Tim?"

"No, of course not."

"Is that so?" she replied. "And what about Thursday two weeks ago, eh? Whose birthday was it then?"

"Well, I could say it was Tim's – but that would be to deceive you, Mrs Campbell. As Reg just said, we wouldn't try that."

"I should think you wouldn't try *again*, anyway!"

"Deceive a lady?" said Reg. "That'd be lower than a snake's belly!"

Mrs Campbell said nothing, but favoured Reg with a withering look.

George decided to try another tack. He shrugged: "Well, boys, I guess that's it. There's nothing else for it. Let's admit it, Mrs Campbell's right. There's others to consider. We've got to go. We'll spend all our spare time this week looking for somewhere else."

"But," exclaimed Tim, "the bank will be furious! We'll lose our jobs!"

Mrs Campbell knew that this was at least half-true, but she made an attempt to resist the blackmail. "You should have thought of that before you made that hullabaloo!"

George said, "No. It's up to us to do the right thing now. In fact, we'll go and apologise to the neighbours first, and we'll move out by Wednesday."

Reg looked at the ground and then turned an innocent face to the light. "Yair, y'r right, George. We'll find somewhere. No worries. Give us a coupl'a days and we'll be home on the pig's back. We'll work out some excuse to tell the bank why we moved. Maybe we can get closer in, nearer to work. Then we needn't say we had to go. We can say it was to save travelling time."

George adopted a look of deep concern. "Well, I don't know about that. There's nothing to let much in Brisbane now – not unless we go halfway to the coast."

Tim cried in a sort of anguish, "It's really going to spoil things. It's our careers!"

Mrs Campbell could feel herself weakening. "Look," she said in a quieter voice, "the truth is I'm sorry about this. I don't mind you boys myself, but I can't have the neighbours complaining all the time."

"No, of course not, said George. "As we said, of course we will go."

Reg was still in his cheerfully repentant mode: "Yes, I suppose so. It's only fair. Look, Mrs Campbell, won't you come in and have a quick drink with us – just to show there's no hard feelings? Fair dinkum, let's stick the hatchet in the log. Then we can go without any nastiness left over."

Tim added his voice: "Yes – of course you must."

Mrs Campbell wavered: "It's a nice thought – but no, I don't think I should."

George insisted: "Well, we have known you for quite a while now. We don't want to part bad friends. Just a quick one. You wouldn't like us to go leaving a sour taste."

"Well," she agreed, "perhaps a very quick one. But don't think you can get around me."

A bottle of beer was opened for the boys, and a sweet sherry was poured for Mrs Campbell.

"Campbell's a fine old Scots name," said George, making conversation. "You've still got that burr, you know. It's very attractive. What brought you out here to Queensland?"

"Dugald Campbell brought me out here, God rest his soul. Thirty years ago, to work with the wool-classing that he'd learnt as a boy."

"I don't want to pry," said Tim, "but what happened?"

"The same as happened to all the men. He went to France to fight and never came back."

Reg was genuinely touched. "George," he asked, "d'you reckon …?" and he nodded at the piano.

"Maybe not the moment, Reg" said George. "We're not celebrating."

"No. It'll be OK. Do you know this tune, Mrs C.?"

He sat at the keyboard and launched into *Scotland the Brave*, and Mrs Campbell tapped her glass in time. Then he went on to *Marie's Wedding*, and *I Belong to Glasgow*, and *Roamin' i' the Gloamin'*. She began to sing along. Reg tried *The Northern Lights* of *Auld Aberdeen*. George noticed that her glass was empty and proffered a new, brimming one, and she accepted almost unconsciously. Reg invited her to play which, protesting her inability, she nevertheless did with an unexpected competence that made Reg's efforts sound stilted as she lent a haunting beauty to slow ballads like *Oh, Waly Waly* and *I Dream of Jeannie*. Her rendition of *Ye Banks and Braes* would have done credit to any professional. At length, flushed, half-sad and half-merry, she relinquished the keyboard back to Reg.

Reg grimaced, saying, "I couldn't play after you, Mrs C. I'd be flat out like a lizard drinking. You've shown me up."

She laughed, and to his surprise wiped a tear from her eye. "Come on, young man. None of your soft soap!"

So Reg played again while the landlady beat time. He avoided songs that might touch her too closely – *The Scottish Soldier* and *Loch Lomond* and the ballads of the Great War – and shifted to the popular ditties of Al Jolson and Eddie Cantor. Everyone sang, and they went through the Broadway musicals of Sigmund Romberg and Jerome Kern, and moved into the lighter tunes made popular by Fred Astaire. When he judged the moment was right to end the evening, Reg returned to his first theme with *The Road to the Isles* and *The Campbells are Coming* and he followed with *Auld Lang Syne*.

Mrs Campbell sighed, and sat quietly a while, letting memories play in her mind. Then she said firmly, "I've never had so much fun. You boys can stay. Let those other people move away if they don't like a bit of music."

Reg, held up two fingers pressed together. "We're like that, us and you, Mrs C."

They escorted her to the door. She turned and said, "You really are reprobates!" But she smiled. And Tim wondered whether his parents would approve of these two companions. Yet he felt lucky to be thrown in with them.

❖ ❖ ❖

In addition to a working week of forty-four hours, the trio were expected to demonstrate that they could cope with accountancy by completing a preliminary syllabus. They all spent long hours with their books. It was as though work and study formed a near-solid wall into whose few crevices their social life had to be squeezed. Released on Saturday afternoons, Reg and George went like arrows to their golf while Tim fled to his tennis. Tim also went to Mass on Sundays and remained seriously religious.

The days and weeks flew, punctuated by trips home every three weeks. This was not possible for Reg – his home town was too far, and it was as well that of the three he was the least likely to become homesick.

He was also the untidiest. When they had been away, Tim and George would sometimes return to find a sink stuffed with dirty dishes and an ice box bursting with half-eaten food. Tim was irritated, but George simply looked at the debris and then at Reg and said, "Oh, c'mon mate, lift your game". Reg would grin and say, "Sorry, fellers, I meant to do it before you came. I don't suppose the train was early?" Then laughing, he would clean up, and make jokes until Tim laughed, too. It was, in fact, a ménage that worked well. Twice Tim brought Reg to his family home for a week-end, once accompanied by George – who had to sleep in the spare room under the house, with one ear cocked for rats. The three were enjoying life.

CHAPTER 10

Fay
(Brisbane, 1939)

It was at the tennis club that Tim met Fay.

He saw her first on the court, collecting balls fallen by the net. She moved with an unconscious grace that startled him, as though by it a new dimension was revealed. A full figure, not really slim; brown eyes, light on her feet, poised, dark hair falling almost to her shoulders. She was smiling, and he knew that she would always smile easily. Her face had an openness that invited friendship.

As he watched, she walked to the baseline, turned, threw the ball a little higher than necessary and delivered a fairly fast serve to her opponent's forehand. It was returned deep. She met it, totally absorbed, her white knee-length skirt swirling around her legs. The ball crossed the net eleven times before she tried a cross-court volley. It went out over the side line – a winner that turned into a loser. Her reaction caused something to flutter in Tim's heart: she smiled again, as though to say "Well, you won that point – it's all in the game". It was the essence of sportsmanship; and to see it realised before his eyes in a flesh-and-blood woman made him feel curiously lifted, as though a warmth was spread over life in general.

He wanted to meet her, and at once felt a paralysing shyness

– made worse by her being a better player than he was, probably in a higher grade. Still staring, he was suddenly called onto the court, and it was forty minutes later when he could look for her. There was a sort of common area where players relaxed, an affair of benches and wooden tables with a small shop that served snacks and teas and soft drinks. She was there, just leaving to go home, gathering her cardigan and shoulder-bag. Intensely aware, he noticed details – the make of her racquet, the embroidery on the shoulder of her dress, the bracelet she had clipped on. The bag was blue – he saw that it had a nearly broken seam at the bottom. He ran to catch her.

"Excuse me," he said, "but I wonder whether you noticed – your bag – you might lose everything."

She turned and looked. "Oh! Oh – thank you. Yes." She grinned. "That's silly of me, isn't it."

Tim felt himself colouring and tried vainly to prevent it. "No," he said, his voice unaccountably thick. "No – of course not. It could happen to anyone." He hesitated, and forced a smile.

They both stared a moment, communication broken down. "Well," she replied, "I do have to run." As she turned to walk away, he said, "Will you be here next week?"

"Of course. Perhaps I'll see you then."

Later he told George and Reg about this wonderful girl. He described the cascades of dark hair that streamed out as she flew across the court, and the lilt in her voice that would be answer enough to anyone who thought that anything could be wrong, anywhere in this world.

"What's her name?" asked George.

"I don't know."

Reg tried. "Does she have a phone? Did you get her address?"

"No."

"How long did you talk to her?"

"About a minute – less."

"But you said she's wonderful."

"She's amazing!"

"Tim," George said, "You know nothing about her. You can't be in love with a girl you've seen for a minute."

"It's crazy," added Reg.

"In love? You know," said Tim, "I think maybe I am."

Reg and George look at each other. "Hopeless," said George.

"Stunned," said Reg. "Silly as a two-bob watch. Bushed like a joey in the Queen Street traffic."

"She's probably got a fiancé, and three brothers."

"Nasty brothers who wouldn't like him."

"We've got to meet her – check her out."

"How can we do that? He can't even meet her himself."

"I will," said Tim. "I'll see her next week."

"Look, Reg," said George, "do you think we could become tennis players for a week?"

"Na – it's the club four-ball. We can't miss that. Anyway, it'd be too boring. You don't *get* anywhere chasing a ball around a court. Not like eighteen holes."

"Wait a minute," said Tim. "Who invited you two, anyway? What're you talking about?"

George became paternal. "We're looking after you, son. We need to see she's right for you."

Reg shook his head sadly. "And you need help. If you don't have some hide you'll get nowhere."

"Hide! Looking after! Look after your bloody selves. I'm not letting you near her."

Throughout the ensuing week his companions kept up a barrage designed to ensure that Tim would come home on Saturday evening with something accomplished, but he had no need of their sniping. Preparing for tennis he whitened his shoes twice, brushed his hair several times, checked his shave minutely, wondered which shirt to wear, and in the process made himself nervous. When, at the courts, he could not see the girl, his nervousness turned to disappointment. In his memory the bantering of his house-mates re-surfaced. His disappointment became resentment and his resentment became anger.

It leant his play an unaccustomed fierceness in which he seemed to place every ball just so, serving aces and hitting volleys that skidded off the clay to thud into the steel netting. And at the end, the frustration sweated out of him, he turned victorious from the court only to see her smiling face at the gate. She was framed in the opening, with a yellow ribbon about her hair. Her eyes twinkled. A cloud moved in the sky and the sunlight played on her forehead and her arms.

"I've been watching," she said. "You're good."

He swallowed. "Did you really think so? No, I was just lucky today."

"I've seen the whole set. I was impressed."

"Oh, no ... I was really on my game today. Usually I serve lots of faults and hit the net all the time."

She laughed. "You know, I wondered whether you'd be here today."

He felt his bones turn to water. Had she really said that? "I wondered, too." He grinned. "I mean – I wondered about you – not me."

"I bet you'd like a drink after that effort."

She led him to the little shop, he bought her an ice cream and they sat and talked, constantly interrupted by the greetings and chance conversations of other players who milled around and came and went. Her name was Fay, and she was a teacher in her second year of work. She lived with her parents in the next suburb, half an hour's walk away. He learned inconsequentialities – and they suddenly mattered: the flowers she liked, her parents' names, what time she went to work. After a while she went to play, and he watched and waited, thrilled by the fluid movements of her body, wanting her to win. Then she returned unbidden to sit with him again, and his heart leapt. At the very end, as she rose to go he made to accompany her along the road.

"No, don't come," she said.

He was embarrassed. Had he done the wrong thing? Presumed too much? But he spoke, and the words, gauche, slightly croaking, seemed to come involuntarily from his mouth, as though someone else was speaking. "See you next Saturday?"

"I like you, Tim," she replied. And she was gone.

That evening, George and Reg were merciless. Laughing, George said, "At least you know her first name now. Next week you'll get her second name. Then, every week a bit more."

"Yes," said Reg. "Tim's a fast worker. Next year he'll know her address."

George recited:

Ther's little breezes stirrin' in the leaves,
An' sparrers chirpin' 'igh the 'ole day long;
An' on the air a sad, sweet music breaves
A bonzer song —
A mournful sorter choon thet gits a bloke
Fair in the brisket 'ere, an' makes 'im choke …

"Bugger the both of you," said Tim, and went to his room.

To George, Reg said "He's serious, like."

George laughed, and went to Tim's door: "C'mon, Tim. We're sorry – we shouldn't joke. Look, mate – I've got some top beer – Grafton special." He went to the ice box, drew out two bottles, and brought them back. "Look – I got this specially to drink to your girl. It's the best there is!"

"What's this?" said Tim. "Anyway, she isn't my girl."

"Come on, Tim. Have a drink. We're pleased for you." He

held out a brimming glass.

"Pleased for me! The way you blokes are carrying on! I thought I knew you. Bloody vultures! True colours come out, sooner or later."

Reg opened his arms wide in a gesture of helplessness. "Tim … Tim … We're jokers. You know that. We always have people on, you the same as everyone else. It doesn't mean anything."

"Well, you bloody well shouldn't. Grow up! You're not bloody Laurel and Hardy!"

"Are you fair dinkum? D'you really take us that way?"

"Too right!"

George interposed. "We're really sorry. Straight up. We do want to drink to your – lady. Come on, Reg."

"Right. I'll always be in a Grafton!" He took a glass and filled it. "Here's to – what was her name, Tim? Fay, wasn't it? It's a beaut name. Here's to Fay."

"C'mon, Tim. You can't stay out of this. Wouldn't be respecting her."

Tim looked at their deadpan faces. "Nah! I don't trust you. You're smirking inside."

"Tim, Tim, we're your mates! Come on, give us a go. We said we're sorry," said George.

"Well … you blokes reckon you're really sorry?"

"Real as a bag of gold dust."

Tim took the proffered glass reluctantly.

They went through half-a-dozen bottles and, before they collapsed into their beds, made Tim promise to invite Fay to the golf club informal dance – the "hop" – to be held in a fortnight's time.

Which is how he came, three weeks later, to be sitting next to Fay Egan in a taxi, a little uncomfortable in his best suit with a new shirt and tie, thrilled to have just met her parents, awed by the elegance and size of her house, excited to be so near her, overwhelmed that they were actually "going out", desperate to make conversation that would impress her and unable to think of anything to say except commonplaces.

"Are you fond of dancing?" he asked.

"Of course! I love it! Don't you?"

"I guess I haven't had as much practice as I'd like. They tried to teach us a bit at school, and we had dances at home, but I'll do my best."

She smiled. "Your best! Don't be like that. It's not an exam. Relax. Enjoy yourself."

"Well – it's going to be a great night – perfect weather."

"I love this time of year – sort of half-warm. It always makes me feel like jumping out of my skin."

Tim laughed and, glancing at the stole half-covering her bare shoulders, suddenly felt daring. "Don't do that – your skin's too nice to jump out of."

Fay also laughed, and looked at him from under long lashes. "It's horrible, actually. When I play tennis on a hot day, I've got to be careful or it will burn and peel. I have to put cream on it."

To Tim, this seemed a sort of small confidence – a revelation of the sort that invited him into a closer relationship. "Well," he said, "I think your skin's perfect." It occurred to him to add, "And so are you" – but he was afraid that if he overdid the compliments she might think him ridiculous.

She laughed again. "You've had a lot of practice at saying things like that."

He was unsure whether to bask in this totally undeserved attribution of vast worldly experience, or to deny that he could be so insincere. Honesty won. "No, I've never said anything like that to anyone!"

She giggled, wondering whether to believe him. He waited, unsure what to say next and angry with himself that he had no words. The silence stretched, and he was relieved when she spoke again.

"This golf club – I've never been there. Tell me about your two friends."

So he described George, with his quiet charm, and Reg, with his mercurial personality, and told her how they were all brought from their country towns by the bank with the possibility of being selected for special training.

"They sound nice," she said. He was glad of the comment; yet he felt a little apprehensive about the moment when she would meet them. Rationally, he knew that they were genuine friends; but in some part of his consciousness every man seemed a possible rival.

"Now, don't you think they're *too* nice," he grinned. "You're here with me."

"Oooh? Now I *must* meet them. They must really be something!"

The evening went wonderfully. He and Fay danced many times, and Tim stepped on her toes only once. George and Reg were at the top of their form, and both clearly thought Tim had caught himself a prize as they took their turns at swinging her around the floor. She liked them both, and laughed at Reg's anecdotes until Tim had to force himself not to resent his friend's larrikin wit. Others from the club came to meet her, bringing their friends and sweethearts, and laughter went up from the group continuously. The last waltz finally came, and in a sort of blur of tired happiness, Tim took her home. As they reached her gate, she put her hand on his arm. He looked into her eyes and, seeing the smile, kissed her.

"I like you a lot, Fay," he said.

"I know, Tim," she replied, still smiling.

"Can I see you on Tuesday?" he asked.

"What's wrong with Monday?"

Tim could not believe his own happiness. He went home in a daze, and, too excited to sleep for the next three hours, sat on the front verandah, weaving wonderful scenarios in his imagination. Excitedly, he looked forward to Monday evening for the next two days, unable to concentrate properly on his work; and, inspired by what he had seen in a movie featuring Mickey Rooney, arrived at her front door with a large box of chocolates behind his back. He had never given a girl a surprise present before, and when she was delighted he felt that he had reached a new stage of manhood.

"Oh, Tim," she cried, "I'm going to love them!"

The film had just the right blend of romance, comedy, and pathos, and they emerged into the warm evening with Fay laughing as she brushed away a tear.

"Well, look at you!" he grinned.

She smiled. "Tim, thank you. It's been nice."

After leaving her at her door he seemed to float all the way home.

In the following days their closeness deepened – days which, for Tim, passed in a heady glow, as though some new and magical ingredient had been added to the very air. All reality was beautiful. Her mild teasing was a delight and her underlying kindness a greater one. Idiosyncratic features – the way she twisted her hand in her hair, the way she stood, the balance of her body – acquired an intense attractiveness; surely, it seemed to Tim, every man she met must be rendered helpless by her exquisiteness. He realised, when he tried to be detached and logical, that other men did not in fact collapse before her, and that other women had their own personal graces without these touching him in the same way. But these common-sense facts felt unreal: it was as though he was walking in a country of strangers who lacked all sensitivity to what was obvious and wonderful.

George and Reg badgered him to invite her for a meal to their house. "Come on, Tim. She's a great girl – we saw that at the dance. You can't keep her *all* to yourself!"

And when he did so once, they made sure that she would return often. Reg brought a girl called Sylvia from the golf club, and the house became more than ever a place of laughter as the five young people watched their first tentative friendship solidify into something firm and lasting. As a coterie they went out together, to films, to dances, to the coastal beaches, to the hinterland where they rode in the mountains. Tim and Fay always contrived to be alone for part of the time, and they realised in stages that they could share quiet moods and laughing ones, thoughts and feelings, the group and their own company, so that their ease together grew while the thrill of their attraction did not diminish. More and more they felt part of each other, and hated parting.

Tim entered on one of the happiest periods of his life, and, on his next visit home, gave his parents an outline of what had happened, understating his own feelings, and asking whether he might bring Fay to stay one week-end. His father swallowed hard and grunted, and his mother kissed him.

Tim looked in on Willy, who asked: "And what is new, Tim? Your work is going well?"

"It's fine, Bill. I've made some good mates."

"Good. That is not always easy. After your work, it is the most important thing."

Tim had not meant to speak about Fay to anyone except his parents. He had a sense of something sacred in the friendship that forbade allowing it to become a subject of gossip or even of casual conversation; but once in the German's company he felt that Willy was different: there would be a meanness in keeping it secret.

"Bill," he said, "I'm in love."

"Oh, Ja? Oh-oh-oh ... "

"She's fantastic!"

"Of course!"

"No, she really is. She's wonderful. Her name's Fay."

"That is a nice name, Tim."

"I know lots of nice girls Bill. This is different. It's – it's a kind of pain. Like there's something missing inside you. Like you're always hungry but you're not. And it's wonderful!"

"Ach, so. Have you known this girl – Fay – long?"

"No. But there's love at first sight, isn't there?"

For a full half-minute neither of them spoke, as Willy looked unseeing into the distance. Tim, fighting his impatience, listened in silence.

"I have known people who met and married very quickly, and some of them were glad all their lives but some were not. You are in love – that is important; but it is even more important that you can share who you really are; that you can be friends, able to trust. You may find, in ways you cannot think of until events reveal them, that you have made different assumptions – about big things, or perhaps about little things that affect life constantly. Then, you have to be open to considering whether you were wrong, and you need a sense of proportion.

"In all of us there are parts that change and parts that do not. If you marry this girl you should believe that the unchanging parts of your personalities are – not similar, necessarily, but consonant; that they fit together enough to provide a foundation so that the parts that will change can grow together. Your beliefs, your ideals – they must accord. At a certain level, even your reactions. Not that they should be the *same*; but they should not prevent you from communicating and listening with sympathy. They should allow you to share the experience of life.

"And on top of that you must accept each other. You should have an instinct, a confidence, that you can do this. Acceptance – after the first, definitive stage it is still progressive. But it must be real, not an illusion. When it is honest and far-reaching it affects the way you exist. It is something you cannot take back. At least, not without a sort of violence. It is a part of you.

"All love is a mystery. It is a unity between people who nevertheless remain distinct. It is not that one dominates or absorbs the other. It is precisely because they are persons in their own right that they represent to each other that the world is bigger and wider than themselves. And for this they are glad. And yet, the unity is real. In marriages that have endured for a long time, there is an unconscious unity that has become like the earth we walk on and do not notice most of the time."

Tim listened, restlessly, shifting his position several times. "Bill, I can't think like that. I don't want to. I don't want fancy ideas. I just know I go to sleep thinking about Fay. I wake up thinking about her. If there is a telephone call I only care whether it is from her. She is with me all day, not a minute passes even at work when I do not think about her, and wonder what she is doing. That's enough for me."

"Well – you will know soon enough. Do not hurry too much. Not too fast. Not when you are nineteen. For her sake as well as for your own."

It was three weeks later that Fay met Tim's parents. She brought flowers which she had tried desperately to keep fresh in the train by immersing their stems in a can of water and which she had wrapped in tissue paper as Walgabran drew close. Ben at first remained quiet in the background as his wife and his son's girl-friend recognised instinctively that they liked each other, drawn together by intuitions that were mysterious to men. If Fay was at all nervous, she gave no sign of it, but laughed and chattered and admired Walgabran, and before the afternoon had passed she had won Ben's heart.

It was never said, but from a thousand snippets of conversation it became clear that her family was better off than the Rogers. Dinner on Saturday evening was a roaring success, with Ben opening up and reminiscing until Jenny thought to herself, "This is the young man I married – he's back." Sunday morning was Mass and an early lunch before Fay and Tim caught the train. But there were a few minutes when Tim was alone with his parents.

Fay (Brisbane, 1939)

"Do you like her, Mother?" he asked.
"She's sweet. I'm so glad you met her."
"Yes," said Ben. "But she's a cut above us."

CHAPTER 11

The Proposal
(Brisbane, 1939)

The following weeks jumbled together in a confused medley of frenetic activities: work, study, seeing Fay – these filled Tim's life. His sleep was curtailed, his meals were snatched in free moments. On most days they met during her lunch-breaks – themselves uncertain, for a teacher is never fully off-duty – and Tim found that he could just catch the 12.35 tram to meet her in the tea-shop across the road from her school and the 1.12 back without being late for his own work.

His few casual friendships with girls in Walgabran now seemed trivial. In coming to Brisbane he had felt like a sailor heading into an uncharted sea, resolved to surge forward, glad to encounter whatever landfalls lay ahead. And it had turned out well. In the bank he was progressing. He had the friendship of George and Reg and Sylvia and their wider circle. And now Fay. She made him feel complete, fulfilled, confident. That he would ask her to be his wife was inevitable.

But not quite yet. He must wait for just the right moment – one that would be perfect in their memory for a lifetime, a fixed point they would always share.

In this glow of anticipation, he was unprepared when he was summoned by Mr Maguire, the Personnel Officer, and told that the last part of the course on which he was engaged had been re-thought: some trainees would now spend time in places quite new to them. Tim was to go to Cairns, where he would get some experience of the financial conditions of a town that lived on tropical industries – sugar cane, timber, fruit and fish. It was a pity, Maguire conceded, that this decision had not been taken earlier – it meant that Tim's departure would have to be rather rushed. Could he arrange to leave in a week's time?

Tim's thoughts flew instantly to Fay. He couldn't leave her – not now. Cairns was a world away. But Maguire was going on – what was he saying?

"We've been pleased with you, Tim, and unless something unforeseen happens you'll be selected to study accountancy and proceed to a fine career in the bank. This experience should be important to you later on. It's a great opportunity – especially in these times. I wish I'd had the chance when I was young."

Tim uttered a swallowed gasp and replied, in some confusion: "I do appreciate it, Mr Maguire. It's very good of the bank. But ..."

Maguire looked up, surprised to hear any hesitance. "What is it, Tim. Is there a problem?"

He was elderly, with a certain formal reserve but known to the staff as a man of sympathetic character. Tim, looking at his wrinkled face, felt a spurt of confidence.

"Well ... you see, I've met a young lady here ..."

Maguire laughed, not unkindly.

"What? Oh – and you don't want to leave her. Is that it?"

Tim felt absurdly defiant: "Yes, it is!"

"We're not considering sending you to the South Pole, Tim."

"I'm sorry, Mr Maguire, I don't think I can go. This lady is more important to me than anything!"

Shocked at this determination, the older man became wholly serious. "Don't knock this back, Tim. Not after all the bank's already done for you ... I expected you to jump at it. You may feel it's a bit sudden, but as an older man let me assure you – it's the right thing. If you're serious about this girl, the first thing you will want is a steady, lucrative career. Don't throw it away. Of course it must be your own decision, but I want you to sleep on it. Go away now, and see me at four-thirty tomorrow – no, I'll be away – make it Wednesday. Let me know then."

For Tim the appeal to gratitude came from left field. He had to admit that it had some force. But … Fay! If he went away now … what would happen? Would he even keep her affection? A primitive fear gripped him – something akin to panic. He felt a whirlpool of life-forces around him, pulling him in contradictory directions.

He was half out of the office when Maguire hesitated in the action of picking up a file. He looked up at Tim and spoke again.

"There's something else I should say. I hope you don't think I'm intruding, but I've had a long experience. May I offer some advice?"

What else, Tim wondered – had he unknowingly broken some bank protocol? He spoke with a slight apprehension. "Well – of course."

"This matter of your social life. Don't let it become too – heavy. I know you're from the country, and there people often marry young. But they have good jobs, farms. If you get married now you will have no money. Your wife will have five children before she is thirty, and you will not be able to support them. It's not a good idea, Tim, to get really deeply involved yet. Play the field – enjoy life for a few years before you take on too many responsibilities. If you stay with us and do well, you'll be on the way to a secure future."

Tim was momentarily stunned, and then at once furious. What right did this man have to speak like that? In his day people probably got married as they borrowed from the bank, by dry calculation. Now it was the Thirties. Things had changed. In any case, "play the field" was insulting advice. Tim couldn't pretend that his feelings for Fay were the trivial pleasures of passing fun. Besides, a moment ago Maguire had said that going to Cairns was necessary if he really cared for her. Now he was saying something opposite – recommending it as a way of abandoning her.

He had opened his mouth to begin a retort that might have ended his banking career there and then, when Maguire's phone rang and he picked it up and spoke, nodding Tim out of the office. He had no alternative but to leave, still shocked and angry, his thoughts smouldering.

The day wore on, and his mood continued, slowly settling into a dumb determination. Concentration on his work was repeatedly hampered by stabs of anger, and in the midst of these he was visited by a new confusion. Maguire had suggested that it would be irresponsible to marry before he was established. Reflecting, he knew that similar thoughts had floated at the back of his own mind. He had hardly allowed them to come into clear focus. They had remained theoretical, indefinite, hovering on the edge of life, things he could dismiss without really attending to them. Now, to have someone else speak of them as though they were simple fact gave them a totally different force. And his father's laconic reference to Fay's family was suddenly much more than a passing comment.

Unfairly, Willy's words came back to reinforce this: "Do not hurry too much. Not when you are nineteen. For her sake as well as for your own."

There are times when a single short sentence can undermine a large decision. Tim felt a kind of nausea. Was he being unfair to Fay? Had he no right to engage her affections?

Until now a successful banking career had been a pleasant aspiration but hardly a desperate need. Suddenly it became a challenge he must meet, a rare opportunity promising a future to a man who hoped to marry in a depressed economic time.

But the time-scale! A week – Maguire had said he wanted him to leave in a week.

And what could he say to Fay?

He could, of course, simply propose to her – now. It looked as though he would get the traineeship and become an accountant.

They could be engaged while he went north for a few months.

But – he was not *really* assured of the career yet. *Could* he propose – as things were? If she said yes – and he could hardly allow himself to contemplate the possibility that she might not – it could merely be raising hopes in her now to dash them later. For if his prospects did turn to nothing – what was left? Could he still marry her? Could he ask this city girl to adapt to a far more restricted life in Walgabran?

The lonely abstract effort of looking at their relationship from outside – of considering what was best for her in a way detached from his own desires – itself produced a sort of pain. But again, the mere idea that he might in some way hurt her – and that permanently – was abhorrent. It swamped other considerations. He must stay true to that – to safeguarding her – whatever it cost.

Yes – he must do that.

He told her of the bank's offer at lunch in the tea-shop, and his misery was only heightened by her response.

"Tim, of course you must go."

"I hate the thought of leaving you, Fay."

"It'll be all right – it's only for a few months."

"Oh, Fay."

He reached out and held her hand. She looked into his eyes, and he glimpsed the beginning of tears. Every instinct he possessed urged him to enfold her in his arms. He was an arrow in a drawn bow, itching to fly to her, restrained by the merest touch. To obey that urge "wasn't done" in a public place, but what stopped him was not social inhibition – his feelings at that moment made nonsense of polite conventions. It was something else. There was the logic of the heart, of the urge to life – now, immediate, impatient, importunate; and there was also the logic of the head, of everything that Maguire had said. Tim wanted, desperately, to say, "I love you, and I will never leave you." It was on the tip of his tongue then to propose, and to hell with rational, cautionary considerations. Wasn't it gutless to consider them – to allow them to dominate everything else?

But – the damnable plausibility of Maguire's words was there, an ugly post planted across a path into a lovely landscape, bearing a sign warning of disaster. Disaster for them both. Wouldn't that be the real gutlessness – to fail to consider the possibility that he might mess up her life?

Ordinary confidence deserted him; nothing in the world seemed obvious. The dilemma had herded him into a closed corral of self-centred thought, and he hated that feeling in himself. It seemed a turning away from life itself, a diversion of its energy into a sterile caricature. Yet – of course one had to think – had to work things out – sometimes.

Dimly he was aware that he might be putting the accidental before the essential, the secondary considerations before the primary; but he could not see an answer clearly. He could feel any confidence in his own judgment ebbing away as though it was blood and he was bleeding. The capacity to ignore gratuitous by-ways; the intuitive sense of how much risk – for oneself and for others – is reasonable in the conditions of human life as a whole; the simple sanity which rests on a measure of common sense; these were needed by everyone – even by people like Willy, who always tended to chew over details. But in his distress and repetitive thought, he was confusing himself, losing the ability to hold things realistically before him.

Courage? He was exercising a kind of courage – the courage to try to face the alternatives in their fullest dimensions; and in the act he felt he was weakening another kind, one which understands the limits of human vision and takes the risk of making one's best decision and living with the consequences. And he could not tell which courage accorded most with reality, nor where to draw some line between them.

That existential demand for action amid half-certainties was part of the stuff and texture of life. Yet decisions taken too readily could be a way of evading difficult facts.

If he heeded Maguire's warning, a kind of irony ensued. For as he had now thought it out, he could not even say how much he loved her – yet. Even to tell her why he was not at that moment embracing her was, in effect, to propose here and now – in the very act of pretending not to do so. It was to dissemble, to engage her feelings by a kind of blackmail masquerading as something else; and if she accepted, it was to commit them both – whether he could care for her adequately or not. In his mind, she was a jewel who belonged in the right setting. To marry her and *not* to care for her adequately – that, at least, would be a failure he could never get over. He had already decided that.

But – there was also something wrong with second-guessing the simple and great realities of life. He wanted to relate to Fay directly, not hypothetically.

He was going in circles.

He looked at her, and said "I have to go." The words sounded terse and unfeeling in his own ears.

"I know," she replied. And she got up quickly and left the shop.

It was time to go back to work.

Fay was worried.

Why had Tim not been warmer when he told her that he was asked to go away? Yes, he had seemed distressed – but why? Just because of the separation? No, that was not exactly how he had been – there was some reservation, something seriously wrong. Did he really care? Was he actually welcoming this move as a way of ending their relationship as easily as possible? Had he tired of her? Well, if that was the way of it, she didn't want to hold him.

In the midst of these thoughts she missed him terribly. With a distaste that mirrored his own at introducing calculation into the relationship, she felt herself forced to think of him objectively, in a way she did not like. They should have been soul-mates, free of the distancing that begins with judging.

That night, he did not telephone. She had no way of knowing that he was torturing himself with dilemmas he could not solve; that he was going deep into a dilemma, deeper than he had psychic strength for.

They met in the tea-shop for lunch the next day.

Fay took a deep breath. "Tim, maybe it will be just as well."

"What? What d'you mean?"

"Tim, do you love me?"

"Love you? Good God, Fay ..."

And now he saw. This was the decisive moment. He could refuse to admit the depth of his feelings in a sort of effort to protect her from the effects if his career did not take off; or he could let go, tell her the simple truth; and yes – it would be tantamount to an engagement.

He looked into her eyes. And he knew.

At a certain earlier stage, if their friendship had not promised so much, or had been more one-sided, to consider her welfare objectively in the secrecy of his own mind might have been mere common decency. But they really had gone past that. They had left behind hypothetical hopes and attained a sort of bedrock certainty: a thing not romantic in any superficial sense, yet a thing wonderful, solid, satisfying, good – and yes, amazing, quite literally. And mutual.

His hesitation – now it was an infidelity, tearing down the intuitive, responsive, trusting togetherness they shared.

"Fay, I love you so much. Will you marry me?"

Hardly understanding how it happened, she was in his arms, saying, "Oh, Tim, of course!" She looked around at the customers seated at the small tables covered with starched white cloths, blushed and laughed.

Tim grinned. "Don't mind, everybody. We're engaged."

The married couple who owned the tea-shop clapped. The customers joined in. Tim said, "good Lord! I'm going to be *really* late. But now I'll have something to tell Maguire!"

That evening, her head on his shoulder, when he had said, "Fay, of *course* I love you – surely you couldn't doubt it?" she mentioned her own puzzlement at his earlier attitude; and when she had listened to his explanation, she said: "Tim, you and your thoughts! Don't ever try to think for me again! Do you know how close you came to losing me?"

He shivered. "Yes," he said. "I know."

CHAPTER 12

The Cave
(Wildjeree, 1939)

As a rule Tim didn't enjoy trains: with the windows open he was assaulted by spent cinders, and with them closed he was stifled. But this time he savoured the trip, excited at the prospect of seeing Fay again, hardly able to believe that all the love and longing they had both poured into letters would now, at last, magically fly free, released from the restrictions imposed by distance. From Cairns to Brisbane took two days, a journey that went by coast and by mountains, and his impatience increased with every mile.

She met him at the station, alone. George, Reg and Sylvia had tactfully stayed away, but it was a Saturday, and that evening the fiancés were guests at a dinner their friends had laboured over for most of the afternoon. Of the matters that were filling the world's newspapers they hardly spoke. Armies could parade and presidents make speeches – to a young couple flushed with love, Europe's political problems were over the hill and far away – over a very large hill indeed, the hill of their happiness. The evening was one of lightness and laughter punctuated by Reg's antics at the piano.

On the following Monday Tim reported at the bank, and then took a week's leave. It was months since he had been home to Walgabran, and a visit to his parents was well overdue. Reg laughed at his and Fay's reluctance to part even for a few days.

"Don't worry, mate," he said, winking. "We'll look after her for yer."

"Not too well," grinned Tim.

"C'mon – been doing it for the last three months."

But the events in Europe, if they seemed impossibly remote to Fay and Tim, were not regarded by others with the same insouciance. A year ago the German Anschluss with Austria had been signed; now Czechoslovakia was occupied, belligerent noises were being made over Polish independence, Britain and France were full of debate and frantic diplomatic activity. Tim, who had paid only partial attention to all this while he was constantly composing letters to Fay in his head, now encountered reality at his home. Sobered by the concern of his parents, and wondering about Willy's position as a German, he sought out his old mentor and found him deeply depressed.

"Ja," he said, shaking his head. "It is very bad. I have letters from my mother, my father, my cousins. I should be with them. But I cannot. My wife, my child, my life are here. And anyway, they tell me not to come. They are glad I am far away."

"It's unbelievable, Bill. The Great War – the war to end all wars. You think people can really do it again?"

"Yes – they can do it again."

"Bill, if it comes, I could be put into the army."

"No. Australia rejected conscription before. They will not bring it back to fight again in Europe. If it happens you will be asked to go, but you will not be forced."

"Well, I know one thing. After what Dad and you have told me, I won't be going to any war even if it comes. Even if I *am* forced. I couldn't shoot anyone – I couldn't believe it was right."

"I have said too much, Tim. If it comes, ask your father. He is a good man. It is not right that my ideas should influence your mind. Not about something so important. I am only your friend. If it happens, talk to your father."

When he returned to Brisbane, Tim threw himself into work, buoyed by the thought that he was doing it as much for Fay as for himself. When he could, he took her to Walgabran on week-ends, and twice her parents came too, staying at the Drover's Rest; for the rest, he divided his life between working hard and seeing Fay, and whenever there was insufficient time, the answer was simple – he cut his sleep.

It was the long week-end in October when Fay proposed that the whole group – Sylvia, George, Reg, Tim and herself – join a tennis club excursion to Wildjeree, a pretty town eighty miles away that lived by tourism and pretended to be alpine. It had almost-stately hotels with breath-taking views and tennis courts, and it had a splendid golf course; some miles away were the limestone caves honeycombing the Bass mountains, serviced by a small bus that twice each morning ferried customers to the guided tours and returned twice each afternoon.

They arrived late on Friday evening. On the following morning most rose early, enthusiastic for a day's golf or for long walks in bush tracks, though a few late sleepers simply wandered about the town and savoured its tea-shops. They stumbled back, with sore muscles and high spirits, to have dinner and a convivial evening in a room made cheerful by the large fire which, at this altitude, was still needed. Sunday, its activities slowed by the seduction of the broadsheet newspapers and by attendance at various churches, provided a more sedate copy of the same mix. It was Monday when they went to the caves.

The trip took more than half an hour, and the passengers, who had become silent with concealed tension as they rounded hairpin bends on a sharply rising road, reacted by exploding into boisterous life as they finally rolled up to the car park. The reception area, festooned with postcards and miniature carvings in limestone, had an adjoining café whose Devonshire teas were a magnet after the journey. Restored, they had to register for the tour and found that they were in a party of about twenty, ranging in age from seven to seventy. Their chief guide, an athletic-looking man in his twenties whose shoulder-flashes proclaimed that he worked for the Queensland Forestry Department, told them to call him simply "Neville". He briefed them on the geological nature of the caves, emphasising that this was not a stroll but a serious excursion. Initially they would ascend by a rough path inside the mountain and then they would descend to well below their present level; they must take care, and follow the instructions of the guides. Grinning, he added that his own parents had become engaged there, for the caves were as romantic as they were overwhelming. Tim's hand sought Fay's, and – as always now – he was thrilled to feel the ring on her finger.

Neville then introduced Chris, his assistant guide, who gave everyone small shoulder-bags containing some chocolate biscuits and a quart of water. "Yes, he said, "it's just water. You'll need a drink, and we can't make tea up there. We don't want anyone getting dehydrated." He and Neville had much larger packs, and everyone had to put on canvas shoes with soles designed to resist slipping. Then they were given heavy, shapeless, belted jackets, yellow with broad black stripes. These caused general ribbing – "you look like a bumble-bee, Syl"; "zzzz – you're the one I'll sting, then, Reg"; and so on. But they were told they needed the garments because of the underground chill – the late spring weather would not penetrate there. Neville didn't add that the garish design was also a deliberate precaution in case someone strayed – a conspicuous person was easier to find. He made them number-off, and admonished them not to wander alone, assigning everyone a partner with whom they were to remain in close touch. He noticed Fay and Tim holding hands.

"I guess you two can go together this time," he joked, "but don't make a habit of it." Everyone laughed.

They set off. Chris fell back to the rear of the group while Neville led them into a series of enormous caverns, each one opening into another. Arc lights had been installed, in whose glow the walls were glittering white and ghostly grey, with high dim ceilings and indistinct side tunnels branching off into absolute blackness. The group began the walk with the skipping steps of excited young children, their laughter and garrulous talk resonating in the shadowy depths; but slowly they became silent, watching in awe the sculptures and pillars which, they were assured, had taken millions of years in the building. They walked deeper into the system, following curving paths that wound slowly up the inside of the mountain. Their gait changed at length to a sober march and then to a trudge, until some members complained of tiredness. One man said he had to sit down. Others began to say the same. Finally they would go no further. "It's wonderful, but …"

"Around the next corner and then ten more minutes," said Neville, "there are some iron seats and benches. There are some toilets too. Pretty rough, I'm afraid. This is as far as many people go. We'll all rest there, have a drink, and Chris will go back with those who wish to return. For the others, it'll be harder and narrower. You'll need head-torches – I've got some. It'll take us an hour more and the same back to here. And then a couple of hours to the café."

Most, including Reg and Sylvia, opted to return. It was just nine people, seven men and two women, the youngest and fittest of the group, that climbed on through a narrow passage leading upwards to open into another cavern which marked the highest point of their journey. From there the way would be down. They started in single file on an ill-lit descent in which steps had been cut, and Tim saw that they were following a rough hand-rail attached to the wall. There was also a narrow pipe – an electrical conduit, he guessed.

"Careful here," Neville warned. "It's wet and slippery underfoot. Everyone be sure to hold someone's hand. I've got a surprise for you." They formed into pairs and descended for perhaps fifteen minutes in near-silence, one hand on the rail, the other on a partner's, while the never-still beams of their lights were constantly playing on gleaming, damp walls where green slime mingled with rainbow colours. When anyone looked up, a bright streak ran at amazing speed up the walls to flash momentarily onto distant stalactites and then become lost in a gloom too high to discern. Tim and Fay managed to play a little game with their own beams, Tim's chasing Fay's as it bobbed; and when, accidentally, the two bright areas merged so that there seemed only one, they held that unity for a moment, and Fay turned to Tim and smiled.

Whether or not because of this game, a little later Fay was having trouble with her torch: its light began to wobble drunkenly and the band holding it to her head was working loose, and when she tried to tighten it the buckle seemed stuck in one position. She thought of asking the party to stop – perhaps Neville had another – but reluctant to hold everyone up, especially in this gloom, she shrugged and went on.

They were moving down now at an angle steeper than that of their ascent, until Tim wondered how deep they were. If anyone spoke in a normal voice, multiple echoes added mysterious overtones, making the sound blurred and unnatural.

Then they heard something else. "What's that noise?" whispered Fay, in tones hushed for no reason she could have identified.

It was faint but at the same time powerful, like the crash of distant waves against rocks. Neville turned to her, grinning in her head light, his hand over his own to protect her eyes.

"That's the surprise", he said.

They went on, and the noise increased until everyone recognised the sound of fast-moving water. It soon drowned the quiet tones they had fallen into using, and Neville stopped and spoke in a half-shout, slowly so his words would not be confused by the echoes.

There's a corner just ahead," he said, "and around it is a large cavern with an underground stream. We go down a bit of a drop – about six feet down an iron ladder, and then we're on a rock shelf. You'll see a waterfall. The shelf's wide – plenty of room – and the water runs a couple of feet below it. It's slippery, so walk carefully. Everyone stay behind me and move slowly."

They emerged into an opening illuminated by three arc lamps – almost an enormous room. The passage they were following terminated halfway up one of its walls, so that an incautious walker might have fallen, and the top of the ladder was cemented into the rock near their feet. As they hesitated before trusting themselves to it, they could see that water was issuing fast from the limestone face to their left, through a fissure about two feet wide at their shoulder-height. It must, Tim thought, be banked up under pressure behind the opening; only that would explain the force of the flow. It surged outwards and dropped, dividing on a series of sloping rocks and then re-forming into one thick stream that tumbled over a small precipice and fell into a pool of slower-moving but still racing water which passed out on their right through a narrower crack and, apparently, fell again to some new hidden depth in a space beyond the rock-face that was the end of their cavern.

Looking down at the ledge, they saw it was covered with a faint mist; and out on the pool's surface, the falling water rebounded in a spray that rose and fell like a small fountain. In the total absence of wind, this spray remained unnaturally fixed in one position: instead of waving and varying in small, quasi-rhythmic undulations, it seemed to stay for long periods in mathematically perfect lines, as though it was running through invisible tubes, and might have been a delicate glass sculpture; and in the pool where it struck, it apparently produced standing waves so that the endless, repetitive ripples seemed themselves fixed in a single position. This visual, unexpected stillness produced an eerie feeling – as though time itself was frozen. The group stared, no one wanting to break the silence.

The ladder was vertical and cold to the touch, and to Tim it seemed unduly rusty, but they all went down, thankful that the descent was short. As they came to the ledge, the tiny disturbance of the air caused by their movements and their breath destroyed the strange perfection that had arrested them a moment before; but now they were entranced by another effect, for by some trick of the acoustics on the ledge itself, the noise of the stream was suddenly subdued, and this little fountain of spray soared and fell silently, the restless motion of its matter and the constancy of its form blending in a sort of harmony.

It was a place where nature could show its depth and dignity, undisturbed by any rival claim on the attention. This secret river had somehow cut its way through these rocks and was still moulding the shape and structure of its own course; it was part of a dynamic, ever-altering process, but the feeling generated was of something impossibly old and permanent and almost changeless.

"How deep is it, Neville?" someone asked, instinctively whispering to remain in tune with the place.

"Varies; six feet, ten, maybe more. No one really knows for sure. There's fallen rocks on the bottom – see those fast eddies there, like little valleys in the water? That's where it's shallow, maybe just a foot."

Fay felt that she could sit in silence and watch for hours, and she bent to Tim's ear and said "I love it here."

She moved closer to the edge of the shelf, peering down. "Imagine if there were fish here," she said. "Wouldn't that be wonderful?"

"They'd probably be something prehistoric," grinned George. "They'd have six legs and three fins, and walk out of the water and bite your toes."

"I'll catch you one," said Tim.

She laughed, and punched him gently. "No, thanks. Could there be fish, Neville?"

"No one knows."

"I want to find out – I'm going to have a good look." She knelt on the edge of the shelf, peering into the depths of the water.

"No, said Neville. "Don't lean like that. Here – give me your hand."

He spoke a little urgently. Slightly startled by his tone, she half rose and swivelled, reaching her right hand towards him. As she did so, her head-torch came fully loose and, tossed off her head by the quickness of her turn, went arcing towards the water. She reached out her left hand in a futile attempt to catch it, and her foot slipped on the wet surface. She felt herself falling, and knew that she could not prevent it.

The splash was shocking in that artificial quietness. For an instant the group on the shelf froze, and then Neville and Tim had fumbled with their belts and removed their bee-jackets. In moments they were both in the water. By a space too small to measure, Tim was there first.

His ability to breathe seemed to disappear in the sudden cold. Struggling and spluttering, he looked for Fay, and he saw her being swept slowly but deliberately by the current, head-first towards the crack where the water of the pool exited. She seemed to bounce off a hidden rock, and her body twisted so that her face was towards him. He saw blood on her forehead. She was drifting backwards. Half-blinded in the spray, he swam towards her and felt himself impeded by what was unmistakably another body, that of Neville. Neville pushed him off and glanced at him.

In that moment the two men became instinctive partners, like members of a team trained for a single, all-important enterprise, recognising without words their common purpose, their ability to work together. Fay was swimming groggily now, against the current, facing them, but still moving backwards. They swam after her. Tim experienced a sharp headache and his brain seemed frozen. He found his movements absurdly clumsy under the handicap of his clothing, including his shoes. His knee bumped something and he stood momentarily on the same rock that had hurt Fay. It rose from the bottom almost to the surface. He heard a heavy splash behind him, and knew that someone else was entering the pool, coming to help. He teetered and overbalanced, losing that precarious foothold as the current took him. He could hardly swim – he felt he could barely float; and already a numbness was creeping into his hands and feet. But the current was aiding him. He and Neville were near the girl, almost able to hold her. Four or five yards behind her was the crack, the current sucking everything towards it. Tim tried to guess whether she could be swept through – whether she would fit. But he did not have time to calculate, and he ceased to be aware of the cold – of anything except the need to reach Fay. For all he knew, this cavern might be as far as the Tourist Bureau had explored; there might be no other way to reach the place where the water was going after passing out of it. He swallowed water several times, spitting and gasping for air, trying to swim, unable to credit that his arms and legs were so heavy encased in sodden cloth.

Neville, fit from his outdoor life, reached her first. He grabbed her left wrist, holding his own wrist where her palm could close on it in the manner taught to boy scouts. She reached for him with her other hand, but Tim caught it, and the three of them drifted until, like some crazy vaudeville act, they felt themselves in a line pressed against the rock wall, with the men facing it and Fay facing back towards the pool. She had no foothold; her feet were in the crack, her shoulders and hips on the rock.

Tim became more intensely aware of the chill. He wanted to hold Fay around the waist, but dared not let go of her wrist for fear that she would be sucked away. Instinctively he tightened his grip, and for a moment felt unable to think. He felt her answering pressure. Overcoming the chattering of his teeth, he asked, "Are you all right?" In any other circumstances she might have laughed at the ludicrousness of the question. Now she just looked at him through glazed eyes and nodded. But there was blood on her hair and in the water, it was clear that she was dizzy. Whatever had happened to her head was more than a graze.

Seconds later George was there, blundering at first clumsily into Fay and then embracing the three of them. Tim understood: he wanted to make the group into a sort of human lump, a plug too big to fit through the hole. In the way we sometimes have of noticing irrelevancies, Tim realised that George had removed his shoes. That was why he had not been with them at once.

Tim looked at Neville. "We swim," he shouted. "We take her – by her arms."

"The current's – too strong."

"How big do you think that crack is?"

The forester was spluttering. More than Tim, he was speaking in gasps. "Dunno – four feet high – eighteen inches wide – she's not – properly – wedged against the wall – she – could get sucked in. She mightn't go through, but it'd bash her – this other bloke's helping – I think."

"What, then?"

"There's a rope – in my pack. The people – on the shelf – haul her."

Tim nodded. Neville said, "We have to turn – I do, anyway. That means – letting go her wrist. Two people won't fit through that crack – one might. Both of you – try – brace against the rock – for God's sake don't let go. Mate – you move to my right."

This was directed to George, who worked his way past Neville, getting a foot on the rock wall and then a hold, feeling useless. Neville's left hand was grasping Fay's left. He turned, slowly. It meant having no support except that of his body pressed by the current against the wall, pushing his free arm between it and his chest, abrading his elbow, changing his hold on Fay first to both hands and then to his right, squirming to face the way he had come, then extending his left hand outwards, groping with it for some hand-hold on the rock but unable to find one by touch, barking the back of it, then feeling it grasped and held by George. Facing now the watchers on the shelf, unaware of multiple scratches, his words interspersed with deep intakes of his breath, he called out: "In my pack – the rope – make one end fast to something – in the other end make a loop – two feet across – leave a couple of feet free. Then bring it here. Make sure – throw it – right into my hand."

They did as they were told. All of them threw off their coats and, fastening an end of the rope to the iron ladder as the anchor, one man walked along the shelf as far as he could and threw the loop. It fell near Neville in the water, and shaking off George's hold he scooped it up. Turning his side into the wall, he reached over towards Fay with it in his free hand, wondering whether he could get it over her shoulders. It was clearly impossible unless both he and Tim let go her hands – and that was out of the question.

George was now rolling a little, unable to keep steady. Tim strove to overcome his numbness by force of will. He must keep hold of Fay. He cared for nothing – except that he did not let go. But he was afraid – his strength was limited.

Neville called to him, "You've got to turn – like I did. That way you've – got another hand to help. Try to reach over – hold her right hand with your left – before you turn fully. Have one hand on her wrist – all the time."

He obeyed. The movement scraped his arm and shoulder and seemed to twist something in his neck, causing a sharp pain. He felt his left hand close on Fay's, released the grip of his right and turned. The jagged surface had a bruising impact but he was around, around too far, his back against the rock, and his right arm, now free, was outstretched. He groped as Neville had done unsuccessfully for some unseen hand-hold. He realised then that it was not necessary. His back was wedged securely.

"OK," he said, "I can turn sideways. I won't go in."

Both men wriggled experimentally, and found that they could brace themselves against protusions that could resist their hips and shoulders. Neville nodded to George – a gesture whose meaning was plain: let go of me, try to get hold of Fay and keep holding her. George passed his arms on either side of Neville and grasped Fay's belt. Neville, with both hands freed, passed the useless loop behind Fay's waist and managed to fasten it to the main length of the rope, cursing its stiff wetness and fumbling to make a clumsy knot with half-frozen fingers. She was now linked by the rope to the iron ladder. George relaxed, allowed the current to take him, his back now to the rock wall, his feet somehow lodged awkwardly in a small crevice. The position was wrong. He felt a new pain slowly building in his legs.

Neville's attention was brought back from Fay's waist to her face by Tim's cry. He was shouting, "Keep awake. Don't drift!"

She shook her head wearily. Neville, looking, could see that she was losing the last of her consciousness. Between gasps he turned and called to the four people standing near the ladder. "Find somewhere to brace yourselves. Take in the slack on the rope. Then haul in steadily – not till I say."

There was a strong pull on the rope. "No," he screamed. "Not till I say!"

The rope went slightly slack. Neville spoke to Tim. "We'll be letting her go. Can you stay where you are? Use both hands on the wall."

Unsure whether he could do so – unsure, he felt, of anything – Tim nodded. Beyond one thing, he felt too cold to care what happened next. Only – Fay must be taken out of this trap. He spoke to her: "Fay, we'll let you go now. Grab the rope if you can – both hands." Neville worked his way back to the side, took Fay's right hand, led it to the rope.

This was the critical moment. At first, she seemed not to understand, to be moving drowsily in and out of awareness of her surroundings. Then, with a sharp intake of breath, she let go of Neville's hand and gripped the rope. Neville scrambled back past George to the side. At the same time Fay twisted involuntarily towards Tim, but the rope tautened and she was still. Then, with a sudden glance at him, she let his hand go. The action left a gap between her and the crack, and Tim was sucked into it. He swore as he was grazed from shoulder to knee, but managed to use a foot against one wall of the crack to push his body back to precarious safety, steadying himself against a sharp spike of rock.

Fay did not manage to grip the rope with her right hand. The four on the shelf began to haul her in slowly, trying clumsily to coordinate their efforts. She twisted in the water, rolling onto her side, apparently unable to help. George, thinking perhaps of life-jackets, spluttered "She should be on her back – her back, dammit!"

Then, slowly, her left hand left the rope and dropped aimlessly into the water. Her face was below the surface. She spluttered, raised her head, then seemed to let it fall back. Tim watched, aghast, then, with a sudden intake of breath, he pushed himself off the rock wall to swim towards her. The current swept him back, towards the crack. Neville caught his outstretched hand and he wedged himself half in the crack, half scrabbling for some hand hold behind his back on the wall. He tried to swim towards Fay again. Neville and George both held him. George was shaking his head.

Fay was drawn up to the ledge. One man reached down to her armpits while the man behind him kept both hands on his belt. This man in turn was steadied by a third who kept one hand on the ladder. She was hauled up and lay on the shelf, unconscious and bruised where the rope had scored her neck.

"Don't let her sleep," yelled Neville. "Put her on her side – arm out, head down. Try to open her mouth. And throw the rope back."

Then to Tim he said, "You next."

The rope hit him on the head. He got one arm through the loop, then his head and the other arm. As he did so his back left the rock wall, and he slid towards the crack. Suddenly he was wide awake, and his mind went perfectly clear. He realised now that he had the loop around him the wrong way – the rope was at his back. But then ... was it wrong? He remembered hearing George's cry moments ago. Yes ... he would go that way.

Sluggishly he groped for the rope above his head, held it, felt the wall with his feet, and pushed. Heavier than Fay, he was drawn more slowly to the shelf, his face sliding under the water each time the tension in the rope momentarily lessened, and at the end he managed to twist to be helped out face-first. He stood there, watching Fay's still, white face unbelievingly, and shivering uncontrollably as much from shock as from the cold.

Clumsily he knelt, undid the belt of her jacket, and held his hand to the long cut on her head, exerting pressure to stop the blood which still issued slowly. To his touch, her body seemed lifeless. He experienced a sense of absolute helplessness. Tears welled behind his eyes. Instinctively he knew he was looking at something very near death. This could not be real. It was impossible. But also – it was altogether real. He felt incapable of speaking, but croaked out to the others, "Get some dry clothes on her – some of you give her your coats."

"We need antiseptic," said a woman.

"Neville's pack – he must have some," said a man.

"I wonder," replied another. "She must be in shock. Could antiseptic increase it?"

They hesitated, and Tim swore. "Coats! Get her dry coats!"

Obeying, they wrapped her as well as they could. It took minutes for Neville to be hauled in. He pushed Tim aside, and kneeling beside Fay's still body, pulled at the coats, screaming,"Get this stuff off!" George was almost forgotten it seemed, but the two who had thrown the rope got it to him and drew him out. His bare feet were bleeding where they had encountered jagged rock.

Tim scrambled to his feet, trembling, bewildered, unresponsive. His phase of clarity seemed to desert him. The others eased Fay's arms out of her own jacket and pulled it away. Neville turned her onto her stomach with her face to her side. He placed his hands on her back, and kneeling beside her began the fore-and-aft swaying motion known as "artificial respiration", counting under his breath as he applied rhythmic pressure. Some water dribbled out of Fay's mouth.

"What about that cut?" asked someone.

One of the other men put his arm around Tim. "Come on," he said. "Get that bloody wet shirt off. Take my coat." He turned to George. "You, too, mate – here, someone give him a dry jacket."

Tim did not seem to understand, or even to hear. Then, suddenly, his trembling stopped. The clarity was back. He now seemed another person – practical, efficient, detached from the cold and his own emotions; they could wait until there was time.

Neville was apparently made of iron. He was the leader both by his personality and by his skills. Tim knelt beside him. "Let me help."

Neville shook his head. Not losing count. It needed training to do this properly. Then he muttered, "Get everything dry you can. Pack the dry coats back over her legs, yes, but leave me room. Massage her feet. You're her fiancé, Tim – lie near her. Do whatever you can to give her some circulation, get some warmth into her if you've got any left."

Tim lay as near to Fay as he could without preventing Neville from working. He was horrified to find that, cold as he was, Fay felt much colder. He did not know how much time passed. A woman said, "Tim's frozen himself – that's no use," and gently tried to raise him. Tim shook his head, and George, now beside him, said, "It's for Fay, Tim. Let this lady lie near her." Tim seemed not to comprehend, but after a moment he allowed George to raise him while the woman snuggled against Fay. His face was almost dead white.

At length Neville stopped, and felt for the pulse in Fay's neck and in her wrist. He removed his water-soaked watch and polished it against the dry sleeve of a woman's jacket, then held the glass before Fay's mouth. Nothing. He tried the back of the watch. He muttered, "It's no use."

It was Tim's turn to scramble to his knees and elbow Neville aside, and he began imitating the forester's action as well as he could. He felt hands on his shoulders, pulling him back.

Shrugging them off, he continued.

They picked him up, forcing him to his feet. He fought with an unaccustomed strength. Neville slapped his face.

"Tim," he said, "it's over. It's too late. I'm sorry."

As he said this, they all heard something like a faint gurgle. Fay stirred – slightly. Tim dropped again to his knees, holding her hand, rubbing what warmth he could into her. She was breathing, lightly, without strength or consciousness.

They wrapped her with all the dry clothing they could spare, and propped her on her side. From his pack Neville took a first-aid kit, dabbed the antiseptic and expertly bandaged her head.

While Tim knelt and watched, anxiously observing every breath, the others conferred. George, trying to hide the shudders that still travelled intermittently through his dripping body, asked: "How are we going to get her out of here? Even if we had a stretcher, could we carry her? On *this* track?"

"Piggyback?" said the woman who had tried to warm Fay.

"If she was conscious, maybe," said the man who had thrown the rope.

"Yes," said Neville. "Try to get her conscious. Then, maybe, she can hang on."

"You can tie her to me," said Tim.

"You'd never make it the whole way. If we can't revive her, then some of us wait with her while others go for help."

"It's too bloody cold! She can't just lie here shivering."

"Bloody hell!" cried Neville in a sort of exasperation. "I know we're not out of the woods yet – not by a long way. But what else can we do?"

Fay stirred again, and opened her eyes. Her voice was very faint. "Tim?"

"Fay," he said. "Fay, do you know where you are?"

She looked around at the people, the rocks, and back at Tim. She nodded feebly.

"We are going to carry you out – piggyback."

George glanced at the iron ladder and shook his head. His

face was grim. Fay coughed, and said in a faint voice, "I can walk. Help me up."

They tried, and she half-sank to ground on legs that had turned to rubber. "Give me a little time."

And they compromised, waiting as long as they dared to let a little strength return to her limbs. They used the rope to make a sort of sling in which she could sit and a loop in which she could twine her arms. Neville went up the ladder, intending to haul her from above. He made the rope fast to the conduit that Tim had noticed, and did his best to brace himself, using the small undulations of the rough path. George, the strongest and tallest of the others, lifted her from the ground. The sling proved nearly useless but the loop was invaluable. When she was high enough she sat on George's shoulders, and he climbed slowly, taking more of her weight than Neville. At last she was up, and the others followed.

They set off, taking turns, alternately piggybacking her and letting her lean stumbling against Tim.

Halfway to the café they met a party who, worried at the delay, had come to look for them. Neville sent two of them back to ask whether a stretcher and a thermos of hot tea could be brought. This was done, and Fay was carried then, while Tim, Neville and George, released from immediate responsibility, became fully aware of their own exhaustion. George was limping. At length they reached the café, and all four were taken by the café owner in his car, with Fay drifting in and out of consciousness, to the Base hospital at Wildjeree where they were put to bed.

The men were up the next day, shaken but well enough. They were advised to rest for another day, and to see their own doctors in Brisbane. They would have to go back to work a day late. Fay would stay a few days.

The blow was utterly unexpected. She developed pneumonia, and no one was allowed near her except doctors and nurses. After four days, she died.

Tim was at work in Brisbane when they brought him the news.

CHAPTER 13

The Decision
(Walgabran, 1940)

"It's a personality change," said George.

"No bloody wonder," said Reg.

Their concern for Tim had increased during the last two months. They were themselves deeply shaken by Fay's death, George the more so since he had been intimately involved; and they knew that it must be unimaginably worse for many others, especially for Fay's parents. But with their friend they had not fully bargained for the prolonged silences, the inability to smile, the retreat into a private world where no one could follow.

The bank had been understanding, and had decided that Tim must have a month's holiday at home. Not that a month could do more than relieve the worst aspects of his symptoms: the sudden fits of shivering and fear, the waves of profound depression, the sense that every task was pointless. But in the wordless kindness of his parents Tim had an anchor, an unbreakable bridge reinforcing his faith in God; and Walgabran itself had at least this supreme attraction, that it was not Brisbane; for Brisbane was now merely the place where Fay was not, though every corner and shop and street and house was painfully alive with her aura.

Yet his work was there, and after the first week or two he

had no desire to sit at home where his thoughts fed uselessly on themselves. In a disciplined decision that found no echo in his feelings, he accepted that he must try to become involved again in normal activity, and he returned to the bank before he was in fact required. George and Reg, themselves now budding accountants, gave what support they could. But for a time they found they were sharing a house with an automaton, someone who could not sleep, whose instinct for proportion had been jarred into insensibility so that small things became important and serious ones inconsequential; and who went through ordinary life as though deliberately feeling his way through a pointless maze.

Months, however, passed, and this awkwardness at last began to diminish. On the surface he became indistinguishable from others and internally he felt halfway normal. The cycle of the seasons helped, and as spring gave way to summer and summer became autumn and autumn winter, he finally reached a point where those who had known him before Fay's death could recognise the return of the earlier person. His personality remained subdued but he was Tim. And in fact, a trainee accountant now, twenty-one, his life before him, he looked to outsiders like a person to be envied.

One Monday he emerged from the bank into the throng of afternoon commuters. Most were hurrying to catch the white-painted trams. A few were simply dawdling, letting the day's tensions flow from their bodies to dissipate in the open air. There was a blustery wind, and Tim was glad of his three-piece suit. Willy had warned him of the city's oppressive humidity but had not mentioned the frosts that could spread a brittle white morning coat across the grass, or the cool that settled with the darkness on June evenings.

He thought, unusually, that he would walk down to the river.

Turning from Ann Street into Edward Street, he gazed around, half-formed ideas flitting through his head. Ever-present memories of Fay jostled with tasks for tomorrow and with thoughts of home, all mingling with the sights and smells of the city and the clanging of the tram bells and the headlines on newspaper stands that day by day were increasingly disturbing. For in the streets, at work, in pubs, everywhere, there was something new. The whole country was thinking war, and a crackling energy seemed to infect the very air – as though the private thoughts of a million minds somehow combined to exert an unspoken pressure on them all.

Tim, preoccupied though he still was, could not ignore this. His mind ran in unfinished circles that went nowhere and returned to no clarity. War. Fay. Work. Walgabran. War. Fay. War. Each thought interfered with the one it interrupted.

He'd seen Rainier while he was on leave in Walgabran. He remained grateful to the man for the chance to start in the bank, and even more so for selecting him to be sent to Brisbane. But there had been an irony in the visit. Accountancy – some months ago it had seemed a gateway to fulfilment, a participation in some great human enterprise. Now it had the taste of cardboard. He got up and worked and went to bed because everyone else did the same, because it was his habit.

Tired, he let the thoughts drift, unwilling to follow any of them to a conclusion. It was too difficult.

A hand was on his shoulder.

Turning, he recognised the comrade of his childhood. After coming to Brisbane, he had rather avoided Alan. Their worlds and attitudes had diverged, and Tim had attributed to his cousin a sort of professional snobbery. There had been occasional family contacts, but they had not sought each other's company as when they were boys. So now Tim felt awkward – the more so because his confidence had been undermined since Fay's death, while before him was the very model of a promising young man, filled out to an athletic figure, dressed in a quietly expensive suit, with an attractive blend of boyish enthusiasm and maturing charm that surely presaged success. The scar on his cheek had faded; far from a disfigurement, it now lent him a faintly swashbuckling air. And, in his face, there was something else – an excitement that he seemed bursting to share. The enthusiasm was absolutely alien to the heavy weariness that had become habitual with Tim, whose immediate impulse was to keep a polite distance: to say a few words and to pass on.

But Alan was before him. "Tim!" he cried. "This is wonderful!" He stopped, and added, "I'm sorry. Of course I heard about your fiancée. I'm really sorry, Tim. And I'm sorry I didn't know her. There's nothing I can say – only you know what it meant to you. But I'd like to talk. Look. Come and have a drink."

The expression of sorrow was patently sincere. Some fellow-feeling from long ago reasserted itself. Momentarily, Tim's memory scanned a hundred childish scrapes and arguments. He heard himself say, "Of course. We'll go to the Imperial. You can hear yourself there. What have you been doing since Christmas?"

"I'm a full-fledged solicitor now, Tim Boy. Finished the articles, got a job with Davoren and Cooper. Loving it. But – mate, it's not what I've been doing. It's what I'm going to do."

In the present climate, there could be little doubt what he meant. But Tim said, "Same old Alan. And what's that?"

"I'll tell you in the pub."

It was a walk of only a couple of hundred yards, and Alan, studiously avoiding further reference to Fay, filled it with questions about Tim's work and with chatter about his own clients and the eminent contacts he had made. Entering the pub, they found a reasonably quiet corner.

"My shout," said Alan. He went to the bar and came back with a tray bearing two whiskies and two small beers of the type Queenslanders call "ponies".

"Cheerio!"

"Good health!"

They settled. Alan looked, grinned, and became serious. Characteristically, he plunged at once into the heart of the matter. "Tim, you remember the argument we had a couple of years ago? You thought there'd never be another war – that we'd all settle down to being civilised. We all know that's all hopeless now, courtesy of Mr Hitler and his gang."

"Touché. I've got to admit it. We can only hope this one doesn't last as long as the last. I didn't think France would fall. And the British aren't ready. It looks bad."

"It's worse than bad. These Huns are ruthless people, Tim – whatever your father said about the Allies being too hard on them in 1918. They've got to be stopped!"

Though his emotions were now habitually dulled, Tim felt a flash of anger at the personal reference. "My father knows what he's talking about. All this *did* begin with the Allies being bloody-minded at Versailles."

"Ten years ago there might have been something in that. Even that I'm not sure of. I've studied this. Ever heard of the Treaty of Brest-Litovsk? In 1918 Russia was defeated – and the terms the Germans imposed on them make Versailles look trivial! What do you think they'd have done to the Allies if they'd won?"

"I don't know much about it, but I have an idea that treaty got a lot of people out from under Russian domination. Anyway, even if what you say is true, that's no reason why we should behave in the same way."

Alan sighed. "OK. But by the same token, Versailles is no reason for ignoring what's happening now. The Hitler government has changed the landscape. Look at Europe. Austria, Czechoslovakia, Poland, Holland, Belgium, France – all gone. In Germany itself they've destroyed Jewish businesses, smashed and looted; some say they're rounding up everyone they don't consider "pure" – whatever that means. In the last war Russia and Italy were on our side – now they're friends of Germany. America won't come in – they had enough last time."

"You're saying Britain's alone."

"Except for the Empire – and we're a hell of an important part of it."

Tim grinned ruefully: "You always were a good debater, Alan."

"That's bullshit and you know it. This isn't a debate. No one could hold back now – no one with any self-respect. I'm joining up."

Still smarting, Tim could not resist a dig. "To become an army lawyer?"

"Army be damned! Look, Tim – the British want men who will fly. They've set up a thing called the Empire Air Training Scheme. They want pilots, Tim – and gunners and navigators and engineers and radio operators from Australia and New Zealand and Canada and South Africa and Kenya and India and the West Indies. They'll teach some of us to fly – just Tiger Moths or something like that – and then they'll take us to Canada for further training. Afterwards they'll send us on to Britain. Even if you're not selected as a pilot you'll still come along as air crew if you can make it. I've already been accepted for the basic course – it starts next month. I think I could get you in. Come with us – I've already spoken to Bruce, back home, and he's coming. It's the chance of a lifetime!"

For a moment Tim was shocked out of the flatness of his mood. For weeks the question had stared every man of his age in the face – whether to "join up". He had feared to contemplate it. To go meant abandoning his long-held convictions. Not to go meant opposing the overwhelming ground-swell of popular consciousness. That a moment of choice would emerge sometime was inevitable, but he had shelved it, thinking only of Fay. Now the thing was being forced into the open where he must confront it.

Temporising, he turned to a side-issue. "But – but what about your job?"

"Mr Davoren said they'll try to hold it open for me after the war. Can't promise, of course. But Tim – who's going to cling to a job at a time like this? Bruce thinks the way I do. I think I can get Ken and Barry. The old gang. Why don't you to come with us?"

So this was it. His boyhood companions. Alan had always had this curious power to lead them – and to unsettle him, to knock his world for six. How did he do it? Bruce, quiet, solid Bruce, whose opinion he'd always respected. His mind flew back to a cricket match when he had missed a catch because an aeroplane crossed the sky, and to his first feeling of emptiness when, seven years ago, he realised that he would never be a pilot – that he would work in a bank. He had felt then as though he was a brick being cemented into a wall – a wall that would hold him fast from his dreams. In recent years he had entirely forgotten that sense of childhood loss. It returned now, touched his memory – shifted his mind-set back for a moment to a long-abandoned perspective of frustrated ambition.

Accountancy! Why, really, was he in this niche? It was not something he had sought, only an accident of the Depression.

Funny. Reg and George were perfectly happy in the profession. Even for him, three months ago it had a satisfying sense of goodness. Now, since Fay's death, it seemed to weigh him down.

The possibility of *flying*!

Suddenly it loomed as an escape. In the air at least he would be away from normal existence, from Brisbane, from this very earth where all he loved had disappeared.

Fay. Fay was the real point.

Canada, Alan had said. Britain. It would be a relief to get the hell out of the country.

But – war! His father's hatred of it. Willy's strictures against it. His own sense of something false, some deep deception, underlying it.

In the past, the problems were academic. This was reality. Not to be escaped by thought. Alan's words could not be shelved.

It was not so long – three years – since Willy, in spite of his wide sense of humanity, of his idea that to fight anyone was to fight his brother, had warned against the Nazis. At that time Tim had asserted that he himself would never fight even if he was conscripted. But could he salve his conscience by opting out of all this, pretending that he wasn't part of the same world?

He realised that Alan was still talking. "Look – I know it's a big step. I don't really think about things – I just do them. But you're different. You'd have to talk to Jenny and Ben, and chew on it. What about meeting again next week? Phone me at the office." And he scribbled a number on a scrap of paper.

"OK – I'll get back to you. Let's leave that now. But what do you mean – they'll train you in Canada. Why not here? How does all this work?"

They discussed the war, and flying, for the next hour, and parted, it seemed, with their friendship stronger than it had been for years.

After five hours' sleep in two nights, Tim caught the Friday evening train home. He needed to talk to his parents, and he wanted to see Willy. He didn't feel that he cared much, now, about his own life. He did not want to kill. Yet he could see a real argument that as part of a nation one had a duty to defend it – not to let others carry the burden and then himself to benefit.

Hadn't Jesus rejected the sword? Hadn't he said, "turn the other cheek"? Just suppose, he thought, we really took that seriously – if whole nations confronted aggressors *en masse* with non-resistance – what would happen then? Yes, there would be massacres. But for how long? Surely even these Nazis would be shamed; their inner goodness would revolt, and they too would lay down their arms and make peace. Was that a mad thought? And who would be willing to try the experiment? Who, anyway, could get a whole nation to turn into self-sacrificing saints? They would have to be willing to sacrifice not only themselves, but their families – wives, old parents, children. You couldn't ask that of anyone.

Besides, would it work that way? If the world simply let the Nazis walk over them, would not this "thousand-year Reich" of which Willy had once spoken become a brutal reality?

He arrived home at midnight and, exhausted, slept until lunchtime on the Saturday, when he came tousle-haired to the table where his mother had prepared him two lamb chops, a tomato and toast all grilled together. He kissed her and, though his appetite had these days largely deserted him, ate all the food. Chattering, he skirted the subject that had brought him home, sharing instead the trivia of life in Brisbane. Outside, he could hear his father mowing the lawn, and he wanted to retreat from his problem into the comforting domesticity of the life he had grown up with.

But there was nowhere to run. After the meal, sipping tea, he forced himself to speak.

"Mum, there's something I want to talk about. It's important."

Jenny Rogers caught her breath and went still. War had been a possibility for at least three years, and she had worried silently during all of that time. For the last six months, when the Sixth Division was being formed and young men were volunteering in thousands, she had lived on an edge.

Now Tim was telling her how he had met Alan, and what had passed between them. And this was worse – much worse. She had some idea of casualty rates in what she had come to think of as "Ben's war", fought in the horror of the trenches that had lain like endless scars extending across the fields of France and Belgium. But, terrible as those rates were, they had not compared with the ones in the air. Distressed, she said, "Oh, Tim. Tim, you're not going?"

"I don't know, Mum," he replied. "I want to talk to you and Dad, and I think I want to talk to Bill."

"Bill! He's a good man, Tim, but he's not your parents. Why talk to him?"

"Mum, I know he hates war. I think maybe he can help me see what's wrong with what Alan said."

Jenny had gone white. Alan, she knew, had only said what everyone was saying. Perhaps that was not the point. "Tim," she said, "is this because of what happened?"

There was no need to spell out what she meant. "I guess it is, Mum, but that's not the whole of it. I don't know – I just don't know. So many fellows are joining up. A man feels like a coward if he just stays still."

Tim had never before called himself a man in Jenny's hearing. The word shocked her – because of the weight it had carried through history. She felt herself losing her rights to her son – he would always be her son, but something in him was turning to a wider world – and, as always, the wider world would win. She saw him there at the table, still in pyjamas, unkempt from sleep, as he had so often been as a toddler. And she loved him with the same protective love. She had to say something.

"Tim, those fellows are not joining the Air Force! The Army's bad enough – even the Navy would be better! Though with submarines ... the damage they did in the last war ... oh, Tim!"

He could hardly remember feeling so miserable. For the first time it occurred to him that joining Alan might actually be selfish. In the pub he had seen his friend's approach as heroic and generous. But - what was it doing to *his* mother?

At this point Ben Rogers came in, wiping the hands he had just rinsed under a garden tap on a cloth half-stuffed into his pocket. Seeing Tim, he grinned: "Well! He finally wakes up! Just in time for lunch! It's a great life for some people!"

Tim replied in a toneless voice, "Hello, Dad."

"Ben," said Jenny, "Tim's talking about the war. He met Alan in Brisbane. Alan's going to join the Air Force – in England!"

Ben drew a deep breath. "I know, Jenny. I didn't want to mention it. But Jim told me. Louise is upset. Jim's worried, but he's as proud as Punch. He seems to think Alan's going to finish what we started twenty-five years ago."

"Ben, Tim's thinking of going with him."

"What? Go to England?"

"Yes, Ben, in the Air Force."

"Bloody hell! That's crazy ..."

There was a long pause, then he asked, "Well, what do you say, Tim?

"Dad, Mum – I don't think I could stand the army – or the navy. And everyone's joining up. Bruce is going with Alan. Maybe others. I don't know ... I'd like to see what Bill thinks ..."

"Tim," said his father, "this is not ... it's not that you *want* to get killed, is it?"

"Dad! How on earth can you say that?"

"I know you wouldn't ever kill yourself – no matter what. I didn't mean it that way. But sometimes a man can lose his desire to live to the point where he becomes reckless, and he fails to take ordinary precautions more or less without noticing – it's like being just a little drunk. He doesn't care as he should. Even for his own life. I've got to ask. It's not that, Tim?"

"Yes, maybe ... I d'know, Dad. No – I don't think so ... No, Dad, I wouldn't do that."

Ben turned to his wife. "Love, after what's happened ... this actually could be the best thing ... I don't know – what do you think?"

Strength suddenly showed in her face, suppressing the despair that was also there. "Yes, Ben ... it might be best ..."

He looked back at Tim. "Right, son. You know your mother and I won't stand in your way if it's what you really want – but be damned sure that it is. Alan's got plenty of guts, but I wouldn't give him top marks for sense!"

Jenny added, in a barely controlled voice, "Oh, Tim! No, we won't stand in your way."

And she turned away to the kitchen, to hide her trembling. Ben followed, and put his arm around her. Tim stood up, began to speak but caught the words in his throat. He felt as though he had made up his mind but couldn't admit it to himself. His whirling half-thoughts could neither be solved nor shelved. He went to have a shower.

Bill, he thought – Bill will help me.

In the deep recesses of his heart and mind, Tim was sure that Willy would advise him not to fight, whatever the cost – and the cost of taking that stand would be considerable: not so great as in Britain, where pacifists were often regarded as cowards and conscientious objectors as little better than traitors; for Australia, without conscription at that time, did not to the same extent force personal decisions into the public arena. Still, to refuse to join the military on moral grounds required a courage that was probably greater than that demanded of those who enlisted.

To Tim, the dilemma seemed more acute by the hour. On one side was the desertion, as it now seemed, of his family, together with the appalling human destruction of war. On the other, the implications of a Nazi victory and the sense that he could not stand back and let others take the strain. He went to Willy with a kind of belief in the artist's moral superiority. It was a sort of test. If he would not condemn it, then the case for going must be strong indeed – overwhelming.

But his old friend was of little help. He seemed unexpectedly hesitant, and Tim could see tears gathering in his eyes. Surprised, Tim said: "But Bill, you always said that nothing justified war … at my house, you said that when you fight, you fight your brother."

"Ja. I know."

Tim asked a question he had never asked before. "Bill, why did you come here? After the war finished in 1918 …"

"The war did not finish."

"What do you mean?"

"The war never finished, Tim. Oh, yes, there was a pause …

and that was all. A pause to rest for a while, and forget, and make jazz and movie stars and invent new things – wonderful new ships, and great, strong radios, and aeroplanes – new inventions for men to kill each other with … that is what the world has been doing since 1918 …

"The war never finished. Do not blame the people of Germany too much. They were caught between two forces – two evil forces. They were starving, and they resented what the Allies did in 1919 – that was one force; the other was their own romantic tradition of the soldier with his coloured jackets and big moustaches and bright swords. It is not their fault, Tim – at least not their fault only. To an extent all Europe shared that romantic notion. Its nations have been fighting for thousands of years.

"But now the war cannot be left unfinished. The Allies made a bomb, waiting to explode one day again. You know, if you cool water very carefully, it does not freeze when it should. It just gets even colder. Then, if you drop a pebble in it, it all freezes suddenly – at once! Germany was like that, waiting for the pebble without even knowing it. But – unfortunately the pebble was the Nazis.

"Do you know anything about Ancient Rome? Others did not fear that people for nothing. They destroyed nations – swallowed them up! The triumph not of beauty or culture or even intelligence, but of power itself! It lasted for six centuries at least. This man, Hitler, will do the same if he is allowed – and he has modern weapons. He will do worse. Europe will be submerged under Nazi rule and a Nazi idea – until everything else is forgotten, except by a few foolish old scholars! It is not just a war like other wars, Tim. Hitler has confidence. And other nations have confidence, too, in his power. That is why he will win – unless there is a miracle. I have run out of arguments. I think – I think maybe it is better to die trying to stop him.

"But – do not blame my people, Tim. If others had been put in the same situation … it is not the people. In a way, it is not even the soldiers. It is everyone in the world who does not care about other people – everywhere! It is an idea – it is the belief in Force."[2]

For Willy, the effort of bringing these thoughts to the surface and articulating them had been immense. The tears in his eyes dried, but he suddenly broke down, into great racking sobs. Tim, shocked, was instantly ashamed of his own self-pity.

"Tim, this is not only because I am German. It is also because I do not – I really do not – believe in war. And yet, now …

"I do not tell you to go. I am not your father or your mother. If you go to join the Army – or the Air Force – maybe you will kill young German men, and maybe they will kill you. I cannot tell you to do this. I would have to be a monster. But three years ago I would have said do *not* go. Now I do not say that. I cannot.

"Tim – go, now. I cannot talk." And he turned away, a man whose idealism had been defeated, to hide his face.

---

2   See Appendix: Simone Weil's *The Iliad or the Poem of Force*.

Part 4: War

CHAPTER 14

The Letters of 1941 (Walgabran, Honolulu, Canada, New York, Britain)

SS *Strathburn*
Sydney
28th November 1940

Dear Mother and Dad,

Well, we're on our way. I was disappointed, of course. But a lot of us didn't make it as pilots, so I've plenty of company, and it's good to get elementary training over. I think my bit of accountancy had something to do with me being made a navigator.

After Canada we'll go to England for more training, and then join something called an Operational Training Unit. We'll be placed in crews and sent to a squadron. We'll try to stay together, Alan, Bruce and I – all the way. It might be possible with Alan being a pilot and poor old Bruce stuck in "Bombing and Gunnery". That's the worst job. Though I guess the pilot has the most responsibility.

Lots of love,
Tim

_____

17 Nursery Street
Walgabran
30th November 1940

Aus. EATS 2293771 F/Sgt. Rogers, T.P.
Poste Restante
Vancouver, BC
Canada

Dear Tim,

You fellows have started a rush. Ken and Owen are in the navy. John and Barry have gone to save the Canal. Your uncle Jim is cheering them on – he reckons the Sixth Divvy will win the war. Personally I was hoping they'd go to Singapore with the Eighth. They'd be out of danger there.

Your mother tells me I mustn't say we miss you, so I'll just say we hope it'll be over soon and you'll be home. She's made an extra cake this year. You'll still be at sea for Christmas, but you should get it soon afterwards. We've already sent it to the Ottawa address you gave us.

Tim, don't worry about not being a pilot. Navigators are just as necessary. You'll be doing an invaluable job. Remember us to Alan and Bruce. Jenny's adding a few lines.

Love, Dad.

My dearest son,

I won't say much. You are far away now, but you are always close in both our hearts. Always remember we love you and pray for you, and you need never worry about us.

Fondest love my darling,
Mother.

SS *Strathburn*
Pearl Harbour, Hawaii
10th December 1940

Dear Mother and Dad,

It's all real. Lush green islands do rise straight out of the sea, the girls do wear flowers in their hair and leis around their necks! The postcard looks tarted up but it's not. (Sorry, Mum, that's an Air Force expression.)

On shore we ran into some US Navy men who insisted on buying us drinks. I'm afraid Alan got sort of stroppy – he reckoned America should come in with the Allies. Bruce and I just listened to the argument, a bit embarrassed. But the sailors were divided on the question.

We feel like sailors ourselves. They give us jobs on the ship, mainly cleaning but also spotting for aircraft and subs. Not that there's much real risk – not here, in the Pacific. Just as well – this tub does thirteen knots flat out, so we'll be dawdling around this sea for a while.

I'm sending you a couple of small gifts.

Love, Tim.

---

17 Nursery St.
Walgabran
21st December 1940

Dear Tim,

Your mother loves the scarf, but, mate, how am I going to wear that shirt? Black and covered with huge red tropical flowers? I'd be run out of town! I'm giving it to Jenny, and she'll take it in for herself on the sewing machine.

All the best, Dad

Dearest Tim,

Thank you for that wonderful silk scarf. It's really beautiful, but I won't wear it until Christmas, since it is your present. The shirt is beautiful, too. Your father's being silly about it. Don't worry, he'll change his mind.

We'll be thinking of you at Christmas. Bill always asks about you whenever we see him.

Love, Mother.

Aus. EATS 2293771
F/Sgt Rogers, T.P.
Auspost, Ottawa
CANADA
2ⁿᵈ January 1941

Dear Mum and Dad,

I'm not allowed to say exactly where we are, but it's near a place called Broken Lake in Alberta. Cold! I think my ears are going to fall off. I laughed at the long underwear you bought for me, Mum, but it's twenty-one degrees below freezing and I can tell you I'm bloody grateful for it now.

I want to tell you about something that really moved me. Two days out from Vancouver the S/L made a speech for Christmas Eve. Bruce dressed up as Santa Claus and gave out "presents" – not real ones, they were all jokes. In the evening we had our own carol concert in the dining room. It's in the middle of the ship, with no portholes, but still we had the lights dimmed. At midnight we "RCs" had Mass, while the "ODs" hit the sack.

Silent Night – it certainly was. There was snow on the decks, and there was just the ship and the sea and the dark. Once at school we had a poem that spoke of the tabernacle in church as "The secret window whence the world looks small and very dear." That's how I felt. Everything was small and dear and very close. You were close, all the people in the world seemed close. Even Fay. It didn't matter whether they were rich or poor or clever or simple – all that stuff seemed secondary. Only, the whole earth felt vulnerable, like the child Jesus in the crib. And this war seemed so stupid.

Sometimes it's like that in church. You feel connected with everyone around you, you can feel the prayer of others, and you sense that it's all combined into one big prayer, and you know, somehow, that the grace, the love that keeps everything going, spreads beyond the limits we can see, and you feel close to it, and you know that this is what the whole world's meant to be like, with a unity and a sense of going forward in energy but also in peace.

It doesn't last long, does it? On New Year's Eve we went into a bar in Broken Lake and there was a fight with some Canadians. To be honest I'm afraid our blokes started it.

We're hard at work now. Not much let-up. No sign of Mother's cake, I'm afraid. Now you're not to worry.

Must go, fondest love, Tim.

---

17 Nursery St.
Walgabran
3rd January, 1941

Dear Tim,

John's Dad showed me a letter from the desert. Hot days, cold nights, sand getting into everything from weapons to eyes. But, climate or not, he says that the morale of the boys is high.

I said we hoped you'd be home soon. But I'm afraid I can't see it ending quickly. It will be more than one Christmas, I think, when you're away.

Sorry, son – this isn't much of a letter – no news, really. What a pity the mail takes almost two months!

Love, Dad.

Aus. EATS 2293771
F/Sgt Rogers, T.P.
Auspost, Ottawa
CANADA
12th January 1941

Dear Mother and Dad,

I knew the old mob would all join up. Somehow I guess we had to. Was it like that in '14, Dad?

It's hard finding my way around in the air. We train in Oxfords, Harvards, and Ansons – they're all a lot faster than the old Tigers, so I've got to be faster too. The big deflection up here between true and magnetic north doesn't help, and a landscape covered with snow isn't easy to read. The sky is nothing like the sky at home – it's dark and low, and in this climate the wings can ice up or the engine oil can freeze. Once we were caught in a snowstorm! Even Canadian bush pilots respect that sort of weather. And they're a breed apart.

We'll train right through the winter.

Love, Tim

---

17 Nursery St.
Walgabran
5th February 1941

Dear Tim,

I've some pretty disturbing news. Bill's had stones thrown through his windows. Margaret's terribly worried. No one knows what these people might do next. Saw him in the street and said I was sorry. It's a bit awkward with the reports from the front. He's kind of in the middle, going through a private agony of his own. He's completely on our side, but he must feel every bomb that lands on German soil and every bullet that hits a German soldier – more, I think, than if he was part of it. All he can do is listen to the news and keep his head down. There's no way he could write to anyone in Germany.

Love, Mother

Dear Tim,

Yes, some bloody idiots I didn't know we had. Bill, of all people!

We've read that Londoners are sleeping in their underground railway system for fear of the bombs. Shocking numbers – over 1,000 killed in January. In my day civilians were pretty much in the clear. To be honest, we're both glad you'll be away from all that at some Air Force station. They'll be targets, but they'll have better defences.

Your mother and I pray for you every night. In fact, I think Jenny prays all day.

Love, Dad

Aus. EATS 2293771
F/Sgt Rogers, T.P.
Auspost, Ottawa
CANADA
22ⁿᵈ February 1941

Dear Mum and Dad,

Sorry I haven't written – been flat out! How do you like the snaps? That's me and Alan in the distance, mucking about in the snow on the railway line. The white stuff is deep, and the frozen river you see in the foreground still looks solid. Though, of course, it's flowing under the ice.

My instructors say I should pass in April. I guess navigation's not so bad. It feels good when you actually get where you're meant to. The RAF has new four-engined bombers. Stirlings and Halifaxes, they're called. With luck we could be manning them soon.

Do you ever hear from Fay's parents?

Still no sign of the cake that we were supposed to have at Christmas.

I've got to go – the senior flight sergeant's going to put the lights out in a minute.

Lots of love, Tim

---

17 Nursery St.
Walgabran
10ᵗʰ March 1941

Dear Tim,

Two letters from you came together. Jenny says isn't it enough you'll have to fight the Germans without fighting the Canadians, too!

We've read that the Suez Canal has been blocked by mines. Once you're in England it could slow down the mail even more. Though I don't know how much goes through the Med anyway. Too bloody dangerous for most merchant ships, I'd have thought. How did the Jerries manage it with the British holding Cairo? Aircraft, I suppose. Or some bloody good commando work.

The business has picked up a bit. There's not a lot of money around, but people always need hardware.

Love, Dad.

Keep as warm as you can, Tim. I started knitting you a thick sweater, but Ben says you can only wear your uniform.

Love, Mother

Aus. EATS 2293771
F/Sgt Rogers, T.P.
Auspost, Ottawa
CANADA
15th March 1941
2nd January 1941

Dear Mum and Dad,

Only a moment to write. It's shocking news about Bill. And it's got to be people we know, hiding behind anonymity! I've written to him, trying to tell him it's only a few people and that every society has its ratbags. But that won't help much. It would be bad enough in somewhere like Brisbane, but in a town like Walgabran it's going to make him wonder about everyone he passes on the street.

Sorry, there's a Harvard with its engine warmed up, waiting for me.

Love, Tim.

---

17 Nursery St.
Walgabran
27th March 1941

Dear Tim,

It won't be long now before you're on your way to England. It seems the Luftwaffe nearly destroyed a whole town up Glasgow way this month, and the RAF's been doing heavy raids into France and Germany.

Son, you know we love you very much. We can't say things like "keep safe". That would be nonsense, and you know it and we know it. But we can hope.

The other war news isn't good. As I write, the Germans have recaptured Bardia and the Ninth Divvy has withdrawn into Tobruk. Men from the Sixth have crossed over to Greece. It's rumoured Wavell doesn't like it. Menzies and Blamey both think it's a big risk. So do I. Reminds me a bit of Gallipoli. This town is worried about John and Barry.

What's happened to those friends of yours down in Brisbane?

God bless you, Tim.
Love, Dad

Dear Tim,

Your father's said almost everything. But just the same I will say "keep safe", my darling son.

Mother

Casey's Hotel
East 48th Street
Manhattan
N.Y., USA
5th May 1941

Dear Mum and Dad,

We're on our way to England and I'm in "li'l old New York"!

One of our pilots, Vince McCauley, somehow wangled a trip here on a Canadian DC2 for four of us. The trains with the others were delayed by snowfalls back in Alberta, and we've had three days here waiting for them. Vince is rolling, and he booked us all into a posh hotel in Manhattan!

It's been a hectic time. It all started when we got out of a taxi outside our hotel. We were standing on the footpath (sorry, "sidewalk") when a woman looked at our uniforms, pointed at us, and shouted, "fliers!" We were mobbed and cheered and slapped on the back. Someone grabbed my luggage (for all I knew it was being stolen) and someone else took my arm, and people simply took care

167

of us – installed us in the hotel, took us around the city. Half the men said they wished they were coming with us. We've hardly slept. A man named Charley and his wife took us to a nightclub. Vince had the hide to ask the singer to come and sit with us, and she stayed for hours and made us promise to write.

The rest of the men from Broken Lake arrive in the morning, and we join the ship with them tomorrow afternoon. Austpost will forward letters until I give you a British address.

But there's something else. I'm in a funny mood. The others have gone sight-seeing in Central Park, and I'm alone. I mean, really alone. Here in this neutral country I'm away from the Air Force, I know no one and nothing is familiar. In fact it's more than that. It's a weird feeling. Everything seems unreal. It's as though I was detached, looking at life from outside like seeing a picture in a frame. Maybe it's because of that, but there's something I want to tell you.

I used to hate the idea of being a navigator. Everything and everyone depends for their safety on you getting the maths and the wind-drift and the magnetic deflection right. You do long preparations before take-off. Then you work with the engine noise beating in your ears and the plane bucking around. It's really a desk job, a few miles up in the air, and at night there are often curtains around the navigator so his light doesn't affect the night-vision of the others. It's busy and constant, using the simplest protractors and pencils as well as the fancy instruments. Half the time we can't check our calculations because no one can see the ground and the other half no one can see the stars. In fact, often we can't see anything.

This sort of thing has never been my temperament. I wanted to be a pilot. I guess that goes right back to the time I was making balsa models. When I wasn't accepted for that, I told myself that we all have to get on with the job – everyone's important. I didn't like it but I accepted it. At least I wouldn't be like the poor bastards in the stokeholds of ships – they can't see what's going on any more than we can, they just have to keep shovelling coal and know that they are probably in greater danger than their mates on deck. So I said, OK,

I don't want this, but it could be worse.

But now I've changed. We had accidents in Canada – fatal ones. I couldn't write about it because of the censors, but maybe it's brought the realities home to me. For a while I thought this way: as a navigator, at least I won't have to handle the guns or the bombs or even the plane as a whole. I don't want to kill anyone. I guess that's a hangover from Bill's influence. I've thought about him a lot.

I didn't realise then that on some aircraft the navigator actually doubles as bomb aimer. But in any case I know I will be seeking out a target – a train, a factory, a harbour, even a city – and I will be doing it to bring death. That won't be my intention but it will be there, in the result. And I just hope I'm not going to push the buttons that release the bombs. Is it cowardly to feel like this? Part of me despises myself for it. It feels half-hearted in a nasty sort of way. Pretending I'm not really doing what I'm doing.

Especially since I do believe what we are doing is necessary. I honestly believe I'd be better as a fighter pilot, where the role is largely defensive and the targets are mostly enemy planes.

I know this will worry you. I don't think I'm afraid of playing my part, but I'm glad it's the navigator's part and not another one. And I need to tell you this. I don't know why. I just do. It's bursting out of me.

Fondest love to you both,
Tim

---

17 Nursery St.
Walgabran
12th May 1941

Dearest Tim,

The flowers you had sent for Mothers' Day were beautiful – red and yellow roses and dark green lilies and Baby's Breath. You didn't mention them and they came as a wonderful surprise. They're on the mantelpiece now.

Jim was tickled pink at the photographs of you and Alan cavorting in the snow. We all think of you all the time.

With all our love, Mother.

Tim, your Mother cried when she got the flowers, but now, like always, she is so brave. A hell of a fine woman I married!

Love, Dad

2293771 F/Sgt Rogers, T.P.
c/o Base PO RAAF
Kodak House, Kingsway
London W.C.2, U.K.
25ᵗʰ May 1941

Dear Mother and Dad,

Don't take any notice of my last letter. I was just a bit down. I'm enjoying the advanced training. We're based in Gloucestershire, but we won't be here long. Wherever I am in Britain, the above address will find me.

You asked about Reg and George. I had a letter in Canada, and I wrote back a while ago. Mrs Campbell sent the letter back, saying they'd joined up. She didn't know where.

I didn't think I'd ever say this about any place but navigating around this country is actually worse than Alberta! Mostly the winds aren't as strong but they're forever shifting, and there's a hell of a lot of o rain and low cloud, and below us the ground is full of little fields that all look the same. So do the villages and the bays and the hills. You need to be sharp as a tack.

Still, I haven't mucked it up yet – I think. Got badly lost a couple of times but that was early on. Made a mistake that could have landed a Wellington in the Irish Sea but corrected it before anyone noticed. Or said they did.

So I guess I'm in business.

Love, Tim

---

17 Nursery St.
Walgabran
13th June 1941

Dear Tim,

We loved the story about New York. It sounds like the American public is very supportive of Britain. I think they'll join the Allies sooner or later. Your friend Vince reminds me of leave in Paris in '17. A man with money often splashed it around then, too.

Now, I'm going to give you some advice. If your adjutant or petty officer reads it and takes it the wrong way, he can think about this: I was in the trenches when he was probably in short pants, and I know what I'm talking about. My son is all right, and he'll be all right.

Personally, I'm glad that you're a navigator. Yes, some people would say that it's cowardly to be relieved if you don't pull the levers or press the buttons yourself. But I can tell you you're not a coward. I know you, and I know how you're built. There's other blokes that are different.

I understand why you feel torn in two. But if you stay like that too long it will damage you deep inside – try to resolve it. If you ever decide that you won't fight any more, you know Jenny and I will stand behind you – and you'll need us: because then people really will call you a coward. And they'll be wrong.

Love, Dad

> *2293771 F/Sgt Rogers, T.P.*
> *c/o Base PO RAAF*
> *Kodak House, Kingsway*
> *London W.C.2, U.K.*
> *15ᵗʰ June 1941*

Dear Mother and Dad,

Back in February, Dad, you were shocked to read about 1,000 deaths in Britain from air-raids. Well, in April it was 7,000. In May 5,000. It's a horrible business. Where will it all end?

At least the Luftwaffe seems to have eased up a bit recently. We think we know the reason. They've gone to support their ground troops in Russia.

> *All the best, love, Tim*

> 17 Nursery St.
> Walgabran
> 7ᵗʰ July 1941

Dear Tim,

Everyone here still well, but there's more trouble. Someone painted a swastika on Bill's house. People go all stiff and embarrassed if he goes into a shop. There are some who won't speak to him at all now. And the worst of it is, they avoid Margaret, too. I see as much of her as I can. She needs a lot of support.

Last week we went to Brisbane shopping, and we visited Fay's parents. They are bearing up well, but Mrs McWilliam has aged ten years. Dan doesn't look that much better. They asked after you and sent their love. They also said that guide at the Wildjeree caves – Neville, wasn't it? – has joined the navy.

We're sending you a food parcel. Hope it arrives

safely. All the butchers here have signs saying "Meat for Britain – we have the meat and we'll see that they get their share." We have our own rationing, but we know it doesn't compare with over there.

Love, Mother

Dear Tim,

Nothing I can add. That damned swastika speaks for itself.

Well, at least the Aussies are still holding out in Tobruk. Your uncle Jim is puffing out his chest. But this bloke Rommel's a problem. Clever and unpredictable. It seems he showed a lot of initiative in the last war (which probably meant ignoring orders). It's a worry. Auchinleck has been winning, though. That's something.

Love, Dad

2293771 F/Sgt Rogers, T.P.
c/o Base PO RAAF
Kodak House, Kingsway
London W.C.2, U.K.
21st July 1941

Dear Mother and Dad,

We had some leave and Alan, Bruce and I went to London and stayed at the Strand Palace. Took in a variety show. Alan, of course, picked up a girl. And we had a slap-up dinner at a posh restaurant.

The stage show was wonderful and the food was great. But where does it come from? Salmon, chicken, and there was what we used to call Black Forest cake at home, but because that's a German name it was just billed as "chocolate cake with cherry sauce and cream". Of course we had to finish with cigars. Mine made me sick, and I had a rotten night afterwards, but it was worth it.

You know, these Londoners are half-starved, they're bombed, they put up with blackouts and shortages, a lot of their kids have been sent away, nearly every family has someone in the services, lots of them have someone killed or wounded. The streets are bleak. Half-ruined houses, rubble everywhere. The news is bad from Yugoslavia, Greece, North Africa, Russia. And yet, with all that, they come up smiling with this cocky, defiant humour. If we win this war, that spirit will be a big part of the reason. If only the Yanks would come in, it would all seem so much more possible.

Love, Tim.

---

17 Nursery St.
Walgabran
1st August 1941

Dear Tim,

More bad news. They've interned Bill. A week ago. Margaret's had a letter from him – it came yesterday. It was very short – just a few words. She's distraught.

He was ropeable when he was taken. He's in a camp at Tatura, in Victoria. It's a hell of a long way from Margaret and Jack, and it's a cold place in winter. You remember he came here because he needed a warm, dry climate? But I think maybe he was too proud to tell them about his lungs. When we have more news I'll let you know.

Fondest love, Dad.

2293771 F/Sgt Rogers, T.P.
c/o Base PO RAAF
Kodak House, Kingsway
London W.C.2, U.K.
13ᵗʰ August 1941

Dear Mother and Dad,

There's still so much to learn before we go to the OTU, and we'll be there in no time now.

Everyone says "thank you" for that food parcel. All those tins of fruit and ham, cakes, chocolate! We're sharing them around. The pineapple was a special success – even before the war it was a rarity here. Some of the fellows asked whether I had cigarettes. Actually, I think they could put up with no food so long as they had cigs. They're not supposed to smoke in the air, but a lot do.

You mentioned the rationing, Dad. Yes – it's tough, especially on civilians unless they're nursing mothers or something. They've put more things on recently. Each week each person gets one egg, two ounces of butter and the same of cheese, two bobs' worth of meat, three pints of milk. Not only food – other things like clothes are restricted. Those who can afford to eat out are better off, though the restaurants aren't allowed to serve fish and meat at the same meal or to serve any meal costing more than five shillings. It's a bit easier out in the country where the farms are.

Of course, this is nothing compared to the Continent. There are stories. One bloke was shot down and with the help of some amazing people in Holland managed to get out. He says that starvation is a real possibility there.

Well, that's it for now. We're all off to the "Red Bull" now before we turn in.

So fondest love,
Tim

17 Nursery St.
Walgabran
14th August 1941

Dear Tim,

I've gone into this business about Bill. Germans living here are investigated for Nazi sympathies, and it doesn't take much to convince Army "Intelligence" that they're all secretly heiling Hitler. Half the time it's tenth-hand gossip. Some damn fool complained about Bill calling young Jack "Hans". And you'll find this hard to believe, but apparently someone told the military bureaucracy that he used to put an old spiked helmet on top of his house – just to show how German he still was. That was enough to clinch it for them! At first your mother said not to tell you this bit, it would worry you, but we decided it's important – you might even be able to help by telling them the real story about that bloody helmet. A letter from a serving airman training for Bomber Command could carry weight. There's a lawyers' thing called "The Aliens' Tribunal" where you can send a protest, but the whole show is under the Minister for the Army, and it might be better to write to him. The Hon. Percy Spender, Ministry for the Army, Parliament House, Canberra, A.C.T., should get him. I'll find out the camp commandant's name too, if I can.

Love, Dad

2293771 F/Sgt Rogers, T.P.
c/o Base PO RAAF
Kodak House, Kingsway
London W.C.2, U.K.
18th September 1941

Dear Mother and Dad,

The OTU is full-on. We're practicing operational tactics. The instructors here have been in the thick of it, and most of them want to get back. They're working us really hard, and we're all pretty tired.

Your last came quickly. It's horrible about Bill. I've written to Spender in Canberra and to our High Commissioner at Australia House in London, but I'm not hopeful. I asked the Wingco here if he could help, but he gave me a funny look. I guess the Brits have been fighting too hard to have much sympathy for any German, even one like Bill.

We're off in a few minutes. Sometimes there's too much time here but at others it's hectic, and then we sandwich our letters in when we can.

Love, Tim

Nursery St.
Walgabran
19th September 1941

Dear Tim,

We've been reading about your "slap-up" dinner (you're picking up Pommy slang, son – watch it) and we hope you have more of them. It sounds wonderful. What you said about Black Forest cake being given a different name – well, don't laugh, but maybe it isn't a joke any more. Here, German Shepherd dogs are all "Alsatians" now. But we still have hamburgers, and frankfurters as well. No one seems to have thought of them as unpatriotic yet.

Good news from Tobruk. Half the Aussies have been relieved by the Poles, and the Brits have agreed to try to relieve the rest. Even Jim's glad. He realises now that Australia can't win the war by itself.

Love, Dad

2293771 F/Sgt Rogers, T.P.
c/o Base PO RAAF
Kodak House, Kingsway
London W.C.2, U.K.
3rd October 1941

Dear Mother and Dad,

It's so long since I've written a proper letter. I'm sorry.

Our final test at the OTU was to fly over enemy territory dropping leaflets. A strange feeling – suddenly the war is more real.

So now we're posted. We thought all the Aussies would stay together, but they've dispersed us. Alan, Bruce, I have been sent to make up the numbers in an RAF squadron, and we're expecting the new Halifaxes soon.

We managed to stay in the same crew. So Alan will have me as navigator and Bruce as mid-upper gunner. (Actually, Alan did so well in the course they nearly made him an instructor. He'd have hated it.) There's also Tony Scanlon, he's our Sparks, and Phil O'Toole who's Revs, and Ron Evans as bomb aimer, and poor old Don Faithful at the back. It's so cold for the gunners in their turrets that they have to wear electrically heated clothing. Apparently – you won't believe this – they can be court-martialled if they get frost-bite!

I can't tell you exactly where we are, though the Huns must know anyway. But the nearest town (village, really) is Netherholme, and the nearest real city is Norwich. They say it has one of the best climates in England, and it's certainly nothing like as cold as Canada, but to a Queenslander it still looks bloody bleak right now. Maybe summer will be better.

Sixteen blokes in my hut. We new chums are looking forward to our first "show". That's what everyone says, anyway, but we're nervous underneath – except of course for Alan. He doesn't know what nerves are.

Netherholme has a pub and a picture-house and a dance hall. There's a bus that takes us in, all jammed together, and the blokes sing on the way. There's always someone drunk coming back. I guess it's that kind of life – flying, letting our hair down, drinking, sleeping, flying. There are plenty of girls – mainly WAAFs – and I think the war has made some of them pretty reckless. They're living in a crowd of young people which is also a lottery of life and death. (Now don't worry, Mum – I'm still your good boy.) We'll get to Norwich sometimes – especially if we can get hold of a car. We'll even get to London once in a while.

Catholics can attend Mass in Netherholme if we're free on a Sunday. I've met the priest – Father Johnson – a man of about sixty, I suppose. A quiet, scholarly sort of bloke, a gentleman and also a gentle man.

There's a kind of humour that seems to work at home but not here. You know, that Aussie "ribbing" which joshes people but really expresses friendship. It's odd – the English do something similar, but in a different style, somehow. You've got to be careful or you can offend people without knowing it. And one or two of the officers are a bit snooty – they have a way of making you feel you don't count for much without actually saying anything. Maybe it's what they don't say. Most are OK, anyhow.

And you've got to admire them. They won't even think about losing this war, and they're damned brave – quite often, the sort of fellows you wouldn't pick have a DFC. (That's for officers – sergeants get a DFM. That's a bit of England some of us don't like much – I mean, their making that distinction.)

Where is that cake you sent a year ago? I dream about it coming in a big Arnott's tin. I don't think a real, dark, fruity, moist Aussie Christmas cake is something the Poms have never seen. It would make me king for a day!

We have our first operational sortie tomorrow, laying mines. A daylight job. They call it a milk run – that means it's easy. Not much serious flak or Jerry fighters – so they say. Well, we'll know soon.

With great love for you both, Tim

17 Nursery St.
Walgabran
4th October 1941

Dear Tim,

Glad you've written to try to help Bill. They aren't interning all Germans. Only the ones they regard as suspicious. But it's hard for the others, too. In Brisbane there's a respected old doctor from Stuttgart called Hertz. He's been there thirty years. He was interned in the last war. He's free this time – but his practice has virtually stopped. I suppose he makes just enough to live. No one wants to be seen talking to him, even people he fixed up. And the government has put all sorts of restrictions on people like him – how far they can travel, what work they can do. It's all sickening.

Margaret says that a lot of people interned with Bill don't even know why they were picked. But apparently these camps are run on the inside by the inmates, and some of them do sympathise with the Nazis, so the anti-Nazis like Bill have an even harder time. No one seems to bother to separate them. Maybe they will if a serious riot breaks out.

Love, Dad

———————————

2293771 F/Sgt Rogers, T.P.
c/o Base PO RAAF
Kodak House, Kingsway
London W.C.2, U.K.
5th October 1941

Dear Mother and Dad,

We've just landed, and I can't sleep. If that's light flak I don't want to meet the heavy stuff.

But I have to admit to finding it exciting. Flying at

night, dodging the searchlights; moonlight coming in through the pilot's windscreen and the astrodome. Everyone nervous, tense. Alan's voice on the intercom, calm, settling. The gunners looking out for fighters, the sudden lift when we released our mines, the crude remarks on the way home, me feeling that I mustn't make the slightest mistake, checking everything four times, the relief to hit our base and get down safely. The trip took longer than I expected, yet I wasn't conscious of passing time.

Everyone hopes we'll get Halifaxes soon. They're bigger, tougher, faster.

There's a bus going into town, and after the raid I don't want to sit around here alone. Not after that. So I'll close and catch the fellows up.

Fondest love, Tim

2293771 F/Sgt Rogers, T.P.
c/o Base PO RAAF
Kodak House, Kingsway
London W.C.2, U.K.
6ᵗʰ October 1941

Dear Mother and Dad,
I didn't know when I wrote yesterday. One plane didn't come back. Two blokes I've been with all the way from Brisbane were in it. Jack Ferguson and Dick Rigby. I wasn't particularly close to them, but I feel close now. Dick wasn't twenty yet. It's pretty sobering. We can only hope that they'll turn up safe and sound – or at least, that we'll hear they're POW's. I'm sorry for the S/L – he's got to write to their families.

But that's not the whole of it. Last night it was worse – three planes. Twenty-one men. In one go. I don't think I'll ever get used to this part.

Sorry this is so short. Forgive me. It's hard to write, sometimes.

Love, Tim

---

17 Nursery St.
Walgabran
14th October 1941

Dear Tim,

It'll be autumn there now. You'll see all those colours and bare trees – you'll see a lot of things we never will. In Flanders, all the trees were dead stumps. I hope that Hitler's left enough of London for you to enjoy when you're on leave.

Your mother's cake has either been snaffled for the black market or is still floating somewhere in the postal systems of three countries and two air forces. We hate to think of it going missing! It was too damned good! We'll send you another cake for this Christmas. Maybe this time it'll reach you.

Son, I've a request. Since you wrote from New York you haven't mentioned those doubts you had then again. I think you're trying to protect us. Don't. It's obvious that a bomber is one of the most dangerous places to be in this war, and it's obvious that it's a bloody difficult job. We know you can't say everything, but we want to know the truth – how you are coping and how it all affects you. Even your recreations. Don't forget, in my own way I've been there.

Fondest love, now, Tim.
Dad.

2293771 F/Sgt Rogers, T.P.
c/o Base PO RAAF
Kodak House, Kingsway
London W.C.2, U.K.
30ᵗʰ October 1941

Dear ones,

Forgive me. I haven't been writing. It's hard to explain why. We've been doing a lot of flying.

Cologne and Hamburg were bombed three times in six days. Our crew wasn't on the last raid, but the fellows say that they really pounded the city. Some came back as excited as though they'd just beaten Australia for the Ashes, but others came back very quiet and silent. We lost several aircraft, but it wasn't only that. To be honest, I'm glad I wasn't on that last show. Just how many people did we kill?

It's a strange and terrible thing to say, but I really think some of us couldn't do it if it wasn't for our own losses. They make us feel we are replying, defending the country – and yes, civilisation – they only way we can.

I don't think like this much in the air – not in the middle of the action. It's afterwards, when I've slowed down. Maybe, if I wasn't going in a few minutes, I'd throw this away.

I know we'll be OK, Mum. Keep up the prayers.

All the best, love, Tim.

---

17 Nursery Street,
Walgabran
1ˢᵗ November 1941

Dear Tim,

It's All Souls' Day. At Mass this morning Father Sullivan prayed for our people who've died; but just at the end, he prayed for the others, too – the ones on the other side. A few parishioners didn't like that but I know you would understand.

Days like today, and Anzac Day, and Armistice Day – they remind me of the loss and waste. This war – you have to wonder where it all started. Sure, the things that happened in 1914 and 1919 and 1933 and 1939 are part of it. But they didn't just happen. Not out of the blue. They too grew out of something, out of earlier events. Partly, at least. I don't mean they *had* to happen. But there seems to be a chain of evil that goes back and back.

But there's a chain of good, too, son. That's in our faith. Somehow, somewhere, we believe that the good will triumph. Hold on to that.

Love, Dad

2293771 F/Sgt Rogers, T.P.
c/o Base PO RAAF
Kodak House, Kingsway
London W.C.2, U.K.
20th November 1941

Dear Mother and Dad,

It's getting cold again. November seems a dreary month here. The nights are long and the days are grey. All this low cloud helps protect us from flak and fighters, but it increases the risk of getting lost. And that's my responsibility.

The three of us managed five days' leave in Ireland. Great to be in a country where there's no war. Wanted to just stay there. Not seriously – that'd be desertion, of course – but the idea certainly crossed my mind.

We needed the break. We have been thrown in at the deep end recently. Raids every night when the weather allows. Not a lot of sleep, stomach upset with the tension and the flak and the evasive bloody action and then off again.

We're going tonight. There's low cloud, rain and lightning, and we didn't expect to go in this weather, which the met report says should extend across Holland and Germany, but we've been ordered to take off at 1900, and all navigators go to the first briefing in a couple of minutes. We're all dog-tired. Everyone hopes it's not Berlin. Whatever it is, someone must think it's important.

And yet – what's the alternative? What's the bloody alternative to what we're doing?

I'll try to speak to you on a trunk call for Christmas, but don't worry if I can't – it's not easy to get through, and there's a lot of competition for the phones.

I know we'll be OK, Mum. Keep up the prayers.

All the best, love, Tim.

---

17 Nursery Street,
Walgabran
12th December1941

Dear Tim,

Suddenly, it's a new game. There's a war in the Pacific now. The Japs were fools to take on America. And now Germany's declared war on America, too. So the Yanks'll be "over there" (as they said in '17) with you. I think it's the beginning of the end.

Hard to believe it's more than a year since you left! We'll be thinking of you at Christmas. Maybe this time the cake will reach you.

Everyone is well. Margaret's gone down to Victoria to be as near Bill as they can. How she will survive is a mystery. There is plenty of work for women now, but she has two young kids to look after.

Love, Dad

2293771 F/Sgt Rogers, T.P.
c/o Base PO RAAF
Kodak House, Kingsway
London W.C.2, U.K.
20ᵗʰ December 1941.

Dear Mother and Dad,

Sorry for the writing. My hand seems a bit shaky after we've landed from a raid. Nothing to worry about. Well, you asked me to tell you all about my life. So here goes. I'm afraid it'll be a long letter.

On a raid I can see out a bit through my porthole or the forward turret but my curtains restrict this. There's not much fun in this half-blind flying.

Actually there's a lot of boredom in the air – a funny kind of boredom mixed with constant tension. Even though I'm constantly busy. There are even times when it's hard to stay awake. But mostly I really get nervous trying to get us to the target, and even more nervous about getting home, especially if there's much cloud (and our weather reports don't really cover the Continent). We do have help. We get radio bearings from stations in Blighty, but they can be jammed by the Jerries or affected by static. The worst kind's a thing called "precipitation static" when electric charge builds up on the metal of the plane, especially in rain. Sometimes we do drift a hell of a lot, and I often feel it's by guess and by God. There are rumours of new hush-hush electronic aids but no one at our level really knows.

The crew's become close. Everyone's afraid (except maybe Alan) but no one admits it. It's kept under control by a sort of pincer-movement of informal jokes and formal discipline working together. We use first names – rank doesn't matter. To the Poms in the crew Alan is "Skipper" or "Mac", but to me and Bruce he's still Alan. And he is a bloody good pilot.

Sometimes I can hear shell-bursts above the engine-noise and I wonder how close they are. Thank heaven we haven't had any night-fighters nosing around. Not yet, anyway. The intercom's a lifeline, but as a rule everyone's quiet on the way to the target. On our first raid, once we passed the occupied coast on the way home everyone chattered like a cage full of excited monkeys. Reaction and relief, I guess. We didn't do that again.

As we come in to land, Ron and I have to leave our posts and move aft a bit, just in case something goes wrong. The first thing when we're down is debriefing for Alan and breakfast for all of us. After all those hours in the air it takes a while to feel steady on the ground, and we want to unwind even though we're tired. So we don't go to bed at once.

Nearly every day someone doesn't come back. Often more than one. Mostly we are confident that it won't happen to us, but sometimes a man has a sort of conviction that his number's up. Then, if anything does happen, you can't be sure: did he have a bee in his bonnet which made him careless, so that what he feared came true by a sort of ironical accident? Or – do we sometimes get a sort of warning that it's time? I don't know. If it happens to me, my dears, always remember I loved you.

Of course, if a crew doesn't come back they could be prisoners, and it takes weeks for that information to get to us. A few manage to evade the Germans and eventually make it home only to find someone else in their bunks. New faces arrive to fill the empty places, and we carry on as though it was ordinary not to grieve. You'd think this impossible – but sometimes I worry that it has become the opposite – too easy. I feel like two people. One, the one I rely on for deliberate control, has no heart. It's a sort of dry me, walking through life mechanically, moving my arms and legs, directing everything I do without involving my feelings. Actually this is the real me, I suppose. It's the me that acts and takes responsibility for what it does. The other person has a heart that I try to leave behind somewhere while I do my job but it still bothers me.

It's not only the danger. It's not just our possible deaths. When those bomb doors open I feel sick. I don't talk about this with anyone. Very occasionally someone mentions the people on the ground in Berlin or Cologne or Hamburg or Essen or wherever. But *when you're flying, the target is a factory or a city – not people. I suppose that if we thought much about the human beings we'd go mad. Even an enemy fighter plane is just a machine out to destroy you, and our gunners don't have time to think – they just fire at the machine. The pilot's an afterthought if he's thought of at all, and generally he isn't. I heard of a fighter pilot who shot down a one-oh-nine and saw the German pilot bail out. Something went wrong, and the parachute didn't open. That British pilot was never much good after that.*

How is it that all the force of life – our urges and drives and cares and ambitions and loves and compassions and instincts – can be so different in different people? The men around me are good men – very good men, brave, generous, loyal. They are genuine heroes – virtually all of them. I certainly don't think I'm better than them. Most, I think, do face these questions in their own way, and if they come up with a tough answer, that doesn't mean they don't care. They just accept it and all it entails. I don't seem able to do that. I guess it's similar to the detachment a surgeon needs in the theatre – the sort of strength he needs. Alan said something like that, a long time ago. There are a few fellows who actually thrive on it. Not the killing, but the business of defending Britain. The more intense the fighting and the danger, the more they seem alive. Alan's one, I think. They want to be part of it, the way a footballer wants to be in the game and not on the sidelines. But most of us just want to survive and to get the damned war finished. We keep going, doing the job, sticking to it, hoping, not thinking too much.

I've spoken to the priest in Netherholme, Father Johnson, about all this, and I suspect that he agrees with me that bombing cities is at least questionable morally, but he won't say so – maybe for fear of putting a burden on my conscience that I couldn't cope with. Is that how the Church works with the whole population? Helping us do our best in an imperfect world? Maybe the Pope or someone should just tell us all we must stop – that the whole business is un-Christian. How many would accept that? But then, nations have a right to defend themselves. I guess you can't impose on people

what is not a moral demand but a sort of deeper ideal. How does
it all mesh together with the love we're all supposed to have with
each other, and the way God touches everyone? The way we're all
supposed to be united in God's embrace? It's as though humanity
can't be what it should; as though a great hampering net is holding us
all down.

Isn't that net what Christ came to lift? It's taking a
bloody long time.

It's a terrible mess. It must have been like that in the
trenches, Dad.

Don't misunderstand this. I still believe in this fight. I
still want to be part of it. But I loathe it.

Of course I'll smuggle this out to the civvy post. You
can't talk like this here. Even if you said that Chamberlain had to try
his way before we could really know what the Nazis intended; or that
many German people probably don't want a war – not unless they
were stirred up to it; you'd be suspected of sedition. You wouldn't
be keeping up the right attitude. That's how far the evil of this goes.
Even simple truths have become crimes. "Spreading alarm and
despondency". No one's supposed to do it – least of all someone in
aircrew.

I suppose there's self-pity in this letter. Mustn't do that.

Well, that's in the air. About on the ground: I told you
that we sometimes have dances. I can't enjoy them. Fay's still with
me too much. You know, every time someone fails to return I think
of her. To be honest I don't think I feel anything properly since she
died. I think you know that joining up seemed a way of leaping into
a new world, starting life again. It's kept me busy, but the pain never
really goes away.

The truth is that, while I can see that other girls are
nice, they don't really affect me. It's as though there was a wall of
glass between me and them. They're real enough, but it's not my
reality, if that makes any sense. I can see a woman, and imagine how
I might have been attracted to her three years ago – but that's only
in my head: the part of me that was attracted has gone cold. If a girl

seems to like me I just back away. At times I feel really low. When that happens I find that little actions I should do automatically – even picking up a pen to write a letter, taking my boots off to go to bed – require a deliberate act of will, and life, instead of flowing naturally, becomes an endless succession of forced decisions.

Recently I've even become a bit distant from the blokes. I just don't seem able to be a good mate.

That's it, my dear ones. Maybe I shouldn't have told you all this. I'm not holding anything back. I'm pretty sure I can speak to you by phone in the next few days.

Love, Tim

---

17 Nursery Street,
Walgabran
29th January 1942

Dear Tim,

It was so wonderful to hear your voice on the phone at Christmas! Jenny cried, and I shouldn't tell you this, but so did I.

Thank you for that long letter, son. It worries us more if we don't know. In ordinary life, most of us cope with our ups and downs by not giving them more attention than they deserve. But a situation like yours – extreme stress and danger alternating with nothing to do – is like constantly stretching a rubber band and letting it go and then stretching it again. It's a recipe for a break-up – or a break-down. In Flanders plenty of blokes wound up with shell-shock. You aren't facing constant shelling, but I'd bet that you've got men with problems that aren't too different. Even without all that you'd be exhausted just from the long journeys at night. But you've got this added thing – you can't stop worrying about what you feel as a moral dilemma. And that must drain whatever energy you have left.

There's not a lot I can say, except that you have to find a source of strength somewhere. The Service discipline probably helps you cope. And your faith has always been strong. Beyond that, your comrades are vital. Even if you feel yourself a bit different from the others, don't withdraw from them. And never forget we love you.

Tim, I feel this has to be said some time. You have lost Fay. You are still grieving. I know it's hard to believe but it will pass. I don't mean that you will stop loving her. But the loss and the pain will one day be put in a sort of back pocket of your soul, in a place where you can handle them, where they do not prevent you from being enthusiastic for life.

You say you can't be interested in anyone else. I think you feel a sort of fidelity to Fay in that. And yet, is that what she would want? I'm not saying you should go charging off trying to make yourself fall in love again – that doesn't work, and it's dangerous. But you're not Robinson Crusoe. So many in these days have lost husbands and wives and sweethearts. We hope you keep safe, both from the Jerries and from those wild girls you mentioned once. But not so safe you hide yourself in a cupboard. Sooner or later you must make an effort. You can't stay within your old horizons. When we're in love everything seems centred on one person – but now you have to accept that the world is wider. Sorry if that seems hard, Son, but it is life. Don't force it, but give it a go when you can.

You're doing your best. Nil carborundum – don't let the bastards get you down – not even the bastards inside yourself.

So I'll leave it there. I'm sorry if this is a tough letter, Tim. Remember the cake you never got? We've sent you another one for this Christmas. Maybe this time it'll reach you. We love you so much.

God bless you, Dad.

2293771 F/Sgt Rogers, T.P.
c/o Base PO RAAF
Kodak House, Kingsway
London W.C.2, U.K.
29ᵗʰ January 1942

Dear Mother and Dad,

The weather's wild, the snow's deep, the ceiling's about eighty feet, and everyone's rejoicing because we can't fly in this. So with any luck we'll get a few days off for New Year.

And there is news you'll never believe. I have received two cakes! The one you sent this year has come, and the one from last Christmas turned up on the same day! It has stamps from all around the world – Australia, Canada, Brazil, Portugal, The United States, Iceland, Ireland, Scotland, Liverpool and here. I'd hate to blame your handwriting, Dad, but if it wasn't that then I don't know what. Perhaps the war caused a ship heading across the Atlantic to divert to South America, and then everyone got confused.

Anyway, that cake kept going, no matter what! And so can I. And I know you can.

OK, I'll make a big effort.

Love, Tim

---

17 Nursery Street,
Walgabran
3ʳᵈ February 1942

Dear Tim,

Everyone is well. Margaret thinks she might be able to get work in Wangaratta, from someone a cousin of hers knows. Then she'll "only" be fifty miles from her husband! But I suppose she'll be able to visit on week-ends, at least.

Singapore's the big worry here right now. The Jap

advance has taken everyone by surprise. The Eighth Division's there. Australia feels threatened and Curtin's bringing the Sixth and Seventh home, but I can't see it affecting men in Bomber Command like yourself. They'll leave you where you are.

Over there the desert war's been going back and forth like waves at the beach. The same in Russia. But Napoleon couldn't take Russia, and neither will the Nazis. You'll see.

What a year '41 was. Best wishes for 1942.

Fondest love,
Mother and Dad.

CHAPTER 15

Alan's Therapy (Britain, 1942)

"How's young Rogers going?"

Wing Commander Nordale's question was shouted, projected through the snow fluttering across the airstrip, as he watched the exhausted crew trudge from the Halifax towards their hut. Alan, surprised and off-guard, responded with a double-take. "Er – fine, sir" he replied. "He's a bit thoughtful, but that's what we need in a navigator."

The senior officer grunted. "To be honest, McCleary, I'm worried about him. Aircrew need to be on their toes."

"He's fine, sir. I've known him all my life. He's my cousin. The three of us – Rogers, Tosh, and I – we all come from the same town in Queensland."

"Well, I don't know anything about towns in Queensland but I know about men in this damned war. He thinks too much. Doesn't get off the station enough. His moods swing all over the shop. Probably moping about something. Keep an eye on him."

Alan knew that the CO's words conveyed a serious message. On the surface a casual expression of mild concern, they really expressed something like an ultimatum. That was "Naughty's" way.

He would have to take it up with Tim. "Young Rogers,"

Nordale had said; but he and Tim were the same age. As if fighting the Jerries wasn't enough. Being a nursemaid wasn't what he'd joined for. Since they were kids he and Tim had been half friends and half at odds. It all went back to that Hun cleaner-handyman when they were at school. He'd been interned back in Australia. Bloody good thing.

Alan fingered the barely visible scar across his cheek.

Well, damn it, it could wait until after tonight's raid. He looked at the dark sky streaked with pearly grey. It would be dawn soon – dawn at nearly 9am. What a country!

"The radio's U/S, Skipper." Tony Scanlon's Glaswegian voice was thick when he was stressed. "She started screechin' then just stopped."

Moments earlier the crew, in spite of the weather, had been alert but relaxed. Phil had been muttering in satisfaction over his array of dials recording engine temperature and revolutions, fuel and oil pressure, generators and oxygen supply and de-icers and a dozen other systems. Bruce, idle in his turret, had been watching St Elmo's fire dancing along the wing-tips and reflected in the constant rain-spatters. The others had been hovering over their routine jobs. Only Alan had been irritated, swearing softly at small lightning-flashes moving between the clouds.

Then, without warning, the Halifax shuddered briefly under the impact of a thunder-clap that drowned the sound of the engines. In the same instant Bruce had glimpsed a brilliant light playing along the aircraft's metal skin.

Momentarily deafened, no one spoke. It was Tony's report that recalled them to normality.

Alan answered him: "Nothing you can do?"

"I'm lookin'."

"Well, we've got power. The intercom's all right. Instrument lights are on. But the bloody compass is waving all over the shop."

Tim came on: "So's mine. Dancing like Fred and Ginger. It's like the air's all charged up. The CRO's off as well."

"Jammed by the Huns?"

"No. Dead."

Alan's bad temper vanished, to be replaced by a cold decisive calm. "You mean we've no navigational aids at all? Phil, go and help."

The engineer found Tony squirming around his set with a screwdriver and an ammeter. The wireless operator looked up and shook his head. Phil probed in his turn, examining the connections and peering at the dark coating covering the inside of the vacuum tubes; then he turned to Tim, who moved aside to let him investigate the cathode ray oscilloscope. After some minutes he reported: "I don't think we can fix them, Skipper."

"Shit!"

A pause, then Alan spoke again: "We're flying through muck. There'd be more visibility down a sewer. But we should be home in less than an hour. Tim, can you get us there without a radio bearing?"

"I'll try. My compass has gone steady now. All that twisting and turning over Holland didn't help. There's a hell of a wind. We might have to put down at some other strip."

"We'll be lucky!" responded Alan. "How the hell are we going to find another base in this?"

"Well, we know where they are. And Andy Stevens did it last week."

"For God's sake, Tim! He had everything working. Anyway, everyone knows Andy has more lives than a cat and he's probably used them all up, the way he flies. I'm not Andy! Get us home!"

"I'm trying. I'm not a bloody miracle-worker. How's the fuel? Can we hang around until there's more light?"

Alan grunted without replying. The crew now tense, the

bomber droned on. Their last clear reference point had been the target at Düsseldorf. Since then they had flown for three hours, weaving between clouds repeatedly torn by fierce gusts into tattered clear spaces before closing again. In the brief intervals of clear moonlight Tim had taken rapid and rough star sightings. Their real course and ground speed, modified by the strength and direction of the wind, were always partly a matter of intelligent estimation, but tonight they were wild guesses. An error of a few degrees could put them fifty miles from their base, or even down in the sea.

The men in the forward and rear turrets, whose view of the ground was best, strained their eyes for some landmark showing through a break in the weather. Phil left his panel and went to the cockpit, and with Alan he peered ahead for a glimpse of the coast which must surely be approaching. Moonlight alternated with thick darkness as cloud patterns dissolved and re-formed, and their greyness intermittently merged with the darker greyness of the sea in a monotonous rhythm.

No one spoke for a full twenty minutes until Ron Evans came on the intercom. "Bomb-aimer to Skipper. I can see surf. Left – nine o'clock."

"Recognise anything?"

"No, Skip. Just surf and a dark bit that might be cliffs."

"Roger. Where are we, Tim?"

"I hope we've hit Norfolk. Can anyone see which way the coast runs?"

Ron answered: "Seems to be pretty well east-west. Almost parallel to our course."

"Good. The north edge of Norfolk is almost the only bit that does that – unless we're way down in Kent. And that's impossible."

Alan objected. "That's too confident, Tim. It might be just a local turn of the land. You'd need to see thirty miles clear to be sure."

"We'll have to assume it, then. We've nothing else. If I'm

right we're nearly home. Head east for five minutes then steer oh-one-three-five. That way we should be hugging the coast as it veers south-east. We might be able to recognise a bay or even a promontory. Then if we go a little inland we'll be heading near the smaller towns. Get a bit of altitude. We'll pass Walsham, Stalham, Hemsly, Brundell … might see something."

"OK, Tim. Your play. Everybody keep watch."

They fell again into silent vigilance for ten minutes, then Ron yelled: "A flare-path! Port – ten o'clock."

Phil O'Toole laughed. "I see them. That's not our station. Ruddy string o' pearls, they are. Laid out for us. Just as well we're not Jerries. We could smash that station to bits."

Tim could almost feel everyone relaxing. Silently he muttered a prayer. His relief was short-lived as Alan took up Phil's thought and twisted it. "Let's hope their ack-ack gunners don't have the same idea!"

But no searchlights flashed across the sky. The Halifax moved away to describe a wide arc and began a descent, levelling as it lined up on the flares, slowing and dropping rapidly. Tim listened to the changing engine-note, wondering where they were. It had to be an RAF station of some sort. From his navigator's seat he could see the lights approaching through the forward gunner's perspex.

Phil muttered, "That runway's a bit short. If it's grass it mightn't take our weight."

They knew that the Halifax had a reputation for being difficult to control at low speeds. Alan said nothing. Descending steeply to give the huge, bucking aircraft as great a run as possible after touch-down, he held the controls with absolute steadiness. They felt the impact – it was double, a bounce – and there was a sideways lurch followed by a quick recovery. The bomber rolled on and came to a stop with its brakes smoking and its nose projecting absurdly over the grassy verge at the end of the runway, and at once there were men running towards it. The flares which had guided them down became black nothingness, switched off by a remote controlling hand. A car approached, the faint glow of its dimmed lights stabbing ineffectually ahead through the now light rain. It stopped near the main door of the Halifax, and three armed airmen got out and waited, followed in a moment by a man whose sleeves bore the white, black, red and grey stripes of a Squadron Leader. The officer's rank was not in itself surprising, but it seemed ridiculous in someone who looked barely twenty-one.

The crew remained slumped in their positions, reacting now, letting tension give way to lassitude, unwilling to make the effort to move. Alan chivvied them onto the tarmac and saluted. "Sorry to come down on your runway, sir, but we had no choice. It was that or make a great mess of your countryside round here."

"Well, we're not used to these bloody great things on our turf. Where've you come from?"

Alan grinned. "Depends what you mean, sir. Queensland once upon a time. Last fix was Düsseldorf. But our station's near Netherholme."

Tim looked around. The moon was again hidden behind cloud. Against the blackness of the overcast night sky he could see darker patches, the humped shapes of hangars and other aerodrome buildings. Around him fugitive gleams of light resolved slowly into reflections from the propellers of small aircraft.

"All right, Flight Lieutenant …?"

"McCleary, sir."

"What happened?"

"Radio's out, sir. No Gee. Feeling our way in the soup. Couldn't find our base."

"Well, you're welcome. I'm S/L Featherstone. I'll get our Wingco to phone your squadron commander and you can talk to him. Damned lucky to get down safely on our runway – it's used by Hurricanes and a few light aircraft. You did well. You can leave that huge crate here until the morning. It's practically on the perimeter anyway. We'll give your men somewhere to kip." He turned to one of the airmen. "Arrange it with W/O Evans, Ivory. Take these chaps to the Senior Intelligence Officer and then get Bennett to give them some eggs and bacon."

Alan spoke. "Wonderful, sir. We can do with it. Sorry to give your Intelligence Officer extra work, especially at night."

"I'm afraid he's used to it, McCleary. You're not our first visitor. Our biggest, maybe."

How far are we from our own station, sir?"

"You won't use any altitude – it's hardly a hop. This is Little Coring. We'll want you away first thing. If you can get off, of course."

"Should be right. We've no extra weight – no bombs, not much fuel. Oh – sir … ?"

"Yes?"

"We saw your flares, of course. We wondered why they were on. There didn't seem to be any other aircraft."

"There was one. The lights were on just long enough for a Lysander to get down. Ten seconds more and you'd have had no help from us."

The Halifax crew absorbed this with a slight shiver. They might have been unable to land safely at all. Bruce commented, "We were worried you'd think we were Jerries."

For a moment the other's military bearing relaxed marginally, and he smiled. "Nearly sent a couple of Hurricanes up after you, just in case. But we weren't too worried. Corporal Ivory here claims he can tell the sound of Merlin engines from anything the Huns have. He bet another man a pound you were British. Still, you might have been anyone. You'll notice that the men do have rifles."

Featherstone and two of the airmen got back into the car and drove off. As Ivory led them towards the CO's hut, he clearly felt it his place to take up the conversation where his superior had left off. "Quite a do, sir," he said. "Coming down fortuitous-like. It's your lucky day. You'll feel quite at home here, being Aussies. We've got a couple on the strength."

Tony Scanlon laughed. "Can't get away from the blighters, can we, Ivory?"

"Not in this war, sir, we can't. But one of our men is, sort of, *more* Australian. Talks a sort of lingo no one can understand. Pilot Officer Billingsly. And there's Flying Officer King. They came here together, sir."

Tim's exclamation was a shout. "What did you say? Billingsly and King?"

"Ay, sir. I did. Fine men they are. Liven up the station a bit, if you know what I mean."

Tim's weariness vanished. He was laughing. "You wouldn't have an idea, Corporal, of their first names? Could they be Reg and George?"

"I believe they are, sir – not that we'd be using them."

"This is wonderful! When can I see them? "

"Well, sir, they'd be asleep, I think. But in the circs – I'll see whether we can rouse them. Here's the CO's office, if you'd just wait a minute."

Tim's nerves were dancing while they met the Station Commander and were led away for their small-hours breakfast. He was about to bite into a piece of toast when he was interrupted by a joyous shout: "Starve the flamin' lizards! Look what y' meet around the traps!"

Jumping up, he embraced first Reg and then George, who had followed his voluble companion into the mess. Grinning, they all spoke at once. Then, realising that they were hardly communicating, they all sat and slowed down, while the rest of the Halifax crew looked on with the absorbed detachment of an audience at a play.

"Mate, how's things? When the Corp said it was someone I knew from Australia I guessed it had t' be you!"

"I still can't believe it's you two. How'd you get here?"

"It was you did it, Tim. Straight, it was. When you left we decided to join up, too. Y'd think it would be easy to keep in touch in the same Air Force, but you know how it was."

"You weren't worried about your careers in the bank?"

"Pshaw! The bank'll be there when all this is over."

"Yes – and someone else'll have the job you'd have had."

"Yeah, I know. Some galah. What the hell! It'll be the same for everyone – we'll all be behind the game like a cow's tail."

At this point George added: "We couldn't just sit there in the bank, Tim. Not now. Actually, they're supposed to hold our jobs for us. But who knows? You know what happened last time."

On the face of it he was referring to broken promises made during the First World War. But there was a second level to his words. Who, indeed, knew whether they would return at all? By a shared, unspoken intuition the question was swept under the conversational carpet. And in a similar way neither Reg nor George mentioned Fay. They had no way of knowing whether the wound of her death was still raw in Tim's soul. Better not to ask. If he wished to mention it, he could.

So they talked of current matters. The Halifax crew were introduced, and notes compared. Reg and George had followed the Air Training Scheme path through Canada, and had become fighter pilots flying Hurricanes. George had also become an expert Lysander pilot. He was sometimes employed ferrying senior officers to meetings. But he had other work, when, in the dead of night, he would descend onto rough, short fields lit by the improvised flares of a small group of French men and women turned by war into something to be feared; he would unload supplies and he would pick up or leave very ordinary-looking civilians whose names and business he never learned but whom he admired immensely.

The talk faltered as delayed tiredness hit the Halifax men, and they drifted off to bed, leaving Tim wide awake with Reg and George. They continued for hours, reminiscing, bringing each other up to date, making plans to meet, until finally Tim too, suddenly and without warning, was overcome by a weariness he could not fight. When Corporal Ivory led him to his own bed he slept, as Reg might have put it, like a wombat on a wet day.

It was two days later when Alan, steeling himself, mentioned Wing Commander Nordale's oblique warning. "I'm sorry to pull rank on you, Tim," he said, "but Naughty's asked me to speak to you. He seems to think you're too much inside yourself. And, to be honest, I wonder myself, sometimes."

Tim, taken by surprise, looked at his boyhood friend. He did not speak. Alan went on: "I know you're a bloody good navigator. I never worry about you in the air. But on the ground …

"Look – maybe you'll never get over Fay's death completely, but how long is it now? Getting on for two years? This isolating way you live isn't right. You hardly ever come out with the rest of us. It's not healthy."

Tim thought of a letter in which his father had said almost the same thing. But Alan wasn't his father. His first impulse was to tell him to bugger off. But with the Wingco involved he had a right to an answer.

"It's not only Fay. Well, yes, it is her. Mainly. I thought that crossing the sea – all the sea between here and home – might wash something out. Well, it didn't."

"You wouldn't be the first. You've joined a long line there. There's even a biblical precedent."

Tim did not even hear. He went straight on: "I mean, being in a new place, with new people, having a new purpose – all that does help. But … it doesn't matter how important, or wonderful, or beautiful any place is; to me it's empty, bleak. These trips to the pub, dances – I just don't have any feeling for them."

"I can understand that. OK, you're still in love. But are you going to devote the rest of your life to Fay's memory?"

"Maybe."

"Don't be damned silly. Anyway, what did you mean, it's not only Fay."

"I don't think you'll buy the rest."

"Try me."

"Well, it's the bombing. Spraying death all over a city. I hate it."

"No one likes it. But we didn't start it. You know what the Blitz did to London."

"Actually, I've even heard that questioned. Our side bombed Berlin first, you know."

"For God's sake! Don't hedge. What about Warsaw, Rotterdam, Guernica? Look, this is total war. And we've got to win it. If we can destroy their morale they might rebel. In the meantime every Messerschmitt and every gun we face is one the Huns can't use in Russia. If they win there we're done, and they'll be in a position to take on America and the whole Middle East. You don't want Europe and the empire to be governed by those thugs, do you? Some Aussie cop telling you you're driving too fast is one thing, but do you really want the Gestapo and the SS knocking on the door in the night? Taking all the Jews wherever they take the poor buggers; arresting people because they're Gypsies or handicapped? Or your dad because he hasn't shown proper respect to the Führer? You and I talked about that stuff once, back in Brisbane."

"We did. And I decided to come. But then it was ideas. Now it's people. You talk about destroying morale. You remember Bill? Billo, at school? He was a good man – a really good man. There must be millions like him in Germany. Old men, women, kids. Our bombs don't choose. They just kill. They tear human beings apart. Just like the Hun ones do here."

"Tim, you could be arrested if you said that in the pub. Maybe Naughty's right. You're trying to have it both ways."

"Think what you bloody well like. But look at the Yanks – they aim their bombs at military targets, not cities. Yes, they get people along the way, but that's a sort of accident.[3] You know what I reckon? We don't understand death. We don't even understand suffering – what it's like to lose a limb, to be

---

3   This was US Air Force policy until very late in the war.

blinded, to have shrapnel through your guts – not unless we've been there ourselves! And if we had we wouldn't be flying! I don't think we should inflict things we don't understand on other people."

"So – you want to lie down and let the Nazis walk all over the rest of the world?"

"No – I can't accept that, either. So I go along. But there are questions I can't answer, and they're too bloody big!"

"Tim, you think you're special! You're not! Do you imagine everyone's wrong except you? Ordinary men don't want to kill others. But we look at the situation and make a judgment that it's necessary and after that we get on with it. And that's what's expected of a man – it's moral courage!"

Alan was unknowingly echoing one of Tim's own abrasive doubts. But in Alan's words it was a pure assertion, and it was a repetition of one he had made long before. As then, Tim reacted, unwilling to submit to this cocksure certainty.

"It can be. And it can be sticking our heads in the sand."

"For some people, maybe. But most are more honest than that."

"Alan, I've tried to accept all that. What about the few – the conchies, the ones who refuse to kill, whatever? Aren't they the ones with real courage?"

"Tim, we have to win and there's only one way. Look, this is classified stuff, but I've heard whispers from some pretty good sources that when we aimed at factories and airfields, most crews couldn't get their bombs within five miles of the targets. It was a waste of men and resources – a fool's paradise, or a fool's hell if you prefer. Harris is right. The logic's simple: either we flatten Germany or we have the thousand-year Reich. Don't you understand – they'll keep going until we stop them! And if they win it'll be a brutal tyranny that slaughters a lot more people than the war. So we do it and we don't drive ourselves around the bend. That won't help anyone."

Tim looked hard at Alan through blurred eyes. "No. It won't

help," he said. "It's not practical. But I can't help it."

Alan said nothing. Tim paused then repeated the words: "So I go along." Alan, returning the directness of his gaze, was shocked to see the distress in his face.

"Tim," he said, "I won't say anything to Naughty. But – I *can* rely on you?"

"Bugger it, Alan! You know I'd never let you down in the air. I just try to face facts."

"Well face some of these. I'm taking you to London next chance we get. We're going to have a binge. I'm taking the whole crew. But first we're going to visit a hospital. I'll show you some facts! And you'll come! That's a bloody order."

Alan kept his promise less than a week later. At base, this visit to London wasn't a recreational one. The crew wandered through Guy's hospital and the Royal National Orthopaedic during visiting hours. There were patients blinded by the bombing, patients with limbs amputated, patients suffering from burns, patients permanently disfigured.

Alan's strategy was sound, as far as it went, but he could not have foreseen the help he would get from the Luftwaffe. The air-raid sirens howled as they emerged, forcing them into the Underground where they propped themselves against the wall and chatted to the Londoners who could not do enough for men wearing wings. Tim felt himself drawn into unity with the whole mix of them: men, women, children, rich, poor, cockneys, professionals, aristocrats, huddled against a common enemy; he felt himself taking sides, resenting the men who rained destruction from above, warmed by the spirit of resistance as they waited for the "all clear" and listened to the muffled noises of exploding bombs. When they emerged, there was before them a nondescript open space a hundred yards long where a terrace of five-storey residences had stood hours before. Beyond this was a curious landscape of damaged houses – in one of them only a corner chimney remained, narrow at the top, but it remained to its original height, so that it seemed a lonely spire, standing with defiant dignity like an ancient ruin. It appeared a symbol of resistance, a flag against oppression.

The airmen walked along the street. Then they stopped.

Before them lay a woman, half-covered in rubble, her spine possibly broken. Beside her a dirty child cried. Two ARP men were removing the masonry. They finished and lifted her ever so carefully onto a stretcher. One of them picked up the child. The other glanced at their uniforms and then full at Tim's face. Tears were in his eyes and anger hardened his mouth.

"Get the swine back, mate," he said.

CHAPTER 16

Reg and George's Therapy (Norfolk, 1942)

"What'yer reckon, George?" asked Reg.

"He's lost weight."

"So've we all. But he's thin as a swaggie's story."

"And he's changed – he seems – not old, exactly, but as though he's fighting something inside."

"So'd I be. So'd you be. He was there when his fiancée bought it. He's still doin' it tough."

"So ... we've got a case on our hands."

"Too right. That skipper of his – you know, the bloke who parked that Halifax on our strip – he rang me. He's worried too, he wants someone to shake him up. Someone outside his own squadron, he said."

"And now he's found us."

"That's it."

"Tall order. What's he suggest?"

"Suggest? He doesn't know what to suggest."

"Pass the job on – that's the Air Force."

"You're telling me. So – what'll we do?"

"Go on the town? Take him down to London?"

"Dunno. It'll be hard to match up our free time and his."

"Well ... they get a week every six. Mightn't be *that* hard.

Netherholme's not far. Bring him here for some of our do's – dances and the like."

"Bit dicey, isn't it – dances and women, I mean. You don't think it's too soon?"

"Well … it's getting on for two years. He's got to take an interest some time."

"Tell you what. In for a pound. Get him to a hop, introduce him accidentally-like to some WAAFs – we could brief them a bit first – and then we'll get some bikes and do a bit of touring around the local traps. Us, a girl or two, and Tim. You know, English countryside, old houses, lunch at a pub – the main thing's the company. Barb'd be good. Might scrounge some petrol for the Austin and do a bit of a tour."

"Well, we can try."

Their benevolent plotting proved easier to implement than they had imagined. Little Coring had a cinema, two very small pubs, and a dance hall; the town was linked to Netherholme by thirty-five miles of rail, and the stations were within cycling distance of their RAF bases. Joint evenings out would be possible, though for Tim to return in time he would need to be, as George put it, "sharp with the trains". And when petrol could be found for Reg's battered and patched Austin Seven they might even share a day out.

In the event, bad weather conspired to aid their purposes, sometimes restricting flying for days. Tim was inveigled into attending gatherings "for drinks": laughing, chatty evenings that left everyone sorry when they drew to a close.

It was at the third of these that he was introduced to Barbara. She worked in the ops room, where she maintained a strict concentration that sat oddly with the irrepressible light-heartedness she brought to the rest of life. Plump and pretty, her warmth and cheerfulness had persuaded Reg that she was the antidote Tim needed. How much she guessed of this, and whether Tim would be as good for her as she for him, were factors hardly considered by Reg or even the more thoughtful George as they worked at promoting the relationship; and that, in a way, was a tribute to her – to her openness to anyone in need.

It took three more weeks, during which George dropped hints of such subtlety, and Reg ones of such broadness, that in the end, Barbara laughing and Tim forcing a laugh, they agreed to go out together to a Norwich restaurant when they could get leave.

Tim knew nothing of the city, but taking George's advice he booked a table at Song Lee's where they could watch the river Wensum while they ate such pretend-Chinese food as rationing allowed and sipped very un-Chinese wine. Tim was immediately comfortable with Barbara. He suspected that in another life he might have been attracted to her more intimately; there was no question of that now – only Fay, he felt, could ever be *real* to him in the way that can work a deep, inner transformation in a person. Barbara, for her part, found Tim pleasant enough, in spite of his recurrent tendency to drift into an abstracted muse. She did not understand this, but she was conscious of her ability to lift him out of it, and kind enough to think it worth doing so.

So from Song Lee's expansive window they watched the early spring twilight deepen and they talked simply and easily. "I've always lived in Norfolk," she said. "I've always thought it's beautiful, and people who come here say so, too, so I must be right."

"Of course it is. The Broads are fantastic!"

"I don't think I could live anywhere else. Oh! Sorry – that doesn't seem very nice to other places. Well, I mean, to Australia."

He laughed. "You can't imagine how different my home town is. This country is sort of – moist – even when there's plenty of sun. Walgabran's dry and hard."

"Tell me about it."

"Well … the landscape has a breadth about it, and there's a lot of long grass that's green but not really green – it's sort of half-grey – and the properties have fences to stop cattle and sheep wandering, and our houses are built on wooden stumps and they have verandahs right round; and the flowers are different; to be honest, I think they're brighter …and the birds and the animals are all different. And even in Brisbane it's different – there's a river I left behind there – nothing like this – in mid-summer the heat can hit you like something solid and then it's almost – metallic. By comparison, anyway."

She wondered, trying to imagine the picture he painted. "Birds … I love birds. Do you have many songbirds – like our nightingales and larks?"

"No, but the Aussie magpie and the butcher-bird would give them a run, and the lyrebird can imitate anything – even a train. Like this." He made a "choo-choo" noise.

She laughed. "What about the fashions? Or are you one of those men who doesn't notice?"

He grinned. "I guess I am … no … I think really the fashions are the same as here but somehow the cloth seems lighter."

They discussed films and sports, and the foibles of their superiors and which of them was good to work for, and all the trivia that a man and a woman together make surprisingly interesting – their thoughts about the stars and the weather, what had happened that morning, what they liked for breakfast.

He left her quietly and pleasantly at the gate of her barracks. During the train ride home he felt an after-glow of their time together, but it had a dreamy quality as though he had been watching a film or acting in a play.

He was again aware of that division in his soul he had mentioned in letters home. Two distinct levels. The upper was clear-headed, active and efficient: he was able to respond to briefings and maps and officers with deliberate control. But the lower, where he yearned to rest peacefully, was full of turmoil. Oil floating on troubled water.

It says worlds for the openness and tolerance of Barbara's heart that they nevertheless became warm friends, and that, in the coterie which George and Reg worked to set up, they developed a special closeness.

It was three weeks later, and full spring, when a rare coincidence in the leaves of several people prompted Reg to propose a group trip to Norwich. The party would be six – Barbara and two other WAAFs, Sally and Bronwyn, together with Tim, George and Reg. They would have lunch at Song Lee's, then go to the races. This would be followed by a visit to the Criterion – an expensive establishment with several bars and a restaurant opening onto a large dance floor.

They set off, crushed into the Austin with Barbara sitting on Tim's lap and Bronwyn on George's, while Reg drove and Sally sat demurely beside him. Reg burst into song at the wheel, running through a comic repertoire that started from Flanagan and Allan and ran backwards through the Mills Brothers, George Formby and Harry Lauder to wind up with half-a-dozen old sea chanties. The others joined in, but fell silent when Reg turned to tunes that the girls had never heard: *The Old Bark Hut*, *Click Go the Shears*, *The Queensland Drovers*, *The Road to Gundagai* and of course *Waltzing Matilda*. This nostalgic Australian note remained with them at the track, for they had hardly entered the stand when Reg noted that the second race would have a horse named *Colonial Boy*. It was priced at fourteen to one, but the odds did not deter him. In a burst of antipodean patriotism he approached the nearest bookie. "Two quid on the nose", he said; "we can't let a digger go without a bit of support." The girls laughed at him for risking half a week's salary on an outsider, but drew in their breath as Colonial Boy leaped first out of the box and settled into what promised to be a solid race. There was a stir among the spectators, and raucous calls which increased in volume until at length everyone was shouting while, at the far side of the track, the jockeys began to use the whip furiously.

"Garn, show the Poms," called Reg, and "Come on, Colonial Boy" yelled Barbara, caught by his enthusiasm. She grabbed Tim's arm excitedly. "I do hope he will win!" Then she grinned. "What'll you do with the twenty-eight pounds?" But as she turned back to the race, her face fell. Colonial Boy was slipping back, horse by horse, with every appearance of being exhausted at the five furlong mark. The whole party went quiet, and the horse continued to fall back until, at the end, he came home three or four lengths behind the field.

"Bit of a dog, mate," grinned Reg as he threw away his ticket. "Never mind. Get it back on the next."

And through the afternoon they did well enough, Tim and George more or less breaking even, all the girls winning slightly, Reg losing a little. "Well, said George, we'd better start for the Criterion."

"Can't make tracks yet," said Reg. "Last starts in five minutes. I've got to get my money back." He hesitated, staring at the field on a bookie's indicator, then exclaimed "Stone the crows!"

"What is it?" asked Tim.

"They're running that animal again!" And sure enough, there was Colonial Boy in the last race.

"Can they put a horse in two races?" asked Sally.

"Sometimes," answered Tim, "but it'll be damned tired."

"Wait a minute," said George. His eyes narrowed. "Reg, back it!"

"What? Do me dough again?"

"Back it, mate. I've seen this game before."

"Anybody but you," said Reg. Shrugging, he went to the bookie. He was astonished to be offered forty to one.

"What are you up to?" asked Bronwyn.

George grinned. "Just watch."

And watch they did, in unbelief, as Colonial Boy settled comfortably in the middle of the field until, with three hundred yards to go, he began to stride out easily, passing first one horse then another on the outside until he loped ahead to finish clear with what looked like undiminished zest, running on and nodding his head against the rein. Reg was ecstatic. "Ripper!" he called out. That'll be at least eighty quid. The Air Force is a mug's game. I'm becoming a punter!"

"The crooks!" said Sally, in disbelief.

"They'll all be mad as cut snakes," said Reg.

"Everyone except the bookies," said George.

Tim grinned. "Yes. I don't know that I'd like to be the owners right now – or the jockey! There's got to be a protest."

They waited a while but there was no announcement. "It seems not," commented George. Well, we've done well. Come on – let's go and spend some of it."

"Too early to go to the Criterion yet," said Sally. "Let's go back to Song Lee's for a while – just get some tea."

They did so, and Song Lee, recognising them, ushered them to a table where he removed the tea-bowls and produced two bottles of Bordeaux out of a cache saved, he claimed, since before the war. It was under the influence of this wine and George's win that the party trooped off to dine and dance in the highest of spirits.

And it was those high spirits that led to the fight.

Reg whistled. "Criterion's right. Flash as a rat with a gold tooth – that's what you'd want to be here," he said, overawed by the opulence.

While the WAAFs disappeared to "freshen up" the men waited, propped against the smallest and most intimate of the bars with half-pints of bitter ale. Beside them, a young, cloth-capped civilian was arguing with an older man.

"By all accounts he's a decent cove," the younger man was saying.

"He's a bloody Hun. They're all the same."

"They're not all the same. He keeps the rules. You fight him, but you respect him."

"I tell you there's no difference. None of them would have followed Hitler if they weren't all sodding hounds."

Tim was brought up cold. He was back in Walgabran, listening to his father disputing with his uncle. For a few hours the war had been forgotten, the constant ache of Fay's memory had receded a little. He had a momentary sensation of falling as in a dream. The mood was relieved by the reappearance of the girls and Reg's invitation to "come and put the nose-bags on." They moved to the restaurant and were seated around a table close to the band. Reg, celebrating his win, ordered a magnum of champagne, and asked Sally to dance. The others listened a moment to the infinitely evocative strains of tunes which, whatever later generations would think of them, in the desperation of those times captured the heartbreak of separation and the courage of British defiance set against the background awareness that sudden death was always near; and they felt themselves relaxing into the rhythms and the mood. George and Bronwyn got up. "Come on," Tim said to Barbara, and smiling they went to the floor.

Reg danced extraordinarily well. George was competent, and Tim sufficiently so, and with Barbara it was easy. Waltz followed quick-step, fox-trot followed waltz, and the floor cleared of all but the experts for the rumba and the tango before everyone got up to jive or to try to jive. At length the six returned to their table, where George poured champagne for everyone. "Cost me a packet," he grinned, but we're flush." They became animated, laughter mingling with the raised voices of Reg and Sally speaking together. George summoned a waiter and asked what meal was the best the Criterion could provide. Tim felt himself recapturing old feelings, warming to life in a way he had almost forgotten.

As the evening progressed, the noise from their table increased. An imposing man of perhaps fifty-five, impeccably dressed and with a sleek mane of greying hair, approached. They hardly noticed until he was at their elbows.

"I say," he began, "could you chaps turn the volume down a bit?"

As the group turned to him, he stopped and stared at the single wing on Tim's breast. His eyes travelled to the sergeant's stripes on his sleeve.

"I say," he repeated, "this won't do. Only officers are permitted in here. You can go to the public bar, of course."

There was a stillness. The surrounding tables seemed to sense the sudden tension. They became quiet and listened.

George looked at the man. Adopting his most "correct" voice, he said: "I beg your pardon?"

"This man shouldn't be here. This restaurant is only for gentlemen."

George's voice was ice: "I think it's best if you return to your own table." Reg, however, spoke up: "Mate, the sergeant's as much a gentleman as you are. Back off. Go and enjoy your meal and leave your betters alone."

No one who heard Reg speak could doubt his nationality. "Oh," replied the man, "Australians. I wondered what those darker uniforms meant. Playing up as your fathers did in '17 … And just as uncouth. No breeding at all."

Reg began to get up, anger in his face. "Who the hell are you?"

Tim put a restraining hand on Reg's arm. The stress of months of bombing missions, the sudden release, the enjoyment of the day, the pain of memories, and the champagne – all exploded in him. He stood up. "I'm the sergeant you object to, so I'll answer you. I and my friends are having a rare night off. We've earned it. You spoke of our fathers. Yes, my father was here in 1917. He fought in Palestine and in Flanders. My uncle was wounded on the Somme. For England. It's the same now. What do you think we're doing here? Who do you think we're fighting for?"

A woman at a nearby table applauded. "The young man's right. Leave them alone. Those boys don't get much time to relax."

Her escort added, "Yes. That's right. Damn it, they're putting their lives on the line."

The man who had protested would not give it up. "We must have standards," he said. "And by heaven we need them. You heard the way that fellow spoke."

"Mate", said Reg, "if you weren't over the hill that fellow as you call him'd knock you flat."

"Over the hill! You need to be taught a lesson. Come on then."

The woman who had been with him came up and stood near him. "You're not going to do this again, Gavin," she said. "Come away."

She was followed by a younger man. "Don't interfere, Mother," he said. He turned to Reg, "Pick on someone your own age."

"I s'pose that'd be you" said Reg.

It was out of character, but Tim began to relish the idea of a fight. "I'm with you, Reg," he said.

A youngish man from a table approached. He spoke with an Oxford accent. "Well, there are two of you chaps, so I'd better even our side up. Spot of fair play and all that."

Barbara gripped Tim's arm. "Don't be silly. They'll tell your CO."

"That'll probably happen anyway," said Bronwyn. "Men!"

Sally put a hand on Reg's shoulder, but he shook her off. "Well?" he said to the young man.

"Don't, Derek," said his mother.

Looking at her, he shrugged. Then he turned away, muttering "Sons of convicts – what can you expect?"

"Better than sons of people who would send a man to Botany Bay for stealing a chook," rejoined Reg.

The band had stopped. The manager came. "Gentlemen," he said, "This is a restaurant, not the Wild West. If you don't sit down I can get the police here very quickly."

"Did you call those fellows gentlemen?" asked Derek.

Reg spluttered. "Leave it, Reg. I'll handle it," said Tim.

"No, mate," said Reg to him. "You other blokes keep out of it. This is just me and Derek here." Turning to the young man, he added, "Let's go outside. There must be somewhere nice and private."

"No!" Sally was white-faced.

Derek ignored her. "Very well."

The man who had offered to "even the sides up" held out his hand to Tim. "I s'pose he's right, Sergeant," he said. "Truce?" And he held out his hand.

Sheepishly Tim took it, and smiled. "Wait 'till after the war. When we take the ashes home."

"Never!" said the other, grinning.

Reg and Derek insisted on going outside, and the others followed. They found a large park, deserted at this time, and fought there, the men and Sally forming a rough circle around them while Barbara and Bronwyn and Gavin's wife refused to come anywhere near. The contestants were evenly matched, but Reg had drunk more. The fight lasted no more than a minute, and ended with Reg sitting foolishly against a hedge, bleeding from his nose and muttering "At least the bugger can fight."

Sally spoke to Derek. "I hope you're satisfied. These men came across the world to risk their lives for us. Just because one of them's a sergeant!"

Derek shrugged. And walked away with his father.

It was rare for Netherholme's station commander, Group Captain Thomas, to become involved in disciplinary matters. On the phone to Squadron Leader Featherstone, he could barely contain his exasperation. "Damn it," he was saying, "we can't afford to lose trained men because of a stupid incident in a Norwich night club! You know those Australians of yours. What are they like?"

"The best, sir. Both of them. King does special jobs."

"And the WAAFs?"

"I gather they tried to stop the argument."

"Well, we've got to let the public know that we're handling it. Trouble is, there's not much you can do. We can't kick them out over something like that – and in any case we wouldn't if they're the valuable men you say."

"I suppose we might cancel some of their leave, sir. But they need it. We both know that."

"Yes. Well, I'm giving young Rogers a hell of a rocket and a warning. Actually, I'm told he's a good navigator, but Nordale's been a bit worried about him in other ways. I suppose I'll have to use kid gloves a bit. Goes against the grain."

"Well, sir, I don't think he was much involved. But in a way it started over him – he's an NCO and there's a sort of custom that the restaurant is reserved for officers – and generally for people of that class. Nothing official about it."

"Rubbish! It's not as though the place was invaded by hundreds of Bolsheviks bent on revolution. Anyway, if a man has some manners no one will notice. Dammit, half the time it's a sergeant in charge of our bombers!"

"I rather gather the civilian involved makes a point of this sort of thing, sir."

"I know the type. He'll probably push it and make more trouble. Very well, Featherstone. Just so long as they don't get into trouble again."

"I wouldn't worry about it, mate," said Reg.

"It'll be alright," said George.

"Don't be silly again," said Barbara.

"Men!" said Sally.

And Tim settled down sufficiently to satisfy both Thomas and Nordale. He and Barbara became firm friends but hardly more, and the summer of 1942 came and rolled away and the year at last merged into 1943. In November there had been a BBC report that, in one sense, made things easier – not that the horror of bombing went away, but Alan's arguments were reinforced: heroic Poles had managed to smuggle an even more heroic messenger to London with first-hand accounts of what was happening to the Jews. Even though it was well-known that they were persecuted wherever the Nazis were in power, these reports almost defied belief.

He tried to let the normal mentality of the squadron seep through him, and to harden himself against the loss of men who never returned, and against the devastation – of London, Cardiff, Birmingham, Plymouth, but also of Cologne, Dortmund, Essen ... he met some Americans and was in awe of their daylight raids ... he flew and relaxed with the others, played and mourned and drank, and tried to resist the thoughts that lurked a little below the surface of his mind.

CHAPTER 17

The Last Flight (Britain, 1943)

The fighter looped and rolled, quickly returning to the attack from above, this time using its cannon. In the night it was all but invisible, and of the gunners only Bruce in the mid-upper turret could bring his weapons to bear. He fired at a momentary glimpse of exhaust flame. Whether or not he scored a lucky hit no one knew, but after one more pass the German withdrew, veering away from the points of fire streaming towards him in a lazy arc, pausing only for a Parthian shot almost without aim – a freak burst that struck the control system in half-a-dozen places and knocked splinters off the tailplanes.

As the Halifax slid sideways in a desperate attempt at evasion the crew reached for hand-holds, cursing. They were already crippled. Flak over Augsburg had buckled a ventral plate to open a narrow gap through which the wind entered in a keening whistle, and both ailerons were jammed, one in an up-position. Alan was finding the controls rebellious. It was as though the aircraft had a mind of its own, stubbornly banking to port. He tried to counter the tendency with the rudders and with the engines, throttling back on the starboard side and repeatedly losing height before struggling back to a position from which he could again descend in curving stages. The irregular motion threatened to become a disastrous spin, and the process was wasteful of fuel. The compass wavered erratically as the aircraft twisted and bucked, and Alan was forced to abandon the attempt to maintain a strict course. Like a rider alternately fighting and giving his horse its head, he made frustrated and half-successful attempts to progress homewards.

Normally Phil or Ron would now take over, but Alan could not leave his seat even momentarily. Phil hovered beside him, anticipating his needs – an extra pair of hands and eyes, working levers, monitoring gauges.

For Tim navigation became almost guesswork. To reach Britain they had to head north-west, which the aircraft refused to do. He reported that they could be heading towards Paris.

"Always wanted to see Paris," said Bruce.

"Could even be Barcelona," replied Tim.

"Shut up!" said Alan.

The crew obeyed, and their eyes, constantly alert for fighters and searchlights, were sharper than normal; but their other senses were correspondingly subdued. That is why no one noticed the smell for perhaps twenty minutes. Bruce detected it first. He spoke into the intercom.

"There's a bit of a pong – sort of smoky …"

Alan responded at once: "Tony, go check it out. We'll try to hold her steady."

Of the bomber's crew of seven, five had cramped positions neatly stacked in compact spaces below, in front of, and behind the pilot. Tony left this forward section, twisting and scrambling past bulkheads and wing spars, to make his way aft. In a large open compartment containing bunks, flares and hydraulic accumulators, he found little pools of light-coloured liquid sloshing on the floor and the bulkhead, dancing crazily in the gusts entering through the damaged hull each time the plane rocked and recovered. The atmosphere had an acrid quality and he wondered where it came from; possibly, he thought,

222

smouldering seals, insulation, ammunition tracks. He checked the batteries for leaking acid. No. The starboard rest bunk, he saw, was wet. He drew back and moved on, looking for the source, steadying himself with his hands. Moments later, he was hit on the sleeve by a fine stream, and raising his eyes he saw oil squirting from the upper accumulator. It was holed and the lines leading from it were cracked, spilling their contents onto the metal hull and making a slippery mess on the floor.

Removing his glove, he touched the oil on his sleeve. It was warm. But it would be, under constant pressure. He tried the casing of the accumulator. No, it was definitely hot.

Returning, he reported to Alan, who cursed volubly and spoke into his intercom to the tail gunner: "Don, come forward. The hydraulic system's shot up. If it fails your turret won't turn. You'll be trapped there in the arse-end."

Phil chipped in: "That bloody fighter. What was the bastard, anyway?"

"Don't ask me," replied Tony. "One-oh-nine, Focke-Wulf. Not a one-ten anyway – they'd go for our belly. Thing is, oil in the reservoir could be burning if it was hit by tracers."

"Burning in there? No, mate – no air in there."

"Must be some. Especially if it's holed. And tracers use phosphorus. How much oxygen do you think they'd need?"

"Not phosphorus – magnesium. Anyway, it could have been a cannon-shell."

Alan intervened: "For God's sake, you two – don't have a bloody debate! Tony, get the extinguishers onto it. See if you can tape those oil leaks up. Phil, you'd better go too. I'll manage here for a while. But get back."

Phil slipped off his parachute to give himself freedom of movement, and the two men played the extinguishers on the accumulator. For good luck they sprayed the floor and walls. The atmosphere became thick with foam. Phil wrapped heavy tape around the damaged casing, almost sealing it, and then did the same for the hydraulic pipes. Scrambling back to the cockpit, he reported, "We've tied it up. But there's something else."

"What?"

"I think that fighter damaged the heater duct."

"Shit!"

Alan said nothing more for a long moment. When he spoke it was as though he found it hard to open his mouth. "Get Tim."

When Tim came, sliding into the folding seat vacated by Phil, Alan asked, "You have any idea where we are?"

"God knows. We've managed to go south-west continually, I think. I wasn't exactly joking earlier. We're heading for northern Switzerland or southern France – but I think we'd still be well in Germany."

"We've poor controls and no heating. We've lost height and we'll lose more. Switzerland and France have great bloody mountains. Can you get us around them?"

"Alan, I'd be shooting a line. Keep going south-west and aim somewhere between the Alps and the Vosges. Keep a good look-out and hope we don't fly into the bastards. That's the best I can do. We're hundreds of miles past the range of Gee, and I don't have any reference-point unless you count Augsberg. It hasn't been possible to keep track of our course."

No one spoke. The reality had to sink in. Tim thought of all that he and Alan had shared. The past years came back, condensed into a single sharp vision. Then he murmured, surprised that his voice was so calm: "So – this is it."

Alan risked taking his eyes momentarily from the night ahead to glance at his boyhood friend. "Could be, mate."

"But," he went on, "not yet." He spoke to the intercom. "Everyone get parachutes on. You too, Phil – you shouldn't have taken the damned thing off. Don, get Bruce. If we have to jump you can all go through the forward hatch. Get braced against something. Ron, we still need your eyes. You too, Tim, back to your cubby hole – you've got work to do. We might see something – try to give us some sort of course."

Quickly the rearmost part of the Halifax was emptied of

people. Alan thought: leave it like that – and no one can be cut off. But – cut off there – might that be better? No. Done now, anyway. Up here second thoughts betray you.

Tim bent over his desk for a time and then took a sextant to the astrodome.

Alan spoke again: "Bruce, Don, get off your backsides. See if you can pitch stuff out. Ammo, everything that weighs anything. Oxygen bottles. Things that might burn. Flares, flame floats. Those rest mattresses off the bunks if they'll go. Never use the damned things anyway. Use the door if you can; the bloody hatch is only big enough for a cat and you'd muck up Tim and Ron getting it open."

The constant howl of the wind through the opened doorway mingled with the noise of the engines and forced them to use sign-language. The machine-gun ammunition, stored in a compartment behind the forward section of the plane, was the most difficult to move, and much of it they left. The slip-stream hindered their efforts, and the mattresses had to be twisted and compressed and shoved precariously into a position from which they could be heaved out, but finally they flew free, dropping into the night behind them. Don pulled Bruce back from the open door as he almost followed. Then, as the heavy oxygen bottles were jettisoned, there was a lurching response from the lightened aircraft. Tim was reminded of a car kangarooing. Thrown backwards from where he stood to take observations, he extended an arm to save himself and felt the hot metal casing of the accumulator against the back of his bare hand – he seldom wore gloves; they hampered work with slide rules and protractors and pencils, and he did not need them because his seat was in the one area of the plane that was effectively warmed. He put a hand to his mouth and sucked at the burn.

"That everything?" Don shouted.

"Dunno," replied Bruce, as they returned to a shuddering but steadier course.

"OK," said Don. "I'll go see him." He climbed to the cockpit and crouched in the narrow space: "What's the gen?"

"Everything's getting worse."

Ron called out: "I see a light. Could be anything. Farm house, maybe. But we're nearer the ground than I thought. Three, five thousand."

Phil said slowly: "That loss of oil – the undercart mightn't work. Flaps could be immobilised."

"Don't expect to land anyway. Be a miracle to find a place, and there's this bloody drooping wing. We'll go as far as we can. Did you lighten her?"

Don looked at Alan and nodded, bracing himself with his arms. From somewhere a new thought forced itself into Phil's consciousness: they were probably heading for rough, heavily wooded country – and at night; if they had to jump it would be safer to turn east … but that would be deeper into Germany. He kept it to himself.

Each man felt increasing heat. Don went to look. "Skipper," he said, "those tapes Phil used – they're holding but they're charred and loosened."

The plane continued erratically, swerving, losing height, rising, descending, trying to keep a south-westerly course. There was a prolonged silence until Alan spoke again: "It's time. Don, go and tell them we're bailing out. You go too, Phil. I'll hold it till you're gone." He accompanied the words with a sharp, angry gesture that set the alarm lights winking.

Phil hesitated and shook his head. "I'll stay, mate. You need my help here."

"No. Go. Hurry. Go now."

Phil did not move. Tension raised the pitch of Alan's voice. "Go. You can't help now. If you get back somehow, tell them what happened."

Phil sat still. "Get stuffed!"

"Bugger off!" screamed Alan. "What the hell can you do? They'll need you – the bloody crew needs you. Go! Now!"

Phil looked at Alan wordlessly, rose and went to the others, clustered now around Don. "Quick," he said. "Get organised. We're going."

"We can't leave him!" said Tim.

"Move it! On the double. He'll follow. The longer we take, the less chance he has."

In a dream, Tim obeyed. The men gathered at the hatch. Bruce was first out. Muttering "I've always been terrified of this. I can't look", he edged his feet over the sill and for a moment sat clumsily as though frozen. Then, with a cry that died in the wind, he was gone.

"Don't go like that," said Phil. Do it properly. I'm right behind you. Don next. Then Tony and Tim and Ron. Hurry up."

There was no logic in the order except that Phil, an officer and occasional co-pilot, was going last. Tim looked around. Fire or no fire, damage or no damage, he did not want to leave. His instincts clung to the plane. It was familiar, a place of safety, a link with Britain and home.

His instincts were wrong. He had a momentary vision of himself as a boy, clinging to a tree watching Alan fall onto Willy's roof. He saw Don leave in text-book style, waited for Tony to follow, and then he rolled out.

He was too close to the plane. Somehow he forced himself fall free for the first seconds. His parachute opened with a crack. Swinging in the dark he could see nothing except the plane moving crazily through the sky away from him. Into that moment there broke a rattle of machine-gunfire and an explosion. The Halifax became a helpless lump of metal, marked by a not-very-large fire streaming upwards as it fell through the sky. It seemed almost to be separating into two halves.

Suddenly he could no longer feel the tug of the webbing suspending his body. He could feel nothing. He was crying uncontrollably as he hung alone in the night air, lost between heaven and an unknown earth.

CHAPTER 18

The Hospital
(Tannhofen 1943)

The sheets smelt white and starched, the bed was warm. His left hand was like a club, and the pain in his right leg, which had been a dull, distant consciousness, was suddenly sharp. He opened his eyes, and closed them at once against the headache which rolled over him.

There was a voice. A woman's voice. He could not hear the words.

A sound of steps. Approaching him. No, they were passing. An answer by a man.

Their speech was indistinct. He was too tired and too sick to care.

The voices became a little louder, and he heard clearly: "*Ja, Herr Doktor.*" And then, "*Bis nachher, Sie sehen bis morgen.*"

His mind was not alert enough to understand. Again he opened his eyes. They seemed reluctant to focus. The blur cleared sufficiently for him to make out a white ceiling, a curved metal arm over his bed. It was all too difficult. He closed his eyes. Uneasily, he slept.

❖ ❖ ❖

The headache had almost gone. His leg hurt abominably, his hand throbbed, but he was awake. He opened his eyes and stared for a long moment at the white ceiling. Then, experimentally, he turned his head from side to side.

A pearly light told him that it was early morning. Moving, he felt a tug on his arm, and glancing saw a needle connected to a drip. So he was in a hospital, and the realisation returned that he had heard German speech.

Memories flooded back. The rush of cold air, the jerk as his parachute snapped open, the discomfort of the harness, the noise as he hit – what? A tree?

Where were the others? An image came before his eyes – the Halifax broken and falling. That everyone had escaped was impossible.

A layer of depression slid underneath the pain and nausea. He tried to retreat into its dullness.

But no, he must think. Make an effort. Could the hospital be Swiss? The disabled plane couldn't have travelled so far. Probably it wouldn't have had the altitude.

Glancing down at himself, he saw that he was dressed in a loose white gown, and he wondered what they had done with his own kit. His leg was curiously immobile. How bad was his injury? Raising the sheets to look, he saw that his hand was bandaged and his leg was in plaster apparently from the calf to the thigh. Across it ran a tube that disappeared over the side of the bed. A catheter.

This was appalling. Yet the simple pleasure of relaxing, of lying back and letting others take charge, overcame him. He dozed a little while his mind drifted between thoughts and dreams.

Alan was dead. He had no doubt of that. There might possibly have been time for one man to follow him out of the aircraft. Ron, probably. The others – Alan, Phil – there was no hope. Alan – his lifelong, half-discordant, ambiguous, friend. At the end he'd shown great strength, trying to help the others. A hero.

Would these people let him write – to Australia? There must be some way of informing his parents that he was alive. The normal conduit for prisoners' letters was the Red Cross.

Back in Walgabran, they would get a letter to say that he was missing. Time would pass while they kept hope alive somehow, until he could write. Louise and Jim – they too would get a letter. For them hope would slowly fade until they knew that it was against all reason – but they would continue – unless perhaps he could himself tell them what had happened.

That is, if he ever made it back.

Damn it! Who was going to win this bloody war, anyway? Did it really matter? Did anything matter?

Another patient stirred and muttered, grumbling through sleep. There was a woman's voice. "*Schlaf Dich aus, Dieter. Bleibe nicht wach. Es ist zu früh zum Aufwachen, bald gibt's Frühstück.*"

A deep gravelly reply as the man struggled awake: "*Bereiten Sie mein Frühstück vor?*"

"*Sei brav.*"

Startled by the exchange, he was suddenly fully alert, and the airman's instinct of caution returned. Looking around surreptitiously, he saw a long room with two rows of beds head-to-the-wall, over which ran rails for curtains. A nearly continuous line of low, clean windows ran along both sides of the ward, and he wondered why these seemed out of place, until he realised that they reminded him of something that might be found in an Australian bush hospital. Here in Europe he would expect small, high windows set in the heavy and grimy stone of a nineteenth-century building, at least if he could judge from what he had seen in England. In the middle of the ward were three tables, a large one bearing medical equipment, another and even larger one with bowls of flowers, and the third covered by a profusion of papers onto which a desk lamp still shone in spite of the growing daylight. His own bed was apart in a small recess at one end of the room, out of line with the others and perhaps twenty feet from the nearest. His eyes roamed until they encountered two nurses in white and grey at the far end. They were murmuring over a patient. One of them nodded with finality and walked to the small table, where she sat down and busied herself with paper-work. The other continued to bend over the patient. It was clear at once that the first nurse was the authority: in her bearing was that self-possessed, restrained alertness that settles slowly on anyone who commands. She was tall. Distantly, she reminded him of a film star he'd once seen playing a nurse … was it Garbo? In his mind he gave her a name: Greta.

The room was silent again, except for the breathing of sleepers and a faint snore. He could see Greta clearly now, writing at her work station. She raised her head for a moment and glanced around the ward – a quick check on the sleeping patients before she returned to her work. The lamp had shone full on her face: from beneath her veil a wisp of blonde hair had escaped, shining where the beam caught it: she looked young – under thirty, certainly – and Nordic, very beautiful, and very tired. As he watched, she clipped some papers together and slid them into a pigeon-hole. Then she bowed her head, placing her face in her two hands while her shoulders sagged. This lasted for no more than a few seconds. She gave a little, shuddering wriggle, stood up, and began a parade round the beds, speaking loudly at each one.

Men were waking, coughing, beginning to converse, calling the two nurses. Both women were now hurrying from bed to bed with urine bottles, bowls of water, towels. There was a clatter of trolleys, a laugh, a groan. Some plates were placed on the central table with the flowers. A smell of bread and ersatz coffee made Tim realise that he was both hungry and thirsty. The ward, as it warmed up, was filled with conversation and guffaws and, occasionally, feminine laughter.

Greta was coming towards him. She looked down at him, and he stared back. "*So,*" she said, "*Sie sind wach?*"

Her professional calm was a mask hiding her soul. He

shrugged, and shook his head.

"*Verstehen Sie? Sprechen Sie Deutsch?*"

He understood the last words. "No," he said. "They didn't teach much Deutsch in the bush."

She regarded him with distaste, and walked away, returning in minutes with the younger nurse. This was a girl of perhaps twenty, small, dark-haired and oval-faced. She looked like someone who laughed easily, and she moved with a light, feminine grace. Why, he thought inconsequentially, do nurses imagine that their uniforms are unattractive? She half-turned and Tim saw, for the first time, that there was a blemish behind her right ear – a purple-red birthmark, not large. It would be partially covered when she loosened her hair off duty. So, he thought, not quite the ideal of Aryan perfection.

"I know to speak English," she said. "I interpret. *Schwester* wishes to know – have you bad pain? How is your head?"

"I feel bloody awful. What happened? Where is this? How did I get here?"

"You are in the *Sonderspital.* The nearest town is *Tannhofen.* But here we are in higher country."

"Tann … what? Where the blazes is that?" But Greta at once spoke sharply, and it was plain that the girl had been rebuked. When she spoke again her face was flushed.

"You must tell us your pains, Flight Sergeant Rogers."

So they knew his rank. For some reason it seemed a violation. She seemed to guess his thoughts.

"We have your uniform, naturally. And your money and the documents which were in your pockets. Also a letter apparently addressed to you from Australia, your watch, your compass and the food you carried. Tell us please about your pain."

Of course – they would take his escape kit at once. Somehow it seemed symbolic in its significance, as though to emphasise that he was indeed a captive. And he shouldn't have been carrying that letter from home. He shrugged: "My right leg hurts like hell, and so does my left hand. I have a headache, but I guess it's bearable. I'm bloody hungry!"

The young nurse translated for Greta, stumbling over the colloquialisms but managing the gist. Then she translated the reply: "It is not surprising that you are hungry. You have slept for two days. But if you are hungry, your pain must be not so bad. Men always complain."

In disbelief he tried to raise himself, and a wave of weakness passed through him. He sank back, his puzzlement plain. But Greta spoke briskly to the younger nurse, and the two women left him abruptly.

For perhaps an hour he lay, staring at the ceiling. The sight of urine bottles made him think of the tube over his leg. Again he felt a sense of violation. The universal humanity that his family, his school, Willy, had instilled into him – it seemed long ago – entirely deserted him, leaving pure resentment. His privacy, he felt, had been invaded by these enemies – the ones who had killed Alan and the others. He began to curse them mentally – a train of thought arrested when two men in white coats appeared at his bedside. The older had a benign appearance, while the younger looked like someone trying to seem stern but succeeding only in appearing uncomfortable. Greta joined them, her posture subtly conveying respect.

The older man spoke in accented but correct English. Again, Tim thought of Willy. The voice was almost exactly the same.

"Ah, Flight Sergeant Rogers. At last you can talk. Do you remember the house?"

Tim was puzzled. "House?"

The other smiled in a regretful way. "You descended into our village with your – *Fallschirm*. On top of a house. You hit your head – I know it sounds absurd – it seems on the chimney, to judge from the blood you left there. And you shattered your tibia. We had to operate. Your right leg has eight centimetres of steel in it, it may heal slightly short. I am afraid that you may always limp a little, but it should be barely noticeable. It will take time. Months. Your hand is nothing – a small burn, not too deep. It will recover. A few scars, perhaps."

"Eight centimetres – what do you mean? How much is that? A couple of inches?"

"It is eight centimetres. I do not know inches. It is not so much. You are very lucky."

"Lucky! Shit!" And at once, Tim felt embarrassed to have sworn in front of the nurse, even if she could not understand.

"I am sorry."

Tim looked at the gently smiling face. Could he trust their doctors? Were they competent? Would they make a real effort for him? A wild thought flashed across his mind – if they *had* shortened his leg, had that really been necessary? Was it, perhaps, a touch of German humour – a gesture of revenge for the bombs? In fact, could he believe anything they had said – even about the house he was supposed to have hit?

Then common sense asserted itself. Such things were not impossible – only not worth considering seriously. He asked, unnecessarily, "You did the operation?"

"*Ja.* I und *Herr Doktor Weiss* here. Forgive me. I am doctor Berndt. We did our best. Your kneecap was mangled, the bone was exposed. You will stay here until you can go to a camp for soldiers – prisoners-of-war. Now, you would be trouble for them."

"How long will I be here?"

"It depends how you recover. At least two months. Perhaps four, five. The fracture was not simple. Now – you have not eaten for two days. Perhaps you cannot eat. You must try – a little. First you will be given an injection for the pain."

He turned on his heel and was gone, followed by Weiss.

Left again to himself, Tim found his isolation unnerving. For the first time, his situation came home to him with total clarity. Disabled, in an enemy hospital, unable even to communicate – except with the girl and Berndt and perhaps Weiss – not knowing what had happened to Bruce and Tony and Don after they had jumped, or whether any of the others had managed to get out, not knowing even where he was. Nothing to read. No radio – nothing. He was in a curious sort of solitary confinement, surrounded by humanity; and he was almost grateful for his pain: it provided a focus for his attention, an excuse to rest in a half-aware world.

Only then did he realise that he had not even thanked the man who had probably saved his leg. Germans ... he was so conditioned to think of them simply as the enemy. Again, he thought of Willy ...

But – Willy was different ...

He was embarrassed when Greta gave him the injection and removed the catheter, and glad when she left. Like a sulking child, he turned his head to the wall, only to hear his name spoken softly.

"*Herr Feldwebel* – you can eat?" It was the younger nurse.

He was again aware of his hunger. Twisting, he nodded, hardly trusting himself to speak.

She smiled grimly. "There will not be so much. That is your doing – you RAF."

She left and returned with a trolley from which she took a tray and placed it on his table. "You can sit up?"

He reached for the handle dangling on a chain above his head to haul himself up, and at once fell back in a wave of dizziness. The nurse said, "You wait now," and after a couple of minutes put her hands behind him and helped him to sit. The dizziness was less but the ward moved like a ship in a rough sea.

"I will help you."

"Help me?"

"You have only one hand you can use."

He was not going to be helped like a baby by this German

girl. "I can manage, Sister".

He had used the title in the ironical fashion made popular by American films, but she missed the hint of contempt, thinking instead that he had called her a senior nurse, and she laughed. "No, I will not be Sister for two years. You – promote me. Are you sure that you need not help?"

Suddenly he was ashamed. With Greta beside her, she had been formal and correct, but alone she seemed artlessly friendly. More than that – there was an openness in her that was the opposite of defensive: she was, he sensed at once, one of those people in whom something irrepressible rests on a kind of unconscious courage.

Still, he wasn't going to be fed. He smiled. "Thank you. I am sure."

"*Bitte.*" She smiled and wafted away.

The food was, as he told himself, nothing to write home about, but he wolfed it, drinking the appalling *ersatz* coffee out of the thick mug and wishing for some English marmalade to put on the bread. Using only his right hand was not too difficult, but it made him wonder: how would he do ordinary things – dress himself, write a letter?

Then he lay back, and thought. Now that he had eaten, the pain seemed curiously worse, but it was not unbearable, and it would get better. He had hit his head, Berndt had said.

Fay. Fay, too, had hit her head. So much had gone wrong. A wave of depression swept over him.

He recovered himself and fought it. Think!

His mind turned over, in low gear but focussed and practical. Could he escape from this place? Of course, he now understood, that was why the girl had been rebuked: they did not want him to know where he was. Not that the name she had given meant anything … it certainly wasn't a big town – not one the average Englishman would have heard of.

She returned, again without Greta. He realised, with horror, that he was going to have to ask her for a bed-pan. A young girl like that! And use the thing, here in his bed. Could he get up to go to a toilet? Not with that plaster on his knee. Could he even sit on the pan?

There was no alternative. The need was becoming urgent. "Nurse," he said, "I'm sorry – can I go to a toilet?"

She grinned. "In a week perhaps – you will be able to use a chair, you know, with wheels." She disappeared and returned with a pan. "You can use this *Schieber?*"

He nodded, and she drew a curtain around the bed. "Call me if you need help." Her footsteps, mercifully, retreated.

Painfully he managed, and waited for her return. She removed the pan. "Now you wait."

She returned with a bowl and a washer, removed the gown from his back, and wordlessly sponged and washed him.

"Thank you", he said, looking up at her.

"Today you still wear this. Tomorrow we get you something else."

"Where's my kit?"

"Your … ?"

"My kit – my clothes, my things."

"Do not worry. They are safe."

He believed her. Then he asked "Why is my bed here, away from the rest?"

"What do you do if a German pilot is in an English hospital?"

He did not know, but his question was answered. Not that he was a pilot, but that didn't matter.

She was speaking again: "I go now. I will see you again tonight." She paused. "You have Herr Doctor Berndt. It is good. He is very good."

He nodded, and watched her retreating back. Then he lay back. He could still feel the touch of her hands, and he was glad. She did seem a nice girl – what was her name, he wondered.

Then he jerked his mind back to reality. These were Germans – nice-looking girls or not! He must think … damn this pain! It seemed to be subsiding and returning in a slow rhythm. Ignore it! His job was to think – to think clearly … the doctor had said nothing about the others … perhaps they were in the countryside, escaping … he must not mention them … he needed plans …

But instead, unwillingly, he dozed.

He was awakened by a nurse he had not seen before. At her elbow were two men: one, tall, thin and elegant, wore the uniform of a Wehrmacht captain; the second was in civilian clothes but somehow gave the impression of being in uniform nevertheless – his eyes seemed unnaturally still in an expressionless face surmounting the hard muscles of a squat body. He had to be some sort of security agent – SS, Gestapo, SD, Abwehr, something of the sort.

The officer spoke: "*Morgen, Herr Feldwebel. Ich bin Hauptman Franz Platt. Willkommen in Deutschland.*"

Tim shrugged. The man in civilian clothes spoke – in an accent obviously learned in the back streets of Brooklyn. His voice was gravelly. "This is Hauptmann Platt. Captain Platt to you. He says 'Welcome to Germany'".

Startled at the accent, Tim looked at him without speaking. The other waited, and then said: "While you're here the Hauptmann is responsible for you."

Something in man's demeanour irritated Tim. An absurd mood of recklessness gripped him. "No one's responsible for me."

His tone, at least, must have conveyed his attitude also to the silent Hauptmann, who looked at him with something like disappointment. The civilian spoke again: "Can it. Say, you know if it'd been farmers hauled you down from that roof you probably wouldn't be alive now. Platt's men got to you first. You're lucky to be a prisoner. That's the deal."

Tim did not know what to say. If it was true that Wehrmacht discipline had saved him … He looked around at the hospital and then at Platt, whose face and demeanour conveyed something quite different from those of the security man. He nodded towards him and mumbled something about "I'm sorry – I appreciate your help."

But the Brooklyn voice rasped on: "That's a lot better. You know what we call a British flier in Germany these days? *Terrorflieger*. I guess you can work out what that means."

He could indeed work out what it meant. It was hardly a week since he had been debating the morality of bombing cities with Alan. But the other's approach was challenging, and his accent irritated Tim because it was so unexpected here. It was difficult to believe that those tones could belong to an enemy – he was conditioned to think of Americans as allies, though he realised that some would have German backgrounds and, possibly, German allegiances. In any case, he certainly wasn't going to tell this man of his doubts. So instead of answering he said, "I thought you Yanks were supposed to be on our side".

There was a flush of anger in the other's face. "I'll remember that, Buddy. And – I ain't a Yank. Now as I was saying, so long as you behave you'll get from here to some Stalag Luft … So far you ain't done yourself any favours."

Tim was silent. A "Stalag". Squadron chit-chat had conditioned his mind: the word inevitably caused another to leap forward: escape.

The German seemed to read his thoughts:" Come on, Rogers. Don't play heroic games. There's no way you can slope out of here with a busted leg. Anyway, these guys" – he jerked a thumb over his shoulder – "are soldiers; they'll keep an eye on you. Besides, the folks in the village and on the farms know there's a British prisoner in the hospital. There's no way you could get far."

Everything the man said made sense. Tim felt his courage ebbing but was determined not to show it. "Well," he said, "they say there's always a first time."

"Rogers, you just don't get it. You oughta thank us you're here. You know that?"

Neither spoke for a full ten seconds; the immobile face of the security agent lent the silence a hard quality. But when he spoke it was softly: "So long as you behave, I said. That's going to be important. I got just four questions for you, Flight Sergeant. Where's your base in England? What's your squadron? Where's the rest of your crew? What were you doing in this part of the world?"

Tim tensed: "You know bloody well I can't answer those questions. You already have my name and rank. My number is 2293771."

"Sure, sure. The Geneva Convention. I've got news for you. I don't have to speak to you here in this hospital. Nobody's going to complain if you're moved. There's no one back in England knows whether you're alive or dead. Now there's things I need to know. Your plane was a long way from the regular British bombing raids. Why were you there?"

Tim retreated into formal language: "I cannot give you information." A wave of dizziness came back. There was a fog beginning to swirl over his mind, and he knew that it was related to the anaesthetics he had been given and to the fact that he had been unconscious for – what had the girl said? – two days. He felt hesitant, and was aware that his depression was mingled with fear.

The expressionless face permitted itself a slight raise of the eyebrows. "We do this the easy way or the hard way."

Damn the man. There seemed little doubt that he could do what he liked, and little doubt that he would. Tim struggled to think clearly. He wondered – couldn't he answer some of it without saying anything of use to the Germans?

"Look," he said, "There was a fire in the plane. I was the tail-gunner. The fire cut me off. I couldn't talk to anyone. The heat got me. I bailed out. I don't know about the others – for all I know they got back to Blighty."

The other regarded him quizzically without speaking, then said: "Could be. Or could be a nice story. Anyway I don't believe it. It's too simple. Besides, you give up easy. I don't know's how

I trust that. So where was your target?"

Telling him that could tell him nothing. There had been a big bomber force, and the town had been pasted. "Augsburg."

"Oh yeah? So how'd you get here?"

"Look, I don't know where 'here' is. The flak had damaged our controls. We couldn't turn west – not properly. We couldn't maintain height. Maybe we were well off course. The pilot didn't tell us much – he didn't have time."

"Yeah – about ninety degrees off course. So if that's what happened, how come you think your crew might have got back?"

Tim knew that he had been stupid. "I don't think. I just hope."

"Sure. And your base?"

It was enough. He felt guilty, though what he had said was of no use to the man. The jibe about giving up rankled. "Go to buggery."

His interrogator looked steadily at him, and murmured "Buddy, we'll see. Now I'll tell you what I think. You were dropping supplies – some place there's bandits; 'underground soldiers', you guys call them; France, Yugoslavia – maybe even Italy. Not everyone there loves Germany. I'd like to know just where your drops were."

This was so far wide of the mark that Tim actually laughed, and stopped as a sharp pain shot through his leg and made him draw in his breath. He coughed and stammered, and rested a moment. Then he said: "Yugoslavia! What sort of range do you think a bomber has? And why the hell would we go to France via Germany even if we could?" The dizziness came back, stronger than before.

"Good. Good man, as they say in England. Your Intelligence Officer back home would be proud of you. Listen, Buddy – I *know* what range a Lancaster has. Two thousand miles at least."

Tim was pulled up short. He knew that Lancasters could fly greater distances than Halifaxes, though he did not know how much greater. But even if his interrogator was correct, two thousand miles would hardly be enough to reach Yugoslavia or Italy and then return. He said nothing.

"'Sides, it's only you says that you went to Germany first. Maybe you were off course the *other* way – maybe you went to the south of France and got lost."

The man was fishing in the dark. And a round trip to the south of France was still a long way. With an effort, Tim recovered his control and some of his confidence. "Sure. We just happened to fly over Switzerland without noticing."

There was a small commotion at the door, and Dr Berndt followed by a group of students, swept into the ward. At the sight of the man leaning over Tim, Berndt started and then spoke sharply to the Hauptmann – evidently a question, to which he received an equally sharp answer. Then, turning to the security man, he unleashed a battery of rapid German speech, finishing with the word, "*Raus!*"

To Tim's surprise, the Hauptmann turned to his companion and jerked his head towards the door. The security man hesitated then walked out, saying over his shoulder: "OK. For now. I'll be back." The Hauptmann followed.

Berndt approached Tim: "Dachs has been talking to you. Do not worry about him."

"Easier said than done."

"I am in charge here. You are my patient. Hauptmann Platt is the military man who will take you when I discharge you. Dachs is nothing."

Tim was dumbfounded: "But – do you mean you'll protect me from him?"

"Do not worry about him." Berndt swept away and, with an irritated gesture, summoned the sister accompany him on his rounds.

Tim lay there, wondering, unaware of the passage of time. The senior nurse had rebuked her subordinate for mentioning the name of the town, but in any case it was unknown to him … and that fellow – what was his name? – Dachs – had actually revealed more by his questions than he had learned. The hospital must be in a southern corner of Germany, somewhere within reach of France, Yugoslavia, Italy ... But how could Doctor Berndt, or even Hauptmann Platt, have sufficient authority to over-ride one of the Third Reich's feared security organisations?

Then, as though remembering an oversight, Berndt returned unexpectedly and summoned the nurse with a brief word. She went out of the ward and, moments later, returned with a needle.

"Morphine," she said. Gratefully he accepted the injection.

He kept drifting off. It must be the morphine.

The sun was high, the ward was full of chatter. There was a stir of activity, and two nurses were laughing as they wheeled in a trolley. One called out *"Essen"*, and a few of the patients came to sit around the large central table. These, evidently, were the privileged ones – the walking sick, who could roam the ward and have their meals in style. Bowls were placed in front of them, and then the trolley began to travel around the beds, beginning at the end furthest from him, with the girls smiling as they fielded half-flirtatious jokes and compliments.

He glanced around at his fellow patients. Most seemed cheerful enough, but the atmosphere lacked the chirpiness he felt sure would characterise a similar group in an English hospital. There were other differences: a couple of the walking patients were wearing grey military trousers in lieu of pyjamas, and there was more of that curiously clean look that goes with fine skin and close-cropped blonde hair. Dachs had said that they were mainly soldiers, and there could be little doubt that he had told the truth: they were young, and though damaged they looked strong. A few were smoking. There should be more of that, he thought; soldiers always smoke.

With an absurd element of hope nudging his mind he looked for the girl. There was no sign of her.

The trolley came last to him. "*Können Sie ohne Hilfe essen?*"

He shrugged. The nurse indicated the food. "*Essen?*"

He nodded, and she placed the tray on a bedside table. He raised himself on his right elbow, wincing with pain. She helped him to sit, and took the cover off the bowl, exposing a thin soup and some black bread. "*Brauchen Sie Hilfe?*"

He guessed that she was asking whether he could feed himself, and for answer shook his head and took up the spoon. The soup proved to be based on potatoes. It was far from satisfying, but he enjoyed it. When he had finished, he watched as a new trolley was brought and a second course served – scrawny potatoes, cabbage and a minute helping of liverwurst. He had heard that rationing in Germany was even more severe than in Britain, and this seemed to bear it out.

A new thought surfaced. From Dachs's questions he guessed that they were in a location far from cities and major centres. These men around him, perhaps invalided back from Libya or the Russian front – why were they here, if the place was so remote? Simply for safety? Were there so many casualties that they had no room in their major city hospitals? Or had those hospitals been hit … perhaps by bombs dropped by Tim's friends, even his own aircraft?

His bed was separate from the others … What had the nurse said – how would patients in an English hospital feel about a German flier in their ward? He would not altogether guarantee that the man would not be quietly murdered – an unsolved mystery that no one cared greatly about.

A sense of urgency crept through him. He could not walk. And some of these men could. The famous German discipline might save him. Or it might not.

At least they weren't civilians – back home, they'd be the worst. Though when he thought about it, some Tommies …

Should he worry? Berndt, the young nurse, both had been more than kind.

This was the nation that had crushed the Jews and had

marched over Europe to the East and West, ruthlessly repressing civilian resistance. He remembered the bitter comment of the distraught ARP man in London. "Get the swine back ... " Yes, it was hard – almost impossible – not to feel like that. The combative instinct, once aroused, fed on the desire to hit back, until it over-rode other feelings and became a habit. Was that how people survived as airmen, soldiers ... whatever? Was that how they reconciled themselves to their work?

At least, it helped.

And these people around him must feel the same.

A nurse brought him his potatoes and cabbage. He shifted onto his hip to eat, watching the other patients carefully. Through the language barrier he could recognise the badinage, the conversations about the war. Yes – it would have been much the same in England. In spite of his anxiety, it required an effort to resist a certain fellow-feeling with them. They were so ordinary. He was a casualty of war. So were they.

Enemies ... comrades ... no, he was their prisoner; the lines must not become blurred.

It increased his pain to sit like this, propped on an elbow. In his discomfort he shifted – and slipped. Potatoes and cabbage scattered themselves over his bed, while his tray clattered to the floor. At the sound the other patients looked. In one man's eyes he could see pure hatred.

There was no nurse in sight. One of the walking wounded stumped across to him, picked up the vegetables, replaced them on the plate and offered them to him. That was when he realised clearly how precious food was. The man wiped away the worst of the mess with a rag, nodded roughly to him, and plodded back to his table.

He wondered ... all his dilemmas returned in force, with the stimulus of the German accents reminding him of Willy's voice and arguments. Not that most of them sounded as gentle as Willy's – except those of Brandt and the younger nurse.

Again he thought of the Halifax crew ... *could* Bruce and

Tony and Don have escaped? Might they have linked up after landing? It was easier in pairs, or so they had been told in a lecture by a man who had actually returned from the famous Colditz. He could hope – he could cling to that hope. As for the others – surely they must be dead. All of them. Ron, Phil, Alan.

Alan. He suddenly felt like a very young child knowing that it is about to cry.

He could do nothing. Absolutely nothing. He could not even ask whether the crashed remains of the Halifax had been found, whether there were bodies in it, or whether Bruce and Don had survived; to do so would give too much away and destroy any chances they might have of escaping.

But they could be lying somewhere, hurt, burned, needing help. *Should* he tell?

He tried to put himself in their place. If he was at large and it was, say, Don in the hospital, what would he want? Would he want Don to tell? If he was able to walk, he would regard that as a betrayal. If he was hurt, he would regard it as a necessity. Unfair – but natural.

He felt unequal to the decision.

No, leave it. Say nothing. Follow the highest hope. That was the military way … wasn't it?

In his enforced inaction, with no distractions, he went over the problem many times in the day, always returning to the same result. For the rest, he tried not to be obvious as he gazed at his fellow-patients, and attempted to dominate his pain by parading a thousand memories before his imagination. Walgabran. His childhood. Fay. Barbara's ebullience. Reg's cheekiness. Again, his childhood. He prayed silently. In the evening a nurse he had not previously seen brought him a morphine injection and a sedative. In a half-awake way he slept.

CHAPTER 19

Anna
(Tannhofen 1943)

I t might have been about two in the morning when he was
awakened. He had been dreaming of Fay, and for a moment
it was Fay's face he saw dimly behind the beam of the torch
focussed on the drip in his arm. The illusion passed, and he
recognised the young English-speaking nurse, who turned to
look steadily at him. Fuddled and off his guard, he blurted out:
"What is your name?"

"I am Nurse Bauer, *Herr Feldwebel* Rogers."

He laughed briefly. "*Herr Feldwebel* ... No, that is not me. I
am Tim. Who are you?"

She seemed embarrassed, and shook her head. "You can
sleep?"

He nodded, and she began to walk away. Then she returned,
and said quickly, "I am Anna".

The days followed with a certain monotony, broken by the
attentions of nurses and doctors, and later by occasional visits
to his bedside of some of the walking patients – motivated
largely, he suspected, by curiosity. Through their few words

of broken English and his barely existent German, somehow a little communication was achieved, marked more often by misunderstandings than by clarity. He found them at first hostile, then reserved, then uncertain, and finally in some cases prepared to regard him more as another casualty of war than as an enemy. The time came when a couple of older ones showed him photographs of their wives and children, but most were unmarried. He was, in fact, astonished at their youth.

This relieved his loneliness a little but also sharpened it – it seemed a parody, mocking real companionship. The same was true of the almost wordless attentions of the nurses, some of whom conveyed their dislike even while they attended to him. Berndt's rounds and the rare visits by his offsider, Weiss, became a blessed opportunity for a snatched conversation. They spent some frugal moments by his bed, and he grabbed an early opportunity to ask whether he could write home. Berndt mused a little with pursed lips, and said that it would be very difficult, but he would make enquiries.

The appalling Dachs had not so far re-appeared, and he wondered why. He had little faith in Berndt's ability to override the man's authority, whatever it was, and he expected some rough treatment if he could not satisfy him. He felt very unsure of his ability to resist serious pressure. Rank, name, number: beyond that, Alan, he thought, would have told the Germans nothing at all; neither would his father. Perhaps a waiting game was being played – to increase his anxiety, to soften him up.

But it was not that. He had mentioned his anxiety to Doctor Weiss, and that young man had answered, "Your story was not implausible. It would be serious if Dachs had some other reason to think that you were lying ... but apparently he had no such information. He is busy. For him you are just a little fish. Besides ... you are fortunate to have Doctor Berndt. He is a true doctor. To him, you are not an Englishman – you are a patient. He will not tolerate interference from outside."

"But," Tim had countered, "surely the police ... "

Weiss grinned. "Dr Berndt has connections. He was able to straighten the spine of a grandchild of a Reichsmarschall. It took several delicate operations. Many surgeons would not attempt it. He is now a friend of the Reichsmarschall's family. Everyone knows this. Platt, Dachs, everyone."

This was highly encouraging, but Tim was not wholly convinced that even a Reichsmarschall had the necessary authority in Nazi Germany. He continued to be uneasy until, after ten days, Berndt told him that the tail section of a crashed bomber with twin rudders had been seen from the air by a low-flying transport aircraft. It was almost hidden in rough, well-treed country. No German plane had gone missing in the region. No, he did not think a search had been made. But three half-starved Englishmen had managed to cross the Rhine in a stolen boat and make it to the border – oh, a couple of hundred kilometres from here – only to be captured in France. He was sorry to bring bad news – but at least that fellow (Berndt hated even to use Dachs' name) appeared now to be satisfied that Tim's story was substantially true. He would not be back.

Tim had no doubt that the aircraft was his own. He himself had seen it falling towards the ground. If the fugitives were from his own crew, they would surely be Bruce, Don and Tony, who had bailed out before him. Ron had been scheduled to follow him. There was the ghost of a chance that he'd made it. But that would be four, not three. And it still left Alan and Phil. He could not know. In all human probability they were dead. Alan would not have left the controls while anyone else was alive in the plane. It was a virtual certainty: Alan was dead.

The ward seemed to become physically darker, as though these depressing reflections affected even his eyesight. He stared at the ceiling, and his thoughts drifted in circles, filled for a while with images of Alan and the others before playing aimlessly with random trivia and then returning to his comrades. In sheer exhaustion, a kind of numbness supervened, stealing across his mind, and he accepted it gratefully.

In an hour the lassitude passed, and he resorted again to rehearsing memories – especially memories of home and of Fay, memories that sustained him even while they reminded him of his loss. His parents. Walgabran. Its heat, its smells. Fay's joy, something innocent and wholesome, something to cling to, something in the universe stronger than this war.

This unrelenting attempt to dominate the stresses of isolation was harder than physical work.

After nearly two weeks Berndt gave him an answer to his question about the possibility of writing home. Apparently someone with sufficient authority had decided that it would be good propaganda for Germany that a wounded British flier was being cared for in a German hospital. He would give a letter to Berndt. Its delivery would be slow and tortuous, and he must not write anything to reveal where the hospital was – hardly possible since Tim could only guess that the crash had been somewhere in the south-west of the country – or anything that would be to Germany's discredit. On getting this news he wrote at once, stumbling over the words, anxious not to disturb his parents more than he must.

In this desert there was one other oasis. He waited, with an expectancy that grew every day, for Anna's arrival. Initially it was merely that her kindness and her snippets of chat were his principal relief. But increasingly he began to admire her. Not in a way that conflicted with his memories of Fay. On the surface she was very different, and different too from Barbara. Yet she shared with both an unaffected and frank simplicity that looked out on the world and saw, even in the midst of war, a fundamental goodness. She was shy, but her shyness was of the kind that hesitates only momentarily before it is over-ridden by a vivacity that shines suddenly out, and her reserve would frequently dissolve in a merry laugh. That birthmark, he thought – even for a growing boy, let alone a girl, it would have been difficult to accept; but she seemed to have risen above it. Had that involved a long struggle? Or had she been able to brush the blemish aside? His own first reaction to it had been something like pity – but he felt now the wrongness of that. It was not actually attractive, but neither was it unattractive: it was simply part of her.

And – yes, she was attractive.

During her nursing ministrations she allowed him to use her Christian name, almost as a private joke – a concession to someone who did not understand German formalities and could not even pronounce "Bauer" without making her smile. To him this small intimacy somehow removed her a little from her professional role and made nonsense of the word "enemy" – at least as applied to her.

When the hospital's schedule transferred her to a later shift it gave her more time to pass a few words with him. He fretted on her day off, but he tried to disguise this, for he realised that the rough welcome the ward had come to show him would not extend to approving anything like a friendship between him and a German woman. Especially this diminutive pixie who seemed to carry with her a light-heartedness that infected all the patients.

He was immensely grateful when Greta one day dumped some English books by his bed. They bore a stamp proclaiming that they were supplied by the Red Cross for English-speaking prisoners of war. Greta's attitude made it clear that she disapproved of this concession and that she was acting under orders – Berndt's, perhaps. He must remember to thank him.

As time passed, he became dimly aware that he was crossing a boundary. The time he had spent unconscious, emerging to a sudden and total change of physical and human environment; the removal from the fighting; the daily trivial kindnesses showed him by some prisoners; the slow diminution of pain; all this combined to make him feel that he was entering a new reality, one where fresh tastes and thoughts were possible, where the native energy that had deserted him for three years might be able to return. He had said to Alan that he had hoped crossing a vast ocean might help him to regain some sort of enthusiasm for life after Fay's death. It had not; but now, at least, there was something – the beginning of a new perspective.

And then he was placed in a wheel-chair, with his hand unbandaged and one leg stretched out straight before him. It had taken much longer than the week Anna had predicted. He felt weak, and he tired easily, and when the plaster was changed he was shocked to see how the flesh had shrunk where the muscles had been without exercise for weeks. But he felt a surge of excitement to be able to move out of bed and around the hospital.

Because she alone could understand his speech, the other nurses left the job of looking after him to Anna as far as possible, and usually it fell to her to wheel him outside after lunch. She would leave him for an hour, with one of the books which, eventually, he had read at least four times; but there were also days when she was less busy, and then she would come and wheel him around the hospital grounds.

His first view of the surroundings astonished him. What had Dachs said? – "difficult country". They were facing rugged slopes and valleys, and he understood for the first time that the nearby village, wherever it was, was in the foothills of something approaching an alpine region.

And the hospital itself – something in its structure had reminded him of Australia, but by a fugitive impression he could not catch. He saw it now. His first view from the outside revealed a cluster of timber buildings, steep-roofed with big windows and verandahs protected by gaily painted wooden rails. The main ward, the only one-story building in the complex, was, except for the steep pitch of its roof, not unlike the verandahed timber houses found in many parts of his home state. There were other, larger buildings of brick and stone which puzzled him both by their number and their elegance until Anna told him that the place had originally been an expensive sanatorium. Most of it was now closed, and the rest converted to the hospital.

Anna (Tannhofen 1943)

The view was charming, and sharing it with Anna became his delight. She would wheel him to different parts of the grounds, often a little remote from other staff and patients and at times out of their sight. The summer was beginning to decline, and he was delighted by the play of the sun through the curling, yellowing leaves of maples and oaks. He watched elms, copper beaches and poplars slowly drying to autumn colours while the firs remained a deep velvet green. With Anna he chatted ever more freely. It was inevitable, as it had been with Barbara, that their earliest conversations would contrast their backgrounds: pine forests and gum trees; snow-topped mountains and expansive plains; Bavarian songs and bush tunes; the Baltic and the Pacific. These and a thousand other differences – Miller and Mozart, Gershwin and Lehar, common, domestic things – became items in their little, shared mind-village. He described his childhood in an Australian country town, and she hers in Hildesheim, and they recalled treasured family anecdotes of the doings of their uncles and aunts and grandparents, each claiming the more outrageous store. The tin-roofed dwellings of his childhood were utterly foreign to her experience, and her imagination clothed them in rich colours far from the reality. She taught him a little German and giggled at his accent.

One subject they avoided: the war and all that the Nazis had done. It was too real. And it did not fit – not into the world they were unconsciously making for themselves. If Tim, like Alice with her looking-glass or Gulliver on his travels, had stepped into a place apart, then Anna was following. But as yet neither of them knew it.

One day he asked her why she seemed to welcome him when some of the other nurses resented him. For answer she took the hand he was learning again to use and stroked the scar tissue that covered its back like a choppy sea. "Perhaps," she said, "It is because you are hurt. It makes me see you as … just one of the people in a war."

The touch of her hand then was not the professional touch of a nurse. He closed his fingers over hers, and they looked at each other's eyes. After a long moment he grinned. She smiled and blushed, dropped his hand and turned quickly away. "Tim'", she said, "I will take you back now to the ward."

"Must you?"

"Yes, I must." But turning she brushed her hand over his hair. Then she said, "I am your nurse. But you are big boy now. You can comb your own hair." And laughing, she mussed it up.

That night she was restless. This foreign boy – this enemy. She was seeing his face in the midst of other things: hearing his voice as she gave an injection, or did her washing; or as she relaxed, tired, after assisting at an operation. He belonged to the force fighting her country: the force whose aerial bombardment had killed God knew how many people. And more than that – he was a part of its spearhead. She knew this; but that knowledge was detached from her other, more personal knowledge: on that intimate level, he was just another damaged young man, and one she could not help liking.

She was in one way glad that other nurses could not speak his language: it increased his isolation, but it also locked him with her in a virtual country that could not be invaded. She wanted to heal him – to use her skills to build him into the man he should be – with a longing that was becoming too personal to be wise in a nurse. It had sneaked up on her, gripped her quietly with a strength that was now a threat. While she was concentrated on work she could forget him sufficiently to remain efficient, but the moment she relaxed, her thoughts flew to him, as though in a curious sense to her home, to the place where she naturally reposed.

Tim was not to know that she was beginning to feel a deeper loneliness when she was away from him, but he could not escape the suspicion that she was manufacturing opportunities to be with him. He became aware, too, that his looking forward to these times was no longer a matter merely of needing company. There was a freshness, a lift to his heart, that belonged to another level of human experience entirely. The dawning sense that life could, after all, take a new turn, one that would draw the sting of the past, converged now on Anna as on a focal point. He knew he would never forget Fay nor cease to love her; but he was like a man after a long and wintry trek entering a new sun-filled valley whose existence he had not suspected.

Barbara: Barbara had tried to bring him to this same place. Barbara the generous one, the one with the courage of joy. She had been a good friend and a pleasant companion, someone to admire. But the impact of her friendship had been nothing like this. Not that Anna was necessarily a better person or even a prettier one. There was no simple logic to it.

To be alone together for any time was nearly impossible in the hospital and in its grounds. But, very slightly, they began to flirt – wordlessly, by looks, if anyone else was in earshot, and by timid allusions if no one was near. In that infertile soil, the attraction grew, attended by an underlying pain because of the contradiction between it and their circumstances. Nothing intimate was said openly. They realised slowly, by osmosis, that they were falling in love, but each feared to speak of it – the thing was impossible. To remain silent was to pretend that neither the developing friendship nor its difficulties were real – and so to allow it a sort of limited life.

Even so, there were dangers. Tim was aware of them, Anna less so. Her Cordelia-like simplicity prevented her from noticing that among her colleagues some might be watching her very closely indeed. Greta already had an idea that she might become too attached to the British flier, and had restricted her access to the extent that she could.

But the attraction strengthened until for each it became an ache as though part of their soul had been snatched away. Inevitably this was more self-centred in Tim: the melancholy side of his temperament asserted itself more when he had no one else to speak to, and he had endless hours to brood. For her, the pain was purer, more simply a matter of loving.

One morning Berndt handed him a letter, half from his mother and half from his father. He read it many times that day and on days long afterwards. The relief that they knew, now, that he was alive, was immense – like the final lifting of a great burden to which he had become so accustomed that his conscious mind had ceased to notice it. He had not realised, until then, how much of his tension and chagrin had been due to concern for them. And he was given permission to write – once each month; the Red Cross would send the letters on.

His spirits, already rising, jumped upwards to a new level. It was soon afterwards that the next step was taken.

Anna wheeled him right to the back of the sanatorium buildings, where he had never been. It was, unusually, empty of other patients and staff. He found himself facing a broad expanse of lawn and trees surrounding a small lake. A low stone wall marked, as he guessed, the perimeter of the hospital property. Beyond that the ground evidently fell suddenly into an enormous valley, and in the far distance a great range of mountain peaks seemed to salute the sky.

It stirred something. Slowly it came together. At first he thought he was recalling an image from some film or even some dream, and then, as detail after detail slotted into place, he felt it was undoubtedly very like a place he had seen, but of course not the same. Against the convictions of common sense, he felt an increasing sense of *déjà vu*. His gaze wandered and his memory stirred to a shrub here, an oak there, a patch of lawn between. The shape of the body of water fitted a pattern he was recognising rather than encountering. Of course it was impossible but, bit by bit, the conviction grew that he had seen it before.

Yet it was different. The trees were larger, the flower-beds neater, the distant mountains lacked snow. And beyond that something vitally important was missing.

And as he continued to gaze, it leapt into his mind: what was missing was the loitering ladies and gentlemen – the colours of the gowns and parasols, the black of the frock coats and grey of the top hats, the elegance and grace and vivacity. He was seeing Willy's garden again. In an instant he was back in primary school. Almost hysterically, he began to laugh.

The spasm over, he looked at her face which had become anxious as she wondered what had happened to him. With excited, shining eyes he contained himself and asked: "Anna – do you know what this is? ... No, of course you couldn't ... "

She did not understand. She knew only that his wild excitement made something in her respond as she had not done before. Leaning to his face in the wheel-chair, she kissed him.

He took her face in his hands, and she kissed him again, and laughed as the arm of the wheel-chair hurt her when she tried to embrace him. He laughed too, and she then sat on the grass, holding his hand, leaning against his knee. He drew her and kissed her and knew that he must not do so again. Not then.

They sat close, knowing that they were in love and it had been admitted between them. He told her then of the garden which had captivated him as a child and of Willy and his parents. The war they had feared to mention receded even further – it became the fantasy, the unreal backdrop to the reality of their love, a bad dream from which they were awakening. Until now the memory of Greta's rebuke had prevented her from telling him the location of the hospital. Now that reservation seemed part of the nonsense world – of the mad illusion gripping humanity. She told him that they were a little south and east of Freiburg, which itself lies in the south-west corner of Germany, almost in France and almost in Switzerland, where a small area is elevated to around three thousand feet. The nearest village was Tannhofen and some thirty kilometres away was Donaueschingen – where, she told him, the Donau rises; it actually originated, she said, in a basin in the garden of the palace of Prinz Fürstenberg.

He was puzzled. "Donau?"

She laughed and hummed a few bars: "Da-da-da-dum, da-dum, da-dum ... "

He joined in her merriment: "Oh – the *Danube!*"

Had the river ever featured in a raid on which he had been the navigator, he might have reacted by being jerked back to the war. But it was too far south, and that association did not enter his mind – he thought only of the Strauss waltz.

"Is it really blue?"

She told him that when it was a clear mountain river it could be silver or grey or blue, and far downstream it was sometimes brown; but that even there it was blue to people who were in love, and she joked that now it was blue to her. She told him too of the nearby Titisee, into which their own garden lake dribbled, and the Feldberg, the local hill famous because from it the snow on the Alps was clearly visible.

After that morning they came here whenever her duties allowed, and though they were never again absolutely alone together for long, they snatched kisses and light caresses, and they kept their love a secret, and it was all the sweeter for that. But one day – they knew – one day, after all this unreal folly called the war, they would marry.

At times their bodies yearned to be closer, but he had been brought up a Catholic, she a Lutheran. Each of them was half-glad for the unconscious chaperoning of other patients in wheel-chairs and soldiers on crutches and hospital staff wandering not far away. And this wordless pact between them, in spite of its inevitable stress, added another dimension to their love.

Because he was excited, he did not notice the fear which attacked her when they took the plaster off his wasted leg for the last time and slowly got him walking. He had momentarily forgotten that, if he could walk, he could go to a POW camp.

They could not hug or say a proper good-bye. He was taken quickly, almost suddenly.

He never saw the town of Tannhofen. Enclosed for an hour in a covered truck he was aware that they were descending, slowly at times around hairpin bends and then moving fast. After that there was a long journey by train into a profound sense of loss.

CHAPTER 20

Liberation
(Germany, 1945)

After the bombing of Hildesheim all possibility of communicating with Anna ceased. Berndt was no longer willing to transmit her messages via the dentist. Those messages had sustained Tim over eighteen months of camp life. Without their support, he felt himself walking on the edge of a psychological pit – an absurdly enticing one. Gripped by anger and frustration, he knew that he could slide into despair.

He resorted to intense activity. He studied German, played volleyball, worked hard at every job that offered, and entered into the life of the camp as fully as he could. Sometimes wild thoughts of escaping and making his way to Anna flitted through his mind, but in sober reality he knew that the chance of success was zero. No: his job was to hang on, and to foster his own physical and mental health against the time when he could hope to be reunited with her.

One thing counted in his favour. As the particularly bitter winter of 1945 gave way to early spring, there was an increased restlessness in the stalag. At first it was felt subtly. Among the prisoners a cheerful energy began to assert itself, even though Red Cross parcels – the lifeline of camp existence – were no longer coming regularly. Small jobs, long regarded as tedious, were now done with something like enthusiasm. Often-mended and at times motley uniforms were brushed and pressed beneath blankets. A lightness in the step, a cockiness in the greeting, a satirical jibe about the food – these put new life into every-day interchanges between men who were far too used to each other's company. Even a renewed irritation with off-beat personal habits – with the man who splashed soapy water over others, or the man who finished every sentence with "d'y'see?" – was in one way a symptom of fresh vitality. It was as though some hibernating creature forgotten for ages beneath a vast snowscape was stirring. It could not be long now – that was the hope expressed again and again. Everyone knew that Germany had lost. The war was merely being played out like a hopeless chess game in which the loser will never consent to resign.

Yet there was a counter-current, an anxiety dampening these expectations. No one knew what the Germans would do when the end came. It was assumed that the Commandant would try to behave with propriety, but his authority was not absolute. These concerns became acute when the surrounding compounds were suddenly evacuated. The soldiers could be seen leaving in numbers that indicated they would not return. The Commandant would tell the Senior British Officer only that they were being moved to the West. Why, then, not the airmen? Someone started a rumour that a last, vicious penalty might be imposed on the "terror fliers". And, if it was, it would have to be something extreme – something that would leave no witnesses. A few worried kriegies proposed that they try to anticipate any such move by launching their own rebellious assault.

In the face of machine-guns and German discipline, they would have had no hope, and as it turned out, the rumour proved unfounded. On a May morning the stalag awoke to an eerie quiet. The accustomed sounds – banging mess tins, crunching boots, German voices bawling to line up for an *Appell* – were stilled. There was only the subdued noise of those few prisoners who always rose early, trooping to the latrines and wash-rooms the moment they were let out of their huts. The others began to stir restlessly, and those whose normal habit it was to stay in bed until the last possible moment began instead to throw off their blankets. In small groups they emerged to find the watch-towers emptied of guards and the gates swinging open. There was no sign of any grey uniform. Bemused, they moved around, hesitant to walk past the trip-wire that defined a forbidden margin inside the fence. It had become second nature not to do so, for the action would attract machine-gun fire. They stood, staring, unbelieving, unable to comprehend; then, slowly, a buzz of muttering built up and passed around and became a crescendo until everyone was laughing and shouting, and they went outside the camp into the region, a couple of hundred metres wide, that had been cleared of any vegetation that might give cover to an escaping prisoner. There they danced and joked and cried and rolled on the ground and ran around and brought each other down in rugby tackles for sheer unbearable joy.

When the Senior British Officer was called in his shirt-sleeves from his shaving-mirror to see the situation, he too stood as though dazed; and then sent the nearest man running for Dukes, his Warrant Officer Discipline. "What'd'you make of it, Mister?" he asked.

The Warrant Officer looked around, his gaze sweeping the camp from end to end, and at last he said: "It's a miracle, sir. It's actually happened! They've gone. The whole bloomin' lot! Scarpered. Gone AWL – in a manner of speaking."

"That's it!" The officer drew in his breath. "They've run. Get everyone paraded – everyone. Senior officers to report to me. At once. And mount a guard over the Jerry kitchens and any Red Cross supplies. Get men who can't be pushed around."

The command called for instant obedience. Yet Dukes hesitated. In managing men he was the expert. They were facing an unprecedented situation, a release from years of captivity, and he wondered whether it was wise to try to impose order

without first letting the mood play itself out. "Sir," he began –
but he was cut short, and that too was almost unprecedented.
"Bob, you know what I think this is about? I think the Jerries
took the army first and they meant to take us as well, but they
ran out of time. They've gone without much notice – and gone
to the West. Why would they do that?"

"Well, sir, there's only one thing in the East they'd run from.
The comrades."

"Yes. And they'd rather surrender to our chaps – or the
Yanks. They've jumped ship. That means the Russians must be
practically here – maybe today."

"You think we'll be liberated by Uncle Joe's men?"

"It looks that way. We must get the men on parade at once."

There was a moment's further hesitation. "Sir?"

The officer spoke impatiently. "Well?"

"These Ruskies. Unknown quantity. I've heard they're a wild
bunch. If we could follow the Jerry guards west ourselves we
might save a hell of a lot of red tape."

"*Red* red tape?"

"Well, yes, sir."

"We can hardly march through Germany hoping to meet a
doughboy tank. We don't know where the front is. It could take
weeks. And we've sick men. We can't stand here talking. Get
everyone paraded at once. And get that bloody food secured.
On the double, Bob!"

And that was the problem – information. They were working
in the dark, with no knowledge of what was happening outside
the camp. The SBO's immediate concern was that of preserving
some sort of order: he was determined to keep the men together
until they could be transported back to England. Particularly he
did not want them wandering out into any villages within easy
reach. After years behind barbed wire, various forms of mental

illness were certainly present, and some prisoners might simply disappear – deliberately or by accident. There were those who were quite capable of exacting revenge on any German man – or worse, any German woman – they met.

The Officers' conference was divided over the main question – to wait or to walk? If the Germans had left without a word, the Russians must be very close indeed, and the obvious course was to sit tight until they arrived. But when, or even whether, they would come could be doubted, and Warrant Officer Dukes' distrust of them was not without reason; it was even suggested that the prisoners might not be liberated, but held as hostages against the repatriation of Red Army soldiers who were rumoured to have defected. It could be safer to move carefully and steadily to the west.

In the end they compromised. The SBO summed up: "We'll send a dozen men out on a recce. German speakers, if possible. They'll have to be bloody careful. Stay in groups of three, back by fifteen hundred. We wait for their reports. But we only stay for two days – three maximum – after that the men will be too restless. In the meantime they're to be ready to move at thirty minutes' notice. All of 'em. Whatever basic kit they've kept or accumulated packed up and by their beds. We're not taking junk. But see whether you can scrounge some carts, bikes, wheelbarrows – anything that we might be able to use for transport. We'll need them for our worst sick. Keep a close eye on the men in your huts – anyone missing, tell me at once – wake me if necessary. WO Dukes reports the Huns have obligingly left a little food in their stores, we've some Red Cross supplies, and we might be able to detail a few chaps to scrounge some more from nearby farms or towns. Our cooks will be hard-pressed: volunteer some men who understand how to keep their hands clean."

When Tim pleaded to be allowed to stay behind to search for Anna, his superior was very logical. "Do you know where this woman is? How can find you her? How can you travel? Flag down a lorry? Are any still running? Don't speak German – not proper German, anyway. Why should anyone help you? More likely to attack you. Country must be in chaos. Even the Huns need papers to move about their own country – what have you got? Identity discs, paybook if you haven't lost it, that's all. You'd be in jail within two days. Back to England first, Rogers. Apply for compassionate leave. See if you can get some money, then work through this Doctor Berndt. Don't want you turning into a bandit robbing old ladies for your lunch. Hard enough now when we're all together."

"But sir," he countered, "Hildesheim's not a big place. Surely I could make my way there and ask around. Someone must speak English."

"No, Rogers, it's not some village with one-and-a-half streets. Personally I'd advise you to forget the whole business and go home and find an Australian girl. But if you're really bent on some quixotic search, you're going to need enough money for weeks, at least. I expect you'll be getting some back pay in Blighty."

Did money matter? Tim had only a little "Lagergeld" – the camp currency issued by the Germans – and a stock of cigarettes which might be accepted in small transactions. The SBO was right. The difficulties were appalling. It was crazy to take them on.

But in the midst of these reflections a new thought struck him like a blow. The Australian ex-prisoners might not be demobilised upon release; they might, instead, be sent to fight in the Asian-Pacific war. The possibility was obvious, but his mind had been so thoroughly focused on Anna that he had blotted it out. It would make things twenty times worse. To be so far from her, not as a free civilian, but navigating bombers again – it would be unthinkable.

To find Anna had become the driving force of his life. To deny it now would render tasteless any later successes – as though he had stepped out of the only game that mattered in order to play one that did not. The penalty for obeying the SBO could be a lifetime of regret. And worse – it would be to desert her after the risks she had taken for him.

He would have to go without permission. It was a fair bet that if he eluded the half-hearted watch now being kept by a few British soldiers, who after years of confinement had no stomach for becoming guards themselves, he would not be alone: some prisoners had no intention of knuckling under to military restrictions in what they regarded as, in everything but name, a post-war situation.

He would be going AWL. It would have to be done very quickly. More or less at once. The escape kit carried by all aircrew had been taken at Tannhofen but he was a navigator, there were stars, and he knew the general direction of Hildesheim from the camp – whose own location the Escape Committee had made common knowledge. He would have to go west-south-west.

He went to his hut and emerged with nothing to betray his intentions except bulging pockets stuffed with chocolate and cigarettes, and he walked nonchalantly around the compound, quietly observing. His watch said ten o'clock. Scouts had already been sent out on a reconnaissance mission and a couple of men were posted at the gate. He approached them and said, "When we were outside earlier I lost a wallet. It's important. I need to look for it. Back in an hour."

The sergeant shrugged. Strictly he should not let even anyone through. But in his opinion it was bloody stupid. Tim had a marginally higher rank than he did. He shouldn't be manning this bloody gate anyway. Turning into a bloody goon. What could anyone do, here in the bloody middle of bloody Germany? "I never saw you, Sarge."

Tim made a show of searching the ground, gradually moving further from the compound and nearer to the sparse forest beyond the cleared area. Every few minutes he glanced back furtively at the guards, and choosing a moment when the two men were staring away from him, he slipped into the trees.

He had seen the scouts departing earlier. They had moved

south-west. It was his only lead. He did the same.

He was surprised to find how quickly he tired. His limp was a by now a small handicap, a barely noticeable peculiarity of gait. But two years in Bomber Command followed by two in hospital and a POW camp had done little enough for his physical fitness. Remembering his basic training he forced himself to walk hard for fifty minutes, to rest for ten, and then to go on. He had not had the time, nor even the clarity of mind, to form a studied plan, and as he walked he wondered what to do. He could not get a train without German money. Perhaps he could change cigarettes for a ticket. Well, he had started. His thoughts swung this way and that, now telling him that his enterprise was worse than futile, now telling him that he could do nothing except go forward hoping for some favourable circumstance to emerge. But beneath every rational consideration was the driving undercurrent: he knew he would go on.

At first he was intensely alert. But increasingly he felt a light-headedness, almost as though he was drunk. There had been no food since yesterday. He staggered a little, and took a savage grip on himself.

Eventually his tiredness seemed to pass. Progress through the trees became easy, and easier still when he came on a small track. He followed it, and skipped his second rest. He came to a T-junction, where the track met a sealed road. Faced with the need to choose he turned right, towards the West. There was no traffic to speak of – some young boys walking in the opposite direction glanced curiously at him, and a little later a woman riding a bicycle did the same before suddenly accelerating. He wondered why, and then saw that in the tension of absconding from the camp he had neglected the most elementary of all precautions. Chagrined at his own unbelievable folly, he took off his battle-dress blouse and hung it over his shoulder with the insignia turned inwards. There was some small advantage in its Australian dark blue – an RAF uniform might have been even more instantly recognized – but probably the damage had been done. Those people would report him when they got to their destination. He looked constantly over his shoulder, ready to run off the road if a truck or car approached from behind him.

But it was from the other direction that trouble came. Breasting a hill he came without warning to the outskirts of a small town. Dead ahead were a few thatched cottages, and further on were terraced buildings clustered solidly around a square where two main streets intersected. He debated whether to skirt the place – so close to the camp, the inhabitants would be very conscious of escapers. But as he looked he was aware of something moving in the distance: smoke, travelling above the low horizon. There was a railway line, then, and it seemed to run roughly at right angles to the road he was on.

Ignoring the slight pain which vigorous exercise could still sometimes cause in his right leg, he ran to the square and paused at its entrance. Gasping and with a stitch, he leant a moment against a wall. Then, breathing deeply, he crossed the open space and saw a sign saying "*Bahnhof*". Forcing himself to a measured pace, he followed the arrow and passed into a much smaller square where he almost bumped into a group of loungers. There was a burly man leaning by a door, wearing the trousers and boots of a Wehrmacht soldier topped with a ragged high-necked sweater. Other men sat on walls and a stone bench. Several of them seemed to be staring at nothing, looking fixedly into the distance. The first man heaved himself off the wall. He moved into Tim's path, an arm's length away. Tim smelt the beer on his breath.

"*Kalt, Ja?*"

The words were friendly enough, but the tone was not. The man went on: "*Sie kommen nicht von hier. Wie heissen Sie?*"

Tim thought quickly: he could see smoke rising beyond the buildings ... the train was invisible ... it must be stationary ... if he ran ... no, he was too late. It was pulling out. He must say something. He searched desperately for German phrases. "*Ja, den Zug ich muss nachlaufen – jetzt.*"

His grammar was abominable and his accent worse. It could not be helped. He stepped aside to go past. The burly man was looking at the blouse under his arm. The others had by now dropped their lassitude and were taking an interest. One said, "*Stammlager – daher kommt er.*"

"*Nein,*"said the burly man; "*Durchgangslager der Luftwaffe.*" He moved directly back into Tim's path, silent, challenging. After a gap of several seconds he spoke. "*Terrorflieger? Sind Sie ein Terrorflieger?*"

"This is it," Tim thought. "This is the pay-back." He shrugged. He was tired of pretence. The frustration that had been smouldering flared, and a sort of recklessness surged in him. "Go to buggery," he said, and the Australian expression brought a satisfaction to his own ears.

"*Engländer! Sie sind ein Engländer! Sprechen Sie Deutsch?*"

"No," said Tim. "*Nein. Kein Engländer.* Australian."

The other approached close. "*Engländer!*" And he pushed Tim in the chest, advancing as he did so.

Tim retreated a half-step and then his anger snapped into an active force, concentrated, building somewhere behind his back, blinding him, pushing him forward. For some reason he thought of Alan, and of Jim Nolan. He charged into the man, not with any plan, careless of the outcome, fists flailing. There was a stab of pain in his knee. The two of them fell to the ground, wrestling and punching, neither having the space to do any real damage. In the midst of the struggle, Tim could hear the sound somewhere of running feet. They were close now. He felt strong arms encircle his neck and he was drawn backwards. Something – fists, feet, a club – crashed into his diaphragm. The pain seemed to go right through him, and he wondered whether he had been stabbed; it was not right that a simple blow could hurt so deeply. A red light spread in front of his eyes. He was on the ground, and something crunched into his shoulder. He realised that he was being kicked – on the side, the back. His neck seemed to snap forward, and the world dissolved

269

into something a little like sleep but much deeper, yet with a headache throbbing through it. He was two people: one, the one at his centre, was crumbling into nothingness; the other, detached, it seemed, not really belonging to him, was aware of the groaning of a siren. And then consciousness vanished completely.

He had been here before. When? Where?

Painfully it came back. He was in the hospital at Tannhofen. He had never left. There had been a long, vivid dream. About a POW camp. He heard a voice: "He's very restless." It was not Anna. Something bad had happened.

He inclined his head, and a surge of pain swept behind his eyes. There was nausea. Breathing seemed to hurt his chest – low down.

But behind the mist – was it Anna?

He tried to speak, but the effort was too great.

"Be quiet. You are in hospital. Rest. Rest."

He heard the voice rather than the words, and the sound reached him and made him happy. Pain did not matter. Anna was here, caring.

Then a measure of reality intervened. No, that was impossible. Through opening eyes he saw a large, long room, blurred but definitely not the hospital he knew. Some other clinical place – ugly two-tone walls, railings overhead, perfectly clean.

Two people. A nurse in uniform. Not Anna. There was someone else a little behind her, a tall, thin, moustached man in uniform. With an effort he focussed. An RAF uniform. The SBO became clear, present.

He was speaking. "Can you hear me, Sergeant Rogers?"

Tim began to nod, and stopped as his eyes seemed to hit his skull. He managed a croaking whisper, surprised by the weakness of his own voice. "Sir?"

"This isn't much good. When can I talk to him?"

"Come back this afternoon, *Herr Oberst*. Late ..." There was a moment's hesitation, and the speaker continued: "I have a request, also. Perhaps, if the Americans come you can get us morphine. You know our supplies are low."

"I will see what I can do. There may not be much time."

The blurring returned. They all receded. It all did not matter. Anna was holding his hand. He was tired. He dozed.

"*Herr Feldwebel*. Wake up." He looked at her, fully awake. With an effort that hurt his side, he raised an exploratory arm to his head. He felt bandages. There was something about his neck. A collar of some sort.

There was someone else. An English officer.

"Can you talk now, Rogers?"

He found that he could, though his throat felt as though it had been sandpapered.

"Yes, sir."

"Good man. Can you tell me what happened?"

"I was jumped, sir."

"What were you doing in the town?"

Tim had no answer.

"You say you were jumped. Not that surprising, is it? What the hell were you doing – trying to start World War Three before Two had finished?"

Tim could think of nothing to say.

"Don't ever take up poker, Rogers. All right, I'll tell you. It's that girl of yours, isn't it? I've already told you – now listen to me: I don't have time for this kind of caper. You're in the local hospital – the German police brought you here and, not knowing what to do with you in the circumstances of a war about to finish, sent a delegation to the stalag. We expect to be liberated any moment. What you tried to do was stupid. Our goons might have given up, but this country is crawling with ex-Hun soldiers and SS units who'll still be fighting like hell, and in a week or two it'll be lousy with our own bloody MP's and Yank and Russian ones. And you're a bloody deserter. A fugitive. How the hell can that help your girl? She'll have to hide you. Half the camp knows you want to marry her. Well, instead of that you'll be the biggest burden she's ever had! And at the very moment when you might be able to do something legitimately if you've a little bloody patience!

"Now – the doctors have told us you can move: no bones broken except for a hairline crack in a rib, no serious internal bleeding. Concussion's slight, no brain injury – you'll just have to cope with that. You'll be back with us this afternoon – fit or not. In the meantime, there are two airmen outside this ward who will see that you behave."

With an effort Tim spoke again. "D'you reckon I'll be able to get back to Germany, sir? I've got to find Anna. And I'm afraid they might send me to fight in the Pacific."

"Hell, Rogers! You're bloody incorrigible!"

He turned to go, but stopped at the door and looked back. "Is that what's worrying you? I don't think it'll last that long. We've all been here a long time, and I understand what you did. I'm not going to report it – this time. Don't try to bugger off again or I will."

He paused and spoke again. "Come back, Tim. It's your best chance. Your only one, damn it. Come back with us. We'll fix it somehow."

It was perhaps the hardest decision Tim had ever made, and it as much as the beating left him exhausted. But in the end he admitted to himself – yes, the SBO was right.

And in one way it freed him: he had half-neglected the news and the gossip that was all around him, but now he listened avidly. Okinawa and Luzon had fallen to the Americans. The British were advancing in Burma. It would take several months to repatriate men like himself and then get them to these theatres. No one knew how much longer the war would last, since Japanese resistance was still incredibly determined, but it seemed extremely unlikely that he would be sent. That part, at least, of his mind relaxed. Another question remained: could he apply for demobilisation while remaining in Britain? He was not sure. But one thing he knew: if they ordered him back to Australia before he could return to Germany, the ship would sail without him.

The camp was in fact liberated by Americans, a day before the Russians arrived from the other direction. Almost at once an airlift of ex-prisoners began, the men huddled on the floors of bombers stripped of armaments and bound for clearing camps in Britain or France.

Part 5: Aftermath

CHAPTER 21

Repatriation
(Britain, 1945)

The transition from stalag life could be abrupt. In a clearing camp at Eastbourne ex-prisoners were examined medically, deloused, given new uniforms, demobilised and dismissed. Some stayed longer, some were sent to hospitals or convalescent homes. For these the camp, set up in principally the interests of order, functioned incidentally as a halfway house.

Tim was referred to a clinic which confirmed what the German doctors had said: his skull was intact, no bones were broken, he had suffered internal bruising but there was no sign of rupture. In the tedious periods of waiting demanded by the battery of blood and other tests, he spent the time writing home, reading paper-backs, and planning how to get back to Germany. He wrote to Berndt care of "The Hospital, Tannhofen", but he had little hope of a reply. He was able now to tell his parents of things that he could not have risked the German censors seeing – above all, of Anna; and, hoping they would understand, he unfolded the whole story.

During this period he had a recurring dream. In it he could see but could not hear a Lancaster caught in the beams of several searchlights, struggling to escape. Flak was bursting around it. Smoke streamed from an engine and there was an explosion. As in a film the scene shifted. A wide pattern of bombs falling on a city. As their trajectories curved towards the target their noses slanted down and their fins wagged in what seemed mockery. But no, they were dumb things, only obeying the laws of physics: the scaffolding of the universe – turned now to destroy, to serve this madness. Where they fell they started pinpoints of light that grew into one great fire.

He woke sweating. *Was* it necessary – *was* it even justifiable? Alan had believed so, honestly. So had many others who had sacrificed their lives. He himself had been persuaded – enough to act, but not enough ever to be at peace. And now ... did Germany have to be crushed for Nazism to be defeated?

Well, it was over. But not the dreams. Mercifully they were fading. One thing he knew – he would not do it again – not in any circumstances.

The clinic sent him back to Eastbourne with orders to rest pending a final check-up; and it dawned on him now that he had been a fortunate prisoner. Unlike most airmen, he had escaped interrogation. Unlike most soldiers, he had not been transported for days on end crowded in cattle trucks or goods wagons with no sanitary facilities except buckets. Bad as his food had been he was not, unlike some of the worst cases, little more than a walking skeleton. Above all he had missed the horror marches in the winter of '45, when men had died of cold, malnutrition, illness or even bullets as they walked and stumbled westwards through hundreds of frozen miles to holding camps at Fallingbostel or Moosburg.

During those marches men had absconded. They simply had walked across Germany, stealing or begging food from houses and farms, continuing until they met Allied troops or even until they reached Belgium where they were given lifts on ships. Learning their stories made him wonder whether, with more luck, he might have succeeded in his effort to remain in Germany until he could find Anna.

He had been in this limbo for a week when letters addressed

277

to him came in a bunch. Some had been sent to the stalag and forwarded by the Red Cross, others had gone directly to his service address in Britain and made their way through a bureaucratic maze which was surprisingly efficient. He found himself answering questions from home that were seven or eight months old. He wrote too to Willy, for he learnt that his old friend had at last been released and reunited with Margaret, and that they had returned to their home in Walgabran; but he experienced an almost superstitious reluctance to mention that his hospital had been the one whose garden the German had painted on the school wall – perhaps because until he found Anna again it was somehow an incomplete story, one which might easily end in failure.

And now, at last, he received news from his father of the men who had bailed out of the Halifax ahead of him. Bruce, Don and Tony had managed to remain in contact. Over six days they survived on their escape rations, crossing the Rhine in a stolen boat. They were caught and taken to Strasbourg and held briefly in a special section of an ordinary jail. But an Allied air-raid came at just the right moment, attacking the railway yards as they were being marched from a covered truck to a train bound for Germany. A bomb fell close enough to make prisoners and guards dive for cover, and before the dust had settled Bruce had grabbed Don's hand and with Tony following they were running, pursued by confused shouts that died in the darkness. It took them another four days to get into France where, starving and at dead of night, they knocked on the door of the priest's house in a small mountain village. They did not know how they would be received; as it turned out, the curé put them in touch with a "link" – part of a chain of people who, at constant risk to their own lives, passed allied airmen on to the next link and the next and so on until, if they were very lucky, they might reach a neutral country. They were eventually smuggled across the Swiss border, where, since they were not now "evaders" but "escapers", they were interned until the end of the war – but in the considerable comfort and relative freedom of what was, in effect, an Allied club. Tony, in fact, enjoyed this enforced holiday so greatly that he courted and won a local girl and took out Swiss citizenship. He was still there, happily married.

Tim was cheered immensely to learn this. Even more important, his fears of being sent home to fight in the Pacific were finally quelled. Troopships were hard to come by, and Commonwealth ex-POWs could expect to be stranded in Britain for months. They had little to do, and leave was readily given. Thousands roamed Britain on extended holidays with their pockets full of back pay.

Leave, however, was one thing. Permission to go back to Germany was something else. It certainly could not be obtained at Eastbourne.

"It isn't what you know but who you know." The highest-ranked person in Britain with whom Tim could claim any personal contact was Group Captain Thomas, the station commander at Netherholme; but he had a remote quality. "Naughty" would be more approachable. After his check-up in the second week he handed the Commanding Officer his certificate of fitness and headed for Norwich.

He passed through London, and old memories flooded back as from the train window he gazed at elegant squares and grimy streets, all half in ruins. When he telephoned from Norwich railway station, he was warmly invited to visit the base at Netherholme the following morning at eleven. This meshed neatly with his plans; for there was another errand he looked forward to and at the same time shrank from.

Close to half of the men he had known in his flying years had died, and it was only too likely that his friends at Little Coring had followed. This fear had dogged him ever since his capture. It was a minor but persistent theme in the turmoil of his emotional life, largely submerged under his obsession with Anna but never wholly forgotten. The apprehension was irrationally deepened when a new letter from home, arriving just before he left Eastbourne, contained bad news: his boyhood friend Ken was lost, his ship sunk in the Indian Ocean. The nearer Tim got to the fighter station the more he was attacked by an absurd pessimism. At the end it took him a conscious effort of will to direct his steps through the gate.

"Strike me bloody hooray! George!"

Reg Billingsly stood on the tarmac, his head framed by the propeller-blades of a Hurricane and his legs braced apart. He looked steadily at the lean figure walking towards him, and called out again, "George! It's him!"

A voice called from the cockpit of the aircraft. "Who?"

"*Him*, y'r birk. Tim! Tim Rogers!"

"*What?*"

George emerged and dropped to the ground, and the two of them watched Tim approach. Reg coo-eed, and Tim answered. Then they were embracing, laughing, back-slapping and swearing in that Australian way that expresses affection.

"Shick tonight, boy! We're getting full tonight."

"Just one night," said Tim. "I've a story to tell."

"I bet y'r have. We've got a few, too. But yours first, y'old bastard!"

Tim was flooded with relief and surprise to see them alive. He had made the mistake of translating a fear into a near-certainty. To his further astonishment, he discovered within seconds that both had accepted the offer of staying temporarily in the service. George explained: "Most chaps want to get out quickly, and that suits the Royal Air Force. But they still need people for odd jobs. Mainly we're delivering superannuated aircraft around – the RAF's flogging them. Won't last, of course."

"So what'll you do when it runs dry?"

"Well, for me it's back to accountancy. Remember that? It's still my real job. Not for Reg. He wants to fly – something in civil aviation."

"And I'm not waiting too long," put in Reg. "Soon all those jobs will be gone. There's a lot of good pilots with nowhere to go."

Tim did not even hear Reg. Excited at what George had told him, he asked: "You can't get a flight to Germany – with room for me?"

"Well – so far it's been Portugal and Turkey and Finland. What the hell do you want to go back to Germany for? I'd have thought you'd have had enough of the place."

Tim told him the story.

"My word," said Reg when he had finished, "A Hun girl. That's one for the books."

"I've got to get to Germany to find her. I'll start in her home town. If that's no good I'll try to get back to the hospital. A search like this could take – forever, I guess. Every day I can save ..."

"At the moment there's nothing."

"I suppose it was a crazy hope. Well, tomorrow I'm seeing my old Wingco. Maybe he can help somehow. Can I bunk here overnight?"

"No worries. But the rest of your crew – you still don't know what happened?"

Tim hesitated: "Four of us bailed out. I lost contact. I heard just last week – they made it to Switzerland. The other three couldn't have survived. Alan was the pilot – we were kids together."

These words were dredged up from some deep place. George could see that Tim was tired in a way that had little connection with sleep. And he merely replied, "Let's all go out."

The trio descended on the smaller of Little Coring's two pubs where they ate, drank and talked for hours and then, returning to the station, yarned on with no thought of bed. They broke up at four in the morning, half-seas over. Bleary-eyed a few hours later, they piled into the old Austin and departed in a cloud of dirty exhaust as Reg drove Tim to meet his deadline of eleven am. It was on the way back, when they were alone, that Reg asked George: "This *Fräulein* – what d'yer reckon?"

"Sounds wonderful!"

"Sure?"

"Sure I'm sure – you remember how he was over Fay. Maybe this has cured him."

"If it works. Look – how well does he know the girl? A few months in hospital – that's all they've shared. He's an incurable romantic. And people can do silly things – about marriage, I mean."

"Well, at least in some ways she's seen him at his worst. Probably had to hold the basin while he vomited. *She* won't have too many illusions."

"That doesn't count. It's not real life."

"I think we should leave it to him. He's a big boy now."

"I guess ... "

At Netherholme Tim found the station a sort of ghost town, with most of the airmen gone. Nordale, however, was still there with a skeleton staff, "mopping up", as he put it. Poker-faced, he looked up from the papers on his desk. Suddenly Tim felt foolish. What help, really, could he expect here? But he saluted smartly and said, "Sir."

The CO, for his part, had not forgotten what he had once referred to as Tim's "moping", and he assumed that a POW camp would have made it worse. He was surprised to find the opposite. Young Rogers, he saw, was thin and weary but he had a new energy about him. It was a little unexpected that he was paying this courtesy visit. Probably he wanted something.

"Good to see you again, Rogers." For some minutes the talk dwelt on the crash of Tim's Halifax and on shared memories. They recalled men they had known, those who had survived and those who had died and those were still simply "missing".

Hardened by two years of squadron life, where one coped with the comment on the notice-board, the stranger who filled the vacant place, by not becoming too close, Tim was surprised now to feel a pressure of tears behind his eyes. Only yesterday his feelings had seemed frozen when he had spoken of Alan, Phil and Ron, and they were much closer to him. He shook his head as though he could literally shake the subject away, and asked about his ground-staff, but Nordale had barely known them. There was a silence. At length the Wing Commander said, "I won't ask you what it was like over there – I've heard too many stories. Well, what're you going to do now?"

Tim had said nothing about travelling to Germany. Worried that the CO might regard his romance as close to traitorous, he had hoped somehow to avoid the subject; but try as he would, he could think of no way around it if he was to ask for help. He took the bull by the horns.

"Sir – I have a favour to ask – a very big one. There's a friend I want to find."

"Glad to be of assistance if I can."

Tim swallowed: "Sir, this friend – she's in Germany. She's from Hildesheim."

"*What?*"

"In Germany, sir. You know I was six months in a hospital there. Well, she nursed me."

"You mean a *German*, Rogers? A German *woman?*"

"Sir, she wasn't a Nazi. She hated the war. And sir, I want to marry her. I was hoping that you could get me permission to travel there. You see, I don't know where she is now – or how to contact her."

Nordale stared, then threw back his head and roared laughing. "I didn't think you had it in you, Rogers. But this sounds mad. If I *can* help you – which I doubt – how will you manage over there? By all accounts there's not even much food – I don't suppose you can drop into a café any time you want a meal."

"I've been told that, sir. But – do you think there's a chance?"

"Probably not." Nordale paused a minute, musing, then seemed to come quickly to a decision. Young Rogers had had a bad time, and if he was showing a bit more get up and go now, the CO did not wish to dampen it. But some realism was needed.

"Well, look, I can give you some gen. Some of it's good. It's not hard to *get* to Germany – there's endless air-traffic, mainly American. The Yanks have the petrol. And they're either fiercely strict about rules or very easy-going – depends who you strike. Plenty of the second kind – chaps who'd give you a lift."

The words implied that all would be well. Tim relaxed – just a little. The Wing Commander went on: "And some of it's bad. This business of chasing your nurse around the country – difficult, Rogers, difficult. Damned difficult, in fact. With your military papers and with a valid leave-pass, you won't need a passport. And provided you give advance notice you may be able to eat and stay at Allied military establishments. But fraternisation with Germans by the Occupying Forces is out. In fact it's a military crime. The Americans are even forbidden to speak to German children. I don't think there's any way you'd get compassionate leave for your personal quest."

"A crime?" Tim's discipline cracked. "That's mad, sir – that's – that's absolute bullshit!"

Ignoring the slip into vulgarity the clipped voice continued: "Rogers, you were a good navigator, good in the air, but on the ground you brooded, didn't mix terribly well. Something's happened to you – something good. Maybe it's this *Fräulein*. I like your new approach. I think I should help you to carry it on.

"Now, look. You can't go charging into foreign countries without proper arrangements like some hitch-hiker. What you need is an official reason for gallivanting about Germany – and even for staying here, for that matter. And there's just a chance I can get you one. But it'll tie you down in the Air Force for another year or two."

"But sir – I've got to find Anna – I mean, I've got to find her now, not in two years!"

"Sergeant Rogers, *sit down!*"

Surprised, Tim hesitated momentarily.

"Come on, lad. Sit!"

Tim did so, and at the same moment Nordale stood.

"Hear me out. If I can get you into the scheme you'll probably have a better chance."

"Sir – what scheme?"

"Searching. It's run by a Canadian – Maclaurin – he's a group captain now, and among his new jobs there's something I think you'll find interesting. He wants men to help him. They'll go in pairs, or threes, and they'll fan out through the continent, looking for evidence of fliers who went missing. Families need to know what happened to their husbands, sons, brothers. These chaps – there won't be many – will collect everything they can. It'll be pretty – well, depressing – work, I fear. But it's important. How do you fancy yourself as a detective? If you're interested, I'll ask Mac to consider you."

Tim felt dazed. "But sir – I need to go to Germany at once."

"I hadn't finished, Rogers. If he accepts – if, mind you – I may even be able to dream up some excuse for a quick prior trip to our base in Hanover: interviewing someone there with special knowledge, that sort of thing. Two or three weeks. It's only an hour or two away from Hildesheim. Should give you a start, at least."

"But – didn't you say that we're not allowed to fraternise with Germans?"

"The occupation forces aren't. You wouldn't be part of them. You'd be well advised not to chatter in the wrong quarters about your lady friend, of course."

Tim could not believe that "Naughty" was doing this for him. Yet it was not enough. "Sir – it still wouldn't solve my problems. Even if I can find Anna in two weeks – well, you're suggesting that then I leave her again – come back to do this job. I don't know if I can do that. If I can't get leave now I think it might be better to get demobbed and go as a civilian. Then I'll be free."

"Can you do that – get demobbed – without going home first?

285

I don't know what arrangements the Australians have. Might be easier if you had a commission."

"I think so, sir. They're only sending us home because they assume that's what everyone wants. Overseas Headquarters London could discharge me and the Australian High Commission would get me a passport – I hope."

"Well, of course, if you decide that's best. I don't know how long it would all take. You realise there wouldn't be anything I could do for you in that case."

"No. I see that, sir."

There was a depressed silence. Then Nordale sighed. "What were you before you joined up?"

"I worked in a bank in Queensland. I'd started studying accountancy."

"How far did you get?"

"Six months."

"So – you'd barely started. You have some experience working at a relatively junior level in an Australian bank and no other qualifications except those of a navigator. You want to go to a foreign country choc-a-bloc with refugees and half-starved citizens competing for work that isn't there, a country that will be in absolute chaos for years, and marry a girl and set up a family – and I suppose you don't even know the language. What sort of job do you think you will get in those conditions?"

In Tim's memory a remote nerve was touched. Maguire in Brisbane; the SBO in the stalag; even, in a way, Willy … Older men had given him this sort of advice before – they had all said something similar – and he was fed up with it.

"Bloody hell, sir!" he exclaimed, "I can't just give up! Anyway, I'd hope to take Anna to Australia – or even stay here."

"Have you asked her to do that?"

"No, sir."

"Rogers, no one's suggesting that you give up. But you really *do* need to think longer-term. If you join Maclaurin's crowd, it's a job, and the experience might help you in civvy street afterwards. For what it's worth, it's what I'd do in your position."

Nordale was prepared to go well out of his way to help – that much was clear. And the work he spoke of *was* interesting: when Tim let himself seriously consider it, it drew him at once. At Eastbourne he had felt fortunate to have escaped the brutalities experienced by some prisoners; now, talking with Nordale, remembering the men they had reminisced over, remembering especially Alan, Bruce, Ron, he felt fortunate merely to be alive. The relief was mixed with something like guilt. This work – it was a little like giving something back to those who had not survived as he had.

And if he wanted to marry Anna – a job, any job, *would* help.

But the bloody delay! Again!

Nordale was speaking: "Sleep on it, man. Come back at fourteen-hundred tomorrow."

"Sir."

"You have somewhere to stay?"

"I have some old friends near here – fighter boys at Little Coring. I can stay for a few days."

"Oh, yes. Featherstone's the CO. Good man. Two o'clock, Rogers."

That night Tim intended to discuss the offer with George and Reg. But before he could begin George excitedly forestalled him. "Just hold on to your seat. There's a chance I could be asked to take an old Swordfish to Zurich. Can't think why the Swiss want it – they can hardly go dropping torpedoes in Lake Lucerne. But anyway I'll know on Friday. It's slow as a wet weekend, and the cockpits are open, but it'll take three and it'll fly a thousand miles. The flight plan cuts off a bit of Germany, near Strasbourg. I can put you down. Be like the old days. I could drop you, of course, but after your last experience with a parachute I doubt you'd be too keen."

287

"Like the old days …" What could George mean? Certainly not Brisbane. Was he referring to his Special Operations jobs? Suggesting a clandestine landing? If anything went wrong – especially any damage to the aircraft – his career in the Air Force could be finished. The opprobrium could follow him even into accountancy. Tim couldn't accept.

"Impossible, mate. Anyway, that's Black Forest country – trees, hills, gullies. You can't land a Swordfish on a split-level cow-paddock. In the war you had a Lizzie. And you had a strip marked out."

"Dunno about that. Fleet Air Arm landed them on tin-pot carriers that started life as merchant ships. But anyway, I don't mean sneak in. Do the whole thing above board. Find a proper airfield. Ask the Zurich people if we can stop at Colmar, Karlsruhe – they won't object. Neither will Featherstone. Only add ten minutes to my journey, not even out of my way. Piece of cake."

Tim was restless, the prospect was tempting, it was immediate. But there was still Nordale's offer. He told them of it. To his surprise it was Reg who agreed with Nordale. "Well – maybe you'll impress her relatives more as a flight sergeant in good standing than as an unemployed civilian drifter."

"Or maybe they'll see me as a *Terrorflieger.*"

"Yeah – hell of a choice. But Germans do like uniforms."

Group Captain Maclaurin was the image, almost the caricature, of an RAF officer. Short, stocky, with a bristly moustache and a merry facial expression that one could guess concealed a formidable toughness held just a little in reserve.

It was a slight shock to hear him speak – in a mellow Canadian accent.

"Wing Commander Nordale recommends you, Flight Sergeant. That means a lot."

"Thank you, sir."

"Well, I've looked at your record. You did a good job. And for this work it helps that you were shot down yourself – puts you in the club, as it were. Do you speak German, by any chance?"

"Some, sir. It's pretty slight, really. Attended classes in the camp for well over a year, though."

"Well, it's something. French?"

This was beginning to go badly. "Schoolboy stuff, sir. I'm sure some of it has stuck."

"Yes – enough to get a cup of coffee, I suppose. But real people don't talk like text-books. Dutch? No? Oh, well, hardly anyone speaks Dutch. Except the Dutch, of course. Pity."

He paused, musing over some papers. Then he said: "I would expect the local authorities to lend you every assistance, though. And in Germany you could get help from the occupation forces – they'll have people who can interpret."

Tim breathed a silent sigh of relief. He seemed to have been accepted. But then Maclaurin commented, "Nordale says something about "preliminary" leave. Bit of an odd request, isn't it? I'm sure you need a rest – to get back on your feet, as it were. But he seems to want me to accept you in the scheme and then give you leave *before* you've actually started."

Once again, there was no help for it. Tim told his story. When he had finished, the group captain asked questions about the hospital and its staff and about life in the prison camp, showing far more interest than Tim had expected. "But," he said finally, "I don't know about this notion of special leave. If I take you on you'll be expected to toe the line. You can't waste time running all over Germany at the British tax-payer's expense."

"Sir – I'd take the job seriously. I realise its importance. But – I really need this chance. And you just said I'd need a rest before starting work. I'd waive that rest. I'd go at once. If I could have just a couple of weeks – right away …"

Maclaurin looked at him steadily, then again at Nordale's letter, reading carefully. He leaned back. Tim sensed that this was the moment when everything hung in the balance. "Look, Sergeant, you do seem determined. You've got something in your belly – I'll say that. I hope it's the right stuff. I'm going to take a chance. You're in."

Tim wanted to shout. But he said in a controlled way, "Wonderful, sir."

"Now – about this leave. In a way it could be a practice run, and I suppose that incidentally you might find something of use to us. I expect you to be alert for anything of the sort, and before you go I'll do my best to get you the particulars of men who didn't come back from that Hildesheim raid.

"But that's not why you're going. You could have a hell of a task sorting it all out – finding your friend, working out how the two of you will proceed ... if at all ... I'll be interested to see how you do. You'll start at the *Rathaus*, of course. That's where the Huns have their *Einwohnermeldeamt* – their residents' registration office. But the records could be destroyed; or they could refuse to co-operate. After all, they have to be careful: there are people looking for other people all over the shop now, and some of them have nasty intentions. What then? You seem to think you can just go and ask around. The city isn't *that* small – fifty thousand, maybe. And that's only your starting-point. You might have to travel. Most rail yards and lines are already repaired – you have to hand *that* to them – but the trains'll be crowded. It will be pot luck ... and this is an affair of the heart – unpredictable. You could get tangled in a network of vague leads that would never end. That is *not* to happen. However it goes – Rogers, *however* – I want you back here – three weeks, absolutely on the dot."

"Sir, Wing Commander Nordale mentioned the possibility of liaising with our people in Hanover."

"Forget Hanover. When you get back you'll be assisting a squadron leader. He'll be your immediate chief, answerable only to me. You'll have a car – be careful of petrol – and you'll go to a town, a village. Present yourselves to the Mayor, the police, churches – the parishes should have their own records of burials. Show them your credentials. Ask whether they know anything. See whether you can interview likely citizens, local farmers, anyone that can help. Don't be too naive – it's always possible that someone salvaged something from a kite and wants to keep it quiet. Keep your eyes open. Follow things up."

He paused. "You may run into all sorts of things. Be careful. For all we know, some of our men may have been murdered. It could get sticky. Questions?"

Tim had a sudden inhibition. "Damn it!" he felt. "Not now!" But the mention of murder raised an issue he hadn't thought of, and if he didn't voice it now he never would.

"Sir – I'm prepared to do everything I can to find what happened. But I'm not a policeman. If I unearth, say, evidence of a betrayal, I'm not prepared to hand anyone over to French or Dutch reprisals – whatever they've done."

Maclaurin looked up: "You *do* want this job?"

"Desperately, sir. It's just that I – I was brought up with a strong Christian perspective, maybe my own take on it – I don't believe in vengeance. Ever since something that happened when I was a kid. Anyway, I don't think we can stand in judgment. I reckon they're all victims – those that were caught by the Germans and those that let the secrets out. At least they took damn horrible risks in the first place."

The Canadian looked at him steadily for a long moment. Then he shrugged. "I don't suppose I want anyone hanged because he cracked under pressure or when his family was threatened, Rogers."

"Yes, sir. But even if it wasn't that – if it was for money – or a Frenchwoman with a German soldier – I couldn't turn them in. Not to the vigilantes or to the law."

"You take this 'not judging' pretty far, don't you?"

"Yes, sir."

Again a pause. Then, "All right. I suppose I do agree. But I expect you to tell *me* of anything you find relevant to our work."

"Yes, sir."

"Very well."

Breathing another sigh of relief, Tim was again struck by a possibility he had not yet envisaged. "Sir, what about my own Halifax? I told you we were hundreds of miles off-course – badly shot up, and our skipper could hardly steer, so we came down somewhere near a place called Tannhofen in the south-west corner of Germany. At least, that's where I was put in hospital. Two of our crew came from my home town. Our sparks and our gunners got away – I know that from letters from home. But I don't think the others got out. Could I try to find our plane?"

Maclaurin considered a moment, his lips pursed, before he answered: "I don't think so, Rogers. I understand you'd want to, but – look, we've all seen hellish things in this war, but I don't know about this. You'd be too close to anyone still there. I don't think the psychiatrist chappies would advise it."

"Sir, know a couple of people – I mean German people – over there, in a way. There was a Hauptmann Platt I saw in the hospital. Bit stiff, but he didn't seem a bad type. The medico in charge was a good man – it might seem funny to say that, but he was. And one time he told me that what was left of a plane had been found. He said three men had been captured, but I never heard any more."

"Well – I suppose that you will be within striking distance anyway – a hundred miles or so … late in the war the south-west *was* bombed. And no one else will be able to do it …

"Look, Rogers: it's worth checking. You may find something. But about your own aircraft – I want your chief to conduct any close investigation – not you, Rogers. Repeat not, emphasise not. I mean that – and I'll tell him the same. Now – I want you here at oh-eight-thirty tomorrow morning ready to sign some papers. And we'll get this leave organised. I'll try to find you some transport. You don't want to spend a week getting there."

"As a matter of fact I think I already have transport, sir. I'd rather not say too much about it."

Tim felt he could *hear* a tense reaction. The pause was ominous. Then Maclaurin smiled. "Hidden depths in you, Rogers. All right. Initiative is what I want.

"And – I think I'd like you to get some promotion. I'm sure it'll be approved. You'll get more co-operation from everyone with a commission. Congratulations, Pilot Officer Rogers."

Shocked, Tim stammered his thanks. Maclaurin grinned openly. "Now go and take the day off."

Tim said to George: "Mate, that Swordfish. Are you taking it? I've three weeks' leave – official. It'll be legal and above board!"

"I'm going tomorrow. Coming? I'll need to ring Zurich at once if you are."

A far memory floated into Tim's mind – a small aeroplane flying over the school, and him dropping a catch.

Those wonderful old, old machines.

Aircraft had changed beyond recognition. But – a Swordfish! It was almost one of them.

He smiled. "Try and stop me."

"Wonderful! But how'll you get back?"

"I'll ask the Yanks."

"Why not go both ways with them? A lot more comfortable."

"This'll be quicker. And – you know, I've always wanted to fly in a – a *real* plane."

293

CHAPTER 22

Tim's Search
(Germany, 1945)

Tim had flown to Germany many times and seen little. Droning through the night twelve thousand feet above the earth he had been able to glance through the forward turret or the side ports, but mostly into a dark nothingness, at times relieved by the play of the moonlight on clouds. To cover the same ground in the Swordfish took twice as long, but the height was halved and it was daylight, and the view of the ground was limited only by the lower wing and by the discomfort of peering over the side in a slipstream laced with the smell of oil. The fragile aircraft had an intimacy, and Tim surrendered to its charm as he ignored the cold and stared at the fields of Belgium which, a generation earlier, had been blasted into a lifeless landscape; and which twice in the last five years had again been the scene of untold human tragedy.

They put down for lunch at Namur; but Tim fretted at every moment's delay, and George laughed as he gave the pilot's seat to Reg and they took off less than an hour after landing. Four hours later, tired and cramped at Karlsruhe, his friends packed Tim into a train which would cover half of Germany before meeting the branch line to Hildesheim. He had no chance of a sleeping-car, and propped on a seat he dozed a little and woke often, turning quickly away from the faces that met his eyes whenever he stirred. The faces of a defeated nation. As an Allied airman – for he was still in uniform – he had expected enmity, perhaps even violence; but he encountered only silence.

He felt a deep loneliness, and for the first time allowed to surface in his mind the repressed fear that what he was doing was crazy. Fiercely he drove it from his thoughts. It was a barking dog, harmless, to be ignored.

Steadying himself against the rocking of the train, he washed and shaved early, and at the station he had some *ersatz* coffee and thin slices of stale bread whose sawdust taste took him back to the stalag. He looked eagerly for his first glimpse of the town that had nurtured Anna. Neither large nor small, it was a nodal meeting-point for road and rail. But he was not prepared for the impact of his first sight of a bombed German city from the ground. Well over half of the buildings had been damaged or destroyed by the series of raids culminating in the heaviest attack in March of 1945. Much of the old city centre was flattened.

Shock and fear for Anna gripped Tim anew. Under a late summer's sky, using the crude German he had learnt as a prisoner, he at length found the *Rathaus* and spoke to an official who, in answer to his request, delved into papers in a back office and returned triumphant. Unlike the passengers on the train, this man was chatty and helpful. Moreover, his English was much better than Tim's German.

About the men that Maclaurin reported as missing after the raid, he had no news at all. Tim could try the police station. But the Bauer family – which Bauers? It was not an uncommon name. Oh, there was a daughter Anna, about twenty-two? And at least one sister? Let me see – yes, there was a record of such a family. Frau Bauer had died in the raid. Herr Bauer had survived, but he had been badly injured. His lungs had been affected by the smoke; he had, in any case, been a sick man. The girl Anna? They could make enquiries. Of course the old address no longer existed – living not far away, the official had seen the street himself and noticed a particularly large crater at number twenty-seven – but there would be someone: cousins, friends, acquaintances. Perhaps those people knew where she was. In theory anyone who moved was obliged to inform the authorities; but in these times … so much of the city had been obliterated … perhaps half of the citizens were homeless … and the gentleman must understand that there were many enquiries, they were very busy. In the meantime, perhaps he might be interested to visit the grave of Frau Bauer? Could he return the next afternoon?

The cemetery was well cared for. Many headstones had recent dates, and their silence reflected the stillness that clung even now to the damaged city. He found the grave and felt more bewilderment than anything else. He turned, almost with relief, to the immediate problems facing him.

He did not have much time, and he had no clear idea of how to proceed. But he had seen, stretching around corners, long lines of people patiently queuing – to get to the meagrely-stocked shops, he supposed; or, for all he knew, waiting for hand-outs or seeking work. A new thought struck him: might one of these people act as a guide? Some of them must be bilingual in German and English, surely.

He returned to the *Rathaus* and asked to speak to the same official. Yes, it might be arranged. There were people anxious for any employment. The gentleman could pay?

He did not have to pay much to get the services of a youth for a few days. Werner was close-mouthed about his past. He could not have been more than eighteen, but he spoke briefly of retreating before the Russians. Tim could believe this – he looked like a soldier. His bearing was erect, and he did not have the ill-nourished and depressed appearance of the older people in the streets. It was all to the good: Tim would feel less guilt in asking him to work for perhaps several longish days.

And, as it turned out, the difference between floundering

alone with his half-mastered German and having an interpreter was immense. Werner insisted on pay in advance, but beyond that the young man was obliging – it was as though his capacity for hatred had been exhausted along with his energy for fighting, and had given way to an amused irony. At one point he looked around and shrugged, saying: "For two years I have been in danger from the Russians. Now, with you, I can be in danger from my own countrymen. Among these people we pass in the street some have been trained to kill – silently, with a knife. All it needs is someone who hates your uniform enough – someone in a dark corner who thinks he is safe, or maybe someone who does not care whether he is safe … there are people like that. And there are gangs. Some from the streets. Some from refugee camps. People who want to survive." And, for reasons utterly mysterious to Tim, he laughed.

They tried first the telephone directory, and found several Bauers listed, one at the address that the official had said would no longer be standing. Five telephone calls were enough to confirm that none of the others belonged to Anna's family. They went to the shattered street, and Tim fought back anger as he stood gazing at the hole that had replaced number twenty-seven. He had seen many craters; but this time it was absolutely personal.

They knocked on the door of every remaining house, Tim removing his tunic and rolling it under his arm. The people at number forty-one knew Anna. She had become a nurse, and gone to work in a hospital away in the country, a hospital with a fine reputation. But she was here during the raid – it was terrible, no one could describe it. She had been a tower of strength. Did she go back to the hospital afterwards? No, perhaps she stayed with her father. Where did they go? One woman thought Cologne. Where in Cologne? No one knew. Perhaps the local post office could help.

Tim cursed himself for a fool not to have tried this before. The postmaster did have a forwarding address, and yes, it was in Cologne. Might Tim have it? Well, the postmaster was not sure. These were confidential matters. Could Tim write a letter that he could send on, and wait for a reply? Of course, the postal service was struggling in these times, like everything else … there could be delays. Tim explained that he represented a British organisation set up to make enquiries. What enquiries, the postmaster wanted to know. Werner intervened. He begged, he urged that Tim might soon have to return to the other side of the world, that he had very little time, that it was immensely important … the enquiries had nothing to do with reprisals or pursuing criminals; the *Engländer* was not a policeman. Of course, normally the postmaster would not dream of revealing the address, but in these circumstances … Werner had been decorated at the Russian front, and he would consider it a personal favour …

In the end, their combined efforts extracted an address: *375 Blumenhöhe, Köln.* Slapping Tim on the back Werner said: "Now we eat. You have cigarettes? Chocolate? Like the Americans?" On being told that Tim was well supplied, he suggested a small café where, in exchange for some American cigarettes, they were given turnip soup and more stale bread.

The train to Cologne would leave at six-twenty in the evening. Tim's conscience stirred: he had thoughts only for Anna, but Maclaurin had told him to enquire about crashed aircraft, and he had a duty. The official at the Rathaus had suggested the central police station. They found it quickly, and a police sergeant stared curiously at them, but went to get his superior. A man wearing four stars on his epaulette came and invited them to an office, where Tim explained that he was deputed to search for missing allied airmen and handed the official his authority. Werner was hardly necessary – they dropped quickly into English.

"We can enquire," said the policeman. "But you understand that many people died on that night. Not every body was identified. It is possible that some British or American fliers could have been buried without our knowledge. I know that we Germans have a reputation for keeping meticulous records, but in those circumstances ..." He shrugged. "If an aeroplane had crashed *in* the city I would know. Perhaps the police at nearby villages will have more news. As I say, I will try."

"I have very little time," said Tim. "I have to go tonight to Cologne – to Köln."

"You can telephone me from there – in, say, three days?"

"Yes. Certainly."

"*Gut.*"

On the train Werner dozed peacefully, but Tim was again restless. Time became somehow unreal, at once foreshortened and extended. Things were rushing forward faster than he had expected, and his impatience, so long held in check, surfaced now, but mingled with a sort of numb fear of what might be the final outcome. In all bombed cities it was impossible to evade the feeling of sadness hovering over the half-standing houses whose forlorn remnants of kitchens and bedrooms were absurdly exposed forty feet in the air. London had been bad enough, and Hildesheim much worse. But to set foot in Cologne would be to face a new test, for in May 1942 he had taken part in the first thousand-bomber raid that Britain had launched, a raid whose target was this city. He was in some part responsible for the ruins he knew he would see. He was afraid for himself, and he was even more afraid of Anna's reaction, of how she must feel and of how much of the destruction she would attribute to him.

He sat staring from the train window into the slowly fading darkness, his own reflection at times superimposed on shadowy fields and distant lights, his thoughts crowding each other out before they were fully developed, so that when the train puffed and sighed its way to a stop he could not believe that it was only 6.24 am. He wanted to go straight to Anna's address and sought a shop that would sell him a map. There was one on the concourse – it seemed to be both a café and what in England would be called a paper-shop – with books and charts displayed in its window; but it was not yet open.

Werner, still tousle-headed and sleepy, looked at him and laughed. "So – how far from here is her apartment – her house? How many kilometres? How will we travel?"

"Let's find out."

"How?"

Tim tapped the window of the shop. Werner smiled: "You wish to break the window? How do you say, to thieve the shop?"

"Not thieve, burgle. No, I don't want to do that. I just wonder when it opens. But why don't we ask at the ticket office? They might know the way."

"Possible. Not probable. We will ask. But if you could see yourself, you would not be in this hurry to present yourself to her sight. You will frighten her. Is there no smartness in the RAF? Did not your *Oberleutnant* inspect your uniform? We try to find somewhere for you to stay, to wash … to make you look right. Besides, will you call on a lady before she has made herself beautiful for the day? I need to eat. We eat here – at the station."

They did so, stale bread and soup from a trolley, Werner covertly watching as Tim glanced every few minutes at his watch. At last the shops opened and they were able to buy a small map. It told them that *Blumenhöhe* was some five kilometres away. As they started into the street, they saw around them large areas swept clear of buildings except for some jagged remains and a jumble of untidy bricks that no one had bothered to remove. Fringing these bleak spaces were terraced houses, some undamaged, some whole on one side and crumbled on the other, as though a monstrous animal had partly eaten them and then, sated, left the rest in a chewed ruin. Soaring close by was the cathedral. Indicating it Werner said, "To build that church took six centuries." It could have been destroyed in hours. Tim was glad that it, at least, had largely survived.

They approached the river, the Rhine. In 1942 Tim had
seen it reflecting the glow of burning buildings; now he could
inspect the result. A bridge had fallen into it, the tops of two
cantilever towers still showing above the water, all symmetry
gone, beauty become ungainly, like the carcass of some great
slain beast. Surveying this symbol of his enemy's defeat, he was
surprised to catch in himself a feeling he had not expected – a
triumphant satisfaction, the nihilistic gloating of the conqueror;
and simultaneously there was disgust and shame that this gut
reaction should surge in him. Then both emotions receded as he
was struck suddenly by something more like pure guilt: a heavy
plane approached, an American transport, apparently about to
fly directly overhead; as it roared near, an old man near them
in the street suddenly ran to the shelter of a low wall and flung
himself down. He remained there until the plane had passed
and then, trembling and stuttering uncontrollably, rose slowly,
muttering half-formed words which Tim realised were some sort
of apology.

They walked in silence, asking at several hotels only to be
told that they were full. At last, in despair, they turned into
a side street which was clearly the beginning of a less affluent
district. Werner stopped a thin, hungry-looking man and spoke
quietly. The man nodded and pointed. Werner took Tim's
arm and told him, "I am your guide, but in *Köln* I too need a
guide. He will show us a place to sleep. You must give him the
equivalent of one American dollar but in marks – you have? He
says the street – what do you call a small, narrow street? – is not
far. One-and-a-half kilometres. We must cross the *Rosenstrasse*
and go straight for ten minutes along the *Birkenweg*. Then the
little street. *Vogelweg*. It will meet us."

They accomplished this and the man led them a few more
yards to the door of a dirty but intact tenement. The words
"*Pension Vogelweg*" were printed over the door in large and
somewhat tattered gothic letters. "*Warten Sie*," he said. "*Ich
werde ein Zimmer für Sie finden.*" They followed their guide into

the block where he spoke to a woman. She jerked her head disinterestedly, indicating a passage, and the man, apparently knowing the building well, led them down it to a room. "*Hier*", he said. "*Haben Sie Dollars? Sie hätte gerne Dollars.*"

Werner answered: "*Nein. Mark. Wir bezahlen ihr später – Ihnen bezahlen wir gleich. Ein Dollar für eine Stunde Arbeit. Das ist ein sehr guter Tarif.*" And he signed to Tim who paid the man for his services in German money. He accepted it with a bad grace, but brightened when Tim added a packet of ten English cigarettes. It was only when he looked at the ground, and left them with his head down, and Tim realized that he was a tout only out of desperation, and suddenly was again ashamed – he had despised him, despised him for a defeat Tim himself had had some part in causing.

Raising his eyebrows, Werner asked Tim for more money for the landlady, and took it to her. She pocketed it without looking at him or uttering a word. He was not a person, merely a client.

The room had two beds, none too clean. "We must be careful," said Werner. "Do not again show cigarettes openly. It is good that there is a lamp near the door in the street. You rest a little, and then you wash and go to your lady. I will stay awake. We will not both sleep at the same time here. Not in this place."

"I cannot rest."

"Oh, women! What they do to us! Very well, *I* must rest. You *Flieger*! Soldiers are not like you. In Russia we slept when we could, often for one hour only, in the snow, and below the snow were rocks. Did you know that sometimes rats can still look for food when a man would freeze? You will guard me for two hours. Anyway, it would not be polite to arrive at – what do you say in English? – at the time for eating. No, we rest, we find your *Fräulein*, and then I will go."

Removing his shoes he collapsed on the bed and was quickly asleep. Tim, again alone with his thoughts, sat on a battered sofa, and the restless anticipation that until now had urged him onwards seemed to desert him. He realised that he was after all unutterably tired. His eyelids kept closing, and he had to force them open. In order to stay awake he got up and walked around and thought of Anna, remembering what she had written in letters, things she had said, the way her hair curled to her neck ... after a while he felt more awake. He would sit for a moment, he thought ...

He was aware of no more until he felt Werner was shaking him awake. "*Idiot! In der Wehrmacht hätte man Sie dafür erschossen! Wie konntet Ihr nur gewinnen?*"

Tim did not understand the words but the general meaning was plain enough. "I'm sorry" he said.

"Sorry! *Verzeihung!* It is not a matter for sorry. It does not happen!"

Tim shrugged. "I'm sorry. That's it."

He looked at his watch, and was suddenly on his feet, wide awake. "We are late! Bloody late! Let's go!"

Werner sighed, and looked at him speculatively. "*Nun gut.* You must have a coat, a long one. You stay here. I will find something. Lock the door until I am back."

It took the young German an hour to return with a light and grubby dust-coat of the kind used by the drivers of early motor-cars as a sort of cover-all. "I gave the man who was wearing it seven marks. I hope you can pay."

Tim nodded. It was less than a dollar. His uniform masked by the coat, they descended to the street. Trusting the guide's instructions, they made their way to *Blumenhöhe.* As they went, his tiredness vanished. They were passing house after house, door after door, with nothing special to distinguish them. It could have been tedious. But – soon, behind one of these doors, just above one of these short flights of steps, might be Anna.

Must be Anna. Surely he had found her.

Number 87. Steps. Apartment 14.

The fear that had been dogging the recesses of his mind returned intensely. After so long, what right had he to expect Anna to welcome him?

He looked again at the door. The blank wood told him nothing. To raise his hand to it took a deliberate effort. Werner, sensing his tension, watched him curiously.

He knocked. Too softly. He knocked again.

A female voice called.

Anna's voice.

Nothing. He waited. There was a crash, as though something had fallen. A soft exclamation of irritation. The voice called again: "*Ich komme ja schon.*"

More delay. Then the door opened. In the stillness it came suddenly.

Her astonishment was heart-stopping, the silent equivalent of a scream. She looked at him with widening eyes, her hand went to her mouth, and she seemed unable to speak. It was clear that momentarily she was in a place where reality seems too shocking to be real, where one must fight off the trickery of imagination. She seemed to become smaller. There were tears that gave way to sobs.

He was afraid now with a different fear, afraid to touch something so fragile. He felt he could crush her.

She looked up, recovered herself.

The dam burst, and she whispered "Tim". Then she said even more quietly, "Tim".

She was in his arms. They clung, feeling each other's warmth and wanting never to let go.

She pushed him a little away and stared. "What are you doing here?"

He shook his head. Werner stood quietly watching, forgotten. When he spoke the world was real again. His ordinariness broke the spell. "You can find your way back?" He turned to Anna: "Fräulein, I have brought your friend here. I will go now."

She turned and offered Werner her hand. "Who are you?"

He bowed and gave the hand the ghost of a kiss. It implied that she was married. "I am no one."

"Where are you from? Why are you with Tim?"

"I do a small job for a few marks."

"What is your name?"

"Werner."

She looked searchingly at him, noting the thinness of his face and the straightness of his back. Then she asked, "You were in Poland?"

He nodded. "Poland, Prussia – Debrecen."

Tim realised that in two days of close association he had not asked these questions of the young German, and Anna had done it in moments. This boy, a veteran of savage battles, perhaps seven years his junior, who had been so useful to him. Even beside Anna he looked absurdly young as she laid a hand on his shoulder. "Werner, thank you so much. I can never repay you."

"*Bitte.*" And he was gone. Tim had no chance even to thank him. He ran into the street, and called after him. Werner turned, waved once, and disappeared quickly around a corner.

Anna watched him go, sad for a moment, and led Tim into the apartment, making futile attempts to straighten her hair and her clothes. "Tim," she said, "to come now, when I am like this. You wait. I will go and make myself as I should be. Tim … Oh, Tim …"

Dimly he was made aware that she wore some utilitarian and shapeless dress, a dull grey affair probably reserved for housework. He had not even noticed. He held her and said "Just stay here."

"No, you wait. Tim, you are very bad. You have caught me. Oh, I am so, so glad!"

Smiling, she took the coat off his shoulders – "What is that rag?" – and pushed him onto a sofa and left the room, returning after ten minutes in a primrose frock and with a little make-up, and they looked at each other in silence. He stood to embrace her, and as they did he was aware of tears. She pushed him away into the chair again, and sat beside him, and then they began to talk.

It was not the talk he had intended.

"Tell me – the *Stalag*. It was very bad?"

"It was bad. But I had your letters. Anna, you were crazy to write them."

"I did not care if I was crazy. Herr Doctor Berndt helped. I needed him."

"He must be very fond of you."

"Fond?" She did not know the word.

"He must – love you."

"He has been wonderful, always."

"The risks – I worried for you all the time. But without those letters – you know, some men went a little mad. I might have been one of them."

She smiled, and he kissed the smile. Laughing, she said, "Yes, you are a little mad – to be here. But the – camp. You must tell me."

So he spoke of how some prisoners could trust each other and some not, and of the small things of daily life, and of how some guards were friendly and some angry, and of the dentist and of Berndt's final anger. Again they sat a little in silence, contemplating all that he had said and knowing that it scratched the surface, that there was much more that could not be put into words even if they had a long time. But sense of something shared drifted through their small world and gently subsided like the dying strains of distant music.

Then she told how it felt: death being rained from aeroplanes far overhead, dropped by men secure in their untouchable world. Tim knew that this was a false image – that the crews were far from secure, and that a man who joined Bomber Command had little better than an even chance of surviving the war. But he recognised that to those on the ground it would have felt like that: the inhuman remoteness of the machines, their impersonal clinical detachment, contrasting with the dreadful immediacy of the destruction around them. He had known that feeling himself in London. And he knew that she understood all this. But that understanding did nothing to assuage the felt human cost when those who were killed and maimed were people you could see ... When your mother died, and you had to leave your home ...

And – her father was very ill. Ever since he had returned from the first war, he had been frail. He needed her, present with him. He was out now – he had gone to find some food. They had heard of a shop that had a few eggs. If he was very lucky, they might get one. They could share it with a neighbour.

"Did you say 'one'? One egg? *Share* one egg?"

"Yes, an egg."

In English cities people could not count on more than one each week, though it was better in the country. Tim knew that. But still he exclaimed: "*One* – for two people *and* a neighbour?"

"Tim, I know of a family of five people. Last week they shared one egg between them."

"Good God!"

It brought him back to full reality – to the realisation that there were serious questions to be asked. But now he feared the answers. Instead of speaking he took her and held her and they kissed and kissed again.

This could not last. They had to speak of the future, and there was little time. He took her by the shoulders and she looked into his eyes.

"Anna, I have waited for this moment for two years. I love you. Will you marry me?"

She looked away a moment: "Tim, I will marry you – if I can. But not now."

"Yes – now! Of course now! What do you mean?" She shook her head, and he knew what she would say before she said it.

She must remain with her father. They would not stay in Cologne longer than necessary. This was her sister's house, and her sister had a husband, now returned from the fighting first in Italy and then Germany. The couple were kind, and said nothing, but it was obvious – one simply *knew* – they hoped that they could have the house to themselves, and be relieved of the added financial burden of their relatives.

Anna had been in contact with Doctor Berndt, hoping that she could go back to work at the hospital in Tannhofen and take her father with her; but her place had been filled, and the hospital – already operating on a shoe-string during the war – was in fact putting off staff. It was in the sector occupied by the French; in the American sector there might have been more money to help running costs.

And Tim? Of course he could not stay in Germany. He could not even speak the language well. The country was flooded with returned soldiers looking for every job that could somehow be cobbled out of this beaten, impoverished shambles.

"Besides, you still have uniform. You are still in your British – Luftwaffe. You are not free. Not now. How long is your leave?"

"My Luftwaffe? You have no idea how strange that sounds. We say the Air Force. The RAF. The RAAF. Whatever. It doesn't matter anyway. To hell with leave, to hell with them all! I'm not leaving you again!"

"Tim, you cannot stay."

He had not yet mentioned his job in Maclaurin's group. And now he became reluctant to do so – it would only reinforce what she was saying. At that moment he had no thought for his promise to Nordale. He would learn German, sweep streets, whatever it took.

"You know, Anna – we both know – if I leave you now, I will lose you – forever."

"No, Tim. You will never lose me. Not in my heart."

Her reply was interrupted when her father came wheezing up the stairs. Tim had expected someone of, perhaps, fifty, sixty at most. He saw a man who looked eighty, frail, stooped, with tremors in both hands.

But a change passed through Herr Bauer's body as he saw this stranger and then dropped his eyes to inspect the uniform. He drew himself up into a semblance of standing straight. A dignity fell on him. He tried to speak and failed, shaking his head. At the second attempt he succeeded. There was no mistaking the fury in the hoarse voice that demanded, "*Was ist das?*"

"*Papa,*" began Anna. But she got no further. " '*Raus! 'Raus!*"

The old man advanced on Tim with fluttering hands, as one might drive sheep or dogs away.

Tim stood his ground. "Doesn't he know, Anna?" he asked.

"I could not tell him. I do not think he will live very long. His chest … Tim, you cannot stay here. Do you have somewhere to sleep tonight? Somewhere to eat?"

"Anna, that's not important. You and I – we are important."

"Of course it's important!" She was suddenly angry. "What will you do – curl up in what is left of some bombed house?"

"For heavens' sake! I have a room. That young man, Werner, found someone who got us a room."

"Good. Do what I tell you – like you did when I was your nurse and you obeyed me always. There is a garden at the end of this street – a little – what do you say? A park. To the right. Go there now, and wait for me. I will bring you some food."

He could not have cared less about eating, but her last words threw his response off course, and it was to them that he replied: "But you have so little!"

The old man interrupted. *"Raus! Anna! Was ist das? Dieser Mann – warum sprichst Du mit ihm? Raus! Raus! Wo ist mein Stock?"*

She pushed him out, both of them forgetting the dust-coat. He waited for nearly an hour, scowling at his own thoughts, fretting in case he had mistaken the place. Then he heard her heels on the pavement. He knew the sound of her walk – he had heard it so often moving through the ward.

They found a bench and sat close, her head on his shoulder. Placing a neat parcel beside her, she looked at him with a curious smile. "Tim, you found me. It must have been very difficult. I will never forget that."

"Don't talk about forgetting. You won't forget *me* – ever again. I'll be too close to you."

"I have told you, Tim. We cannot stay together. Not just now."

"Why? Anna, is your father bad to you?"

"No, Tim, you do not understand. I will talk to him, I will

try to make him accept you. But it will take time. You must see that. Even I – I have sometimes hated you. Even when I loved you. Because of the bombs. And then I have thought, we are all victims, and I have thought of you, and I could not hate you. You must give me your address in the – the RAAF, was it not? I will write to you there. Give me your address in Australia, too. Your family's address. That will be good."

"Australia! Have you any idea how far away it is?"

"It is nearer than starving in the streets of Cologne – believe me. There is nothing for you here."

"There is you. I have found you, Anna. I will not leave you again."

Ignoring him, she pushed a piece of paper into the pocket of his battle-dress blouse. "If you write to this address it will always reach me. Even if I am not still here."

"No. I will stay near you."

"Tonight. See me here tonight. Exactly here, if no one has stolen this seat. At eight. But first give me the address of your home. Your Australian home. You told me in the hospital – it had a strange name, and I forget." She rummaged in her handbag and produced a small notebook. "Here – write it on this. These are times when nothing is certain. Not even what will happen tomorrow. Give me all your addresses – now!"

"Anna ... "

"Tim, please."

"Shit!" But, choking back an angry protest, he wrote his address in Walgabran and added his Air Force address in Britain. "It doesn't mean I'm leaving."

"You will. You must."

It took him forty minutes and three false leads to find the street where he and Werner had spent the night. As he went, thoroughly absorbed by what had happened, his mood ran

310

through wild changes. He had not eaten since morning, but he felt no hunger, and Anna's parcel remained forgotten in his pocket. The problem was obvious enough. Anna felt responsible for her father, and in that commitment there was no place for Tim: the older man would never accept a British flier who had caused untold German deaths and suffering.

Yes – he could understand. But it was unfair. Anyway, the Germans had started it ... No, not Anna – but the Nazis ...

But – where and when did it start? He remembered: once his own father had written to him that there is a chain of evil, stretching back and back, through history. Evil begets evil.

Anyway, that was now the past. Damn it. He was not leaving, Anna's father or no Anna's father. The old man had his needs – but he and Anna had their lives in front of them.

So what could she do? Desert the old man?

No, she would not.

And – no, he could not want it, could not want her to want it.

But – there must be some way ...

Entering *Vogelweg*, he turned towards the pension. There was a man by the door. He experienced a renewed awareness of his uniform – the dust-coat must still be in Anna's apartment; in the flurry of his thoughts it had been quite forgotten. For a moment he was apprehensive, conscious of Werner's warning. But then – no, he thought, in the street around him he could feel a dark mood, but it contained no danger. It was something else. A tangible depression. He resolved to leave this place of despair. Tomorrow.

It was still light at eight, with the cool light that remains after the sun has gone. A balmy warmth, the subdued afterglow of the August day, flowed around them. The park bench was transformed into a magical seat in fairyland.

"Köln is beautiful," she said, gazing around.

He was surprised: "But – it is ruined!"

"Yes. It is ruined. But it is still beautiful."

A memory flitted across his mind – when he was a boy: something Willy had said to the class about beauty where we do not expect it.

Anna brought him back to practicalities. "Tim, have you thought? What we need now – my father and I – is work, and food, and somewhere to live. I cannot take him from Germany. When our situation has changed enough I will marry you if you will still have me. But for now I cannot. And – I have something to ask you. I would not ask this for myself, not of anyone, not even of you. But for my father …"

She looked at the ground, and Tim, puzzled, could see that what she was about to say cost her terribly. He could not imagine anything that could embarrass her in front of him.

"I have seen the – what do you say? – the occupation forces. There are Americans who seem to have everything – and British, too, though they do not have so much as the Americans. If you were part of that – Tim, do you understand that you could help us? Or – I do not know whether you will stay long in the – RAAF; or whether you can get other work in England. But if you can send us clothes, food … "

She was not looking at him. He could see fugitive, suppressed tears and knew that they were tears of shame.

He was stunned, not so much by what she had said as by his own reaction. Anna had said that she would marry him. And then she had made this request. Until now he had been moved primarily by longing for her. Now he felt something no less primitive: the desire of a man to expend his strength for his family; to support its structure, to be a pillar, one of two, in some ways the stronger but probably in most the weaker.

Evil, no matter how strong, was never fundamental. *That* was the heart of what his father had said. What then of the other chain, the chain of good? Surely it was still there, handed on by ordinary decent people, everywhere rising above the layers of hatred. A living energy. The Holy Spirit. There must be, now, a chance to resurrect something fine out of these ruins surrounding him; out of the spent fury of the war. Perhaps he could help to repair what he had helped to destroy. He ... and Anna ... and their children ... they could be part of the new work.

He took her in his arms. There was no need to speak.

After a while, he said one word: "Anna." She knew it meant "I am happy".

It was only then that he told her of Maclaurin's group, of his acceptance of the job, of his deadline to be back in England. She looked and smiled sadly. "So – you must go again, soon?"

"I do not want to."

"Do not think about it now."

For the next seven days they met in the park, twice each day. On the Sunday Anna, Lutheran though she was, took him to the cathedral. In the times between, he walked in a golden daze of happiness, but he was repeatedly brought up short by the devastation around him. For the first time he noticed clearly how many people were damaged, and how greatly women outnumbered men.

The city was in the British sector, and he saw plenty of Tommies and NCOs and junior officers – the senior ones presumably being too busy in offices to be much on the streets. At the local British Army of the Rhine headquarters he was given a bed when he showed the documents confirming his leave and indicating the task on which he would soon be engaged. Remembering his promise to Maclaurin, he phoned the policeman in Hildesheim, who assured him that he had enquired extensively, but was able to give him the particulars of just one man who had been buried there – a British squadron leader. Others, he said, might be found later but there was little hope. Tim felt a stab of remorse at not probing further, but he would not leave Cologne again. He wrote to his parents and to Willy, giving him Anna's address and begging him to write to her father.

Anna for her part had to tell her father something to account for the sudden appearance of this *Terrorflieger*. She outlined the story: how he had arrived in her hospital, his wounds, his revulsion from all bombing. She presented him as a friend without saying more than she must. This mollified the old man a little, and he was grudgingly pleased when Tim, instead of being brought food by Anna, was able to take her some parcels carefully salvaged from the British sergeants' mess. The obvious inference was that Tim was with the occupation forces, and Anna did nothing to dispel the illusion, for to say that he had sought her out from England would have been to pour petrol on a fire.

But he stayed close to her as long as he could. And then, suddenly it seemed, he was due to start work for Maclaurin next Monday. The British were not able to offer a flight in time. With three days to go he made a day-trip to Frankfurt and presented himself to the American military government.

He was surprised by the warmth of his welcome. They had their own uncounted dead, and the Eighth Air Force their own history of courage, blood, and flying aces. But among Americans some quite special respect lingered for the men who had defended Britain in the air for those first lonely two years, and they tended to extend this even to those who, like Tim, had not encountered the enemy until the Battle of Britain was well over. A young army major insisted on buying Tim a drink and promised him a place on a Dakota if he could get back to Frankfurt by midday on Saturday.

Anna persuaded him not to risk relying on an early morning train. They were too crowded, too much could go wrong in Germany now. He could stay at the American base overnight. He must catch a train on Friday evening.

At the station he was gripped by a reluctance to leave her, rational or not. He did not mention it. She did not need to be told.

"Go, Tim. Go while I can still say this. It is better. Go now. Go quickly."

They kissed. And gently but firmly, she took his shoulders and turned him away from her and pushed him towards the carriage. He took a step, turned and looked. A single tear in her eyes would have brought him back. There was no tear. "Go," she said.

The next morning an American Lieutenant put him on the plane, and he stared moodily out of the window until the co-pilot, beside himself with joy and yelling like his confederate forebears, came to tell him: "It's over! Buddy, it's over!" The Japanese surrender had been reported on the radio.

What did it mean for him and Anna?

Peace – finally. A chance.

But also – the atom bomb.

The chain of human evil and counter-evil.

Where was God in all this?

That Christmas Mass on the ship, four years ago. That sense of universal love …

He thought: the world, our struggles, our desperation – these hide God, mask his warmth. But we are wrapped in love … God feels every hurt we feel, even the hurt to creation when we smash it with bombs … that is what Christ means …

Yes – Anna and I … we will build a small chain of goodness somehow. And in the end it will prevail. "That's our faith, son." His father had written those words.

And he was glad then to be joining Maclaurin's team.

CHAPTER 23

Maclaurin's Search (Western Europe, 1945–1946)

Tim found to his delight that his immediate chief was to be the man with whom, four years earlier, he had shared days in New York.

Vince McCauley was made to be a leader. He had arrived in Britain from Canada already a competent pilot and a little older than most members of the Empire Air Training Scheme, and was quickly made an instructor. Disappointed with the posting, he had made repeated applications for a transfer to operations, and in the end had spent most of the war in Coastal Command. Physically he was slightly under the average height, broad-shouldered, handsome, with a body trained in the surf club at Bondi; by education he was unfailingly a gentleman; by temperament he was decisive and humorous. But his decisiveness could become impulsiveness, especially in the wild mood of reaction from stress at the war's end. This may explain his response when Maclaurin approached him. Though he had already been offered a job as a pilot with KLM, he shrugged and fell in with the Canadian's suggestion to allow the toss of a coin to decide; and in effect he had sacrificed a commercial pilot's career to join the search for missing airmen.

It was with this man that Tim was to trace a course that,

beginning in Belgium, would veer north through part of Holland and then south into France and finally into Germany. Sometimes following a specific lead, more often taking potluck, over eight months they would enter more than fifty towns and villages, staying in each a few days or occasionally a week.

Emotionally, it was a difficult journey. They gathered information which, almost always, would result in the confirmation of tragic news to some family who both expected and feared it. The local authorities opened their records and took them to cemeteries, and helped them to question citizens who had seen planes come down. Before they were finished they would be led to numerous wrecks – fighters, bombers, British, American – buried in offshore mud near Dutch harbours and broken in French forests and perched like grotesque monuments in lonely cols; and sometimes they would find what was left of the crew. Tim felt that he could hardly have supported the burden of the work if he had not managed to find Anna first.

Not all the information came from officials. There were times when the starting point was their own observation. If they saw a girl wearing a flier's fur-lined jacket, they made enquiries; if the wheels on a barrow looked like those from a British fighter, or if they heard of a two-way radio with an American brand name, they investigated. On one occasion the suspicion arose that a man had salvaged such material secretly and failed to report the presence of bodies on his farm. Vince and Tim informed the local police, but when they learnt the man had been arrested and savagely beaten in the course of questioning, they turned and left the town in disgust without pursuing the case further.

It sometimes happened that the crashed planes turned out to be German. Tim wanted to do the same job for them – to send information to Germany. Vince was at first reluctant; it was not their brief, and their time was limited; but he recognised that the enemy dead were enemies no longer, and over a beer agreed so long as it would not divert them too far from their proper job.

His sympathies were not in fact markedly dissimilar from Tim's.

"But," he said, "who do we contact?"

"What's still working?"

"Courts. Police. Bits and pieces."

"Surely they've got someone doing what we're doing?"

"You'd think so. But most high-up central admin's being done by the Allied Control Council."

"Would they help? Wouldn't someone German be better?"

"Well, the Luftwaffe hasn't been disbanded – yet. We could try them."

They did so. And from each town Tim wrote to Anna. He could not be certain, as he expressed it, when he would be where, nor whether the postal services had been fully restored, but he asked her to write *Poste Restante* to towns he was sure he would visit. It was clear enough that he would not be writing so often to anyone but a sweetheart, and rather than put up with Vince's raised eyebrows and unspoken questions he took the risk of telling him that the lady was German. In fact, he hoped to see her when they reached Germany.

Vince looked quizzically at his aide. "Well," he said, "that explains why you wanted to help the German families."

So Tim's first call was always the post office, and when there were letters he devoured them greedily and then put them aside to read again slowly at night, when he could savour each word.

Her first message poured out her feelings and was filled with longing for him. Her second, perhaps fearing that the first had given the wrong impression, reaffirmed her commitment to her father. Her third however was simply joyful. For her father had softened his attitude – unexpectedly. Apparently this was Willy's doing – Tim had asked his old friend to write to Herr Bauer, and the result was a glowing reference on Tim's behalf.

Willy assured Herr Bauer that Tim had hated the war, and that his capture, however great his feeling for the rest of the crew and his chagrin at his own loss of freedom, had not been without a certain consolation – for it had relieved him of the task of guiding bombers to rain death. Willy had laid it on a bit thick. He had not added that Tim nevertheless believed in the Allied cause. Nor had he mentioned anything that might alienate Herr Bauer – his own pacifist convictions and his anti-Nazi sentiments. But he had reminisced a little about the *old* army, the army of the Kaiser, and about the Germany of his boyhood. He had also emphasised every German-Australian connection he could think of. He wrote that Germans came with Captain Cook, that the first governor was the son of a German; that there were areas in Queensland and Western Australia where the current population derived from nineteenth-century German immigrants; that there was a district in South Australia where German settlers had set up a wine industry, concentrating especially on adapting the whites they had grown on the slopes of the Rhine, and that many towns in that state had German names – even the capital, Adelaide, was named after a German princess; that there were Germans famous in early Australian history – the explorer Leichhardt, the botanist von Hugel, and Jakob Alt who planned early Sydney; that the anthropologist Strehlow, whose father had been a Pastor at the famous Hermannsburg mission, had recorded the languages of central Australian Aborigines and defended their culture against criticism; and that more recently a Catholic bishop in Western Australia had invited German missionaries to work in the sparsely populated north of the state. Finally, Willy had mentioned something that Tim himself had not yet learnt – that in Australia ex-servicemen, who had passed a matriculation examination, could get generous scholarships to the universities – hoping that this might make Tim seem more attractive as a future husband for Anna.

The result was that Anna's father was prepared, just a little, to consider Tim as something better than a monster. Anna felt sure she could get round him. It was probably good that she and Tim would not see each other for a few months, all things considered. Regular letters and the passing of time would help her to change the old man's attitude step by step.

For the first time in six years, Tim began to feel really happy in a settled way. This showed. He had always been a conscientious worker, but now Vince noticed a new engagement, an effortless energy he brought to the job.

Still, their progress remained painfully slow, and for Tim the tragedy of airmen killed before their prime was symbolically underscored by the pathos of the wrecked planes they found. Since childhood he had been attracted by aircraft; and the elegant lightness of their structure, their intrinsic *goodness* simply as machines, unfailingly touched a nerve in him. Even on bombing runs, he remembered, there was a sort of comfort in the rhythm of the motors, in the delicate mathematical relationship of wings and fuselage and tail and weight and power, which was part of the *rightness* that had to be there if the aircraft was to fly. And there was a greatness in all their deployment of chemistry and metallurgy and electronics and of heaven knew how much else of accumulated human wisdom. But the brilliance of their design was enlisted in the service of that insanity which leads men to kill each other *en masse*.

Goodness turned to evil. It was far wider than the aircraft. Back in Brisbane he had experienced a youthful sense of wonder at the miracle of community itself – at the power of human co-operation, at the way quite disparate activities could mesh together to achieve a viable and complex whole. He had felt the nobility of the ordinary: of common effort and work and courage and leadership and practical, ordinary small tasks and decisions. All this spoke of a goodness in the very structures of the world. But, too, all this could so easily be corrupted. And that corruption, when it happened, was something men and women could not face – they somehow took a perspective that blotted it out. That was the human failure. That was war.

❖ ❖ ❖

During the next months, Vince and Tim moved across northern France and then nearer and nearer to Germany. They were to cross the Rhine at Duisburg, for there and nearby – at Essen, Düsseldorf, Cologne – massive British raids had encountered heavy losses. They would then go further south, through the country around Mannheim, Karlsruhe and beyond, concentrating on small towns rather than larger centres. This would take them first from the British-occupied zone into the American and then into the French, where they would go to Offenburg and Freiburg and last of all to Tannhofen. For Tannhofen was near Freiburg, and Tannhofen would be the starting-point in the search for Tim's Halifax.

As they neared their point of entry to Germany, Vince said: "OK, our itinerary takes us right to this lady of yours. You'd probably desert if I didn't give you a couple of days off then. Don't tell Maclaurin."

In those two days Tim and Anna were formally engaged, though they had no idea how or when they could marry. They both knew that it was a mad thing to do, but they did it. And the effect on Tim was utterly unexpected, even by himself: he had recently become much happier, but now he felt a liberation that embraced his whole being, and a sense of emotional freedom that he had not known since childhood. The stress of the work remained, but there was a part of him that seemed immune from its effect.

The effect on Anna's father was equally startling. He made a huge effort to accept Tim, and when Anna told him that Tim had persuaded his chief to send information on crashed German aircraft to the Luftwaffe, he finally gave his reluctant blessing. He wrote to Willy, asking for more information about Australia. Willy replied, stating that generally the country was not highly sophisticated but had its very successful scientists and writers and theatres and universities, and that it was developing; that the people were tough and in some ways rough, but decent and with a certain old-fashioned gentility which they managed to mix with casual attitudes in what was really the invention of a new culture; that Tim should be forgiven if he did not understand the proper formalities in addressing an older person – his heart was in the right place; that the government was eager for immigrants from Europe, and that Germans were beginning to come in considerable numbers.

The last piece of intelligence struck the old man in two ways: he would be a fool not to see that it might provide the answer for his daughter and her fiancé. And he remembered what had happened to Germany after the Great War. But for himself – at his age, and indeed in his state of health, how could he think of leaving the country where his wife was buried, the country he had always loved, all his friends – those who still lived – everything he knew?

It placed an intolerable burden on him. It took him three days of anguish. Then he said to Anna, "I know what you must do. You must leave me and go to this new country."

She refused. They argued until he had only one card left to play against her stubbornness. "All right, damn it! I will go there too."

No, she said, he was not really fit for a long sea-journey. "Rubbish!" he retorted. They argued again, and again, and both wept. And yet, there could only be one final result. Sooner or later, Anna, her father, and Tim would all come to Australia.

Unless Anna's sister changed her mind. But that was unlikely.

CHAPTER 24

The Wreck
(Germany, 1946)

The city of Freiburg was spread out in a plain nestling among range after range of steep hills – young mountains, they would have been called in Australia. Tim tried to imagine how it would have looked before the war.

He could not. Vince and he were tired, their energy depleted both by the months of travelling and the challenge of their work, and they were glad that the journey was almost ended. They would enquire in the region, then one last task would remain; and as it came close Tim was apprehensive, knowing that he might find the remains not only of his Halifax but also of his comrades.

Their work in the Freiburg district done, they passed again through the city and continued the thirty-odd further miles to the hospital. Tim had written ahead to Berndt, and before long he was introducing Vince to the doctor, who to his disappointment received them frostily but politely. He seemed to regret having agreed to the meeting.

"*Herr Doktor*", Tim said by way of opening, "I remember your anger after the bombing of Hildesheim. I ask you to believe that I did not personally approve. And I cannot tell you how grateful I am for all you did for me."

Berndt clearly thought that these were empty words, formalities not to be taken seriously. "Ja, Ja," he said with some impatience. "What is it you want now?"

So Tim explained the task on which they were engaged, and Vince pointed out that they had performed the same service for the relatives of German fliers where possible. Berndt warmed a little at this.

"Sir," went on Tim, "we have spent eight months in this work. We now have one last task – to search for the plane from which I parachuted. When I was here as your patient you told me that a wreck had been found. Obviously there is a very good chance that it is my aircraft. In any case, it is a lead that we should follow up. Do you know more exactly the location?"

Still somewhat surly, Berndt shrugged, but he made a visible effort of thought: "You know it is more than two years. Much has happened. In these days one aeroplane which crashed two years ago is – how do you say? – small beer. If I remember, I was told of it by Hauptmann Platt, and he has gone. Perhaps you can trace him. But he has disappeared into the chaos" (here he made a sweeping gesture with his arm to take in the whole of Germany) "and in any case could tell you little unless he remembers the source of his own information. I think he said it was twenty-one kilometres south-west from here, towards the French border. I can make enquiries. Yes, I will try. I am not so hopeful. In the meantime you must go to the *Rathaus* in Tannhofen. Perhaps they can help. Someone will be able to speak English. These country people – they remember things longer. There is a small hotel in the town where you can stay. I will send word to you there."

"We will. Sir, as I said, I appreciate the help you gave me, when I was in the hospital and when I was in the Stalag. I would be honoured if you would have dinner with us tonight at the hotel."

Berndt still looked like a man in two minds, but after a pause he said, "Ja, I will come. At half-past seven." It was a concession.

Tim hesitated. A fragile *rapport* had been achieved, one which he could easily destroy now by speaking, but there was another imperative: Berndt had a right to know, and to delay would be to lack respect. "There is one more thing. I have to tell you that I have seen Anna Bauer, and I have asked her to be my wife, and she has accepted me."

The German looked at him steadily for a long time, and it was impossible to guess his thoughts. And then he said, "I hope – for Anna's sake – that you will be very happy. Ja." Then, for the first time, he smiled just a little. "Anna. We will toast her in good *Rheinisch* wine tonight."

Tannhofen, an insignificant town in a remote area, had been immune from bombing, and their first glimpse revealed to the Australians just how charming the towns of the Black Forest could be. There was a small, winding river spanned by a bridge with ornate balustrades. On either side, houses three or four stories high were mostly white, but some were of a red that Tim had not seen before – he thought of stewed quinces as an approximation. Brown fretted stonework or black timber framed their windows, and their shutters were thrown open to the early spring sunshine. Balconies and bay windows projected over the street, and here and there circular towers rose clear above steep gabled roofs. The whole seemed huddled contentedly beneath the spires of the church like sheep around a shepherd, and the general effect contained an element of playfulness. Tim had never seen a Franz Lehar operetta, but he could easily associate the scene before him with the dimly remembered music emerging from the gramophones of his youth in Walgabran, a town that in so many ways was an exact opposite of this.

A cluster of old men in the square greeted these strangers as they entered, and one who had a smattering of English appointed himself interpreter. Gradually, in answer to Vince's questions, they voiced half-remembered rumours of an aeroplane crash in the district.

"Ja," said one. "There was an aeroplane. Twelve, fifteen kilometres, to the south-west. My brother-in-law heard of it from a man whose cattle had strayed."

"Twelve kilometres? Nein. Twenty-five, thirty," said another.

"Poof! Cattle do not go so far. These are the stories to tell children when they are going to sleep. There is no aeroplane." This was the oldest, a man with a long moustache.

In spite of the last sceptic, it was a lead, and it chimed with what Berndt had remembered. The distance was not great, but the search would require a trek through well-treed country which, though not actually alpine, was rugged and full of steep valleys.

Tim's limp no longer slowed him appreciably, and he and Vince were by now used to hard walking; but for this search they would have to camp out. Even to hope to reach the area in a single day was ambitious, and then they had to find the plane. They would need back-packs and hiking gear.

Taking their new-found interpreter with them, they went to see the Bürgermeister. A middle-aged man with a grizzled face, he greeted them with reserve. It was almost possible to see his thoughts: these people – what do they want here?

But the project, once broached, interested him: if such a search was successful, it could publicise his region; and besides, the *Engländer* would surely pay for a guide. He had a suggestion: his niece Katerina was a keen member of a walking-club and knew the country. And she had learnt English at school.

"But," objected Vince, "we can't take a girl. We'd need two tents, for a start. And ground sheets – heavy stuff. Winter's past, but that doesn't mean the ground's dry. It's too much to carry."

The Bürgermeister nevertheless sent a message to his brother's farm, and within an hour a tall girl arrived and kissed him with a merry laugh. But when the project was explained she became as reserved as her uncle had been initially; and in German too rapid for Tim to follow, she began to argue with him. Several times he seemed to insist, and she to object; but finally she sighed and nodded, clearly submitting with a bad grace.

She addressed Vince: "I do not like *Britische Luftwaffe*. But I respect men who die. We go. My uncle says you want tent. You do not need. I haf in der hills with blanket sleep and – how you say? – hot – clothes." And she paused, unable to think of English words to continue.

Vince was still in two minds. "Will your parents allow you to go away with men you do not know?"

"My parents know me. My uncle sees your papers. It is *gut*. You not worry."

"I don't know," muttered Vince. Apart from any concern about proprieties he was beginning to feel a steamroller quality in this girl's personality.

The interpreter spoke to the Bürgermeister and relayed his reply. "Of course her *Bruder* will come. And, of course, the gentlemen will pay. *Und*" – he stared at the Australians' uniforms – "*und* you cannot go in those clothes. He will give you some until you return."

Vince looked at Tim. "What do you think?"

"It sounds pretty good. About paying, a few dollars should be enough. He probably sees it as a token war reparation because we're British. We can't accept their clothes of course. We can buy some – might have to go back to Freiburg."

Katerina took charge – she would always do that without self-consciousness. "No. No money." She spoke again in German to her uncle. Another argument ensued. This time she won.

Vince stared. "Miss, we can't ... "

"If you pay you are boss. In this I am boss. No pay. We help. Clothes – we – how you say? – lend. Not for money. Have you rope?"

"Rope?" Vince felt stupid.

"Rope – for climb."

"No," he said, taken aback. "We're not mountaineers."

"Not mountains – but like baby mountains. I bring good rope."

She waited a moment, then, taking silence for assent, added: "Tomorrow at five we leave. In two days, tree, four, we return for sunset. I bring food. Food that will not – *verderben*. *Wasser*, everyone carries. But *Wasser* we also will find."

Vince was aghast. "Did you say *five*? In the morning?"

She laughed, not unkindly. The warm side of her nature surfaced momentarily. "You are not farmer. I can tell. Is not early. Tomorrow – at five. Here, in front of the Rathaus."

In the pre-dawn light humped silhouettes turned from black shadows to grey ghosts and then to the shapes of hills and trees. It was one of those fresh mornings that suggest an innocent world, and Vince, muttering about getting up in the middle of the night, was secretly enjoying the experience. Bending forward under the weight of his pack, he coped easily with the pace set by Katerina and her brother Dieter, a lanky farm-lad of seventeen. Tim had to push himself a little, but after the first hour they had all settled into a comfortable rhythm, saving their breath on steep ascents, making scraps of conversation on easier ground. Dieter seemed a naturally quiet person. Katerina was polite but formal. Sweat rose on their backs in spite of the morning chill, and as their bodies warmed they felt a kind of instinctive sympathy with the awakening country around them. After a while even the girl began to mellow. Here she was fully at home and fully relaxed. Flowers abounded, struggling to open, and Vince wanted to examine them and to inspect the unfamiliar trees and shrubs, but whenever he paused Katerina said "Nein. We walk."

For a short time there was a half-made track, but it petered out and they entered real forest where the ground was rough and the carpet of pine needles slippery, though the undergrowth remained sparse enough to allow more or less free walking. By nine Tim was both hungry and tired, but he said nothing, unwilling to appear weaker than their guide who seemed as fresh now as when they started. It was a full two hours later when she called a welcome halt. "*Mittagspause*", she said.

The Australians expected to eat frugally, knowing the economic conditions in Germany. They had reckoned without the fact that they were in lush country and that she was a farm girl. They gorged themselves on heavy food, and then she announced that they would rest.

"I didn't know Germans had siestas," said Tim quietly to Vince.

"For heaven's sake don't question it," he replied. "She might think better of it. She's a walking machine. I need a good break."

They ate and lay back, scraping small hollows in the earth and falling into a doze. She let them lie for an hour and a half before rousing them. "We go."

Stiffly they got up and put on their packs. "Not so far now," said Katerina. "But more steep."

They found themselves climbing again, and the terrain became more rugged and the forest thicker, restricting visibility to a few metres. The effort of the day began to tell on Tim. His bad leg protested, a toe was sore inside his boot, under the straps of his pack his shoulders ached, and he stopped often to drink and to massage his calves. Once he slipped down the side of a rock, scraping his side. Dieter looked on, surprised that he could be so clumsy.

"You are tired," said Katerina infuriatingly. "Only one hour more." At the end of that hour they found themselves a hundred metres below the top of a high hill, and she pointed to a nearby brook that wound its way down the hillside. "Here we stop."

Vince's fears of wet earth had been groundless. They spread their blankets and, setting up a little sheltered space to secure the food in Katerina's pack against the incursions of animals, gathered fallen wood for a fire. Then they went to the very top of the hill, and from there found that they could survey the surrounding ridges, indented with depressions and gullies any of which might hide an aircraft. They looked in every direction for signs of the crashed plane until their eyes ached, but saw nothing.

"What is time?" Katerina asked.

Vince looked at his watch. "Nearly five."

She nodded. "We have light one hour. We look – close, near. We go now."

"Now, just a minute," said Vince. "We need some organisation. First, Tim doesn't go near this plane, if it's here. Neither do you or your brother, Miss. There are probably men inside – what is left of men who could have been burnt. Your uncle let you come with us as a guide – that's one thing. But he wouldn't allow you to see that."

She had some difficulty understanding, and she was surprised by the sternness that had entered his voice, but she replied steadily, "What you know I haf seen, haf not seen? I do not wish see inside. I help you find."

"Of course, Miss. We absolutely need your help. I appreciate that. But there are things I have no intention of exposing you to."

Vince's language was too complex. She did not bother to respond. "We lose time. We go now, search. We go four ways. You can find to come back here?"

"No. That's not possible. We don't go alone and we don't go now. What happens if someone has an accident? We're damned tired, and that's dangerous. Especially in the dark. I'm not going into the bush tonight, and neither are you three. We're staying here – all of us."

At once she was angry. "You think you are *Kommandant?*"

Tim felt his thoughts racing, tumbling over each other too fast for him to assess. He agreed with Vince – what Katerina had suggested, though certainly the quickest way to begin the search, was unwise. On the restriction Maclaurin had laid on him, however, he now felt in two minds. Back in England he had accepted it; Air Force discipline was deeply ingrained, and to observe it had often been a matter of life or death. But now, surely to say that he couldn't observe the bodies, if bodies there were, was to treat him as a child.

He interrupted: "I know what Group Captain Maclaurin said about me staying clear. But – look, Vince, I'm not wrapped in cotton wool. I should be there, part of the investigation. I *know* the crew, and I have known Alan McCleary's folks back home all my life. I can't come this far and then fail them because I didn't look properly."

"Damn it, Tim, we can't change the system now! If we find a Halifax, it's got to be yours. And if it's got men inside, you know they're your mates. There's no need to check beyond that."

"There *could* be another plane – from a Stuttgart raid, maybe."

"Not likely. Anyway, this far south it'd probably be a Lancaster, or a Mosquito."

"That's logical, I suppose. But I couldn't be satisfied. Not getting right there and not really checking. I'm pretty well finished with the Air Force. I'll never be back here. This is my only chance. Maclaurin doesn't even have to know."

Vince stared, unbelieving. "You gave the man your word! I'm not deceiving him – not over this. I expect you to do the right thing. I'll have to report you otherwise, and there'll be repercussions. You could be kicked out. If that happens, how are you going to marry that girl of yours?"

Tim could tell that Vince was absolutely serious. He tried to balance things: his obligation to Anna, his obligation to those at home, his obligation to Vince, his obligation to Maclaurin. But before he could reply Katerina spoke again. She was seething at being sidelined. "I wait for your answer! Do you forget you speak to me? If I want orders I get from my *Vater*. In this I am – how you say? – in charge!"

Vince stared. This was not how farm girls addressed squadron leaders. "Bloody hell! Am I surrounded by insubordinate nitwits?"

"Look, Vince," Tim said, "of course it's your show. But if you get to inspect the Halifax – well, it depends what you find. Let's decide then."

Throughout the day Dieter had hardly spoken. Now he intervened, revealing to the Australians' astonishment a grasp of English far better than his sister's. "No, *Schwester*, the major is correct. In this country no one must walk alone."

Vince sighed with relief. "I don't even know which conversation I'm in. But thank heaven someone here's got some sense! Of course we'll go in pairs – young Dieter's right there. And only I approach the plane – if there is a bloody plane! And that's final!"

"OK" said Tim. But still he wondered what would happen if the search was successful.

Hearing her brother side with Vince, Katerina smiled sardonically, undid the ribbon tying her hair and re-gathered it neatly. Then she went some distance away and sat alone, ignoring anything said to her. Vince went to approach her, but Dieter shook his head. "Wait," he said.

They sat too, backs against trees, silent, and waited for what seemed a long time. Until the light began to fade she gave no sign. Then she rose, came to the boy and gave him an affectionate mock punch, pouted, scanned the sky, appeared to find some answer there, and said: "*Du gewinnst, Brüderlein.*" She shook her head, and abruptly seemed to relax. Dieter looked at the Australians and nodded.

With abrupt suddenness, the resentment she had been nursing and suppressing since morning appeared finally to dissolve. She stared at the Australians for a long moment and said, "You haf lost the time for search. Ist late now. What cannot be, cannot be. We make fire, we eat, we sleep. But first we haf this." And she took a mug from her pack, half-filled it with water, and then produced a metal flask and tipped in a considerable quantity. She offered it to Vince. "You drink."

"What's this?" asked Vince.

"You know *Schnapps?*" She was smiling. The girl they had seen kiss her uncle was almost back.

To refuse would be to reject her – and to undermine the search completely. Warily, he sipped the cup, and fell into a spasm of helpless coughing. When he recovered he could not help grinning. "Amazing stuff. Don't know if I like it or not. Pure alcohol, I suspect."

Katerina giggled. And, miraculously, her laughter defused the friction not only between her and Vince, but between the Australians – the first that had arisen throughout their work together. There was something ridiculous in the confused arguments, and the girl had accepted the fact first. An absurd merriment infected all three men. They chuckled, and Vince said "Katerina, until we find the plane, I accept you're the expert – hiking, domestic arrangements, you're the boss. Then it's me. Your call. What do we do now?"

She understood the gist. She took the cup and handed it to Tim. "You try."

Tim did so. "I've never had water like that!"

"Here – I'll have another go," said Vince, taking the cup.

"You keep. Now you make fire. Big one. Not to lose time." And she went to get food from her pack.

"Right, Miss. Very good, Miss." Coming to attention Vince gave an exaggerated salute to her back, but he went about the chores, followed by Tim and Dieter. Later he said to Tim in a quiet aside, "I'm glad it's not *her* you've been mooning over."

The next morning they were on their way before six, watching ceaselessly for anything that might give a clue – a region of burnt forest, a swathe cut through trees, a scrap of parachute silk, a part of an aircraft. Vince went with Dieter, Tim with Katerina – the pairing least likely to result in renewed friction.

They explored two large valleys, one running more or less south, looking towards Switzerland, the other west, towards France; but the real search was conducted in the smaller side-valleys and gullies that opened out of these.

Tim and Katerina kept as far apart as they could while remaining in touch, scaling every small eminence to survey the surrounding country. It was fruitless. They stopped three times to rest and eat a little, and turned back only when Tim's watch told him that darkness might overtake them. Vince and Dieter were minutes before them, and the fire was already going. They, too, had found nothing.

"Is not good," said Katerina. "We must have weeks."

"It's pretty hopeless, all right," replied Vince. "We try for two more days. If we haven't found it by then, we give up."

Choosing new valleys, they followed a similar plan for the second day, and returned dispirited. They had seen nothing, and weariness sapped their optimism. They had one day left, and little real hope.

Katerina was dissatisfied. She approached Vince. "Too slow. Tomorrow we go four ways – like I say when we come here."

"Don't start that again."

"You wish to find this aeroplane?"

Tim intervened: "Yes – I bloody well do. Vince – it really matters to me. We have to try everything."

Katerina interrupted. "Look, Herr Mac-auley. Look at this country. Hills, valleys, forest. I tell you what. We mark where we go – I have red – how you say?" And she rummaged in her pack and brought out a large reel of pink tape. "We tie on trees. Anyone does not return, we can find. We meet here after one day, *und* we say what we see."

Vince hesitated. It *would* double the area they could cover. If he'd realised that they might separate, he could have tried to get some two-way radio sets – US walkie-talkies, preferably. But without contact in this country even a sprained ankle could be disastrous.

"No," he said. "The same pairs. Tomorrow."

"You say I am boss until we find crash."

"Damn it! No! How many ways do I have to say it?"

The next morning they awoke to find Katerina gone. Dieter told them that she had gone alone, leaving before Vince could try to impose his will on her.

Vince swore volubly and said, "That's it! We're packing it in. Finish. Let's make some breakfast, and as soon as she comes back we bugger off – unless we bloody well have to search for her. I bet she didn't tie her damned pink tapes on the bushes, either. We'll need black-trackers, and there aren't any of them around here!"

Dieter shrugged, Tim set about a fire for breakfast, and they settled down to wait. Vince was just lifting a cup of ersatz coffee to his lips – even Katerina's farm had not been able to supply real coffee – when she appeared in the distance, waving. When she was close enough, she shouted: "I find it."

She led them at first in the direction she and Tim had followed the day before, but turned off into a narrow ravine, overshadowed by a ridge that hid the sun. A small stream, little more than a rill, emerged from it.

High in the side of the ravine was a cleft, closed at the top, a sharp gash cut into the ground. Wedged in it was the Halifax, nose down and tipped on its starboard side as though it had been sliding down the main hillside but had skidded laterally into this position. Only the forward section of the aircraft was in contact with the ground, the rest standing free like some sculpted monument. The starboard wing was torn almost off and folded back under the fuselage; the other projected obliquely into the air, its two propellers like stilled windmills stark against the sky. It was this wing that Katerina had first seen. It was charred at the root, and a dark streak ran from there to the inboard engine. The cockpit was intact, but the nose was crumpled and forced backwards, and Bruce's turret had been torn away, leaving a gaping circular hole from which a jagged crack ran halfway down towards the upraised wing. The plane had almost broken in two at that point. Scattered bullet-holes dotted the fuselage, and their tattered edges sometimes pointed outwards.

It was a windless day, and the forest was still; but at the bottom of the wreck, where the crushed nose was forced into the ground, there was a faint sound where the water of the tiny stream emerged from behind the twisted metal and ran on down the cleft, dividing and gurgling and dividing again.

The four people gazed from below. The cleft itself was close to vertical, and directly between them and the plane a smooth escarpment twelve feet high interrupted the steep slope of the ground. It would be easier to go around this, scaling the ridge at the ravine's left side. Katerina said to Vince, "We go. They wait."

They started, Vince boosting her over rocks and she leaning down a hand to him. Tim and Dieter, watching their slow progress as they struggled past obstacles and across gaps, had time to notice small details: blood oozing along Katerina's arm from a scratch; a new tear in Vince's borrowed trousers; dents in the metal of the plane itself; the painted numbers on its side; the aileron still grotesquely raised from the port wing. Probably the jammed one, Tim realised. If he had needed any assurance, he did not now: it was his Halifax. He shivered a little.

Once above the escarpment, Katerina and Vince were soon roughly level with the point where the smashed nose rested, but the cleft-sides were too steep to be negotiated by anything like a lateral traverse. Possibly Katerina could do it, if she had rock-climbing skills, but Vince urged her further upwards. At length the pair stood well above the cleft itself, on a patch of ground that allowed standing without hand-holds, staring down at the twin rudders. Katerina, the watchers saw, had her rope around her waist. Now she unwound it and made one end fast to a protruding rock shaped like a rough bollard. Then she began to fix it around her body, but Vince shook his head. He waved the girl back. They were arguing, and after a minute or so, to Tim's surprise she stopped obediently and gave up the rope.

Vince was looking intently at the fuselage. Those who had bailed out had used the forward hatch. In his present position it was hidden from him, but the watchers below could see that it gaped, in mid-air, a good fifteen feet from any rock or foothold. A team properly equipped with anchors and temporary bridges and climbing gear could get to it and, sometime in the future, probably would. Vince, scrambling alone, would not; nor, Tim judged, could the four of them working together.

Vince moved across the top of the cleft until he could see the plane's belly and evidently came to the same conclusion. Returning he began to put knots and loops in the rope. Katerina seemed to protest, but to no avail, and she sat looking away, the very action suggesting sulking. Probably, Tim realised, she could abseil, while he was prepared to bet that his chief could not. If this was so, Vince was not concerned. He tied the free end of the rope around his own waist and slithered down a small bank that brought him to the edge of the cleft. From here the metal hull plunged downwards, and with a long fishing rod he could have touched it. If he could clamber down the precipice, he could, after a while, steady himself between the aircraft and the rock and continue to the point where the cockpit rested further down the rock wall. Tentatively he began, his feet searching for crevices, his hands grasping the knots. At times he relied on shrubs growing out of the rock wall, and Tim wondered that he trusted them. But slowly he descended more than fifty feet until he had nearly reached his objective. Then, over the last four feet, he slipped, to fetch up with a jarring crunch in a sitting position wedged between the fuselage and the cliff.

For a full minute he was still, obviously in pain, apparently unsure whether any serious damage had resulted. Eventually, seeming to decide that nothing was broken, he waved to the others and looked for a way to stand. Hauling himself by the rope, he wedged his feet into small rocky niches and managed to lie across the aircraft peering in through the perspex of the co-pilot's window.

He remained there for a long time, observing everything he could.

And he could do no more. Twice he looked downwards, obviously considering trying to return that way, but the rope was not long enough. He looked up and began to ascend. The process was slow and dangerous, and at moments it seemed likely that he could not complete it; but he arrived, exhausted, to where Katerina was waiting, and he shook his head.

What the gesture meant was unclear. In reply she said something and gesticulated. Vince spoke and she nodded.

He waved to Tim and Dieter, and he and Katerina began to pick their way down. It took perhaps forty minutes and they arrived breathless. Then, "Everybody sit down," said Vince. "I want to talk."

Somewhat unwillingly, they sat. "OK, here's the drum," he began. "There's no way we can get in the aircraft – not without special equipment that we don't have. I've looked in, and that's all any of us can do. Tim, how many got out?"

"I was fourth. There were three behind me. I don't know whether any of them made it."

"Mate, there were three dead men in that plane. There's no way anyone could recognise them. One was in the pilot's seat and one was sprawled near the back of the cockpit. The other was down below near the escape hatch – I was able to see him through the radio operator's window."

Tim was bewildered. "That's crazy. Alan in the seat – I can understand that. But the others were *all* below. " He thought, and said, wonderingly, "Phil must have gone back somehow to help Alan get out. My God!" And he sat down, slowly, and put his head in his hands.

"They're dead, Tim. Long dead."

"I've got to look."

"I'm sure it's better if you don't. I'll tell you this – you won't know them. Not as individuals. It's just a matter of counting."

"I've got to try. You can lower me on the rope. A couple of loops, a turn around me."

"Yes, we could. Have you ever *tried* dangling on a rope in mid-air? It doesn't behave. You twist around, your weight doesn't stay in the right place, you turn upside down, you fall off. It's not so bloody simple. Especially for a man with a weakened leg. But yes, we *could* do it ...

"But I don't want you to. For a start, I gave my word to Maclaurin, and so did you. And Maclaurin was right. It'll be a long day before I forget this one. Some things are necessary, but they don't help us psychologically. Tim, I assure you – there is nothing you can see that could help. You're going to get married. You and your wife – it's a time for joy, life, love of life. You've already seen too much death, but this is different. There are some memories you're better without. Especially as the last thing you saw in the Air Force. For your wife's sake, if not your own, leave it. I honestly believe even I'd be better without this burden. And I didn't know the men."

Katerina spoke: "Ja, I have seen men return to families – from the Russian front. Men who have nightmares. No woman wants that. If you do not have to do this, do not. It is not *gerecht* – fair – to your – how do you say *Verlobte*? – it is not fair to your wife."

It was a new thought. Could she be right? Could it actually be unfair to Anna? Until now it had seemed cowardice to follow Maclaurin's direction. Suddenly there was a new question – a genuinely serious one.

Then Dieter, the quiet one, spoke. Herr Rogers, men will come here. They will give the men in your aeroplane a good burial."

Tim felt a nausea. Was it, he wondered, his basic weakness – a hesitance that came from entering too deeply, too empathetically, into alternatives? Should he simply look at problems from the outside and judge and act? Like Alan? It would have made the war a bloody sight easier.

Or – could it be an evasion?

Maybe it depended how squarely things were faced.

Anna.

Anna was the most important thing. If seeing his friends' bodies could really hurt her ...

It tipped the scales.

"OK," said Tim. We go now. *Right* now. Let's go quickly."

Vince said, gently, "Of course, we could try to find the others – those who bailed out."

"No, I know – didn't I tell you? They got to Switzerland. I had a letter at Eastbourne. They were interned there – if you call it internment. In a sort of holiday club."

They made their way back, no one speaking until they arrived at their camp. All the way Tim fretted silently, and Vince, guessing that self-doubt was plaguing him, decided to push straight on. Though it was late, they struck the camp and made a four hours' journey towards Tannhofen, until night closed around them and they were forced to stop.

A half-moon was high in the sky. Vince cocked an eye at it and rummaged in his pack for the schnapps. He drank some neat, coughed, and said to Tim, "How do you feel?"

"Bugger it, I don't know. Maybe I should have gone to the cockpit, whatever you said. I don't bloody know."

"Mate, you couldn't have done it anyway without help. And I wasn't going to help you. Neither were the others."

"It's bloody hard, mate. And now I just want to get out of here."

CHAPTER 25

Homecoming (Germany, Australia 1946)

Anna and Tim were married in a still-standing church in Hildesheim. There was no question of his family attending. The war had been over for a year, but for small-business people like the Rogers, a long and expensive sea-voyage followed by an overland journey in war-ravaged Germany was out of the question. So the wedding had a one-sided feel. Anna's father, her sister, and her friends thronged around, admiring the picture of beauty she achieved in a wedding dress that her sister had worn five years earlier. Tim was flanked by Reg, George and Vince, all of whom were carefully out of uniform.

That the reception would be thoroughly formal was taken for granted. The women, in a sort of defiance of the shattered world outside, filled the room with colour, while the men were resplendent in sleek black, in some cases obviously preserved for thirty years and brushed up for the occasion. A four-piece band of old men – accordion, clarinet, violin and euphonium – played with considerable skill. But for all this adherence to tradition, the celebration was in some ways a new departure: it required a determined effort for the company to accept this marriage of a daughter of the fatherland to one of the conquerors – and a colonial at that. It helped a little that Tim had been a captive, though this advantage was offset at moments by Reg's Puckish wit, which in spite of his efforts to contain it escaped now and then like a puppy from a basket.

Beginning stiffly, the party became more relaxed as wine was opened and beer poured – perhaps too relaxed for comfort, George reckoned, fearful that alcohol would liberate insults and perhaps violence. But it proceeded well enough until the time came for Tim to reply to the toast to Anna and himself. His attempts to speak German provoked guffaws, and he quickly reverted to articulating a sentence, waiting for it to be translated, and proceeding to the next. Berndt was his translator, the doctor spreading a sort of everybody's-favourite-uncle aura over the whole gathering; and so long as Tim was expressing his gratitude, the company warmed to him. He apologised for his presumption in taking this beautiful German girl to the far side of the world, and was careful to say how his own German connections went back to the painter who had been his boyhood mentor.

But in the circumstances it was inevitable that the war must at least be mentioned, and this was walking on eggshells. If Tim had referred to Willy's near-pacifism as an influence on him, there were those present who would have concluded that this distant Schultz was after all no patriot, while others, absolutely disillusioned by the disaster the war had proved to be, would have applauded. Tim tried to go carefully, saying that the whole world was glad that it was all over, by now in the Pacific as well; and he touched lightly on his own gratitude for being shot down, because it was through this that he had met Anna. He even went so far as to hint that he had been glad to be relieved of the responsibility of attacking cities from the air. And again, this was delicate: he had to strive for a balance between achieving something like fellow-feeling with his defeated listeners and offending those among them for whom military virtues were paramount – people who would hear such sentiments as cowardice or as treachery to his own side.

The guests generally knew that Tim had been in the war; some did not know that he had been a member of a bomber crew, and there was an audible intake of breath. Two rose pointedly and left. One, an old, distinguished-looking man wearing a scar on his cheek, managed as he did so to convey by his very bearing that he would have liked to slap Tim's face and ask his seconds to call on him.

Anna watched them go, and observed the ensuing moment of tense silence. She jumped to her feet, took a deep breath, and began to address the company. "It is not usual at a wedding for the bride to make a speech. Well, this wedding is different in many ways, so it can be different in that way, too. You all know that I lost my mother in an air raid. I will never get over that. I can never hear an aeroplane overhead without shuddering, without remembering every detail, without remembering her love.

"But I know this man too. I nursed him for nearly five months. I know – I know! – that he hated bombing. And I know, too, that there are women who lost their mothers and fathers and brothers and sweethearts and husbands in other countries – in Poland, Russia, France and – yes, in Britain, too. And those bombs were dropped by the Luftwaffe, and they were not dropped only on soldiers and factories."

She paused, hesitant, surprised at herself. Then she went on:

"People talk of '*Terrorflieger*'. Well, that is us, too. It is every country in this rotten, horrible, monstrous war.

"Now, as my husband" – here she stopped again, looking at Tim, smiling to use the unaccustomed word – "as my husband said, we are not going to continue the hatred of each other – we are going to hate only the war. We are not going to continue the destruction.

"We are going to build something – we are going to build peace!"

She sat, breathless, astonished at her own daring, and began to weep quietly. Tim, who had understood barely a word but who could not fail to guess the import, moved and put his arm around her. The silence seemed to expand to fill the room.

Berndt, tall, slim, impressive in his dress suit, rose to his feet, put aside his cigar, and began to applaud. Slowly the guests followed him in small groups. Then the whole company was on its feet, clapping. And, as the noise began to die away, the band in an exuberant mood struck up "The Blue Danube". Tim, who had thought the piece trivial, was astonished at its beauty when played with delicacy. He took Anna's hand and whispered, "Tannhofen." She smiled at him through the dampness that still clung to her eyes, and replied "Donaueschingen." And they were waltzing – Tim half-remembering the dancing lessons at Walgabran tennis club, not caring if he made mistakes, letting the music take him.

Couple by couple the guests were on the floor. The music seemed to become more alive, the tempo increased slightly, the band was one with the dancers.

Anna looked again at Tim and smiled and laid her head on his shoulder. "I am so happy," she said.

The honeymoon was the six-week sea voyage to Australia. As Tim's wife, Anna was accepted as a war bride. Her father's case was much more difficult. Europe was still awash with "displaced persons", many of whom wanted to emigrate, especially to the United States. Australia wanted immigrants, but from England first and then from virtually every country in Europe. A man of Herr Bauer's age was given low priority – if he had been a refugee it would have been easier.

Of course, he was now a member of an Australian family. This helped. And it was the Returned Services League that did it – the RSL had enormous political clout at that time, and fought hard for anyone who had been a prisoner. They went to bat, as Reg would have put it, for Tim and Anna and her father; and because of their efforts Herr Bauer knew, at the time of the wedding, that in a couple of years he would be able to join Anna – if he still wished to do so; for in the meantime he would stay in Cologne with his other daughter and her husband, and it was impossible not to wonder whether, after that time, he would decide not to leave the country where he had lived all his life.

The last stage of a long journey: the train to Walgabran.

Tim thought: six years … Canada, the Air Force, the raids, the hospital, the prison camp, the search through Europe. Six years packed with experience. They had changed him. And now he was nervous. How would Anna react to his family, his home town? How, indeed, would he?

It was as well, he felt, that they had spent more than two months travelling. From the wedding they had gone to London, where he was discharged from the Air Force. She had met Maclaurin and Nordale, and they had explored the city, often with Reg and George at their elbows. Then they had embarked for Queensland, touching at Naples, Suez, Aden, Singapore, and she had mixed with her fellow passengers. She had visited places wholly exotic to her. All this made a kind of buffer zone between Germany and Walgabran. He was desperately afraid that Anna might shrink into a kind of depression at seeing a regional Queensland town, where the sun beat down on white, tin-roofed houses on stilts, where rough country pubs were friendly but absolutely unsophisticated, and where there were no concert halls or art galleries or elegant coffee houses within a couple of hundred miles at best – and then, only in Brisbane, a city provincial even by Australian Standards, while Australia itself was provincial compared to Europe. Certainly, ever since Victorian times, famous touring theatre companies and musicians had visited the country and been enthusiastically patronised, but it was still a world away from Munich or even Hildesheim.

Not that they intended to settle in Walgabran. It was open to Tim to return to the bank and to his study of accountancy, and that would mean Brisbane. But his enthusiasms had changed. And Anna – where would she be able to feel settled? It was a crossroads, and a bewildering number of choices arose for the couple. Brisbane, Sydney, Melbourne? Would she be too homesick, a fish out of water? Might they, in a year, perhaps return – at least to Britain? Even to Germany?

It was only now that Tim learnt of the existence of ex-servicemen's scholarships – somehow, no one had mentioned them to him though Willy had written of them to Herr Bauer. Australian universities were bursting at the seams with a newer type of student, men back from the war, men who otherwise could never have afforded to spend years studying. Often they were impatient of the light-hearted insouciance affected by many younger undergraduates.

Possibilities opened. Engineering? Law? The thought brought Alan back vividly.

But he had a wife to support. Was there a part-time course?

For the moment, they had his ex-serviceman's gratuity and his back pay, and their love and faith in each other, and little else.

And, right now, they were going to Walgabran.

She was fascinated to observe the country where he had grown up, and to his surprise, she loved it at once. She might have been born to the long dry grass and the tough gum trees and the slow, laconic speech. She warmed to his parents, aged by the stress of the war, as they did to her; and she embraced Willy and Margaret, and chattered in German and English without seeming to notice the transition. A grand meal was prepared in his old home, and even Jim Nolan, whose bitterness against everything German had been reinforced when Alan went missing, came and made an effort to be pleasant to everyone. He mellowed a little after hearing how Anna had risked her life to communicate with Tim in the Stalag, and he went silent when Tim told him that many German families had helped POWs who dropped out of the last brutal marches; though later he muttered something about exceptions proving the rule.

Tim was thrilled to find other guests at the table, ones he had not expected: Bruce was there, and obeying an impulse foreign to their upbringing but true to their instincts, the two men spontaneously embraced; and he found Owen and Barry and John, grinning and shaking his hand vigorously as though to make up for years. Only Alan and Ken had not returned – two out of six. During the meal he heard for the first time Willy's account of his own incarceration, and felt a sense of shame which brought him to his feet to make a mini-speech, one of apology. He went on to thank his old friend and mentor for writing to Anna's father. Willy waved his hand deprecatingly and muttered *"keine Ursache*, nothing – it is nothing." Then Anna rose too, and said "It was not nothing – but there is something more, which none of you know." And with a shy smile she told the company that the first kiss she and Tim had shared had its catalyst – Tim's sudden recognition on a German hillside of a scene he had first met in a Walgabran schoolroom. And she ran to Willy and took his hands in hers and looked into his eyes and said, *"Danke schön, Herr Schultz."* And she embraced him.

The group, small and domestic as it was, nevertheless could not refrain from applause. Willy, in particular, was hugely pleased. Thrown off balance, he smiled, and his old shyness for a moment flashed to the front of his expression. Then he rose with a glass in his hand, and spoke. He described how a small boy had hit him with a cricket ball, and as a punishment had to work with him, and how the friendship had grown and lasted over the years, and how he himself – here he actually winked at Anna! – owed his own marriage to Tim's secret machinations. Nothing in the world – nothing – could give him greater pleasure than to know that he had, in his own way, reciprocated the favour.

"But," he finished, "there is something that you do not realise. Tim, did you intend to show your lady the mural in the stage of your old school hall?"

"Of course."

"Well, I will not tell you. I will let you see for yourself."

Slightly disturbed by this cryptic comment, Tim decided to go alone to the school. He found it smaller than he had remembered, and the trees in the playground seemed dustier. But the children played happily, wholly unconscious of any shortcomings. A curious mood gripped him. It seemed that time coalesced into a single point and yet that his consciousness divided into two parts. He saw himself, there with the children, twenty years ago, and at the same time standing apart, looking on. They exhibited a simplicity, a promise, an instinctive optimism. Something that might, merely by its light-hearted unconsciousness of the destruction, have seemed in the rubble of Europe almost an affront. Yet – something absolutely proper. Where did they get it? A few years ago they did not exist; yet here they were, vital, responding to the world around them.

For some reason he thought of Fay. Ever since she had died he had been aware that she – Fay, the person – was something bigger than the event that had stilled the life in her body. He had seen that in every person there is a dimension that cannot be extinguished, a dimension that is rooted in and reaches towards something unlimited.

And it was the same with these children. They chased and tripped and laughed and fought; and through their exuberance shone something else: their humanity in its mystery and wonder – and the unity that runs through the successive changes of a person's life like a continuing thread and is awesome in its final significance.

He thought: we aspire, we achieve; we have our triumphs. Especially at such moments we can feel self-sufficient. Yet we live only by response: we respond, and need to respond, to others, to the world. We live like the grass: the grass joyous in gratitude reaching upward to the sun. We respond to our Creator. We are not self-sufficient: we are small, and when we understand we are glad to be so.

The Second World War. A fantastic achievement of every admirable human quality – an enormous effort of concerted intelligence, invention, enterprise, courage, cooperation; even, in a sense, of that gladness of life without whose support the scientists could not have invented, the soldiers marched, the squadrons flown; but all – all – enlisted to bring death and destruction. The utter absurdity of it! And in the overwhelming majority of cases it was not done for personal gain, for on every side men and women had sacrificed themselves and endured loss and had sometimes died, resisting even torture. Could the same idealistic effort not be harnessed to eliminate starvation, disease, poverty; could it not be marshalled against rancour and hatred and all that drags down life and relationships? Why could the world rise to such heights for war but not for peace?

Of course, there were those – and they were many – who did spend themselves for peace. But they were never enough to change the world; at least, not quickly. So might these children, and those like them in other countries, come in a few years to kill each other?

A third World War seemed all too likely. Europe divided, America and the Soviet Union armed to the teeth and in frank opposition.

Perhaps war had a sort of attraction because it dramatised life: it gave intensified scope to idealism, enabling individuals to recognise a meaning beyond their personal good, enabling communities to coalesce around transcendent goals; a metaphor for a universal struggle with evil to which people could give themselves.

That struggle was real enough. And desperation under attack did stimulate idealism. But it could be universal only when peace, and working to build, were appreciated as even more dramatic than the sudden destruction which terminated most battles. When all humanity was valued.

Modern war used so much technology, so much science. But science was based on wonder. That alone should draw people together. It implied something greater than us all – something we could converge on.

He remembered something Willy had said – that it was the little failings of many people that made war possible, that allowed the decisions of presidents and kings to set nations on that path. Was he right? Perhaps not in earlier ages, when rulers had absolute power and their people less education. In the modern world? Tim did not know. He knew only that it was right to go on – to hope – whatever the past had been.

As he knew he and Anna would do.

Anna … once he had loved her smile, her kindness, her hair, her personality, her body, her laugh, her sigh – a thousand things. But now he loved *her*. Willy had said this, too, long ago. It would not, he felt, matter if illness or accidents came to change her. His love contained – hope; the intimation of final meaning. It was the person, the essence, that he loved. And somehow this was inseparable from her love for him. The love itself was something shared, almost a third thing, something between them.

Once he had been taught that the Trinity was like that.

Shaking himself from this mood, he approached the children and asked them where to find the Principal. Several adopted him, and, squabbling over the contradictory advice they insisted on giving each other, took him to where a young monk stood watching over the same games he had played twenty years before. In the common manner of religious brothers he had a kind of informal formality, a politeness that grinned. So Tim was an old boy? Might he just have a sentimental look at his old classrooms? Certainly – so long as he did it quickly, while it was still lunch-time. Would he have a cup of tea and a bite in the brothers' monastery? No, if he might just particularly glance in the old hall, where the stage was? Of course.

The mural had been painted over, and the wall was white.

He had been hoping that it would delight Anna, though at the same time he was a little afraid that it could make her homesick.

But – to find it gone!

It felt like vandalism. It must have happened while Willy was interned – some new school principal, not recognising its value, had thought it old-fashioned, or superannuated, or just didn't like it, and had had it painted over. Or – had some idiot thought it a Nazi painting?

He rested against a gum tree in a corner of the school yard. Overwhelmed by an absurd sense of loss, he looked at the playing children. They did not miss the garden: it was not part of their world, and he himself was a distant, anonymous stranger.

When he told Anna, she was sad for Willy. "But," she said, "for me … for me it does not matter. Tim, I love you. Not a painting. Not Australia. Not Germany. It does not matter where you are, what you do, what happens to us, so long as I can share it – that is my happiness. You are in my heart, and my heart is not in Tannhofen, or Hildesheim, or Cologne or Walgabran: it is where you are."

It was as though she had taken the heart out of him and exposed its feelings, for he felt exactly the same for her. But he could not say it. He could not speak.

He drew her to himself and embraced her.

They both knew that embrace would last forever.

Appendix

List of Sources Consulted

BOOKS

Barker, R 2005, *Men of the Bombers*, Pen and Sword Books, Barnsley

Botting, D 1985, *In the Ruins of the Reich*, George Allen and Unwin, London

Boyle, A 1955, *No Passing Glory*, Collins, London

Charlwood, DE 1956, *No Moon Tonight*, Angus and Robertson, Sydney

Dennis, CJ 1915, *The Songs of a Sentimental Bloke*, Angus and Robertson, Sydney

Donnelly, GL 2000, DFM, *A Quest for Wings*, Tempus Publishing Ltd, Stroud, Gloucestershire

Jarausch, KH 2006, *After Hitler: Recivilising Germans 1945–1995, translated Brandon Hunziker*, Oxford University Press, Oxford

Herington, J *Air Power Over Europe*, in *Australia in the War of 1939–1945*, The Australian official history

Leggett, A 2006, *Don't Cry for Me*, Linellan Press, Oldbury, Western Australia

Longden, S 2005, *Hitler's British Slaves*, Arris Books, London

Mackenzie, SP 2004, *The Colditz Myth*, OUP, Oxford

McKibbin, MN 1947, *Barbed Wire: Memories of Stalag 383*
Staples, London. This book, published in London in 1947,
was written at least substantially in the camp. Many details
in Chapter One are drawn from it, and since it is not readily
available, the words on page 12 are quoted from memory.
It contained excellent drawn illustrations, and, if it had a
fault, it must surely be that it under-stated the difficulties
of that life, preferring instead to describe them with a wry
humour.

Miller, HC 1976, *Early Birds*, Seal Books, Sydney

Monteath, P 2011, *P.O.W. – Australian Prisoners of War in
Hitler's Reich*, Pan-Macmillan, Sydney. This book contains
a description of how Wing Commander R.C.M. Collard
at Stalag 3A, fearing at the war's end that the Russians
would wish to keep the prisoners as bargaining chips with
the western allies, wanted them to break out and head west
to meet the Americans. However, he did not have time to
implement this plan. The Germans left on April 1 and the
Soviets came on April 2. As a result, the prisoners were
not released for a further month, and only after repeated
arguments and protests. The website *World War II Prisoners
of War – Stalag Luft 1* says that the prisoners from that stalag
were flown out by Americans against the wishes of the
Russians who had actually liberated the camp. They took
first the sick, then the longest-standing prisoners, then the
others, taking them all to France within a few days.

Pearson, R 1995, *Australians at War in the Air*, Kangaroo Press,
Kenthurst, New South Wales

Ramsay, I 1985, *P.O.W. – A Digger in Hitler's Prison Camps 1941–45*, Macmillan, Melbourne

Ritchie, A 1998, *Faust's Metropolis*, Harper Collins, London

Rollings, C 2007, *Prisoner of War*, Ebury Press (Random House), U.K.

Stafford, D 2007, *Endgame 1945*, Little, Brown, U.K.

The Department of Veterans' Affairs in association with Mullion Creek Productions Pty. Ltd. 2009, *Australian Prisoners of War*, Canberra

Turner, I (Ed.) 1989, *Reconstruction in Post-war Germany: Occupation Policy and the Western Zones 1945–55*, Berg Publishers, Oxford

Watt, D 1995, *Stoker*, Simon and Schuster, Sydney

WEBSITES
B24.NET, *Great Escape – Research of WWII B-24 POW Stalag Lufts*, research provided by Rob Davis, prepared and completed by Fedorowicz, F, translated Strukowska, A. Available from: <http://www.b24.net/pow/greatescape.htm>

Forces War Records, *Life as a Navigator in RAF Bomber Command in World War II*. Available from: <https://www.forces-war-records.co.uk/blog/2014/10/16/life-as-a-navigator-in-raf-bomber-command-in-world-war-two>

Wikipedia, *List of Prisoner-of-War Camps in Germany*. Available from: <https://en.wikipedia.org/wiki/List_of_prisoner-of-war_camps_in_Germany>

Stalag Luft 1 Online, *Prisoners of War – Stalag Luft 1*. Available from: <http://www.merkki.com> (Annotation above.)

RAF Bomber command 1939–1945. Available from: <http://www.elsham.pwp.blueyonder.co.uk/raf_bc/>

Mirror, *RAF's Darkest Night*. Available from: <http://www.mirror.co.uk/news/real-life-stories/rafs-darkest-night-95-planes-3276531>

Wikipedia (and other websites), *Jan Karski*. Karski, caught and tortured by the Nazis in 1940, escaped from a hospital and was later smuggled twice into the Warsaw ghetto and into a death camp in order to report to authorities in Poland and in the West. He was then smuggled out of Poland and reached London at the end of 1942 with his first-hand accounts and a microfilm. He met Anthony Eden and others. In 1943 he went to America and twice met Roosevelt. Later he became a professor at Georgetown University. Available from: <https://en.wikipedia.org/wiki/Jan_Karski>

Wikipedia (and other websites), *Witold Pilecki*. See annotation below. Available from: <https://en.wikipedia.org/wiki/Witold_Pilecki>

History on the Net, *World War II – Prisoner of War Camps in Germany*. Available from: <http://www.historyonthenet.com/ww2/german_pow_camps.htm>

Bill Rudd, Available from: <http://www.anzacpow.com>

OTHER

The Australian Government, *Report on the Directorate of Prisoners of War and Internees at Army Headquarters, Melbourne 1939–1951*. Chapter 2

Moriarty, Biddy (Barbara), *As You Were*, annual, 1947 edition

Blitz Street, British TV series

de Sola, David *The Man Who Volunteered for Auschwitz*, article, *Atlantic Monthly*. This article, and a number of websites, tells of Witold Pilecki, who as a member of a Polish resistance organisation deliberately allowed himself to be captured and interned at Auschwitz in order to gather intelligence about the treatment of prisoners and to help them in other ways which included plans to free them. Information he gathered was sent to the West from 1941, but according to the Wikipedia article "Witold Pilecki", even in 1943 it was still thought "grossly exaggerated". Pilecki was arrested, tortured and executed by the Soviet authorities in 1948.

Weil, Simone *The Iliad or the Poem of Force*. Written in French in 1940 and published in *Les Cahiers du Sud*. English translation in the November 1945 issue of *Politics*. Available in many editions. Willy's reference to Force on page 154 is drawn from it.

www.ingramcontent.com/pod-product-compliance
Lightning Source LLC
Chambersburg PA
CBHW061311170626
46817CB00001B/145